KINGDOM FALL © 2021 A. Zavarelli
Cover Design: Cormar Covers
Cover Photo: Michelle Lancaster @lanefotograph
Editing: Aria J.

DISCLAIMER

1

ALESSIO

The Rolls Royce pulls to a stop in front of Butcher and Son, and Luca meets my gaze in the rearview mirror.

"Would you like me to wait, Mr. Scarcello?"

"No." I reach for the door handle. "I'll call for you when I'm ready to return to the city."

He bows his head and waits for me to exit the vehicle before quietly rolling away. I glance at my phone briefly to note the time before the door to the abandoned slaughterhouse opens, and one of Marchesi's men gestures me inside.

"Nice to see you again, Mr. Scarcello," he says. "Mr. Marchesi is waiting for you in the back."

I nod in response and head for my intended business. My visit to New York will not be a lengthy one, and I'm eager to get it over with, so I can return to my obligations at home.

Behind the aged plastic door curtain, I find Marchesi sipping from a mug of coffee at one of the old butcher tables while he reads the paper. He glances up, startling slightly at my presence.

"Goddamn, we need to put a bell on you, Scarcello." He chuckles. "You always manage to scare the shit out of me."

I don't reply. It's something I've heard many times before, and why it should surprise him that I move quietly, I have no idea. It's to my benefit, and knowing my occupation and reputation, he should expect nothing less.

"It's good to see you again." He removes a white envelope from his pocket and slides it across the table to me. "The Ruin appreciates you making the trip to Desolation to assist us with this case."

"It's not a problem," I answer curtly, sliding the envelope into my jacket pocket. This isn't my first song and dance with the underground network in New York. Some call them a mafia outfit. Some just call them criminals. I don't call them anything except clients. They aren't affiliated with The Society, so we are nothing more than associates.

"There's half up front," he tells me. "I'll be around when you finish for final payment. Just come find me. The client is in the freezer."

I nod and leave him to his coffee while I slip into the back where the old freezers have been left to collect dust. It's not my first visit to Butcher and Son, and I doubt it will be the last. Though I have no affiliation with The Ruin itself, they often contract my services when their more primitive methods fail to gather the intel they need, or the target is a trickier subject that requires discretion. Today, I have traveled to Desolation, New York, to extract information from a man I don't know, one I don't care to know. To me, he is just a number. He is a job to complete. I always complete my assignments, no matter how gruesome the task might be. They call me The Debt Collector for a reason. I never walk away from a target without payment, be it flesh or information.

The freezer door creaks open under the weight of my grip, and the musty odor of dust combines with the permanent decay of blood. This is why they bring the clients here. Time does not erode that smell or the stains on the floor. It foreshadows what's to come, and it does a number on the human psyche to wait in such conditions, uncertain of the outcome.

I lock eyes with the man bound and hanging by his wrists from a butcher's hook. He looks to be in his late forties with thinning hair and a pot belly. He's wearing a yellow fishing shirt and khaki pants that are already stained with his piss. He reeks of desperation as his gaze meets mine, and he attempts to mumble something through the cloth gag in his mouth, but I have no interest in hearing anything just yet.

I waste no time setting down my medical bag and removing my suit jacket, hanging it onto one of the empty hooks. While he groans out muffled fragments of sentences, I roll up my sleeves and slip on some latex gloves. Then I unravel my tool kit, laying it out on one of the shelves before making my first selection, a filet knife.

I always start with primitive torture first. It's not an endgame. It's a warmup. From experience, I have learned that psychological torture wins every time. First, you have to bloody them up and exhaust them by depleting their adrenaline response. The crash will always tip the results in my favor. Despite what many of my contractors like to believe, I don't possess any special talent, and this isn't an art form. I simply understand the laws of human nature.

"I'm here to extract the information you've been withholding," I begin calmly. "And I want to be clear, when you meet with me, you only have two options left. This is a simple exchange of blood and flesh. You will give me what I require, or you will die a slow, brutal death. Do you understand?"

He starts to squirm in his restraints, moaning again, pleading with words I don't care to understand.

"I'm not big on socializing," I tell him. "So, if you decide you're ready to admit the truth, I want you to tap your foot on the floor three times, but only when you're truly willing." I hold the knife up to his throat. "If you lie to me or waste my time, I guarantee the price will be more than you are able to pay."

He falls completely still, and I return the knife to my tool kit, retrieving the plastic case of carbon steel hooks.

"I hear you're a fan of fishing." I pluck a hook from the case and examine it between my fingers. "You've probably filleted quite a number of them, I would imagine. I'm curious, though, if you keep them all for yourself, or do you prefer to catch and release?"

He mumbles a response, and when I turn around again, sweat is beading on his brow. He's renewed his fight against the restraints, straining his arms and his legs as I approach.

"I'm not big on fish myself," I confess as I grab his face and poke the barbed point against his cheek. "I think perhaps it's the texture or the smell. It doesn't appeal to me."

He screeches as the hook pierces his flesh, his nostrils flaring as blood drips down his neck. His muffled pleas resume, but he hasn't reached a point of desperation to tap out. It's human nature to want to believe our love and loyalty for our family will outweigh any adversity, but I know intimately that this is simply not true. Soon, he will understand there is nothing to be gained by trying to prevent his brother's fate.

I continue my task, spearing him with a fistful of hooks, decorating his cheeks like a tacky Christmas ornament. After about two minutes, I suspect his adrenaline is primed, and he's not feeling the same rush of fear as he did initially, so it's time to move on. I discard the hooks and reach for the filet knife once again.

"Death by a thousand cuts," I murmur, examining my reflection in the shiny blade. "I don't know that it's the worst way to die, but I think it might be the most poetic."

More sniffling, begging, and tears ensue as I proceed to carve him up like a pumpkin, slicing off bits of flesh and tossing them to the floor like meat scraps. I take chunks from his arms and move on to his back, cutting through the shirt to gain access. He vomits five minutes in and then passes out. I take the opportunity to adjust his position for the next phase. Tying the rope around his wrists, I loop it through the ceiling hook and use the pre-existing pulley system to leverage his weight.

As I'm considering rousing him for the sake of efficiency, my phone rings, and I glance at the screen in frustration, only to see

Gwen's name on the display. I step out of the freezer for a moment, shutting the door behind me.

"Gwen," I answer. "Is everything alright?"

"Oh, yes, of course," she replies. "It's been so nice to visit with Nino. We've been having such a lovely time together. I do wish I could spend more time with him like this."

"You know you are free to visit us anytime." I stare at a cockroach scuttling across the floor, my gaze unfocused.

"I know." Gwen sniffs. "It's just ... I'm always so sad when I have to leave him."

Silence lingers as she leaves her thoughts to settle over us. This discussion has been had, and she's well aware the circumstances won't change, yet she persists with this topic relentlessly. I won't remind her that her mental health isn't up for the challenge, and that it was already with some uncertainty that I've even allowed her to look after him during these short trips away. This arrangement has gone on for too long, and as much as she might dislike it, Nino needs the stability of a new live-in caretaker who can be there with him when I am not.

"Marianna has been here helping me." Gwen lightens her tone, taking on a wistful note. "She is so good with him."

My fingers stiffen at the mention of her name. "Please thank her for taking time out of her schedule to be there."

"I'm sure she'd love to hear it from you," Gwen says. "She adores both of you. And, of course, Nino soaks up the attention. He really does need a mother figure in his life, and I truly wish you would reconsider allowing her to help you."

I close my eyes and release a quiet breath of frustration. "Is this why you called?"

"Yes," she confesses. "I know you're planning to conduct interviews this afternoon, but I must insist you reflect on the impact of hiring outside The Society. I don't think you've fully considered the consequences this could have."

"I have considered them," I respond bluntly. "But it doesn't alter my opinion on the subject."

"What if this nanny you hire sees something she shouldn't?" Gwen asks. "Then what? Are you going to get rid of her?"

Her question is a trap. She knows how I feel about killing women, and she's leveraging that to make her case.

"She won't see anything she shouldn't," I tell her.

"But if she does?"

"If she does, then I will do what's necessary. I always do."

"Why even risk it?" Gwen asks. "Nino already knows Marianna. She can give him the sort of love and comfort only a mother can provide. He won't get that from an outsider. They don't understand our ways."

"I'm not hiring someone to be his mother. I'm hiring someone to look after him when I can't."

"But Marianna—"

"Marianna has her own motives," I grit out.

We have exhausted this conversation already. Gwen is not my mother, but she's the closest thing I have to one, and she believes it is her duty to look after me. In her efforts to do so, she continues to push Marianna in my direction, hoping I will eventually see her as a wife for myself and a mother for Nino. She still believes I can be converted to the idea of having a family of my own, regardless of how many times I have told her I will not.

"Alessio." Gwen softens her voice. "Please, take it from someone who knows. Family is all we have in this world. You can't be alone forever. I truly believe if you'd just give her a chance, you would see there is so much more to life. It would be for your benefit, but more importantly, it would mean the world to Nino."

"I have to go," I clip out. "My work is waiting for me."

"Please just consider it," she begs. "That's all I ask."

"I will check in later this evening. Goodbye, Gwen."

I disconnect the line and silence my phone, returning it to my pocket. There's a renewed sense of uncertainty in my gut when I open the door and find the client waiting for me. He's bloody, sweaty, and quietly begging for what I'm certain is mercy.

I approach him and remove the gag, staring at him curiously. "You're a father."

When he doesn't reply, I supply the necessary answer for him as I start to pace. "Two children. Ages seven and ten. A girl named Molly and a boy named Maxwell. All things considered, I must ask, do you feel you are doing what's best for them right now? Sacrificing yourself to protect your brother? And for how long? Surely, you must know he can't hide forever. The Ruin will find him, whether you die to protect him or not. And then where will your children be?"

He dips his head and begins to sob as I continue my theoretical exploration. "Your wife would be left alone to protect them. To provide for them on a single income. From your file, I can see that she hasn't worked since the first child was born. I imagine it would be a difficult transition for all of them. But tell me, do you suppose it would be better to have half a mother who is exhausted from her circumstances? Or would it serve them better to have you, the father who provides the structure they have always known? Do you think children need the softness of a woman in their life? Or will they thrive under any adversity, given the right support?"

"I don't know," he shouts. "Please, I don't know."

I consider the questions and shrug. I already know the answer to them, of course. I lost my mother when I was ten and look how that turned out for me. When I arrived here this morning, I was convinced I could find the right candidate with the qualities I needed to look after Nino. Now, I am less certain than ever. Perhaps, Gwen has a point. He does know Marianna, yet I am still unwilling to believe she's not driven by her desire to marry a Sovereign Son rather than her affection for Nino.

Regardless, the interviews have already been scheduled, and I will follow through with them. Now I have to consider that Gwen could be correct in her prediction about the disastrous results. If an outsider doesn't work out, if they fail to be trustworthy, the only feasible option would be to eliminate them. It's a big risk, one The Society would not understand me taking. But the members who have volunteered their services have already made what they want abundantly clear, and I am not in search of a package deal. I don't need a wife and a nanny. I simply need someone to keep Nino on track in the ways I cannot. Someone who can provide the qualities I lack and the empathy to maintain his humanity.

"What are you going to do to them?" the client asks, interrupting my thoughts. "They have nothing to do with this. They know nothing."

"It's not my decision to make," I inform him. "You will have to take that up with The Ruin, should you choose to come clean."

He breaks down again as I walk around to the pulley and start to crank the lever, hoisting his body into the air.

"This is a version of the Strappado," I explain it as if I'm a tour guide who's bored with the whole routine. "You may have heard of it. I will warn you, it won't be pleasant, and you no longer have the ability to tap your foot. I'll give you a safe word, should you change your mind. Do you have a preference?"

He cries out in pain as his elbows start to hyperextend backward, his bodyweight dipping forward from the force of gravity.

"How about Molly?" I suggest. "Surely, you can remember that."

"Please," he whimpers. "Please."

The pulley strains against his weight, and it's a test of my endurance as I turn the crank and pull the rope up by his wrists. I have the stomach for most things, but even I can admit this is a rather gruesome sight. I focus on his feet until I hear the telltale snap of his shoulders dislocating, followed by his screams of sheer agony.

One glance at his arms hanging like useless meat sacks from the hook sours my breakfast, and I'm already considering the next phase when he surprises me.

"Molly! Molly! Molly! Let me down. Please. I'll tell you fucking anything. Oh God, motherfuck. I'm going to die. I'm going to fucking die."

"That's a bit dramatic." I lower him to the floor and stare at him, waiting impatiently. "Spit it out then."

"He's in Miami," he pants, delirious from the pain. "The address is in my phone, under Pizza Hut. He's leaving in two days to try to stash the rest of the money in the Bahamas."

"See, that wasn't so hard, was it?" I walk over to my bag and retrieve a shot of morphine. "You could have saved yourself a lot of pain."

"What are you going to do to him?" he whimpers.

"I told you. It's not my call to make." I lean down and stab the needle in his arm. "He stole from The Ruin. Actions have consequences, and we all have to pay, no matter how much we may not want to. But you get to go home tonight. You get to see your little girl, your wife, and your son. Life will go on, and with some luck, you may forget this ever happened."

"What did you give me?" he whines.

"Just a little morphine." I remove the restraints from his wrists. "You're going to thank me for it when I move these joints back into place."

2

ALESSIO

Luca drives me to my penthouse in downtown Manhattan with an efficiency that reminds me why I pay him so well. He navigates New York traffic with ease, never flustering over the permanent chaos that seems to reside on the streets here. The journey is quiet, as I prefer it, and I take the time to review the candidates I will be interviewing this afternoon. Their names blend together, and my eyes blur as I read through the files, complete with background checks. I have no particular draw toward any of them, but I won't until I meet them in person. I prefer to keep socialization to a minimum in my personal life, but my gut instincts about people are next to none. A side effect of my trade, perhaps. Regardless, I have no doubt I will decide within seconds if any of the candidates are trustworthy. And if they are not, I will have to contend with Gwen when I return home empty-handed.

I lean my head back against the seat and close my eyes briefly, not to rest but to clear my mind. Typically, I would have a long, punishing session in my home gym after an assignment, but there isn't time today. I have contracts to review and two additional meetings with clients I must contend with before concluding my business in New York. For the sake of efficiency, I intend to carry out both contract killings this evening, and still have time to spare to study the new file on my desk before my 6 a.m. appointment in the morning.

"Mr. Scarcello, would you like me to wait?" Luca asks.

I blink and glance at the tower outside. My penthouse is in the heart of Tribeca, and though I do not feel a particular kinship with New York, I can appreciate the location and the views.

"Take a break, Luca," I tell him. "I'll be ready at three o'clock."

"As you wish, sir."

He waits for me to exit, then whisks the car away as the doorman to the building greets me with a respectful bow.

"Dominus et Deus, Mr. Scarcello."

I nod in return and make my way over to my private elevator. This building is owned by *Imperium Valens Invictum*, also known as The Society, and only members are residents. But among them, I am the only Sovereign Son. The title means I am a descendant of one of the founding families. Our organization is powerful and secretive. We have our own hierarchy, rules, and expectations, and we are self-governed. Our members span the entire world and include influential figures in politics, religious institutions, finance, tech, law, and government organizations. The list goes on. In the pecking order, my family name means I belong to the upper echelon, which dictates that other members regard me highly. They often greet me with this common phrase as a sign of respect, but sometimes I wish they didn't acknowledge me at all.

I use a biometric keypad to gain access to the elevator, and it whisks me directly up into the gallery of my apartment. The space is bright and airy, with floor-to-ceiling windows and panoramic views of the skyline spanning the Brooklyn and Manhattan bridges and both rivers. It meets my requirements for when I'm in the city, including a library with a view of the Empire state building, a lap pool, a state-of-the-art kitchen, and a children's playroom. I usually find myself contained to the office during my time here, which is where I head today.

After several hours of reviewing my contracts and making preparations for the busy night ahead, I take leave to the kitchen. I retrieve the chef's prepared meal for my lunch, eating quickly and grimacing at my watch. As I suspected, there will not be time to push my body's limits in the gym. I'm only halfway through the salad when Luca buzzes to announce he's arrived.

Discarding the rest of the meal, I take a few mints from my pocket and suck on them as I step into the elevator. The descent is quick, and the journey to the coffee shop even quicker, given the proximity I chose. Luca idles at the curb and tells me he'll wait nearby for me. I thank him and step out of the car, adjusting my tie. It's only at that point I notice the speck of blood on my shirt cuff. Annoyance at the blemish has me trying to scrub it away to no avail, so with a sigh, I head inside.

A Society daughter greets me at the door with a shy smile. "Mr. Scarcello. So nice to see you again."

I dip my head, avoiding eye contact with her. "Please thank your father for lending me the space today."

"Of course. It's our pleasure. Would you like me to stay and serve drinks while you conduct your business?"

I consider it and decide for my stomach's sake that I would enjoy a coffee, but also because the type of beverage a person chooses speaks volumes to their character. I want to set the tone, and then I want to take my candidate's choices onboard in the decision-making process. Every minute detail matters.

"That would be appreciated. I'll have a true macchiato."

"As you wish." She curtsies before me, and I try to hide my grimace as she hurries off to do my bidding.

I sit at a table in the back and glance over the files one more time, committing the names and photographs to memory. There are already a handful I'm quite certain I won't be considering, and I intend to dismiss them without delay when my gut confirms my suspicions.

The barista approaches with my macchiato and sets it down with an eagerness that betrays her motivations for volunteering her services today. As a Society daughter, she would be expected to offer regardless, but I suspect she envisions me much like I treated my client this morning. A prize fish to be hooked, captured, and displayed like a trophy.

"Can I get you anything else, sir?" she asks. "A croissant, perhaps? Or a cannoli?"

"I'm fine, thank you." I dismiss her without a glance, not interested in sending mixed signals. It would break the hearts of many Society daughters to know I don't intend to marry. Though they aren't interested in me for my shining personality, but rather the status of my last name.

Five minutes pass before the first applicant arrives. Her sickly-sweet perfume blows into the coffee shop when she opens the door, standing there open-mouthed, gawking at the empty space uncomfortably.

"I wasn't sure it was open," she says, lingering near the door as she eyes me off like the grim reaper.

Her instincts are telling her I'm a predator, a threat, and she'd be right. I can't have someone with no backbone looking after Nino.

"Are you Tiffany?" I inquire.

She clears her throat and jerks her chin. "Y-yes. That's me."

"You may leave," I tell her. "You don't have the necessary qualifications for the position."

She stares at me in disbelief for a few brief seconds before relief makes her shoulders sag. Without a word, she turns and goes. And so, the process continues. Some make it through the door. Some even sit down and order a drink. Pumpkin spiced lattes, Frappuccino's, and ridiculous over-the-top drink orders that are far too complicated for my liking. I dismiss one before she can even spit out half of her mile-long list of requirements for a caffeinated beverage. The others that make it to the table have their own set of flaws. Too meek. Too flirtatious. Too much perfume. Not enough experience. Unrealistic job expectations. Questions about the local nightlife in my city and if they'll be drug tested. It goes on and on until my mind is sufficiently numb, and I'm beginning to agree that Gwen was, in fact, right. This is never going to work.

The door opens, and the last candidate comes through, but I'm already prepared to dismiss her. She was on the discard pile before she even arrived, because something about her background check seemed to prickle my senses. I couldn't pinpoint it, but something felt off. It was too squeaky clean for my liking.

"You may leave," I tell her without even glancing up. "I'm done conducting interviews for the day."

I expect to hear her footfalls as she returns to the door, but instead, she approaches the table. I can feel her gaze on me, and it irritates me when I'm forced to repeat myself.

"I said I'm done. No more interviews."

She still doesn't move away, but I can hear her rifling around in her purse. I glance at her shoes out of curiosity, noting the black flats and gray tights that remind me of a schoolmarm. The slow perusal of her body only confirms my suspicion. She's wearing a navy-blue skirt suit that favors the side of modesty, and her dark, cocoa brown hair is pulled up into a tight bun, matching the tense expression on her face. I take note of her features with equal parts annoyance and disdain. She possesses all the natural characteristics of beauty, though she's done nothing to highlight them. Unlike the other women, it doesn't appear that she's wearing much makeup, if any. Her heart-shaped face has a youthful glow that belies an innocence I'm not equipped to deal with. Her lips are pillowy, and there's a faint dimple on her chin that makes her appearance unique. But her positive attributes are offset by the shapeless clothing and silk neck scarf that reminds me of the housewives in the Hamptons.

I don't know what she's still doing here or why she's not speaking, but she doesn't seem to have any trouble maintaining my gaze. It's somewhat surprising and a little disturbing. Most women seem to sense that I'm not the type of man you want to look directly in the eye. I'm not the man you want to challenge. But she is either too bold for her own good or too reckless to care.

She flips her phone screen around to show me a note she's typed out, capturing my curiosity.

You agreed to an interview. I am here for said interview, and I intend to follow through. So, please do me the courtesy of keeping your end of the deal. I don't appreciate my time or effort being wasted.

My lip tips up slightly as I read the words twice to ensure I'm not imagining them. I'm not sure why, but I find myself even more intrigued by who this creature could possibly be. On paper, she was the most boring of all the candidates, but she has managed to capture my interest in person.

"By all means." I gesture to the chair across from me. "Take a seat. I wouldn't want to waste *your* time."

She sits down primly and nods at me before sliding a file folder across the table. Five seconds ago, I was eager to leave, but right now, I'm in no rush to plow through her file. I find myself wanting to know her secrets the way I know my clients'. What are her fears? Her insecurities? More importantly, what trauma gave her such a steely backbone?

The barista approaches again and asks for her drink order, and I arch an eyebrow as she types out another note in the same app. This time, she uses the text-to-voice feature to place her order.

"One espresso macchiato coming right up." The barista makes a note of it and walks away.

I make a careful study of the woman I know as Natalia from her file. Natalia Cabrera.

"Do you not speak?" I ask her bluntly.

Her shoulders tense as she stabs a finger at the file folder before me as if to indicate the answers are all in there. I still don't open it. Instead, I take the opportunity to study the visible scars on her hand and the slim forearm peeking out of her jacket sleeve.

"What are the scars from?" I lean back against my chair and observe her.

Her eyes narrow, and her fingers move rapidly over the keys on her phone screen as she writes a response.

How does that pertain to the job?

Her resistance amuses me on some level, mostly because I am not accustomed to it. A Society daughter would answer my question enthusiastically without delay. She is most certainly not a Society daughter.

"It pertains to the job because you'll be working closely with my son. I need to know if you're reckless or dangerous."

Her brows draw together as if what I said bothers her in some way, but she answers me regardless.

They are from a car accident when I was a child. I was not driving. I'm sure you saw the records in the background check you performed.

"Indeed." I allow my eyes to roam over her freely as the barista delivers her drink, interrupting us briefly. "I read your file, and I'm inclined to wonder how someone could manage to live such an ordinary life. Not a single parking ticket. No indiscretions to speak of on your school reports. No significant relationships in your life. It's all so ... unremarkable."

She seems to understand I'm testing her, but her gaze doesn't waver. Her eyes are clear, her pulse steady. When she writes her reply, there isn't so much as a hint of deception on her features.

My life may not be remarkable, but it has served me well.

I find it an odd thing to say, and despite her assurances, I still can't quell this strange feeling in my gut. There's something peculiar about her. Something mysterious and secretive, and yet, something balancing. I find her honesty refreshing and her stillness even more so. Her inability to speak would serve my needs well, maintaining a quiet home and ensuring no secrets might accidentally spill from her lips, but would Nino like her?

I open the file before me, scanning the typewritten cover letter. She introduces herself as Natalia Cabrera, aged twenty-seven years, with a degree in early child development and education. She has experience in Montessori schooling and references from her time as a nanny. Under the list of her extensive skills, she notes that she is fluent in sign language and can learn and teach other languages as preferred. She is also certified in first aid and CPR. At the end of the cover letter, she notes that she has vocal cord paralysis from damage to the nerve. She makes a point to state that she is unable to speak verbally but can communicate with children through text-to-voice, writing, or teaching ASL if permitted. It all sounds well and good, but I am not certain how Nino might feel about this style of communication.

When I look up at her again, I catch her staring at the blood stain on my sleeve and the faintest hint of her pulse increasing. I wait a moment to see if she chooses to acknowledge it, but she doesn't. I decide it's better that way. I suspect some part of her already realizes this is not the typical business arrangement, and I want that cemented in her mind. If or when I allow her to enter my world, she won't leave until I give her the option. That is if I give her the option.

"I'd like to do a second interview tomorrow." I close the file. "I'll send a car to pick you up."

She shakes her head, typing out a quick reply.

I can make my own way.

I cock my head to the side. "That's unlikely, considering it will be at an undisclosed location."

I watch for any signs of fear, but she does not move. The only noticeable tightening is in the crease between her brows. If she were a smart woman, one who trusted any reasonable instinct, she would tell me no. But for once, I find that I don't want a rational interaction. I want her to pass this test and every additional one I throw at her from now on. She returns to the app on her phone, her fingers moving elegantly as she writes her answer.

Very well. I'm staying at the Paramount Hotel.

"10 a.m." I rise from my seat and peer down at her. "Don't be late."

3

NATALIA

I step out into the cool New York morning, discreetly pausing to check my reflection in the glass behind me. The sun isn't quite peeking through the clouds today, and it feels as overcast as my current mood. My black skirt suit is probably the nicest one I own, but somehow it still feels like a paper sack on my body. I'm a mess of nerves, but I am determined not to show it.

I can never show it.

With a mournful sigh, I decide that I look professional enough. But what does it matter? For all I know, this man could be luring me to my inevitable death. If I didn't have everything riding on this interview, there's no way I would have agreed to let his driver pick me up.

This is a power play by my future employer. A test. It was evident in his eyes as he considered me yesterday, measuring me up like one might examine their produce. He was looking for bruises and weak spots. Signs of malignant decay just beneath the surface. I couldn't hide the obvious flaws on my skin, or my inability to converse with him as he would probably prefer, but I am well acquainted with hiding the deepest rot. The type I can't cut out.

Alessio Scarcello is a dangerous man. If my gut didn't already know it, my research was confirmation enough. There is nothing to be found in his name. Not an address. A phone number. A social media page. He may as well be a phantom. I would be naïve to believe he's not involved in a deeper criminal network. That's why he demands secrecy. A private car to whisk me off to an undisclosed location, just as the job placement required a willingness to work anywhere in the world. New York is not his home, and if I do get this position, I will be working in another undisclosed location. Any sane person would run, but I'm willing to sacrifice my sanity in exchange for what I desire.

A black Rolls Royce pulls up to the front entrance, and a driver gets out, his gaze immediately moving to mine.

"Miss Cabrera, my name is Luca. I am here to drive you to your interview."

I swallow and nod, doing a quick once over of the man. He's an older man, fifties perhaps, but he's very large and visibly strong, a detail I can never miss. A detail that always sets off those alarm bells in my mind that warn me to flee, to survive. I have learned to ignore them, so instead, I put one foot stiffly in front of the other as he opens the back door for me.

Once I'm settled inside, Luca takes his position at the driver's seat and smoothly pulls back into the flow of traffic without a word. He doesn't speak to me the entirety of the drive, and at first, I find that I'm okay with that. Alessio must have made him aware that I can't answer verbally. As we exit the city altogether and put more distance behind us than I'd care for, my hands tangle nervously in my lap. I stare out the window at the passing scenery as a bead of sweat tickles my neck. We drive for what feels like hours, but I know it can't be. It's just that time always slows when those innate fears start to trickle into my consciousness.

Finally, Luca pulls off the freeway and into a town I've never been to: Desolation, New York. It seems like a strange place, too far removed to have an interview, and I can't seem to quell this sinking feeling in my gut. Alessio suspected there was more to my story yesterday, and he was right. Did my lies betray me? Could he sense them beneath my assertions of truth?

Luca navigates the streets easily, directing us past the broken-down buildings and boarded-up windows, completely unaware of my small panic attack in the backseat. I suck in tiny breaths of air, pinching my fingers together to distract myself. Then I repeat the only truth Alessio needs to know, the one I will tell him if he insists on questioning me further. I lost my last nanny position when my employers moved abroad, and I'm living out of a hotel, siphoning off the savings I've worked so hard to maintain. I have no family and no purpose, and this is it for me. I need this job as much as I need air to breathe.

"I'll get your door," Luca says gruffly, pulling me from my thoughts.

When I glance outside, I see that we're parked in front of an old warehouse called Butcher and Son. Panic surges inside me again, but I swallow it down, beat it into submission, and plaster a neutral expression on my face when Luca opens the door. I'm used to pretending, and often, I feel like a Jack in the box. I'm wound up so tight, I could explode at any moment, but not today. Not right now.

I force myself to move, erasing the thoughts from my mind as Luca opens the creaky door and gestures me inside. I stop and stare at the space, nearly choking on the smell of dust and decay that still lingers. Dried blood has seeped into the floor, staining it with the evidence of violent ends. Large sheets of plastic crinkle beneath Luca's feet as he moves along, telling me to follow.

Robotically, I do.

He leads me into a backroom with a butcher table, and I try not to breathe in the pungent aroma that's curdling my stomach. We find Alessio waiting in a chair, casually sipping from a mug of coffee as he stares directly at me.

"You came."

The observation sounds almost taunting, as if he expected I wouldn't show. I'm sure he thought I was weak somehow. Maybe he assumed I'd be too afraid, perhaps. Sure, both qualities can be true at times, but I have no intention of ever allowing him to see that.

He gestures to a metal chair across from him, and I lower myself into it, hoping he doesn't notice the stiffness in my body. Luca disappears without a word, and then we are left alone. I wait for him to speak, letting the silence fill the space between us because I suspect this is a test too.

"You seem like a reasonable woman." Alessio sets his mug onto the table beside him. "I'm sure you have deduced by now that I'm not an ordinary man. The job requirements demanded discretion, loyalty, and dedication. Qualities you obviously must possess since you are here."

He leans forward, his elbows on his knees as his stark blue eyes stare through me. From this close, I can smell the scent of his clean, woodsy cologne. It's a welcome reprieve from the environment around us. I notice the other details of his features too. The angular jaw. The five o'clock shadow. The scar on his chin. His posture, though relaxed, is still somehow rigid too. His smooth lyrical voice lulls me into a false sense of safety. I'm certain he's used it to his advantage many times before.

I don't know what he does professionally, but I know I won't forget that bloodstain on his cuff. It was in my thoughts all day as I sat in my hotel room, and I allowed my imagination to get the best of me. Does he hurt people? Kill them? I suspect he does, and yet here I am.

The truth is, I can only speculate what I'm getting myself into. I know when I look into his eyes, I can see something damaged in him too. Something he has shuttered away from the people around him. He hides behind his intimidating gaze and sharp tongue.

"I have considered your application all night," he tells me. "And I must ask you, Miss Cabrera. Understanding the facts as you do, why do you want this position?"

Cautiously, I allow the slightest hint of vulnerability to leak through the cracks of my carefully crafted armor.

Truthfully? I need this position. As I explained in my application, I've been left without employment rather abruptly. I'm living out of a hotel, and I have no purpose if I'm not working.

He reads my response and challenges it. "Surely, with your qualifications, you'd have no problem finding a position locally. Why respond to my ad? What was it in particular that made you want to interview?"

I tap my finger against the edge of my phone before responding.

I need a change. Your ad specified the position wasn't local. I've wanted to leave New York for some time now, and this seemed like the opportunity to do so.

He leans back and considers me, seemingly satisfied with my answers. Then he jumps to the next question.

"What caused the scars on your arms?"

Irritation bubbles up my throat, forcing me to lock my jaw in place. Calmly, I stuff it back down and type, sticking to my original declaration.

I told you. A car accident.

"Yes, that's what you said," he says. "But I don't believe you."

I incline my head, fingers moving rapidly as I formulate my retort.

Well, I would let you interrogate my parents, but they have both passed on. Cancer took my mother, and my father died from a heart condition. I have no siblings to speak of, and I'm quite certain the deer who witnessed the entire event is long gone, so there is little I can do to change your mind, short of performing a séance.

He doesn't reply. His eyes move over me so sharply, they feel like a physical caress, and I find myself shivering in response. It's the strangest reaction, and he doesn't miss it, but he doesn't respond to it either.

"You are willing to move wherever I require?" he asks.

I nod.

"This isn't a job you can quit easily," he threatens.

I have no intentions of quitting.

His lip tips slightly at the corner like my bravery amuses him. Then, abruptly, he rises to his feet, glancing at me dismissively.

"Luca will return you to your hotel. Pack your things. We have an early morning flight."

4

NATALIA

"Hello?"

I listen to Lynn's crackled voice playing over my messages as I stare at the rain outside my hotel window. It's the last voicemail I had from her.

"Hello, Natalia? I think we have a bad connection. I don't know if you picked up, but Michael and I are bringing home dinner tonight, so don't worry about cooking. We'll be home in a few hours. See you soon. Love ya, bye."

My breath hitches, and a tear leaks from my eye and slides down my cheek. This is all I have left of my friend, but sometimes, I imagine how our conversation would go if she were still here.

I would tell her it was me, and she'd ask if I was okay. I would tell her that I am, but it would be a lie. She'd ask me where I was, and I'd ignore the question. If she knew I was close, she would want to see me, and it isn't safe for her. I know that now, but it's too late to save her.

In my imagination, I'd tell her that I was leaving, and I didn't know if or when I'd be able to call again. That really, all I wanted to do was say goodbye. There would be a long, drawn-out pause before she'd answer, her voice hoarse. "Please, don't do this."

My grip would tighten on the phone as I told her I had to. The line would fall silent, and we'd both know there's nothing else to say, really. She doesn't want me to die, and I don't want her to either. In my reality, I can't go back and make that choice. I have to live with the guilt of what happened. Her willingness to help cost her and her husband their lives, and not just them. There was a doctor that turned up dead too. There could be more I don't even know about, realistically.

I have to live with those wounds. Asking for help from anyone else is out of the question. What I'm about to do, I have to do on my own.

I close my eyes and listen to her message one more time, wishing she could say something else. Hoping that wherever her soul is, she will understand this is goodbye. She's my oldest friend. Someone who knows me better than anyone. More than anything, I hope she's forgiven me for the things I can't go back and change.

The line disconnects, and I watch the rain fall, a raw wave of grief washing over my soul. My bags are packed. The car will be here in ten minutes. I know that there is a ray of hope somewhere on the other side of that rain, because I'm getting on a plane today. I'm going to begin the journey I've spent years preparing for. It can only end one of two ways. Now it's time to do what I must. To leave this city behind and prove my worth to Alessio, clinging to the hope that none of my skeletons come tumbling out of my closet.

I pocket my phone and stand up, brushing my fingers over my clothes to smooth away any wrinkles. I do the same with my face, adopting a neutral expression as I grab the handles of my suitcases and usher them to the door. With one last glance over the space, I accept that this chapter of my life has closed, and the real one begins today.

Downstairs, Luca meets me outside once again, loading my suitcases into the trunk and opening the door to secure me inside. Alessio is absent, and I wonder how he's getting to the airport, but I decide it's best not to overthink the situation. Instead, I watch the city streets pass us by one last time during the journey, taking note of the honking horns and pedestrians. The hot dog vendors. The familiar cracked sidewalks and loud, crowded restaurants. I have no love for any of it, I decide, and I'm not sad to leave it behind.

Luca delivers me to a secluded runway, and I'm not surprised to see that Alessio uses a private jet. By the way he dressed, I could tell he had money, but the salary was a good indication too.

"You may board the plane, Miss Cabrera," Luca tells me. "I'll ensure your suitcases are stowed."

I nod at him and exit the car, pausing briefly at the short set of stairs leading to the jet. Luca gave me permission, but I need to stop for a breath, my anxiety catching me off guard. There's still a part of me that doesn't believe this is real. It's as if I dreamed it up somehow. Touching the railing grounds me and brings me back to reality. I'm here. This is really happening.

I take the steps cautiously, and once I'm onboard, a flight attendant is there to greet me. She welcomes me with a smile and directs me to a seat at the front. As I sit, I notice Alessio in the seat closest to the rear of the jet, paper in hand. He glances up briefly to meet my gaze but doesn't acknowledge me. The attendant sets a folder and a pen onto the table in front of me, and by the time I redirect my gaze, Alessio has returned his attention to the paper.

"This is from Mr. Scarcello," the attendant informs me. "My name is Jennifer, and I'll be here to assist you on today's flight. Would you care for a glass of champagne or anything else?"

I shake my head, and she strides back to the galley. My gaze moves down to the folder and then back to Alessio, but he doesn't look at me again. With a quiet sigh, I lean back, buckle my seatbelt, and then open the folder. It doesn't surprise me to find a contract inside. As I look it over, I would consider much of it to be standard, particularly for high-paying clients in New York. There's the run-of-the-mill non-disclosure agreement, requirements for privacy and discretion, and a carefully detailed plan of the child's schedule, which I set aside. The last document is the one that makes me freeze, my blood pounding in my ears as I read it over. It's a written agreement that I will not disclose my location to friends, family, or acquaintances under any circumstances, emergency or otherwise. I never had plans on doing so, but this only confirms my suspicions about Alessio, and I find it difficult to control my trembling hand as I force a signature onto the paper.

When I set the pen aside and glance up, I find him watching me with a carefully controlled expression and an intensity in his gaze that sends a shiver up my spine again. I offer him a stiff smile, closing the folder and watching him as he rises and comes to retrieve it personally. He does so without a word, briefly disappearing into the galley where he speaks to the attendant. She pops into the cockpit a moment later, and within seconds, the pilot's voice comes over the speakers, informing us we are ready for takeoff and his instructions to remain seated.

I find the entire sequence of events very odd, and I have to wonder if Alessio waited to clear the pilot for takeoff until after I signed the contract. He acted as if I might back out. As if I might run. Perhaps a smarter woman would, but Alessio Scarcello can't terrify me. After all, I've already met the Devil himself.

I lean my head back against the leather cushion and close my eyes, focusing on my breathing as the engines rumble to life and we take to the sky. The whole process is much faster than a commercial flight, but it still depletes my sensory threshold as I force myself to tune out the loud noises and shaking before we reach flying altitude. Once we do, the attendant returns to offer me a fresh fruit plate with some pastries, but I'm distracted by Alessio rising from his seat. He glances at me momentarily, locks his gaze with mine, and I find something disturbing in his eyes. Not that I'm disturbed, rather that he seems to be. His brows pinch slightly, and the vein in his neck pulses as he reaches up to adjust his tie. Then, as if it never happened, he disappears into the bedroom door at the rear of the jet and remains there for the duration of the journey.

Seattle, Washington. That's where I find myself when we step off the plane, and a different driver appears with another Rolls Royce. He introduces himself as Manuel as he whisks us to the car, securing us before he returns for the luggage. It's all so efficient and quiet. I'm not entirely certain what to make of any of it, but it seems Alessio prefers it this way, so I don't bother him as we set off toward the undisclosed location he calls home.

The drive is tense and silent. He sits back against his seat and does not glance at me or speak to me. He doesn't check his phone, or make small talk with Manuel, or even stare at the passing scenery. He just sits there like a statue beside me, his hands resting on his thighs, his back rigid and straight, his face unmoving.

I occupy myself by watching the scenery. Seattle is a beautiful city, although it has a reputation for being rainy and gray. I suppose the same can be said about any location, depending on who you ask.

I can see a large expanse of the city from the freeway, and it looks about the same as any other place. Only, the vegetation is greener. Thicker. Brighter, perhaps. I accredit that to the rain and wonder which places Nino likes to visit here. During the trip, I had a chance to look over his schedule, which was filled with enriching activities as I suspected it would be. There are piano lessons, Italian studies with a tutor, martial arts, scouting, swimming, chess club, and those are just the weekly activities. There is also a revolving schedule with special events that occur monthly or bi-monthly. I felt overwhelmed just looking at it, and I can only imagine how Nino must feel. I do have to wonder if it's Alessio's goal to tire him out by piling on all those activities in addition to his regular schooling, or if he is like many of the upper crust parents in New York, determined to raise the brightest children who excel at everything.

A frown tugs at my lips, but I school my expression as Manuel navigates the car off the freeway and into what can only be described as an opulent neighborhood. The houses are gated, grandiose, and incredibly private. As I'm taking everything in, Manuel pulls up to a gate, rolls down his window, and stares directly into a camera that seems to scan his face before a buzzer signals the mechanism unlocking. It's a high-tech form of biosecurity, and I can only wonder why the man next to me would require such measures. I'm not entirely certain I want to know the answer to that question either.

Manuel drives down the winding road through a thicket of trees on either side of the driveway before he rounds what appears to be an Italian-style villa. The structure is more beautiful than I could have anticipated, with a natural stone exterior and classic Mediterranean-style arches throughout. But it's the waterfront view that captures my attention, along with the accompanying Seattle skyline across the bay. When Manuel opens the door for me, I have a few brief moments to notice the dock and the boat house near the shoreline.

"Come." Alessio gestures for me. "I'll show you to your room."

I follow him across the well-manicured lawn, past a large pergola, and through a stone courtyard to the front door. There is another camera there, which Alessio uses himself to gain entry into the house. I swallow down my nerves as we step inside, and the details become background to what I've been anxiously waiting for.

"I'll give you the evening to get settled in," he tells me. "You can unpack, and my housekeeper will give you a tour before Manuel goes over the security measures with you."

I tap him on the shoulder to stop him, trying my best to contain the noticeable disappointment on my face. He seems eager to rid himself of me as I write out my question for him.

Am I not going to meet Nino?

"He's not here." Alessio stares back at me, his face devoid of any sign of emotion. "I have to pick him up later. You can meet him in the morning."

He continues his brisk pace when I don't reply, ushering me up a long staircase with black and white marbled tiles. The blow of disappointment weighs heavy on my shoulders, but I try to absorb the details because I know they are important. I need to familiarize myself with every inch of this house, particularly the doors and windows. I take in as much as I can from my vantage point before Alessio reaches the landing and turns down a long hallway.

I never thought of myself as a loud walker, but as I hurry to keep up with Alessio's pace, I realize that I must be. I seem to be the only one making noise as my flats make contact with the well-polished floors. I'm not entirely certain how he does it, but Alessio seems to glide right over the marble like an apparition, making little to no noise at all. It's a detail that affirms his deadly nature, and a lump forms in my throat as my hypervigilance kicks into overdrive. I don't know that I'll ever be able to relax around him, but that's for the best. Letting my guard down isn't an option. Not with anyone.

We come to a stop outside an ornate wooden door, and Alessio turns slightly, pointing to the next door along the hall. "That is Nino's room. This will be yours."

My eyes are still on the other door as he opens mine, and I linger for a moment too long in the hall when he steps inside, waiting for me to follow. He watches me carefully as I join him to take in my surroundings. The bedroom is much larger than I expected, with beautiful wood flooring, an intricately carved ivory-colored bed frame, and windows complete with a sitting area and a waterfront view.

I turn to look at him, and he seems to be waiting for a response, so I offer him one.

This room is really just for me?

He nods, and his shoulders seem to relax a fraction as if he's pleased that I'm pleased. I find it strange, but I write a thank you in the phone app. He acknowledges it with a dip of his head, his expression neutral as he heads for the door.

"Manuel will be along shortly with your bags. Angelina will give you a tour when you're ready, and then you can go through security measures."

MANUEL HAS DELIVERED MY BAGS, and I've successfully unpacked the contents of them in the closet. I don't own many clothes, but I have several variations of what I would consider my uniform. Skirt suits, tights, and flats. I have a pair of jeans and a few colors of plain tee shirts and sweaters for the rare days I'm not working. The clothes are what I could afford while I shuttled away every penny I could manage from my salary over the last five years. They served well as far as being functional, but in this house, I'd be lying if I said I didn't feel out of place.

While I wait for the housekeeper, I examine my room, pull out drawers, check the windows' locks, and pick up the decorative items to inspect them. I have a strong suspicion there are probably many cameras in this house, and I'm anxious to know if there's one in this room as well. Upon close examination, I can't seem to find any, which is a relief. Though I know from experience, cameras and listening devices aren't always obvious.

A knock sounds at the door, startling me slightly, and I move to open it, but there isn't time. A young woman steps inside, glancing at me like a frumpy interloper who doesn't belong here. She is stunningly beautiful, with long, sleek black hair styled like she just stepped out of a salon. Her features are modelesque, with angular cheeks and bold red lips. She's wearing a form-fitting black dress that accentuates her every curve and heels to match. I wonder who she could possibly be, but she takes it upon herself to inform me rather coolly.

"I'm Angelina." Her eyes cut over me sharply. "I'm in charge of Mr. Scarcello's household, and I'm here to give you a tour."

I nod at her, my stomach slightly uneasy over the cold greeting. I follow her into the corridor, and I tell myself her opinion doesn't matter. I'm not here to make friends.

She walks as briskly as Alessio, her hips swaying as her heels clip across the floor. She doesn't pause to let me look at anything as she points in each direction, listing off the areas of the home in rapid-fire succession.

"Guest bedroom, guest bedroom, bathroom, supply closet, library." She pauses when we reach the landing, pointing up the staircase as she turns to narrow her eyes at me in warning. "The third level is Mr. Scarcello's. You are never to go up there for any reason. Understand?"

I find my own eyes narrowing slightly in response to her attitude but decide she's not worth the battle. She means nothing in the grand scheme of things, and I refuse to show her that she can get to me.

"Did you hear me?" she sneers. "Or are you deaf as well?"

My hands clench into fists as I force a stiff nod and then type out a message, cranking up the volume so there can be no doubt.

I heard you just fine.

She turns in a huff, continuing with the tour, and I try to listen, but my thoughts are elsewhere as I take in the details as quickly as I can. I don't know if I'm free to explore the house on my own or not, but I decide that will be a question better saved for Manuel.

"There's a playroom down there on the left," Angelina says. "And the rest are guest rooms."

I don't get to see any of them because she leads me down the stairs back to the ground level, where she briefly shows me the parlor room, an indoor pool, a sunroom, the gym, and a wine cellar, which she tells me is also off-limits.

At the conclusion of the tour, she informs me somewhat reluctantly there are chef-prepared meals available in the kitchen when I want them. She also notifies me I'm expected to attend breakfast in the formal dining room every morning. With that, she points at a chair in the hall and barks out a command for me to sit like I'm a dog.

Reluctantly, I do, and I'm relieved when she disappears, leaving me to the silence of my thoughts. A few moments later, like a well-oiled machine, Manuel appears, and I've never been so relieved to see such a neutral expression.

"Miss Cabrera, if you'll come with me, we'll get your security access set up."

I follow him down the hall to an office that Angelina didn't mention. He gestures me inside and pulls out my chair for me before he takes a seat across from me at the desk.

"Mr. Scarcello uses facial recognition software for anyone who requires access to the property," he tells me. "So, we're going to set that up today."

My nerves fray as I squeeze my hands together in my lap. I suspected security would be tight here, but I was hoping for a simple code for my access. Scanning my face means they'll have that information stored in a database later. It will only make it that much easier to find me.

Manuel sets up the camera and gives me feedback as he has me position my face in different angles, explaining that the technology is designed to work in a range of lighting with various hairstyles, hats, etc. When he's finished, I take a deep, quiet breath and watch him input some of my information into the computer.

"Okay." He stabs a sequence of keys on the computer and then shuts it off. "There are a few things I need to go over with you."

I meet his gaze, hoping he can't sense my nerves.

"Angelina should have already told you, but the third level of the home is off-limits. If there is ever a situation that arises where you believe you need access, come to me first."

I nod in acknowledgment, and he continues.

"The neighboring property line outside is well established with a stone privacy wall. You'll see it if you're in the garden. If Nino is not at his scheduled activities outside the home, he is to be within these walls at all times, unless you have express permission from Mr. Scarcello for a planned outing."

My heart sinks as all the notions I had about day trips to explore the area slip away, but I don't let it show.

"When you and Nino leave the house for any occasion of any nature, you will be attended by myself or Mr. Scarcello. There are no exceptions."

Again, I nod, tension seeping into my body as the walls of this beautiful home start to feel more like a prison.

"As expressed in your contract, there are to be no visitors to the home. Your friends or family are not permitted to know where you work or reside. Again, there are no exceptions."

I pull up my app to respond.

That won't be an issue.

He studies me, his expression all business. "Do you have any questions for me?"

Am I free to roam the house, other than the third level? And the grounds as well?

"Yes," he answers. "You can make use of the house and the grounds as needed, so long as it's not disruptive. Anything else?"

I shake my head, and he rises from his seat, moving around to open the door for me. "Then you're free to get settled in, Miss Cabrera. Have a good evening."

5

NATALIA

After helping myself to a prepared salad from the fridge for dinner, I take the opportunity to wander the house some more, hoping I don't bump into Angelina. To my relief, I don't. I study the layout, examining the exits closely. It occurs to me there are multiple options in this house, but upon closer inspection, it looks as if the windows are thicker than normal, and I suspect they may be shatterproof. That familiar sensation of being trapped threatens to suffocate the air from my lungs, but I choose to use the tools I've learned to ground myself and use logic rather than fear to cope.

It doesn't matter if the windows are shatterproof. There are doors I could use to leave, should the need ever arise. That's the mantra I play on repeat as I walk out onto the grounds, noting how much crisper and cleaner the air feels here. I inhale it greedily, making my way through the garden and to the perimeter where the stone wall lies, just as Manuel said. It's so thick and tall you can't see the neighbors. There is no mistaking the cameras lining the property. They seem to be everywhere. The more I look, the more I find.

I know very little about Alessio Scarcello. My research on him produced almost nothing useful, and it was only by a sheer stroke of luck that I discovered him in the first place. Between what I do know and my imagination filling in the gaps, it's confirmation that he's involved in a criminal syndicate. That's the only logical conclusion for all the secrecy. The cameras. The bizarre contract. His rigidness. The quiet way he moves. The almost inhuman blankness I've seen in his gaze. They are all bigger pieces of the puzzle, and it's difficult to ignore the dread taking shape deep in my gut.

I knew when I went to that interview I was walking into the eye of the storm. Despite what he may believe, I didn't sign that contract because I'm a stupid woman. I knew exactly what I was doing, and in the end, my only hope is that I will complete the job I came here to do.

As the breeze picks up, a chill moves over me, blowing across the water and settling over me like a damp blanket. It's still fairly early, but tomorrow is a big day, so I decide it's best to turn in. Back inside the security of my room, I slip into a pair of sweatpants, a tee-shirt, my night scarf, and my running shoes. Then I stand beside the light switch, agonizing for minutes as I stare at the dresser. Normally, I would barricade myself inside with a piece of furniture. It's the only way I can feel safe, but I have a sneaking suspicion that if Alessio were to show up at my door and find it in such a state, he might very well decide I'm better locked up in an asylum.

Anxiously, I turn off the light switch and traipse over to the bed, settling onto the side farthest from the door and securing my butterfly knife beneath my pillow. It's always a difficult task to sleep with running shoes on, but it's made even more difficult with such a heavy comforter, so I drag it up over my feet and stare at the ceiling. I go through the motions of a few breathing exercises to calm my nervous system, and then I close my eyes and imagine the same scenario I have played on repeat for years. It settles me, bringing a soft smile to my face and a warmth to my aching chest.

To my surprise, sleep does come for me that night. I don't know when or how, only that in the morning, I'm startled awake by the sharp rapping on my door.

I bolt upright, my heart pounding as sweat trickles down my brow. My hand reaches for the knife beneath the pillow when the door swings open, and Alessio appears. His eyes move over me, his features tightening when he sees the shoes on my feet. I try to cover them with the comforter, but it's too late. Shame and humiliation wash over me as I realize he already thinks I'm insane. Of course, he's wearing a perfectly pressed suit, ready to greet the day at six am.

"I'll need you earlier than I anticipated," he clips out. "Something has come up that I need to attend to. Can you be ready in thirty minutes?"

I nod, and he lingers near the door, his eyes moving back to my neck. It's impossible to miss the irritation on his face.

"Do you always wear a scarf?"

It's slower this time, but again, I nod. His eyes lock with mine, and I have the oddest sensation that he's stealing my breath from my lungs. I wonder if he can feel this strange tension between us too. Is it just an adrenaline response?

"We'll be waiting for you in the dining room," he says abruptly, and before I can respond, he's gone.

I drag myself out of bed and hurry along to the closet, grabbing my clothes for the day. My nerves feel like they are unraveling as I go through the routine of showering, brushing my teeth, and applying a light touch of mascara and powder. When I glance at my reflection in the mirror, I almost don't recognize myself. In some ways, it feels like no time has passed because my life came to an abrupt halt when I was only twenty years old. Back then, I had a short hairstyle. I spent time on my makeup, carefully choosing colors that complimented my skin tone. I wore clothes that made me feel cute or pretty. I was intro-verted but didn't mind the occasional attention. I could still smile, laugh, and go on with my day, knowing that there was pain in the world but never truly aware of the depths of it. Not until the devil himself came to my door.

A solitary tear slides down my cheek, and I swipe it away, squaring my shoulders and blowing out a breath. None of that matters. I'm here now. I've made it this far. Everything is going to be okay.

I leave my room and head downstairs. Upon entering the kitchen, I wince a little when I see Angelina at the counter, but my attention drifts from her completely when I hear a child's voice in the dining room. Ignoring her gaze on me, I move toward the sound of conversation and turn the corner to find Alessio sitting at the head of the table while the boy is to his left. From my viewpoint, I can only see a head of brown hair and a downcast gaze as he stares at his plate of food. He appears to be upset, but I can't be sure until I glance at Alessio, who also seems to be equally annoyed.

He stands up and gestures for the boy. "Nino, come here. It's time to meet Miss Cabrera."

My breath catches in my throat as the small boy turns to look at me, and I'm met with the sweetest brown eyes I've ever seen. He sniffles, wiping away tears as he tries to hold back his shuttered breaths. His distress pains me, and I find myself angry with Alessio, even though I don't know what the issue is.

I kneel to Nino's level, pointing at my phone screen and writing out a short greeting that the app reads to him.

Hello, Nino. It's nice to meet you. I'm Natalia.

He peeks up at me from beneath his long dark lashes, and then he looks to Alessio for approval.

"He can be ... a bit shy," Alessio says.

I swallow the lump in my throat and write a new message, this time flashing it toward the man in question.

Is everything okay?

"It's fine," he answers dismissively. "Breakfast is always a battle. The chef prepared him an omelet. He doesn't want to eat it."

I glance at Nino's full plate. There's enough food on there to feed a grown man. It appears to be some sort of truffle omelet with fresh herbs. On the side, there are segments of grapefruit and a slice of rye toast. I glance at the spread in the center of the table and then at Alessio's plate, where there are fresh pastries, fruit, and eggs.

May I ask why he's not eating what you're eating?

He frowns as if the thought never occurred to him. "Angelina says this is what children should eat. It's healthy."

My lips pinch together in distaste, and I hope it's not too obvious. *May I talk to him?* I ask.

He stares at me for a long moment before conceding. I write out a message for Nino and play it for him.

I can see that you have some big emotions right now. Sometimes I have big emotions too, and that's okay. Do you know what I like to do when I'm feeling sad or mad or upset?

"What?" He wipes his eyes.

I ask what I can do to feel better. Maybe I'll take a few breaths, or ask for a hug, or talk to a friend about what I'm feeling. And if I want, I might even roar like a lion or jump up and down and shake it off.

A small smile appears on his face at the idea, and I can see some of his anxiety ebbing away already.

We could try it now, I suggest. *What do you think? Would you like to take a few breaths with me?*

He nods.

Okay, let's go on the count of three. Breathe in with your nose and blow it out through your mouth.

I hold up my fingers to count, and he mirrors me, doing the same as we inhale and exhale together. I'm quite certain Alessio is staring at me like I'm a lunatic, but my focus is on Nino. After the first breath, I hold up one finger and count down again. We take a few more breaths, and once he's relaxed, I return to my phone.

That was a great job, Nino. Do you feel better?

"Yes." He glances back at his plate. "But I don't want to eat that."

I rise and write a note for Alessio. *Can he try some of the other food at the table?*

Alessio stares at me, his gaze so intense it's burning into my skin, but I have no idea what he's thinking.

"I suppose it wouldn't hurt," he says.

I move to the space beside Nino's seat, grab the extra plate meant for me, and then hold out my other hand for him. Nino stares at it for a long time, his eyes moving over my face uncertainly before he gently places his fingers in mine. I give them a soft squeeze, trying my best to reassure him.

We start at the mountain of pastries in the center of the table. I look at Nino and then point to them in question. Nino glances at Alessio, chewing on his lip before returning a tiny nod and pointing to a cherry Danish. I retrieve the Danish for him, then move on to the fruit selection, taking time to point at each option and allow Nino to choose for himself. This time, I hand the tongs to him, giving him a choice of how much he would like. During the process, his shoulders seem to relax, and by the time we move onto the platter of eggs cooked several ways, he seems quite at ease choosing for himself.

Alessio watches the entire interaction with an odd expression on his face, but I don't look to him for approval nearly as much as Nino does. Several minutes later, he's settled back into his seat, eating his breakfast without a fight. Alessio watches him take the first few bites before returning his gaze to me.

In my experience, many children do better with family-style options. If they can pick and choose what they'd like, they may even surprise you.

His brows draw together, and Angelina enters the room, pausing when she sees the plate prepared for Nino shoved aside. Her venomous gaze moves to me. "You will spoil him."

My eyes narrow on her, and for once, I'm glad I have to hold my tongue because my patience with her is already wearing thin.

Don't worry. I type. *I'll eat it.*

This idea seems to dismay her even more, and she glances at Alessio as if he should put a stop to this. He doesn't notice her gaze on him, or if he does, he chooses not to acknowledge her. She tops up his coffee with a stiffness that betrays her anger and then leaves.

The remainder of the meal is quiet, and I'm eager for Alessio to tend to his business, whatever it may be, so I can get to know Nino. I suspect that Angelina will be a problem, and I'll have to tread carefully. For now, I just want to spend some time with Nino and familiarize myself with our routine.

"I have a phone for you." Alessio rises from his chair and slides an iPhone across the table. "I will check in with you occasionally through messages, and I would like a prompt answer."

I glance at the device and frown.

I already have a phone.

"This is the phone you will use to communicate with me," he tells me. "And should any issues arise, I expect you to reach out immediately."

Of course.

I reach for the phone hesitantly, knowing very well he probably has some means of tracking software on here. It doesn't matter because I'll only use it to communicate with him.

"I will be gone for most of the day," he says. "You have Nino's schedule. I trust you will not deviate."

I nod my assurance, but he lingers for another long moment. I can't tell what he's thinking, but the intensity of his gaze makes a flush creep over my neck. I swallow, and his eyes dip to the triangle of skin between my scarf and the top button of my suit jacket. Then, before I can convince myself I didn't imagine it, he's gone.

I glance down quickly, checking that the buttons are done, and nothing is inappropriate or out of place, but there isn't.

Nino peeks up at me, and I offer him a watery smile. He's a beautiful boy with such a sweet disposition. I knew he would be.

I'm so happy to be here with you, Nino.

He listens to my message, considering it for a moment. "Why can't you talk?"

This is how I talk, I write. *But I can teach you a new way too. Would you like to learn? It can be our own secret code.*

He seems intrigued by the idea, and I'm glad when he nods. I check my watch, noting we have about twenty minutes before Manuel will drive us to the school to drop him off for the day.

I hear you're a star student. I bet you can say the alphabet in English and Italian.

He giggles quietly. "That's easy. I learned that a long time ago. I'm in first grade now."

Of course. I wiggle my brows at him playfully. *Why don't we try this? I'll show you the first ten letters with my fingers, and you can copy me.*

He watches me curiously as I show him an A, and it seems to take him a moment to work up the courage to try for himself, but he does. He does it well.

That's very good. You are so smart. Should we try B?

He nods again, and I show him B. Within ten minutes, we have gone through each of the first ten letters twice, and I tell him practice makes perfect. I have no doubt he'll learn quickly. Children pick up languages very fast, and Nino is incredibly bright.

I think we need to brush your teeth now. It's almost time to leave.

He leads the way to his bedroom, and I follow him inside, glancing around the space with equal surprise and disappointment. It's almost a replica of my room, right down to the adult-sized bed. The only difference is the bench at the foot, which I presume is how he must climb into it. The color scheme is the same, and the decorative pieces are too. It's completely absent of the vibrant colors I'd expect to see in a child's room. There's no toy box. No superhero comforter. No Legos strewn about the floor. In fact, if I were to walk in here accidentally, I would never guess that a child lived here.

Tension seeps into my shoulders as Nino enters the bathroom and pulls out a step stool to brush his teeth. I watch him with a growing sense of sadness and injustice over the complete lack of insight on Alessio's part. Could he really be so clueless about the needs of children? Is he that emotionally inept?

These are questions I'll have to contend with later. Another glance at my watch confirms we need to be downstairs in two minutes. I help Nino finish up, replacing his toothbrush in the holder and quickly adjusting one side of his hair.

Are you ready?

He nods, and to my surprise, reaches for my hand. That simple gesture stabs at my heart. I can only imagine how starved for affection he is. I want to tell him that it's all going to be okay. I want to make him promises that I'm going to be here for him, but I'll never make a promise I'm not sure won't be broken. I've learned the hard way there are no guarantees in life.

We walk downstairs together, and Manuel seems surprised to see Nino holding my hand already. His eyes focus on that connection for a long moment before he turns abruptly to open the door. He doesn't say much, but I find that I'm okay with that. Once Nino and I are comfortably secured in the backseat of the car, we resume our practice of the letters, repeating them all the way to the school.

"We're here," Manuel tells me. "We can walk him inside together."

I want to tell him that's not necessary, that I can do it myself, but I know it's probably a non-negotiable point. He said he would accompany us anywhere we go, and it's clear he means it. So together, all three of us walk inside, and Manuel watches as I say goodbye to Nino with a promise to see him after school before his piano lessons. He nods and takes his seat in the classroom, and then I force myself to turn and walk back to the car.

As we return to the house, I consider what I'm supposed to do all day while he's in school. Normally, I would plan for some after-school activities, but his schedule is already so packed he'll scarcely have time for dinner, let alone anything else. It bothers me, and I don't know how long I'll be able to keep my mouth shut, but I decide I should observe him for a week or so before I make any snap judgments. Perhaps he really does enjoy all these activities.

Manuel drops me off at the house, and I opt to spend the morning sitting down by the water, memorizing the landscape. I wonder about the boat docked inside the boathouse. I've never driven a boat, but surely, it can't be too difficult to figure out, right? I decide it's something I should research, just in case I need a quick escape, but I'm not certain I should be doing that even on my own phone. Perhaps tomorrow, I can spend some time at the library and use one of their computers.

The time passes slowly, and I find myself wondering what Nino is doing in school. If he likes his teachers. What his favorite subjects are. These are all things I want to ask. I also find myself wondering about Alessio. Why is he so cold? Why is he so oblivious to the needs of a child? There are so many lingering questions about him, and deep down, I know I don't need the answers to them to successfully do what I came here to do. I would be lying to myself if I said there wasn't a part of me that was curious though.

Stuffing those ideas down and locking them away, I decide to eat some lunch. When I walk into the house, I'm hoping to avoid Angelina, but I'm not so lucky this time. As soon as I enter the kitchen and open the fridge, I hear the telltale clip of her heels on the floor. It's too late to sneak away, so I reach for a salad and shut the door to find her staring at me, arms crossed, eyes narrowed.

"What you did this morning isn't going to fly," she snaps.

Calmly, I set the salad aside and retrieve my phone from my pocket.

If you have an issue, perhaps you should take it up with Alessio. He's the one who hired me to work with Nino, and he's the one I answer to.

Her eyes are practically spitting flames as she takes a step closer, trying to intimidate me. "You think I don't know what you're doing, but I do. I can see it clearly, and I can tell you right now, you won't last a month here."

I refuse to acknowledge her with any outward emotion, but inside I'm shaking. I want to tell her I don't care because I have no intentions of staying that long. Instead, I play dumb, even though I'm well aware of her issue with me. She's threatened because she wants Alessio for herself. That was evident the moment I walked in the door.

What I'm doing is providing a service. Performing my job duties. Same as you. Now, if you'll excuse me, I'm going to eat my lunch.

Her gaze follows me, and I can sense she's not done. I'm right.

"I'm watching you," she calls after me. "One mistake and you're gone."

I roll my eyes and keep moving, climbing the stairs and opting for the privacy of my bedroom. Eating my salad alone by the window, I contemplate my plans, and doubt starts to creep in. What if Angelina does get me fired? I don't know how much power she holds with Alessio, but she's been in his employment longer, so reason dictates that it's more than I have, but he doesn't acknowledge her. I've seen it myself. From what I can tell, he seems to be aware of her, but they aren't close. At least, not that I can see. It could just be a farce. For all I know, she makes personal visits to the third level. The thought of it makes me irrationally annoyed, and I'm not sure why.

The one thing I do know is that Alessio seems to value his privacy. He hired me to do a job, and I had no intentions of getting to know him on a deeper level. But if I'm going to maintain my position here for the time being, perhaps I need to. Perhaps I need to form an alliance with him, and I can only hope that bringing my concerns about Nino to him will be the way. Though, it could also blow up in my face. He obviously thinks everything is fine the way it is. Maybe he was raised in a similarly sterile environment, and his mindset is that he survived, so Nino will too. There's only one way to find out, so I decide to test the waters.

Retrieving the phone he gave me, I pull up his name and type out a message, rewording it several times before I think it sounds okay.

I couldn't help but notice Nino doesn't have any children's decorations in his room. I hope you don't mind, but I thought it might be nice if I bought him a gift as a way to break the ice. Would it be okay if I gave him a new bed set, maybe?

Anxiously, I press send, and I'm still staring at the screen when I see that it's been delivered and read. My heartbeat quickens as I wait for him to reply, but he doesn't.

I spend the next few hours convinced I made a mistake, but I can't dwell on it. All I can do is focus on the here and now. Manuel and I return to pick up Nino in the afternoon, and he greets me with a shy smile, informing me he's been practicing his letters all day. I tell him what a good job he's doing, and then we practice on the next ten as Manuel whisks us off to his piano lessons. A few minutes before we arrive, I realize there was nothing in the schedule about a snack.

Are you hungry? I write.

Nino considers it, then nods. "A little."

I reach into my purse and retrieve a granola bar, offering it to him. He unwraps it, and Manuel glances at me in the mirror as if I've broken some sacred rule about eating in the Rolls Royce. I suppose I should have asked him first, but I don't really care. Nino needs to eat.

By the time we arrive, he's finished, and I've stowed the wrapper in my purse and used a wet wipe to wash his hands. His piano lessons are at a residence, but not the type I would expect. It's in a gated community, and upon entry, I can see that it's another upscale home.

Manuel pulls up into the circular drive and glances at me in the mirror before he turns off the car. "You'll have to stay here."

My scalp prickles, and I already know why. This is one of Alessio's associates. Someone else shrouded in secrecy and wealth. Someone else I'm quite certain must be involved in his criminal network too.

Anxiety settles into my chest as I glance at Nino. I know I can't tell him not to go, but that's exactly what I want to do. He's so small, and I don't know how well he knows these people. Quickly, while Manuel is getting out of the driver's seat, I write him a note.

Do you feel safe here?

Nino's brows pinch together, and he nods before his brown eyes meet mine. "It's okay. I come here all the time."

With that assurance, he retreats from the car a moment later, and I'm left to sit there and watch them walk away. I try to imagine who's behind the door, the face of the person giving him the lessons. I can't. And I decide I will have to ask him later when we have some privacy.

Manuel returns a few minutes later and sits in the driver's seat but doesn't start the car. "I wait here for him," he tells me. "Next time, you might want to bring a book or something. There's a lot of waiting in the afternoons."

I nod, but I don't need a book. My thoughts are more than enough to occupy my time, and they do for the entirety of the next forty-five minutes. When Nino returns, I am relieved to see that he doesn't appear to have been put in any danger, but he is noticeably tired. From there, Manuel drives us back to the house just in time to meet with the private instructor who gives him his swimming lessons. By the time we finish that activity, he's exhausted, and when I prepare him his dinner, he doesn't appear to want to eat very much. And still, the day is not over. After dinner, he has a lesson with a tutor for Italian, and then it's time for homework. We complete the task together, and I can't help noticing his bedtime is slowly creeping up, but Alessio still has not made an appearance. I opt to get Nino ready for bed myself, ensuring he changes into his pajamas and brushes his teeth. When I tuck him in, I ask him if he would like to read a story with me, but he shakes his head, yawning.

"Can we do the rest of the letters?"

I smile at his eagerness. *We have time to practice one round. But then you need to get to sleep.*

He nods, and we go through the motions, his hands mirroring mine as I show him each letter. It's amazing how fast he picks it up, even exhausted as he is. I think by the end of the week, he will have them all memorized, and we can build on that foundation. Spelling out letters will fill in the gaps as I teach him a beginner vocabulary.

Alright, little one. It's bedtime. I reach down and stroke his soft hair aside, feeling a rush of emotion as I stare into his innocent eyes. Over the last five years, I have worked with several children, and I have cared for them all. Nino, however, is unique and special. I only hope he can feel it too.

"Miss Cabrera?" He peeks up at me as I stand up.

I nod to indicate I'm listening, and he snuggles deeper into the bed.

"Thank you for coming to live with us. I hope you can teach me all the sign words."

My heart melts as I consider how fast he's warming to me. *Me too, Nino. Goodnight, little prince.*

6

ALESSIO

AFTER A LONG DAY OF DRIVING, I MEET MANUEL IN MY OFFICE for a debriefing, where he goes over the day's events, giving me a rundown of his observations. He tells me about Nino's day. The hand-holding. The granola bar incident. Then he leans back with an expression I know all too well.

"What is it?" I ask.

"I don't know." He rubs his jaw. "There's just something about her. She seems guarded, yet skittish at the same time. She flinches when a door shuts, and she's hyper-aware of her surroundings. I think maybe she observes ... too much."

I can't say that I disagree with him, but I won't admit my suspicions about her are the same. I don't need to add him to the growing pile of people who dislike this situation. Particularly when Gwen has been breathing down my neck all day to visit Nino when I know all she really wants to do is see Natalia for herself.

"Just watch her," I tell Manuel. "And keep me updated."

"Will do." He rises, understanding that he's dismissed for the evening. When he's gone, I glance at my watch. It's late, after midnight, and I still need to take a shower to wash the gasoline fumes from my hair.

Instead, curiosity has me turning to my computer monitor to pull up the security system. Without logic or reason, I watch Natalia's movements throughout the day, replaying the scene from breakfast. I study the video of her and Nino walking down the stairs together, hand in hand, and my shoulders stiffen at the confirmation of his affection for her. It doesn't make sense. Not when he only ever looks at me with fear and uncertainty. She's been here one day, and already, she has won him over.

I pull up the cameras from her room. The ones she looked for but couldn't find. They are discreet and unobservable to even a well-trained eye. She wouldn't have any idea that almost every inch of this house is under surveillance except for the third floor and the bathrooms.

It's dark in her room, but she sleeps with the curtains open, and I don't have to adjust the light to see she's wearing her shoes again. I find it unsettling for a variety of reasons, but mostly because I want to know why. I want to know a lot of things about her that I shouldn't. Since we met in New York, she has been occupying space in my mind far too often. I have questions about her. Now, I want answers.

I go over the footage of her day, watching her emerge from the bathroom and wiping away what appears to be moisture on her face this morning. Was she crying? I replay the video over and over. Pausing and slowing it down, searching for a solid explanation, but I don't produce one. It feeds my interest, and I look for any other footage of her throughout the day. I find her sitting by the water, lost in her thoughts. At the pool with Nino. Helping him with his homework. Tucking him into bed. And then, I move to the kitchen in search of their dinner together. But first, I catch a clip of her run-in with Angelina.

I adjust the volume so I can hear, listening to the conversation, and my jaw sets. Angelina can be problematic. This isn't the first time I've had an issue with her, but it's the first time I've found myself truly considering her value as an employee. She's here because she's a Society daughter and she volunteered for the position. Her philanthropic gesture wasn't out of the kindness of her heart or her passion for running a household. She saw an endgame that was never possible with me, and I've allowed it to continue because I respect her father. But I won't stand for her interference in Nino's care, and this situation will need to be addressed.

I crack my neck from side to side and shut down the computer, locking up the office for the night before I head upstairs. On the second landing, I pause, aware that Natalia is asleep. Something pulls me in that direction, and I stop outside her door, considering how much she has disrupted my life already. From the beginning, my gut told me she was hiding something. Liars are my least favorite life form. If I'm honest, I don't know why I hired her. I wanted something simple and uncomplicated, but already she is complicating things with her inane requests and observations. She's in my thoughts more than I'd care to admit, distracting me from my work and now my free hours too. I consider what I would do in this situation with anyone else. Pests must be squashed. That has always been my motto. It would be very easy to walk into her room right now and smother her to death. It would be quiet and fast, and tomorrow, things could go back to the way they were. It wasn't perfect before, but I'd find a way to make it work.

My hand settles on the knob, turning it slowly. Everything slows as I step inside, closing the door behind me and moving to the end of the bed. I stare down at her sleeping form, her shoes hanging out from beneath the comforter. They look out of place there, uncomfortable, yet I feel like I understand it better than anyone. You never know what lurks in the night.

I reach out and touch the laces, grazing them with my finger. I listen to her breathing, soft and steady. I inhale her clean scent that lingers in the air as my eyes focus on the scarf around her neck. I could choke her with that. It would unravel easily between my fingers before I squeezed it against her throat. In the morning, she'd be gone, and nobody would be the wiser. I could wash my hands of this mistake and hire a Society daughter as much as the thought might irritate me.

Natalia's breathing changes, and she stiffens suddenly as if she can sense my presence. When she opens her eyes and glances up at me, she freezes for a few seconds before she bolts upright, her hand snaking beneath the pillow. I already know what she's hiding under there, and my dick becomes irrationally hard as I imagine her trying to use it on me. There's a part of me that hopes she might. It would give me a viable excuse to sever this cord between us. Admittedly, I would like to know exactly how much fight she has in her.

The lamp light flips on, and she meets my gaze, her expression tight with irritation and confusion. She's waiting for me to speak. Social convention dictates I should have a reason to be here, an explanation for my intrusion into her personal space. Internally, I'm still debating if I need to bother with one or focus on keeping her quiet as I take her life. My mouth seems to decide before I do.

"You gave Nino a granola bar."

She stares up at me, blank.

"He's not allowed outside food. If it doesn't come from the kitchen or the pantry, he doesn't eat it."

She reaches for her phone, her fingers stiff as she writes a response.

This is what you came here to tell me in the middle of the night?

My eyes move over her face, and I wonder what she'd look like with her hair down completely. Right now, it's braided, and during the day, it's in a bun. I can tell that it's long, but I don't know how long, and it bothers me that I don't have that information.

"I need an assurance that you understand," I clip out. "No outside food."

She looks at me like I'm ridiculous, but why wouldn't she? She's not Society. She doesn't understand the danger that comes with being a Sovereign Son. Nino might not fully comprehend it yet, but he is a Sovereign Son. That makes him a target for anyone who might see him as a threat. It might seem crazy to her, but she doesn't know our world.

I understand. She writes. *Anything else?*

"Tomorrow afternoon," I blurt without thinking it through.

What?

"We'll go shopping for a new bed set."

She's still sitting there as confused as I am when I walk toward the door. I don't know that I've ever been shopping in my whole life, not really. If I'm not delirious, I believe I just made an arrangement to go with her tomorrow.

So, I guess she's not dying tonight after all.

NINO IS NOTICEABLY quiet during the car ride to school. By the way he glances at me, and then Natalia, I can tell she senses something is off.

"Why did you come to school with us today?" Nino peeks up at me, and my spine goes rigid when I glimpse the familiar uncertainty in his eyes.

He doesn't like me. Despite my best efforts, I have not been able to gain his trust. I eat breakfast with him every morning. I ensure all his basic needs are met, in addition to a veritable buffet of activities to ensure a well-rounded childhood. Still, he cannot look at me without revealing his displeasure at my presence.

"I have something to do this morning," I bite out.

My tone silences him, and I don't miss the sharp look Natalia directs at me before turning her gaze back to him. She does something with her fingers, and Nino smiles, copying the action with his own. It takes me a moment to realize she's teaching him ASL. She'd mentioned it in her file, and I never objected to it, but now I'm not sure why I didn't. I don't know what they're saying to each other, and I find that bothersome too.

I direct my attention outside the window, wondering again why I decided to do this when Manuel pulls up to the parking space reserved for us at Nino's school. Other than to enroll him, and the occasional parent-teacher meeting, I have not been here to drop him off myself. My requirement of Manuel is that he delivers Nino inside personally, but my mood darkens when Natalia exits the car along with them. Nino holds her hand again, not bothering to look back at me, and I sit in silence, stewing in my growing frustration as I wait for her to return. When she finally does, I turn away from her and ignore her for the remainder of the drive.

Manuel pulls up to the curb at the shopping mall in Bellevue Square. It's close to Medina, one of the few retailers in our neighborhood where privacy is preferred over box stores. I exit the car first, waiting for Natalia as she slides across the back seat and gingerly steps out behind me. She seems as uncomfortable as I am about the prospect of shopping together, and I'm glad for it.

"I'll wait here for you, sir." Manuel shuts the rear door and returns to the driver's seat.

I nod at him and head for the entrance, holding the door open for Natalia. She dips her head and seems to draw a large breath as she enters. Between the two of us, I'm not certain who's wound more tightly.

"Where are we going?" I ask.

She doesn't bother to write a response but points at the Macy's just around the corner. We walk there together, and she finds the home section, examining the offerings while I check my watch several times over. I don't have anywhere to be today, but it's a habit. After what feels like an eternity, she settles on one of the bedding sets, gathering the package by the handle. I stare at her in dismay.

"Aliens?"

She nods firmly. Our eyes lock in a war of wills, and I'm waiting for an explanation. When she clenches her jaw, I can see that she doesn't feel she owes me one. To my horror, her resistance sends a strange thrill through me. I don't know what it is about her stubbornness that fascinates me. Perhaps it's the fact that looking at her, you wouldn't think she'd have such a backbone. She appears to be delicate, even skittish at times, but then she gets an idea in her head and pursues it like a dog with a bone. That tenacity is what got her the job. That steel in her gaze is what I reluctantly admired the first time I met her, and I find that admiration is rapidly transforming into something else. The shopping trip I had been dreading all morning is now more interesting as I imagine how she'd react if I were to bend her over and fuck her right here on one of these display beds.

She couldn't make a sound as I shoved my cock as deep as she could take it. There wouldn't be a noise from her disobedient mouth as I tangled her hair in my fist and shoved a hand into that god-awful suit jacket to grope her tits.

The image in my mind causes my dick to swell painfully, and I wonder if she can sense it. Does she have any clue what I'm thinking about doing to her? My eyes blaze a path over her body, and she swallows audibly, the sound getting lost behind that ugly fucking neck scarf. I want to tear it off. I want to rip it to shreds. And I think if I keep standing here staring at her like this, I just might.

She seems to understand I'm teetering on the edge when she sets the comforter near her feet and pulls out her phone.

He likes aliens, she types. *He mentioned it to me yesterday when he was swimming.*

Aliens? I consider the idea and shake my head. Who the fuck likes aliens?

Somehow, Natalia can sense my disapproval, and she narrows her eyes at me for the second time this morning. Her fingers move faster across the keypad, typing out a note with more force than the last one.

Children need creativity in their lives. There's nothing wrong with a little imagination.

I'm tempted to argue that there's plenty wrong with believing in things that aren't real. There's a reason I've never told Nino Santa Claus exists or given him money from imaginary fairies when he loses a tooth. It's not my job to perpetuate lies. I'm preparing him for the real world, and as such, I keep him rooted in reality as much as possible. It isn't out of cruelty. Rather, I want him to understand that fairytales don't exist.

With this in mind, I'm on the verge of telling Natalia to forget it. He already has a suitable bed set at home, but as I'm standing there at war with myself, my eyes drift to a colorful display of children's artwork. The piece in the front looks familiar in a way, and I don't realize why until it stirs a memory of my mother. I can recall a time when she was painting a mural on my wall when I was a boy. The colors were vibrant, much like this piece, with blues and oranges and yellows. I asked her what it was, and she smiled, telling me I'd have to wait and see. She never got the chance to finish it, so I don't know what it was supposed to be.

The agony of that lost moment in time steals the oxygen from my lungs and makes me freeze. It isn't until Natalia gently touches my shoulder, and I glance down at her concerned expression, that I realize time has passed. I've been oblivious to my surroundings, dragged back to the past, and it's the strangest feeling. I can't remember the last time I had such a vivid recollection of my mother.

My eyes collide with the woman in front of me at present. For the briefest of moments, I consider if my mother would have liked her. Then, I try to forget the idea entirely. I reach down and seize the comforter and then walk over to the art display, grabbing one of the colorful pieces as well. I can feel Natalia's gaze on me as we head for the checkout, but I decide it's best not to acknowledge her. The sooner I can get her back to the house, the sooner I can forget this ever happened.

7

NATALIA

THE NEXT TWO WEEKS PASS IN A BLUR OF RACING FROM ONE activity to another. I've always considered myself an organized person, but between martial arts, Italian, piano, scout meetings, swimming, and chess instruction, even I can't keep the days straight. On Sundays, the one day Nino has to relax, Alessio takes him out of the house, and I have no idea what they do together. Nino barely has time to take a breath, and I'm exhausted just trying to help him keep up.

It's a problem that needs to be addressed, but I've scarcely seen Alessio since the bizarre mall incident. Initially, in his schedule, he stated that he would be present for breakfast with Nino on most days of the week. However, I've only found that to be true on a few occasions. I don't know if he's intentionally avoiding me, or if he's busy with whatever his work entails, but Nino has informed me he's come to say goodnight to him every day this week, so I'm guessing it must just be me.

I tell myself it's for the best. I can't forget the way he looked at me in the department store when we went shopping. The intense heat in his gaze was unmistakable, yet I find myself questioning if I imagined it. Why would a man like him ever want someone like me? I've done everything in my power to make myself as boring as possible. I wear plain, shapeless clothing and minimal makeup. I never style my hair. I hide away under the cloak I've created so men don't seek me out. They don't see me as a potential source of pleasure, but for a brief moment, Alessio did. I can't forget the shiver on my skin when I felt the heat of his focus on me. Even knowing the danger he presents to me, I find that my curiosity about him only grows. It's been a long time since a man has touched me. I swore to myself it would never happen again, but something changed between us that day. I felt it. He felt it. If I'm honest, I haven't been able to stop thinking about it.

I can't go there. I can't. Not unless it becomes absolutely crucial to my plan. I've fallen into a routine here. I've learned the layout of the house and the property. I've gone to the library in my free time and studied subjects I can't look at on my phone. I've avoided Angelina at all costs, trying to fly under her radar at every opportunity. I've searched for weak spots in Manuel's routine, and I'm continuing to learn more about Nino every day. The one person who evades me is Alessio. I don't know what he hides on the third level of his home. I don't know what he does, or where he goes, or even when. I need to if I'm to pull this off. I need to know everything about him. I'm debating exactly how I will do that when Manuel pulls up to the school, and we go inside to retrieve Nino.

Right away, I can tell something is off. He looks flushed, weak, and tired. My lips press together as I glance at the teacher, wondering why she didn't notice. Manuel seems to be aware, too, as he looks at Nino and frowns. We usher him back to the car together, and I sign to him, asking him if he's okay. Over the last two weeks, we've continued to progress his ASL, and he's picking it up at record speed. When he doesn't know the words, he'll opt to spell them out, which keeps us signing often.

"I don't feel good," he tells me.

I gently touch his forehead and realize he has a fever. Before Manuel can pull away, I touch his arm and then write a note for him.

No piano lessons today. He's sick. He needs to rest.

His features tighten slightly as he glances at Nino again. I'm half expecting an argument, but he doesn't say anything else, opting to drive us home instead. When we arrive, I take Nino by the hand, prepared to lead him upstairs to his room, but Manuel stops me.

"No outside medicines are allowed. I'll bring him up some Tylenol and call for the doctor. He'll be here shortly."

I nod, imagining that they must keep the over-the-counter medication under lock and key here too. It says something about their world that they are so concerned about outside food, drinks, or pills. It doesn't take much of a stretch of the imagination to understand they believe something could be poisoned. The very idea strikes fear in my heart as I glance down at Nino and squeeze his hand in mine. I don't know exactly what I've stepped into here, but I can only hope I figure it out soon.

Once we're upstairs, I help Nino out of his school clothes and into his pajamas. Manuel comes in a few minutes later with the children's Tylenol, which he portions out and watches Nino drink. Then he disappears with his assurances the doctor is on his way. I wet a cloth from the bathroom and use it as a cool compress on Nino's forehead. When he's comfortably settled in bed, I type out a note for him and then sign the words as well, just as we've been practicing.

Don't worry. I'll call for your father to let him know you're not feeling well.

He reaches out and touches my arm, gently tapping his fingers over the sleeve of my jacket. "What if he's mad?"

I shake my head. *He won't be.*

A moment passes where he's quiet, lost in thought, his eyes heavy, and his body in need of rest. I'm about to tell him it's okay to sleep when he speaks again.

"Natalia, can I tell you a secret?"

Of course.

He seems to think about it for a while before he signs the words back to me, spelling some of them out.

He's not my father.

The blow of that delivery nearly knocks me off balance. My brows furrow together, and I study him, searching for signs of distress or confusion, but there are none that I can see. He's just a little boy, casually telling me that the man he lives with is not his father. I can't help myself. I have to ask.

Where is your father then?

"Gone," he says without emotion. "Not coming back."

I swallow the pain in my throat and nod, writing out a note for him. *Can I tell you a secret?*

He nods, perking up with interest. I know there are cameras here. Even if I haven't found them, I know they must exist, so I have to be careful. I have to be very, very careful. Acting as if I'm adjusting the cloth on his forehead, I lean in like I'm giving him a kiss on his temple, and with great pain and effort, I manage a choked confession from my broken vocal cords.

A whisper of the truth.

A secret for just the two of us.

THE DOCTOR HAS BEEN to visit several times when Alessio finally makes an appearance. By then, Nino's fever has worsened, and he's so uncomfortable it hurts to witness. I have done what I can for him, and the doctor's assurances it's just a virus doesn't make me feel any better.

I am angry and irrational when Alessio steps into the room, his face devoid of emotion as always.

"The doctor says he's going to be fine," Alessio informs me as if I don't know. "He needs to rest."

I grab my phone and stab my fingers against the keyboard. *I'm not leaving. Someone needs to be here with him.*

He cocks his head to the side, his icy gaze piercing into mine. "I'm here now."

And what are you going to do? Sit here wordlessly? What comfort is there to be found in that?

"Is there a problem, Natalia?" His voice is calm, but his eyes are alight with fire.

Yes, there's a problem. This poor child is so exhausted by the militant schedule you insist on, it's no surprise he's fallen ill. I'm only shocked that it hasn't happened sooner. How can you possibly expect him to keep up with these ridiculous expectations?

His nostrils flare ever so slightly, and he jerks his head toward the door. "A word, outside. Now."

Reality starts to settle over me as I follow him out the door and into the hall. It may have been a relief to let out some of my bottled-up frustrations, but I'm aware I'm tiptoeing a delicate line, and now I've angered the beast.

"Do you make a habit of taking this tone with your employer?" Alessio asks me once Nino's door is shut behind us.

If it's necessary, then yes. You hired me to do a job, and I understand that. However, my job is to care for Nino, which means telling you things you might not like to hear if it's in his best interest.

"And you are the expert?" he scoffs. "What qualifications do you have that deem you as such? You've been in his life for five minutes. I'm the one who has raised him."

He needs balance, I insist. *Surely, if you took a moment to truly listen to him, you would see it for yourself.*

Without warning, his hand whips toward me and latches around my jaw. His fingers dig into my skin as I stumble backward, fear and adrenaline surging inside of me. He backs me into the wall, and I try to remember how to breathe as I stare straight into the storm in his eyes. I don't know what's happening, and I'm mentally preparing myself for a fight when he leans in and does the last thing I expect. He ... inhales me.

A shiver shoots down my spine to my toes, and instead of steeling myself like I should, my body melts into the wall, trapped by his warmth and his intensity.

"I can smell your fear, Natalia." His breath whispers against my ear. "Is it me you're afraid of?"

My chest heaves, and I shake my head, but it's obviously a lie. He knows it. I know it. He fucking terrifies me, and not for any of the right reasons. He terrifies me because I think I like this. I like the hard plane of his chest pressing against me while his scent surrounds me. I like his warmth and the smooth lyrical voice he never raises, even when he's making a clear threat. He towers over me, strong and intimidating, and I should be afraid. Deep down, I know what this man does. I knew it the second I saw the blood stain on his shirt cuff. So why doesn't he scare me? Why is it that somehow, amidst the chaos in my beating heart, I still feel safe with him? Safe to express myself? Safe to stare straight into his eyes the way nobody in his life seems to?

He inches closer, and warmth blooms throughout my belly when his erection presses against me. It isn't a mishap. He wants me to know it's there. He wants to see my reaction. We're so close I'm drowning in the power of his masculinity. I'm breathing him in too. Instinct has me wrapping my fingers around his biceps, but I haven't decided if it's to push him away or pull him closer. He can see the war in my eyes, and he enjoys it. He enjoys it too much. I choke on my uncertainty as I lean forward an inch, just enough to feel the hardness of his want for me digging into my belly. I don't know what the hell is wrong with me, but I know I like it when his eyes flare and then heat with a liquid fire I never want to extinguish.

I should tell him this is inappropriate. I should tell him we can't let anything interfere with our professional relationship. But I can't seem to find the strength to push him away. I think I want to know what it's like to be kissed. To be touched without violence. Control is an illusion, but I feel like I have it with him. He's a dangerous man, but I trust that if I were to tell him to stop, he would. I don't know how or why. It's just something I feel. It's a perilous trap to fall into. I shouldn't. Before I can decide for myself, he makes the call for both of us, stepping back and shaking his head as if he, too, were under a spell.

"Don't test me, Natalia," he clips out. "I told you this is not a job you can leave easily. You might not agree with my decisions when it comes to Nino, but those are my decisions to make."

My jaw clamps down, and his words douse me with a much-needed supply of cold reality. He's back to being a hardheaded ass, closed off and shut down. As angry as the realization makes me, I have an unwanted pang of empathy too. I can recognize this pattern all too well. It's a protective mechanism. He's keeping everyone out, and I have to wonder why. Why isn't he married? Why is someone as handsome as him without a partner?

I catch a glimpse of uncertainty in his eyes before he turns toward the door, like I'm the one who's a threat. As if I could find a weakness in his armor. Two weeks ago, I would have been pleased to know it. I would have immediately planned how to use that to my advantage. Now, the thought makes me slightly queasy, and it occurs to me that this plan was much simpler to execute in my mind. In reality, I'm faced with the very real human emotions I'll have to battle when I betray him. Already, I'm starting to realize I don't want to.

Squashing down those emotions, I neutralize my expression and square my shoulders. Alessio glances back at me, nodding as if he approves, and then he slips quietly into Nino's room, shutting the door in my face. Message received loud and clear.

You aren't welcome here.

8

ALESSIO

Nino spends the rest of the night in a fitful sleep, and I remain by his side, watching him helplessly. It isn't often I encounter a situation I can't control. Power and money can move most mountains. They are the foundation upon which I provide for Nino and ensure his needs are met. Food, shelter, safety. I can give him all these things easily, but I can't protect him from the ailments common in childhood. Over the last four years he's been in my care, I have been reminded of this vulnerability on occasions when he has taken sick, and I always feel guilty for it.

I made a promise to Enzo when I took his son in at two years old. Our Society has traditions and customs that outsiders don't understand, and though I had never considered having children of my own, I didn't hesitate to agree when Enzo granted the customary rite of Nino's care to me. In his absence, I have acted as his parent. I had hoped that I could provide for him as well as a father would. I thought I was giving him a world of skills, special interests, and tools that would ultimately benefit him. That said, I haven't been able to eradicate Natalia's harsh words from my mind.

She tells me Nino is too busy for a child. That his schedule is militant by nature. She speaks of creativity and play as though they are a necessity I have denied him. Every sentence she uttered was like a sharp blade, piercing the one true vulnerability I have. I cannot fail Nino. Everything I have done for the last four years has been to protect him. To guide him. To ensure that he will grow into a capable, well-rounded man who can achieve anything he sets his mind to. I took on this job willingly, but I have had my doubts since the beginning. Natalia couldn't know that. She has no understanding of my relationship with Nino, or his relations, who took me in when my family was annihilated. I owe this to Enzo, but it isn't just that. It's a matter of honor. This is the only way I can ever repay him for his friendship and our brotherhood at a time in my life when I needed it most.

There has never been a question in my mind that I lacked the necessary skills to be a father, but over time I had hoped that Nino could forgive me for the areas I was lacking and respect me for the ones I was better at. It hasn't turned out that way. Anyone can see the boy doesn't like me. He stares at me like he knows I'm a monster, though I have never once raised my voice or permitted him to witness the violence I'm truly capable of. Somehow, he still senses it. He sees beneath the surface, and he does not want to know me. We are two people, co-existing in the same house. I have tried not to force his affection, even as I felt mine grow for him. I did not think it possible to truly care for a child, but when it comes to Nino, he is the exception, not the rule. I have empathy for him. I have admiration for him. I would certainly destroy anyone who wished to harm him. But my greatest fear is that the years he remains in my care will continue to pass us by, and he will never feel love for me. With some reluctance, I can admit that perhaps Natalia was right. He does need more than activities to fill his life.

He stirs from sleep, gazing over at me through bleary eyes, and I sit up in my chair, spine rigid, fraught with tension.

"Are you alright, Nino?"

His little face scrunches up, and he begins to shed tears as he glances around the room in desperation. "Where's Natalia?"

His question is another dagger to my heart, but it comes as no surprise. Whatever witchcraft that woman dabbles in has us both under her spell.

"I'm right here," I try my best to assure him, but it comes out stiff rather than reassuring.

"I want Natalia," he cries.

Frustration makes me stubborn, and I want to insist that he sit here with me. One glance at his face, which he quickly hides from me, and I know it's useless. Wordlessly, I rise from my seat and stalk out of his room, quietly shutting the door behind me before I slam hers open. She bolts upright in bed, a gasp of air the only audible noise as she smacks the lamp to turn it on.

"He wants you," I snap.

She glances over my shoulder as if she expects him to be there. As she does, the blanket falls around her waist, and I'm gifted with a perfect image of her round tits beneath a white tank top. All the other details around us fall away when she catches me staring at her protruding nipples. She swallows, and an unwelcome image of me fucking her comes to mind. I consider what it might feel like if I took her at this very moment, unleashing this strange current of pent-up rage inside me. When she slaps her hands over her breasts in an attempt at modesty, it only irks me more.

"You can spend the rest of the night with him," I tell her. "I have a need to tend to."

Her brows furrow, the only indication she's considering what I said. She slowly pulls herself from the bed, turning her face away as though she doesn't want to look at me.

"Natalia," I bite out.

She whips her head toward me, her eyes wide at my tone. I've always prided myself on remaining calm, no matter the situation, but she tests me in ways I've never been tested before.

I glance down at her feet and narrow my gaze. "Next time I come in here, I better not see you with those fucking shoes on the bed."

I don't wait for a response, and she doesn't offer one as I leave. My intentions are clear as I stalk down the hall and out to my car. I need a fucking release, and my hand isn't going to do tonight. I start the engine with one destination in mind.

There are other ways to get my fix. So long as it's with anyone else but her.

THE IVI COMPOUND is located on the downtown Seattle water-front. In a high-rise tower with mirrored windows, members can see out, but outsiders can't see in. The building is an impressive amalgamation of steel and glass looming over the street below. From the outside, it's anyone's guess what's inside. There are no signs. There are no entrances for the public. The only way in is through the parking garage, where my permit is my fingerprint on a biometric scanner.

From there, the process is streamlined. A valet takes my keys when I pull to a stop, and a host of guards' step aside to allow me entry.

"Dominus et Deus," they greet me in unison.

I nod at them and slip inside, stopping at the coat room where a Society daughter offers me a cloak and mask, which I take. Once I'm satisfied that my identity is hidden, I step out into the main corridor and head for the private elevator reserved for Sovereign Sons. From here, I have choices. Above me, there are floors to meet almost every need a member might have. Rooms for out-of-state visitors or those who wish to stay after they've had too much to drink. There are banquet halls and event rooms, meeting rooms, a business center, a gym, a rooftop pool, libraries, and even children's playrooms. It's a different sort of playroom I'm after though.

I press the red elevator button without a number, and it whisks me up to what the members call the Cat House. It's a den meant for pleasure, stocked full of the finest women money can buy. They are beautiful, elegant, eager to please, and they understand exactly what I want.

A simple transaction.

I was still young, clinging to life in an isolated hospital room when I was left to digest the total destruction of a marriage and family. I had just lost everyone I ever loved over my father's selfish desires. It wasn't something my ten-year-old brain was fully capable of comprehending at the time, but there was an image playing on repeat in my mind. My mother, kneeling before the man who came to kill us, pleading for our lives. Her tears stopped when he uttered those final words.

Your husband's mistress sends her regards.

Seconds later, my mother's brains were splattered across the floor. It wasn't long before my brother and sister joined her in death. That moment cemented one inherent truth in my mind. Love didn't really mean anything. It was just a precursor to pain. Men would always be the weaker sex. I had observed it myself many times over the years, in the aftermath of that event. The male species was easily led astray. Regardless of how high the stakes were, their primal instincts drove them to risk their families for a few moments of pleasure. As much as I wish it weren't true, I was half my father's DNA. The only guarantee I could make to myself was that I would never be like him. In doing so, I avoided relationships altogether, sentencing myself to a lifetime of celibacy.

When I come to this place of temptation, the menu might be varied, but there is only ever one option for me. This option fits my requirements exactly. I don't need to know their names. I don't need to talk to them or worry about their feelings. I come here for what I need, and I leave again with the satisfaction of a release and nothing more. It's a system that has worked well for me, and I find that, like everything in my life, I try not to indulge too much. Once per month is all I usually allow, just enough to remind me that I am human.

When the doors open, I step inside, greeted by the sight of the usual raucous crowd. The offerings here are extensive, so it comes as no shock that I've seen many oddities here over the years. Currently, there is a large orgy taking place to the right, and on the left are the voyeurs. Down the corridor behind me, I can recall a dungeon for those who prefer whips and chains, and it's anyone's guess what goes on behind the private doors. I have seen enough during my visits here to have an intimate understanding of the mechanics of sex. I would often find myself watching, too, fascinated by the full spectrum of human longings. Some were more interesting to me than others, and I'd be a liar if I said I'd never reconsidered my position on the matter. Consistency is the key to maintaining my emotional baseline. I have always known that if I were to give in to anything more, I might go getting strange ideas in my head. Ideas about more than a transaction, ideas about an entanglement or even a relationship, and those are ideas I can never entertain.

"Dominus et Deus." A young brunette who has serviced me several times approaches me when she sees me in the waiting area. "What will your pleasure be this evening, my lord?"

"A table massage."

A secret smile curves her face, and she bows her head before turning on her heel. "Right this way."

I follow her into the back, considering the length of her hair, the curve of her naked hips, and the gentility of her voice. From this angle, I could almost imagine her as someone else. Someone more petite, with amber eyes and a heart-shaped face.

She leads me into a private room, pulling back the sheet on the table for me and then offering to assist me with removing my cloak.

"I'll do it." I want her to stop talking to me. I want her to stop so that I can keep this image in my head.

When I'm naked, I climb atop the table and lower my head onto the cushion, facing the ceiling. My dick is already hard when she starts to massage my feet. She rubs oil into my skin, working in long, even strokes, building anticipation as she moves up my calves toward my thighs.

For a moment, I consider what it would feel like if I were to let my control slip, just once. Just for tonight. If I were to bend her over and fuck her the way I want to fuck Natalia. I could call her Natalia if I wanted to. I could tell her not to speak. I could have her do anything I wanted, but that realization sours the fantasy before it can really take shape.

I could do all those things, but she still won't be Natalia. She won't smell like her or taste like her, and I'm convinced she wouldn't feel the same wrapped around my body.

My breath hisses between my teeth when the woman touches my dick, stroking it without warning. It should come as no surprise. This is what I came here for. This is what I always get. Nothing more, nothing less. Now, it feels all wrong somehow.

"Stop," I command.

Her hand freezes and then falls away as I open my eyes and stare up at her through the mask.

"Did I do something wrong?"

"No." I force my voice to retain control. "It's not you. I've just ... changed my mind."

She looks visibly distraught by my confession, so I try my best to reassure her.

"I'll leave payment and a tip for you at the front."

She dips her head and leaves, slipping out quietly and shutting the door behind her. I curse to myself and stare down at my offending cock, swollen and needy with a new mind of its own. Apparently, not any hand will do.

"Fuck you," I growl, gripping it in my palm and tugging viciously. "You can't have her."

I feel manic, jerking myself off to disjointed images of Natalia. Images I've studied at night in my office from the privacy of my computer. Shots I've replayed over and over. Her delicate hands. Her fucking smile. The way she walks. The way she sleeps. It isn't enough to watch these things from a distance anymore, and that's a goddamned problem. Right now, I don't care. In my head, I'm fucking her every filthy way I've ever witnessed. I'm spreading her legs apart and ripping her blouse open and sucking on her tits through the lace material of her bra. I'm unraveling her hair and biting her neck and making her sit on my face until she soaks me in her pleasure. Only then do I get to feel her, only then do I sink my cock deep into her body and fuck her until I explode.

The imagery is too much. My muscles are tightening, spasming, as air hisses through my teeth. With enough force to shake the table, I blow my load, shooting it across my abdomen. It's a violent release. More violent than any I've had before. I can only credit it to the madness infecting my mind, and as I stand up and clean myself, I worry this is just the beginning.

It's only going to get worse from here.

9

NATALIA

After a rough two days with Nino, he finally starts to show improvement. By the third day, he's happily eating and drinking on his own. My nerves are frayed, and I'm exhausted, but I'm so relieved to see him doing well enough to return to school. Alessio, on the other hand, seems to have alternate plans. I haven't spoken to him since our last encounter, hoping to continue avoiding him, but I know he's been to visit Nino while I've slept in the chair beside his bed. I pretended to be asleep while Manuel and the doctor gave him updates on Nino's progress. However, it would appear my luck has run out. This morning, I found a handwritten note from him taped to my door. It's a far cry from his usual way of doing things, like bursting in and scaring me half to death when I'm asleep.

The note directed me to keep Nino home for the rest of the week, in addition to a request for me to meet with Alessio in the first-floor office at nine p.m. this evening. At the bottom, there was an addendum to go over Nino's list of after-school activities. To my shock, he's given me carte blanche to eliminate the things Nino does not enjoy, except for his Italian studies, which are a requirement. I suspect that's because of his heritage, and perhaps it even has something to do with whatever criminal network Alessio is involved in, but I don't know for sure.

What I do know is that I'm nervous about seeing him today. To my horror, I haven't been able to stop thinking about what he said the other day. He had a *need* to tend to. Those words were specific, and I suspect intentional, as if he wanted to punish me somehow by saying them. I don't know why he thinks I should care what he does or with whom, but it bothers me that he seems to be aware that it does affect me. For three days, I've imagined what she must look like, what he must do with her. It's nagged at me. It's eaten at me. It's ridiculous.

I can't have these feelings toward him, ever. Entrapping myself with unnecessary emotions will only make the endgame harder than it has to be. No matter how I might be tempted to let my guard down, the results will be the same. This can only end one of two ways. Either he will die, or I will.

The only way to resolve this issue is to put it out of my mind and get back to my routine. Since I've been too nervous about leaving Nino's side while he was ill, I've scarcely eaten myself, and I haven't had time to do my morning workout. During my time here, I've made good use of Alessio's home gym. Right now, I am craving that movement. I need something to expend this frustration and make me feel human again.

Once Nino is safely tucked into bed, and I'm certain he's asleep, I change into my gym clothes and head downstairs. It's not often that I wander the house this time of the night, but I find it's always quiet when I do. I've learned that Angelina doesn't reside on the premises, but Manuel does. However, he's usually in his room by seven. As for Alessio, he keeps to himself on the third floor of his private lair. That means I have the space to myself, much to my relief.

In the gym, I push myself through a series of endurance and strength-based exercises I've practiced for years. I'm shaking with exhaustion by the time I finish, and I find it frustrating that just a few days away from my routine has left me feeling weaker. I need to maintain my strength. This is the one area I cannot allow myself to become complacent.

Irritated, I wipe myself with a towel and splash some cold water on my face at the sink. A cold shower would do better, but I find myself glancing at the adjoining glass wall that leads to the pool area. I've sat by that pool many times already, nervously watching Nino as the instructor gives him his lessons. I don't like the water. I've tried to avoid it at any cost. But there's a part of me that knows the water outside might be my only escape when the time comes. I didn't come this far to let one of my fears get the best of me.

I turn around and peek back out into the hall, checking to make sure it's empty. I didn't bring a suit, but I can swim in my bra and underwear. Stripping off my leggings and tee-shirt, I carefully fold them up and set them onto the wooden bench before I open the door to the pool area. The smell of chlorine hits me immediately, and strangely, it is of some comfort. It's a reminder that this water isn't endless. It's not pulling me under, threatening to drown me in its murky depths. This water has a floor and four walls, and I will be safe here as long as I manage my expectations.

I walk to the edge of the stairs and dip my toe inside, swirling it around to test the temperature. It's moderately warm and inviting. At least, that's my mantra as I force myself to descend the stairs and lower my body into the blue abyss.

For a few moments, I just sit there, managing my breath and trying to adjust to the feeling. It's not that I don't know how to swim. I spent every summer at the lake with my father when I was growing up, but those recollections have all been tainted by the last memory I have of the water. Drowning. Clawing. Dying. I didn't think I'd ever get out, and I haven't wanted to return since. But, like anything else, I refuse to allow those fears to stand in the way of my goal.

Slowly, I position my head forward and push my legs out, slicing my arm through the air and back into the water. It's not at all smooth, but I repeat the motion again and again until it is. I swim lap after lap until I'm breathless, clinging to the edge, and truly unable to continue. My fingers have turned to prunes, and my eyes burn from the water, but I can be proud of myself for doing what I set out to do.

One step at a time. That's how I'll get there.

I edge myself toward the stairs and drag my body up to the deck, pausing to wring out my hair. It's only at this point I realize I don't have a towel, and when I glance toward the linen closet, I'm startled by a sound.

There isn't time to process what I'm seeing. It just happens. One minute, I'm standing there in my wet underwear, and the next, I'm witnessing Alessio emerge from the sauna, completely naked.

My breath gets caught in my throat as he pauses, turning to look at me. At least, I think he is. I can't be certain because my eyes are blazing a path down his body, right over the huge cock hanging between his thighs.

Holy shit.

Holy freaking shit.

I have to stop looking. That's what I'm telling myself, but I can't. It's just ... *there.* I haven't seen a naked man up close like this, well, ever really. The one time I was even with a man, he only unzipped his jeans. It was nothing like this. He was nothing like Alessio, who is somehow even more beautiful than I imagined. He's strong, with broad shoulders, a tapered waist, and muscular thighs. On some level, I knew from what I could see beneath his suits, these qualities existed. Now, they are undeniable. His strength is unmatched in any man I've seen before. I wanted to deny it. I wanted to believe my imagination was overcompensating. It wasn't. He's here, and he's real, and I'm still staring at his dick.

Oh my god.

My eyes shoot up, pausing momentarily on his chest when I notice a few round scars there. They appear to be bullet wounds, or at least, that would be my guess. I make a mental note of it and keep my gaze moving, horrified to see he's staring at me too. When I glance down, it's only then I realize my white bra and panties are displaying ... well, everything. I slap my hands over my body, humiliated and ashamed, but it only gets worse. He can see all the scars littering my arms and torso now, and he will know everything I've told him is a lie.

"Natalia." His voice snaps my attention back to his face. "Stay. We need to talk."

Fuck. Fuck. Fuck.

I swallow the painful lump in my throat as I begin to tremble. I'm cursing myself for being so careless when he walks to the linen closet and removes two towels. He wraps one around his waist, but not before I can see the length of his growing erection.

I'm confused and uncertain as he strides toward me and tosses me the towel. I use it immediately, swaddling my body away from his hawk-like gaze.

"You were supposed to meet me," he says.

Shit. I glance around for a clock, but I don't see one. Alessio checks his watch and reads the time.

"Nine-thirty."

I do my best to offer my apologies without a phone. My instinct is to sign to him, even though I know he doesn't understand. His lips draw together, and he points to a pool chair facing the door.

"Sit there. We will have our meeting in a moment."

I stare at him pleadingly, but if he notices, he doesn't acknowledge it. He disappears behind me, and I watch his reflection in the glass as he removes his towel and walks down the stairs into the cold plunge pool. My eyes widen as he submerges his entire body, staying there for what feels like minutes. I've felt the temperature of that small pool, and I know how icy it is. I can't imagine why anyone would want to do that to themselves, but Alessio seems unfazed when he resurfaces and retrieves his towel.

A small part of me wonders if he needed a cold dip because he feels this strange pull between us too. I don't see how it's even possible, considering how I look with all my scars on display, but he must have felt some attraction. That's the only logical explanation for his cock hardening the way it did.

Shit. I have to stop thinking about that. I try to put it from my mind as he reappears, gesturing for me to follow him.

"We'll go into the sauna. Have a meeting as the Finns do."

I hesitate, and he glances back at me. "I have a schedule, Natalia. You disrupted it this evening when you failed to meet me. If I remember correctly, you once lectured me about wasting one's time."

I force a nod, but deep down, I'm wondering if this is it. Is he going to kill me in the sauna? Is he just drawing it out, giving me time to consider all the ways it might happen? I know he's seen my scars. He never believed me from the beginning, and I'm certain he will challenge me now. I don't know what to do because I didn't plan for this contingency. Not so early. If he tries to kill me, I will fight him. I will do the only thing I can and try to kill him first.

He opens the door for me, and we step inside. It's hot, almost unbearably so, but I can't think about that right now. Alessio retrieves a bucket hanging from the wall and dumps some water onto the hot rocks, introducing steam to the environment. He takes a seat on the wooden bench, pointing to the area beside him. It's the space between him and the glass windowpane.

"You can write your responses there."

I release a quiet breath and nod, taking the seat next to him. The space is so large I don't know why he's sitting so close to me. It doesn't make sense unless he plans to confront me. From here, I can smell the clean woodsy scent I recognize as his, and between that and the heat, it's slightly intoxicating.

A few long moments pass where I wait for him to speak. I'm beginning to wonder if he even will when my gaze slips to his large hands. They are so big he could easily wrap them around my throat and snap my neck. It wouldn't take much force from him, but would he?

Even knowing what I do, there's still a delusional part of me that wants to believe he's different. He wouldn't hurt me. I know it's stupid. Once he realizes my true intentions with him, he will certainly want to destroy me. He probably won't even hesitate. He'll just ... kill me.

The silence is suffocating me, and I'm on the verge of a panic attack when he finally breaks it.

"I need something from you," he says.

I swallow hard, repeatedly telling myself not to glance at his towel covered crotch.

"I could use your assistance." He lowers his voice and clears his throat. "What I mean to say is I want you to make Nino ... like me."

My head whips toward him, and I stare at him in disbelief. He seems irritated by my response, but I can't help it. This was not at all what I was expecting.

I turn toward the glass and slide my finger through the condensation, writing out a short message that disappears a moment later in the heat.

What do you mean?

"I thought it was clear. He is afraid of me. He doesn't want to spend time with me. You seem to possess some magic formula, and I want you to use that to change his feelings about me."

My eyes move over his face, and I can see a glimpse of his vulnerability for the first time since I met him. I don't know how I didn't notice it before, but he has guarded it well. I had assumed he just didn't care if Nino liked him. I had assumed a lot of things, actually, and now I am questioning all of them. Regardless, he has to know that what he's asking for isn't realistic.

"I'll give you a bonus," he adds as if this should be the motivating factor for me.

It's not about the money, I write. *What you're asking . . . that's not the way relationships work.*

He grimaces at that word, and I can't understand why. "You can fix it. I know you are capable. You have won him over."

Yes, but it's not for me to win him over on your behalf. It has to be you who does that.

He shakes his head like it's impossible. "That won't work."

I get the sense that what he's really saying is he doesn't know how. He has tried and failed, and now he wants a magic fix. What he's asking goes against every instinct I have, but that human part of me feels empathy for him on some level. He wants a bond with Nino, as any father figure would. But I'm not entirely sure that's the best thing for Nino. What kind of influence will Alessio have on his life? Does he plan to raise him with the expectation that men can't have or express their emotions? Will he raise him to be a killer too? The thought of it twists my stomach. Regardless, his plans don't really matter, do they? I don't even know why I'm taking them into consideration when I know he won't be here to fulfill them.

I don't know what his goals are with Nino, but I have to remember to look at this situation through the lens as he sees it. He is Nino's guardian, and I am nothing more than a nanny. My opinions on his job or his affiliations outside of this house have nothing to do with me. I am here to provide a service, and right now, he is asking me to do just that. The added benefit is that as long as he's talking to me about this, he isn't focused on my scars, and I'm not thinking about him ending my life. Still, I can't force Nino to adapt his emotions to suit Alessio. If he wants that, he has to earn it.

You need to spend more time with him, and it can't just be on your terms. If you want him to like you, find something he enjoys, and do that activity with him. Teach him something. Talk to him without expectations. Allow him a chance to express himself without fear of disappointing you or saying the wrong thing.

I pause for a few moments to let the heat erase the message before I continue.

Praise him. Show him affection. You will find it's not as difficult as you imagine. There is no magic formula. The most valuable thing you can give him is your time.

Alessio watches the words dissipate and then turns his gaze to me. "You say it is simple, but it's not."

Something in me softens at the sadness in his eyes. The irony of this situation is that he's a man who exists in a perpetual fog of dissociation. Now, he is tasked with the job of teaching a child to self-regulate. From the outside looking in, he seems to be in control of everything, always. But I know this isn't the case. When uncomfortable situations threaten him, he actively avoids them. He detaches from everyone around him, shutting himself off as a defense mechanism. I recognize these behaviors because I've used them myself. This is why survivors of trauma often find a bond with each other. Like attracts like. We are both dysfunctional in our own ways. I want to believe that's the simplest explanation for me warming to this man. I don't have to know his history to understand the pain he hides behind those stark eyes. I can feel it every time I look at him.

I will help you, I write reluctantly. *But you have to do the work.*

He nods, and I'm hoping that concludes our meeting so I can slip away into the privacy of my room and cloak myself in the safety of my bed. But Alessio is nothing if not an efficient man. He got the thing he wanted out of the way first, so he could tackle the thing he knows I will resist.

"Why are you wearing this?" His fingers reach up to tug slightly on the tail of my wet neck scarf.

Instinct drives me to stop him. I'm not thinking clearly when I slap my hand over his and freeze.

His eyes lock with mine, and the intensity of that connection makes me sway slightly.

"Show me," he says gruffly. "I want to see what you're hiding there."

I shake my head, pleading silently, and I'm relieved to find he doesn't push me like I thought he might.

"One day, you will show me." His eyes move to the arm that's still holding his hand hostage. "And then you will tell me the truth about these scars."

10

NATALIA

"Good morning, Nino." Alessio rises from his chair to greet us as we enter the dining room. It's bizarre and unlike him, and I'm tempted to glance at the clock to see if I somehow misread the time.

Nino peeks up at him, looking as confused as I feel. "Good morning."

The awkwardness persists for the next thirty seconds, and when I meet Alessio's gaze, I finally realize what's happening. This is his attempt at normal human interaction.

Should we all have a seat? I suggest, noting Alessio is clearly out of his element here.

He nods, pulling a chair out for me, and then repeats the process for Nino. I shoot him a look when he sits down, hoping he can pick up on my silent message to relax. It doesn't need to be so stilted.

Nino, what would you like today? I sign my question and hand him his plate.

"I can do that." Alessio stands up again, and I try to stifle my smile.

"It's okay," Nino disregards his attempt. "I can do it."

I look at Alessio again, offering him a reassuring nod, but it doesn't seem to calm his nerves.

Nino carefully goes about selecting his breakfast, freezing when a piece of melon slips off the spoon and onto the table. His eyes dart to Alessio, and it's clear he needs reassurance that this is okay, but Alessio somehow misses the cue. I nudge his foot beneath the table with mine, and he gives me an odd expression before the realization occurs.

"Don't worry about it, Nino," he responds stiffly. "It's alright."

Nino returns his focus to his task, and once he's seated, Alessio and I dish up our plates. Angelina enters a few minutes into our breakfast, refilling Alessio's coffee cup without even glancing at mine. I'm used to it by now, and honestly, I prefer she ignores me because I don't want her waiting on me. Alessio, however, seems to be more attuned to the situation today, and it catches us all by surprise when he calls her name, and she freezes.

She turns back slowly, peering down at Alessio from beneath her long, beautiful lashes. "Yes, Mr. Scarcello?"

"You forgot Natalia's cup." He nods to my coffee.

Angelina's lips purse and she dips her head. "So sorry about that. I don't know how that happened."

She returns with a tension in her body that wasn't there before, and I'm internally cringing as she refills my cup. I have a feeling she's going to try to pay me back for this later.

When she leaves, Alessio's gaze lingers on mine for much longer than necessary, but neither of us seems eager to break it. I offer him a shaky smile and then turn to Nino, severing the strange connection.

I sign a few questions to Nino, spelling out the words he doesn't yet understand. He answers with his own mixture of spelling variations and words and then beams at my response. When I return to my breakfast, I'm confused by the irritation on Alessio's face.

"Do you not think it rude to have private conversations at the dining table?" he snaps.

I raise my brows at him and then type out a message, holding it up for him to see.

BE NICE.

His lip twitches, and if I didn't know any better, I'd think it amuses him when I talk to him this way. I doubt anyone else in his life does. When he doesn't respond, I take it upon myself to inform him of the discussion I just had with Nino.

I asked him what he'd like to do with you today.

Alessio's brows pinch together. "Today?"

Yes. And he said he would like to go out on the boat.

I leave out the part that I suggested it. Ultimately, this situation will be beneficial for both of us. Alessio can spend time with Nino like he wants, and I can learn how the boat operates.

Alessio glances at Nino, and I'm not entirely sure what he's thinking. For all I know, he could have plans today. After a few moments, I can see he's decided.

"I suppose we could go out on the boat."

Nino's face brightens as he looks at Alessio, and something softens in his expression. That softness tugs at a place deep in my chest, and I try to ignore the feeling that I'm doing something wrong. That I'm somehow misguided or cruel for manipulating Alessio this way. I can't allow myself to care about his feelings. That's the only way I'm going to survive.

We finish our breakfast quietly, and Alessio tells us he's going to prepare the boat. His instructions are to meet him downstairs once Nino is dressed for the water. It's cooler outside today, and that will require a jacket, particularly with the breeze.

I try to hide my disappointment that I won't be able to witness the preparations he's doing. I've taken up studying watercraft operation in my spare time, but it won't be of any use if I don't know where he stores the keys to the boat house. I have a sinking feeling I'm not going to find out today.

Once I have Nino dressed in warmer clothes, I retreat to my

closet to do the same. I don't have many options for boating, so I decide on a pair of jeans, a knitted sweater, and a light jacket.

Nino takes my hand as we walk outside across the lawn to the dock, where Alessio has the boat ready and waiting. From peeking into the window of the boathouse, I've determined he owns a sports cruiser, specifically a Sea Ray Sundancer. It's built for comfort and fun, but I'm certain it will get me where I need to go when the time comes.

Alessio pauses when he sees us, his gaze traveling slowly over my body. By the way his nostrils flare and heat pools in the depths of his eyes, I'm getting the sense he prefers me in jeans over the loose skirt suits that hide my curves.

Nino tugs my hand to pull me forward, distracting me from the moment. Alessio glances down at him, clearly surprised by his eagerness. Then he does something so uncharacteristic it surprises all of us. He reaches down and ruffles the hair atop Nino's head, his face relaxing into the first sign of a natural smile I've witnessed from him.

"Come on, little rascal." He lifts Nino, carries him on board, and then reaches out his hand to help me across the gap.

I stare at his extended fingers for a long moment, my nerves making me pause. It's just a hand, and it's a silly reaction, but I know what that hand is probably capable of. That hand has undoubtedly taken life. That hand is probably well versed in torture, yet when I look at this man, the fear that he first inspired is already beginning to subside. I think, more than anything, that's the thing that scares me.

His eyes implore me to act, and I do, slowly reaching toward him and allowing his massive fingers to engulf mine. The connection sends a tiny shockwave up my arm, and straight to my head, where my pulse is pounding so hard, I can hear it. I wonder if Alessio feels it too. When I look into his eyes, and see the confusion there, I think he does.

Neither of us wants this, but there seems to be some greater force pulling us together. Alessio sets Nino down but doesn't take his eyes off me. Unlike a moment ago, I can't tell what he's thinking. He's skilled at hiding his emotions, but he can't hide the hunger radiating from him.

I swallow and turn my attention to Nino, fussing over his jacket even though I already made sure it was fastened.

"I'm going to start the engine," Alessio tells us. "Nino, would you like to help?"

His eyes sparkle with excitement as he nods. "Yes!"

In another surprising turn of events, Alessio rests his hand on Nino's shoulder as he leads him away. I focus on that connection with a bittersweet warmth in my chest. Perhaps I was wrong before. Alessio might be better at this than I gave him credit for.

I follow them into the cockpit, watching closely as Alessio points out some of the features on the console to Nino, including the start button. I'm taking mental notes throughout the entire process as they start the engine together, and Alessio smoothly navigates us out onto the water.

"You can help me steer when we're out in the open," Alessio tells Nino.

"Okay." Nino sits up straighter, peeking out over the console as if this is the most important job he'll ever have.

The boat picks up speed, and Alessio handles it with precision, guiding us across the lake toward the unknown. The wind cools my cheeks and slowly unravels my hair from its usual bun, pulling pieces out until eventually, it collapses at the nape of my neck. I didn't think to bring a hair tie, so I remove the pins and secure them in my pocket, brushing through the ends of my hair with my fingers to smooth the mess. By the time I'm finished, the tips of my hair fall across my lower back, displaying the length I've been growing for years.

Alessio glances back at me briefly and then freezes, his jaw flexing as he takes me in. I fold my arms across my chest as if I'm cold, but really, I'm feeling exposed. For so long, I've tried to blend in and go unnoticed. I've hidden my femininity as well as I could, determined to keep men away. Right now, I can't hide it, and the longer he looks at me, the more I realize maybe I don't want to.

"Can I drive now?" Nino interrupts the moment, and I'm glad for it.

Alessio nods, his jaw still tight as he slows the speed to a crawl and then pulls Nino onto his lap. I watch the two of them together as Alessio provides instruction, and something in my heart thaws a little. Or a lot. Too much, I think.

God, I don't know what I'm doing, or how to make this stop. This game feels more dangerous with every second that passes, and I'm losing sight of how to protect myself.

I remove my phone from my pocket and type out a quick question, tapping Alessio on the shoulder to show him.

Is it okay if I relax down below?

Alessio turns, nodding stiffly. "If you wish."

I smile at Nino, and he smiles back, and I think this is the right thing to do. Alessio can spend some time with him, and I can get some much-needed distance.

I head for the small door and ease down the narrow stairs to find a cozy salon area. The space is well outfitted with a kitchenette and lounge. Further back, it opens to a stateroom, with a bed and additional loungers. I unzip my jacket and drape it over the lounge before I start my exploration. In my head, I'm reminding myself to look for anything useful, but as my fingers trail over the furniture, my eyes keep drifting back to the bed.

I can't help wondering who else he's brought on this boat. It's a disturbing thought to consider that he's used that space before. That he's had the warmth of a woman next to him right there. I don't want to imagine it, but my consciousness supplies the details regardless. She would be beautiful, of course, and much taller than me. She's probably someone completely at ease in her skin. She wouldn't have a second thought about climbing atop him naked and displaying her body for his pleasure.

A sickening feeling twists my gut at the prospect, and I try to erase it from my mind. I can't think about Alessio's conquests or the bitter resentment I feel over them when I'm not entitled to it. Forcing it from my mind, I collapse into one of the loungers and pull a book from the side pocket. When I see the title, I can't help but wonder at the irony. *The Count of Monte Cristo*. It's been a long time since I read it, but I can remember the revenge theme clearly. If I needed a sign that I'm losing sight of my goal, this is it.

I thumb through the book I've read before, landing on a random chapter as my eyes start to skim over the words. One sentence becomes two, and soon, I'm completely engrossed all over again. I don't know how long has passed before the sound of Alessio's voice startles me.

"Natalia?"

I blink up at him. He's lingering on the stairs as he studies me with concern. Nino is behind him, watching me with rosy cheeks from the wind.

"I called out for you several times," Alessio says.

I shake my head apologetically, closing the book and setting it on the table. His eyes move over it in question before returning to my face.

"It's time for lunch," he tells me.

My stomach rumbles in response, and I rise to my feet, resolved to rejoin them. Alessio watches me as I slip my jacket back on and then holds his hand out again to help me up the stairs. It isn't necessary, but I take it anyway, quietly choking down my tangled emotions when he squeezes my fingers in his.

Upstairs, Alessio leads us toward the stern, where there's a small dining nook and a grill I didn't notice before. It appears he's already started preparations, with a cooler of supplies Angelina must have prepared. I didn't even realize we'd stopped moving, but when I take in the scenery around us, I see why he chose this spot. It's quiet and peaceful.

Can I help? I write.

"I think I can manage," he answers. "You can keep Nino entertained."

I nod and take a seat with Nino at the table.

Are you having fun? I ask.

He nods, a dimple appearing on his left cheek. "I wish we could do this every day."

I try to squash down another surge of guilt as he peeks up at Alessio with clear affection in his eyes. Nino knows Alessio isn't his father, and I was unsure of their dynamic after observing conflicting patterns. On some level, Alessio obviously cares for him, and I can see now that affection is returned.

How long have you been with Alessio? I sign the question using a combination of the words he knows while spelling the rest slowly.

Nino glances at Alessio, and I can tell he's uncertain about answering while he's near him, but he responds by shaking his head. "I don't know."

Since you were a baby?

His brows pinch together, and he nods. "I think so."

I don't want to make him uncomfortable, so I ask him if he wants to play a game or draw. I brought a few things for him just in case, and he seems to prefer quiet activities.

"I'll color," he says, signing the word even as he says it.

I smile at him in approval and retrieve the bag I stowed once we boarded. Nino digs around inside, pulling out a coloring book and crayons while the scent of Alessio's cooking drifts toward us. It all feels so ... domestic. We're out on the open water, enjoying the beautiful day, while Alessio grills like a normal father might. The fresh air and cool water bring me back to my childhood when my father grilled at the lake. I can remember swimming and playing for hours and being so ravenous afterward I'd eat like it was my last meal, only so I could go and do it all over again the next day. Those memories were some of the best times in my life, and I can't help looking at Nino, wondering what his will be.

Right now, he's more relaxed than I've ever seen him. He seems content. Carefree. I can only hope that he holds onto that feeling. That as he grows older, his good memories will outweigh the bad. That he will have a life he loves. It's what every child deserves.

Alessio delivers a plate of grilled chicken to the table and then returns with the cooler, laying out a spread of fresh fruit, cheese, and bite-sized vegetables. He takes a seat across from me, and our eyes meet again as he seems to search for something in mine.

"Hungry?" he asks.

Heat flushes my face, and I find myself nodding too enthusiastically. His eyes flare, and he shoves a plate at me before offering one to Nino. We dish up and eat our meal quietly while Nino pauses between bites to work on his picture. The sun peeks out from behind the clouds, warming my face, but I know it isn't just that. There's something about this moment. It feels like a trap, a possibility that could never be. It would be so tempting to imagine for even a second that I could have this. That somehow, this could be my life. Just the three of us. I try to erase it and forget I even considered it.

That was delicious, I write. *Thank you. I'll help you clean up.*

Alessio nods and glances at his watch. We work side by side, him cleaning the grill while I put away the food in the cooler and wash the plates and silverware in the small sink. I catch him staring at my hands a few times, and I know his mind is turning, the fervent curiosity about my scars burning stronger than ever. I need a distraction, and I find it when Nino starts to yawn, no longer interested in his coloring.

He might need a nap. It's been a busy day.

Alessio follows my gaze to Nino and nods. "I'll take him downstairs."

I concede although I was hoping to do it. If I'm not downstairs with Nino, that means I'll be up here with Alessio. Alone.

I watch them disappear below deck and then resume cleaning to give my hands something to do. I wipe the table and seats down and then clean the sink. When there's nothing left, I wander up to the console, studying it with interest as I try to memorize all the details.

I don't hear Alessio approach me, but I can feel him behind me. His dark energy is a force of nature, and I would be a fool not to sense him. He feels close, so close I could lean back and press his body against mine. I try not to do that. I try not to even breathe, but then he leans into me, inhaling my hair. It's the subtlest of movements, but it penetrates me deep in my core. It sends sparks shooting through my veins, and it only intensifies when he glides a strand of my hair through his fingers and his breath fans across my ear.

"I like it better this way."

My breath catches, and when I turn into him, I'm at eye level with his chest. I always knew he was tall, but I have to crane my neck to look up at him when we're close like this. My only hope is that he can't hear my heart beating violently. When his eyes dip to my pulse, I know he knows.

I study his face, cataloging his brutal handsomeness, memorizing his curves and lines. I want to believe in this strange new feeling. I want to exist in this space where I'm safe with him. I know it's an illusion. He's not my savior. He's my enemy.

"I can't figure you out." He releases my hair, his fingers hovering like he wants to touch my face. "What are you hiding from me?"

I swallow, and he drops his hand, taking a step back and shaking his head like he's annoyed with himself. "I don't know how I'm supposed to communicate with you."

I reach for my phone and reply. *My ears work just fine. We're communicating now, aren't we?*

His frustration ebbs away, but I'm learning that Alessio rarely means what he says. It's only surface level, and there's always something lurking deeper beneath the veneer. While it's true that people tend to tire of communicating with me in a slower fashion than they are accustomed to, I don't think that's his problem at all. He seems frustrated because he wants something more from our conversation, but he can't bring himself to admit exactly what it is. I don't know why I feel like I should bridge this gap, but I do.

You're very tall, I write. *I didn't realize it until now.*

His eyes soften slightly as he looks down at me. "You are very ... short."

Despite my mind screaming at me not to be stupid, I smile. I can't help it. He is so awkward at times, completely at odds with the persona he gives off. I don't doubt for a second that he's a dangerous man, but it's easy to forget during moments like these.

Alessio's eyes move over my face, and something changes in his expression. I can't tell for certain, but I think he seems to relax slightly.

"You don't smile very often," he remarks.

I suppose I don't. But I take my job seriously.

"Yes, well, Nino seems happy in your care."

Nino seems to be a safe topic for both of us. In a way, right now, he almost feels like a safe word. A reminder that we can't fuck this up for him.

He's an amazing child. I don't know how you've managed so long on your own, but you've done a wonderful job with him.

Alessio frowns. "I wasn't completely alone. He had a nanny before, but she was elderly and passed on six months ago."

I'm so sorry. I didn't realize.

I wonder why Nino never mentions her, or why Alessio never thought to mention this. There's a chance Nino is still grieving her loss, and I had no idea.

"He told you I'm not his father," Alessio says.

I stiffen at the observation, wondering how he could possibly know that. I thought we had been so careful with our conversations, but I can see that I was right about my suspicions. There must be cameras in Nino's room. There must be some way Alessio has deciphered our sign language.

Suddenly, I find myself questioning everything. Nino is down for a nap, and I'm out on a boat with him in the open water. Did he bring me out here to kill me? Does he think I'm a threat now that I know the truth?

"That information will need to stay between us." His voice is calm, but his eyes tell me everything I need to know. This is a warning. "As far as the rest of the world is concerned, I am his father. It's my job to protect Nino, and it's important nothing gets in the way of that."

I swallow, forcing myself to nod. *I understand.*

His gaze dips to my lips, and in turn, mine drifts to his. My heart beats a little harder. I wonder if his is too, or if I'm just crazy.

"We have to get back," he says abruptly, taking a step back. "Nino and I have somewhere to be."

I study him for a second, confused. *There's nothing on the schedule for today.*

"This appointment isn't on the schedule." He turns away and takes a seat at the wheel, his intention clear. He doesn't want to be challenged or questioned on this.

I'm not in a place that I could challenge him, but I can't understand where he would need to take Nino. Did he have something else planned that he didn't want me to know about?

"You should go downstairs," he tells me coldly. "In case Nino needs you."

11

NATALIA

I SPEND THE REST OF THE AFTERNOON AND INTO THE EVENING wondering where they could possibly be. Alessio always takes Nino out on Sundays, but until today, I had just assumed it was his attempt at spending time together. Then Alessio told me they had somewhere to be, and the wheels in my mind started to turn. Where exactly is he taking him every Sunday without fail?

Today, they left after four, and it's already past eight. They are usually home by now, and Nino should be getting ready for bed. Concern eats at me as I consider all the different possibilities. Were they in an accident? Are they okay? Is it something else? Something more sinister?

I'm an anxious mess when I finally hear Nino's voice downstairs, and I rush to meet him. Instead of seeing Alessio there, I find it's just Manuel. He glances at me and nods to Nino.

"Go upstairs. Natalia will help you get ready for bed."

Nino does as he's instructed, and I can't help noticing how much his demeanor has changed from this afternoon. There is a sullen, anxious child in place of the quiet, happy boy out on the boat. He takes the hand that I offer, and I lead him upstairs to his room, waiting until we're in the bathroom before I ask him any questions.

How was your day with Alessio? I wet a cloth and use it to wipe his face.

Nino shrugs, casting his eyes toward the floor. It bothers me, and I don't want to push him, but I need to know he's okay. I tip his chin up to meet my gaze, using my hands to sign the words he knows.

Did you eat dinner?

He nods.

What did you have?

Another shrug. "Some gross stuff."

I let him brush his teeth and then help him into his pajamas, hoping he'll open up more with some time between tasks. When I tuck him into bed, it's apparent that won't be happening.

Did Alessio come home with you?

He shakes his head. The only thing that makes sense is they must have had some sort of disagreement. I can't imagine what else it would be.

Where did you go tonight?

He dips his head like he knows he's not supposed to tell me. I'm about to tell him he doesn't have to when he signs three letters.

I.V.I.

My brows draw together in confusion, thinking he must be too tired to comprehend what he's saying. I can't in good conscience push him any further, so I drop it and stroke the hair back from his forehead.

Sleep well, sweetheart.

"Natalia?" He calls out for me as I head for the door.

I turn to find tears hovering on the edges of his eyes, and I rush back to him. *What is it?*

"I don't want you to go."

I'm right here, I assure him. *It's okay. Can you tell me why you're upset?*

He shakes his head. "Just stay with me until I go to sleep."

I will, I answer. *You're safe now, okay?*

He nods, releases a quiet sigh, and closes his eyes.

———

WHEN I'M certain Nino is asleep, I go back to my room and sit on the edge of the bed, staring at the wall. Something is off. Alessio is keeping a secret, and I have a terrible gut feeling I might know what it is. Without confirmation, there's no way to know for certain. I came here with very little information about Alessio and the current circumstances. I don't know why Nino is with him or how it came to be that way. I only know what Nino told me about his father, along with the warning from Alessio about his duty to protect Nino.

Tonight, he took him somewhere he didn't want me to know about. I've tried to rationalize it, but no matter how I look at it, I keep coming back to the same conclusion.

My paranoia is fraying every last nerve, and I don't know how much longer I can do this. If Alessio doesn't know already, if he's not just toying with me somehow, it's only a matter of time until he figures out the truth. I already have my exit strategy. There's no reason for me to wait any longer. I saw him take the keys to the boathouse to the office on the first floor tonight. I know that door is locked, but there must be a key somewhere. I suspect he'll have it on him.

My eyes dart to my pillow as the idea begins to cement in my mind. It has to be now. There will never be a perfect time to carry this out. I'm already getting too wrapped up in this situation. I can't feel guilty for what I have to do, not when I know Alessio would do the same if the roles were reversed.

I don't know where the cameras are hidden in my room, but it doesn't matter anymore. Discretion isn't going to help me, not after tonight. It will either be him or me.

I go into the closet first, packing up my clothing as an idea comes to me. There's an advantage I haven't considered. Alessio will be surprised when he sees me, so I can disarm him. I can lure him into a false sense of safety and tempt him with the thing he really wants, the hunger I see in his eyes when he looks at me.

My fingers hover over the black silk nightgown I never really wear but bought because it felt good against my skin. It's beautiful, with intricate lace detailing and a hem that skims my mid-thigh. I didn't buy it for anyone else. I just wanted to know what it felt like. I wore it once for ten minutes in bed before my fears got the best of me. It went back into the closet, and I returned to the safety of my routine. Sensible pajamas and sneakers, so I could run any time I needed to.

Tonight, I will run. It will be barefoot, and in silk and lace. I will have to come back to my bedroom with the hopes that Manuel won't have awoken by the noise upstairs. If I do it right, the way I imagine it in my head, it will be quiet. Not even Alessio will see it coming.

A wave of nausea rolls through me as I undress and slip into the chemise. I can't think about him as the man I've come to know in my time here, so instead, I think about him as my enemy. That's how I'll do this. That's how I'll harness the necessary rage to end his life.

With the nightgown secure on my body, I glance in the mirror, unraveling my hair and combing through it once more. Just the way he said he likes it.

There's a pit in my stomach as I head for the bed, grabbing the knife from beneath the pillow and slipping it into my palm, tucking it discreetly against my body. It's already past midnight, and I suspect I don't have much time to get upstairs and settle in.

Quietly, I shut my bedroom door behind me and creep down the hall, the marble cold against my bare feet. There's a maniacal part of me that half expects Angelina to jump out of the shadows as I turn toward the banister, parroting her favorite line.

The third level is off-limits.

Tonight, it's not. I grab the iron railing with my free hand, cautiously working my way up into the darkness. When my feet hit the landing, my eyes are already darting around nervously, seeking out traps. It appears much like the second floor. There's a hall leading to Alessio's suite, and the only noticeable difference I find along the way is a series of paintings hung on display. I pause to look at them, noting the details I'm able to distinguish in the dim light. It appears to be a woman and two children. His family, perhaps?

I'm not sure what to make of it, but I don't linger. Looking for too long will only humanize him. It will make this harder than it needs to be.

As I approach the suite with large, solid French doors, it occurs to me that they could be locked. But to my relief, I find that they aren't. When I open them, the first thing that hits me is Alessio's scent. It's clean and masculine, and admittedly, I could see how women might find it intoxicating. I try to forget how to breathe as I examine the room.

I think I was expecting some type of dark lair, but surprisingly, the space is light and clean. The curtains, walls, and area rug are all shades of white and soft gray. The massive bed in the center is cloaked in the same luxurious bedding I have in my room. So white and fluffy, it looks like a cloud. The room consists of the basics, much like all the others in the house, and I doubt he's hiding anything important here. I do my due diligence regardless, snooping through his drawers and peeking into his closet, touching everything I can get my hands on. I'm not worried about leaving evidence. There won't be any way to hide that it was me regardless.

After twenty minutes, I've concluded whatever secrets Alessio may have, they aren't hidden in here. With nothing else to do, I try to determine which side of the bed he sleeps on by checking all three sets of pillows. There is no indication anyone has ever slept in this bed. I opt for the middle ground, carefully tucking my knife under that set of pillows, hoping I'll be able to reach it when the time comes. Then I make myself comfortable in a plush gray chair near his bed. My eyes drift to the clock periodically, watching as the minutes pass. Those minutes soon turn into an hour and then two. By the third, I'm irritated. Where the hell is he?

The first thought that comes to mind is the most obvious. It's the middle of the night, and he hasn't come home. He must be out fucking someone. It's an idea that stirs an unrecognizable emotion in me. I don't want to believe it's jealousy, but the bitterness on my tongue makes me think it must be. Imagining him looking at someone else the way he looks at me is bothersome, to say the least.

I'm not completely emotionally bankrupt. I can recognize feelings when I have them, and I know suppressing them only gives them more power over me. I can admit if I had met Alessio under different circumstances, I wouldn't be so opposed to his uncivilized charm. But acknowledging that feeling and accepting it are two different things. I'm not supposed to like the bad guy, and if I do, it means there is something deeply wrong with me.

He should repulse me. I should hate him with a passion that leaves no room for any sympathy, but I have witnessed him struggle with his humanity. I have seen the way he looks at Nino, the way he wants to protect him and do right by him. That alone has softened me toward him. The way he looks at me ... like he never wants to stop, it has softened me too.

Frustration overtakes me as I reconsider my entire plan. Can I really do this? Can I kiss him, touch him, and give him my body as I stab him in the neck? My eyes burn as I consider it, and I hate that this is what my life has turned into. I didn't choose to be this way. I didn't choose any of this, and I can't lose sight of the catalyst that brought me here or the reality I want more than anything.

I check the clock again. It's past four a.m. now, and I'm beginning to question if he's even coming home. If he has been with another woman, then what? How can I possibly explain my reason for being here in the face of his rejection?

The tumultuous thoughts are giving me a headache, so I do the only logical thing I can. I climb onto his bed and lay my head on the pillow with the intention of clearing my mind and not thinking about anything. Then I smell his scent there, and I realize he does have a side, and this is it. I snuggle deeper, feeling oddly calm as I settle into his space. It's peaceful here, and I can understand why he wants to keep it that way.

My eyes feel heavy, and I try to keep them open at any cost. I count from one to a hundred and back again. I slip my palm beneath the pillow in the middle to touch the blade of my weapon. I roll onto my side and then onto my back, stretching my limbs and breathing deeply. The exhaustion is becoming too much. It's pulling me under, and I think if I can just close my eyes for a second, it will be okay.

A sound startles me awake, and at first, I don't know where I am. Then all at once, a massive surge of adrenaline floods my veins as I bolt upright, squinting into the bright morning light. I glance around the room, unable to see what woke me, but I was certain I heard something.

A muffled grunt reverberates against the door, and I move quickly, tossing the covers off me, preparing for the unknown. I'm standing beside the bed, waiting to see who comes through, but it's taking too long. Someone is still out there, wiggling the doorknob with muttered curses.

Logically, I know it must be Alessio, but the door isn't locked, and I don't understand why he's having such a difficult time opening it. Several more moments pass before I tiptoe toward the door, listening closely for anything else. When I press my ear against the wood, I hear someone breathing on the other side, but it doesn't sound like they are moving anymore. I slip my trembling fingers onto the handle, pulling down slowly and opening it to reveal a sight straight out of a horror film.

Alessio is standing there in a tattered button-down shirt that was once probably white, but now it's soaked in blood. I can't tell if it's his or someone else's, but it's ... everywhere. My eyes move over him rapidly, taking in the details as quickly as I can. There's a cut above his eyebrow and bruising on his jaw. Dried blood is smeared across his throat, and his entire sleeve is soaked in fresh blood. There's so much that it's dripping down his palm and onto the marble floor. I can see now why he wasn't able to open the door.

He lifts his head slowly, clearly exhausted, and his gaze meets mine. "What are you doing here?"

His tone is unmistakably annoyed, and I suspect it's because he didn't anticipate anyone would see him like this, least of all me. When his eyes travel down the length of my body, noting the lace chemise, something changes. His nostrils flare, and then his brows pinch together.

"Were you in my bed?"

That question is a landmine I'd rather avoid right now, so I do the only rational thing I can. I reach for his hand and pull him inside, directing him to the gray chair I was in earlier. I hold up a finger to indicate that he should wait there.

He watches me as I walk into his bathroom. I don't know how to distract him from the fact that I know he has a massive stash of first aid supplies in here. I rifled through them earlier, wondering why he needed so many. Now I know.

I grab everything I think I might use and carry it back to the side table. Then I head for his dresser, where I saw a decanter and a glass. I don't know what's in it, but hopefully, it's strong.

He watches me as I bring it to him, opening the decanter and pouring him a large glass. Suspicion lingers in his eyes as if he knows my intentions somehow, so I do the only thing I can to reassure him. I bring the glass to my lips and take a sip first before handing it over to him.

He takes it reluctantly, and I kneel in front of him, undoing the top button of his shirt. His free hand stills mine, and when I look up, our faces are so close his breath is warm against my lips.

"You should go back to your room."

I narrow my eyes and shake my head. We're locked in a war of wills, and there's still a part of me that thinks he'll insist, but his hand slowly falls away from mine. He tosses back his drink, his throat working in a way I never knew could be so ... erotic.

I force myself to focus on the task at hand, unbuttoning the rest of his shirt and helping him out of it. I saw his chest before in the pool area and the sauna, but it feels more intimate up close. My eyes are drawn to the round scars scattered across the broad expanse of muscle and bone. I don't even realize what I'm doing until my fingers are touching the raised flesh, examining them with equal parts curiosity and sadness.

Again, he stills my hand, his eyes boring into mine, like he's trying to say those are off-limits. I nod at him apologetically, moving on to take stock of his other wounds. He has more bruising on his side, as well as some minor cuts and scrapes. The biggest thing is the gash on his bicep, where it looks like he was stabbed with something.

I'm oddly relieved to find that most of the blood on him isn't his. I'm also slightly terrified. This is the confirmation I needed that Alessio is, in fact, a killer. It's in his nature. I can tell by his demeanor this isn't the first time he's come home bloodied and bruised, and it won't be the last. Today, it's someone else's blood, but tomorrow, it could be mine.

I peek up at him and make a gesture of a writing instrument. He grimaces as he pulls out the drawer of the bedside table and hands a notepad and pen to me. I make a point to ask him what any sane person would in my situation.

What happened?

He's quiet when I set down the notepad and retrieve an alcohol wipe. I tear it open and start to clean his arm first, wiping away the blood. I have to repeat the process, discarding the used wipes into a pile on the table. He watches me, and I don't know if he's going to answer me, but finally, he does.

"What do you think happened, Natalia?"

I pause to look at him. There's an emotion I can't quite identify on his face. This feels like a test, and I know playing stupid won't do me any favors. I can't unsee this, and he wants to know what I plan to do about it.

I discard the wipe in my hand and retrieve the notepad again. *I think you killed someone, and it isn't the first time. I think maybe it's your job for the mafia.*

He reads my response, his face unmoving. "Does that scare you?"

There's a softness to his voice I didn't expect. Almost as if he doesn't want me to say yes. I don't think he wants me to be scared of him, but how could I not be?

Who are the people you kill? I write. *Are they bad? Or do you even know them? Are they women? Children?*

He blows out a breath, shaking his head. "So many questions."

The room falls silent, and I know he's considering what I said. It feels too intense to look at him right now, so I give him space to think as I continue cleaning his arm.

"You shouldn't have been in here," he says quietly. "Now, I'll never be able to let you go."

I stop and reach for the pen and paper, hesitating before I write my answer. *Maybe I don't want you to.*

For a moment, everything else falls away. I don't know if it's an honest confession, but right now, it feels like one. Alessio's gaze burns into mine, the fire warming me from a place nobody has ever touched before. I think I want to taste him for real, and that scares me. The longer we stare at each other this way, the more doubt I have.

I tear my eyes away from him to focus on the paper. *You're going to need stitches.*

Alessio surprises me by reaching out, his fingers grazing my chin before he tips it up, so I'm looking at him again. "The men who meet with me deserve what they get, but to answer your question, no. Never women and children."

I release a shaky breath and nod. Maybe I shouldn't, but I believe him. Still, I know it doesn't change a thing. Just because he hasn't yet doesn't mean he won't. He warned me. He's still warning me. Everything about his energy right now is screaming that he's a threat. I just can't decide if it's to my life or my heart.

He releases me gradually like he doesn't want to, and I resume my cleaning. Once I have his arm washed, I refill his glass and hand it to him before reaching for the suture kit. Alessio swallows his drink and sets it aside while I prepare by re-sanitizing my hands and opening each sterilized pack carefully. His gaze never wavers from me, even as I apply the tissue forceps and drive the needle through his skin.

"It's not the mafia."

I glance up at him in question.

"You said the mafia," he explains. "It's not. The mafia is child's play, Natalia. You should know that before you get any ideas in your head about betraying my trust."

I shake my head to say I wouldn't.

"We make our own rules. We have our own government. We're everywhere. Politicians, law enforcement, federal bureaus. There's no escaping us."

I let that sink in, but I didn't need him to tell me that. I learned it the hard way already.

"I can keep you safe," he continues. "As long as you don't cross me."

I finish suturing the wound and set the tools aside before I write my response.

I understand.

He's looking at me like I don't, like I'm too calm. Am I too at ease with this entire situation? I suppose that's something I didn't consider. The old me would have panicked. She would have cried and felt helpless, but I'm not her anymore. That girl died a long time ago.

I grab another alcohol wipe and lean up to clean his neck. As I do, the warmth of his body penetrates mine. Somehow, even covered in blood, he still smells good. When I finish with his neck, I start to dab at the cut on his forehead, but he reaches up to stop me.

Our eyes clash, and my pulse quickens when I notice him staring at my lace-covered breasts.

"You never told me why you were in here," he murmurs.

I don't have a good answer for that. He'll know I'm lying if I try to make an excuse now. The only thing to do is go for it. This was my plan all along, but it feels different now. It feels less like I'm manipulating him and more like it's happening naturally.

My gaze flicks to his lips, and I lean forward between his parted legs, feeling the length of his erection stabbing against my body. He sucks in a sharp breath, and his grip on my hand loosens as I slowly crawl up onto his lap, hitching up my nightgown so I can straddle him.

He's staring at me like he doesn't know whether to toss me off or kiss me. I choose for him, grabbing his face between my palms and bringing my lips to his. His initial reaction is to freeze, which isn't what I'd expect, but I kiss him anyway because I've already come this far. A soft groan rumbles from his throat when I force his head back, sliding my fingers through his hair.

The tension in his body begins to dissipate as his lips move against mine. It's cautious at first, perhaps uncertain, but after just a few moments, his appetite is unleashed. He deepens the kiss, his tongue delving into my mouth with a growl as his hands start to grope my body. It starts at my breasts, pawing and squeezing before he dips his palm beneath the material to graze my nipple. I startle at the jolt of electricity it produces, leaning into his touch to beg for more. He rewards me with another animalistic sound, using his other hand to grab my hip and roll my pelvis against his cock. It's hot and huge beneath me, and the nerves I thought I might feel are absent. In their place is a need I've never felt before. A need for connection. A need for him inside of me.

Alessio picks me up and carries me to the bed with little effort, his lips breaking away from mine as he lays me down on his pillow. For a second, he stares down at me, a vein pulsing in his neck, eyes dark and hot. I think maybe he's reconsidering, but then he slides his palms up my thighs, spreading me apart for him to see.

I'm vulnerable like this, and my first instinct is to close my legs, but I don't. When I notice the expression on his face ... the undeniable thirst, I know I've got him exactly where I want him. He reaches down and touches me like he can't stop himself. He feels the ungodly amount of wetness there, and his eyes snap to mine, and all bets are off.

"Fucking Christ," he mutters on a ragged breath.

His fingers slide through my arousal, and I arch into him, squirming against the bed as he slips one inside of me. For a few long moments, he just watches my reaction to him, as if he can't believe what he's seeing. It's impossible to hide, and I couldn't pretend to respond any differently right now even if I wanted to. My chest heaves with every breath, drawing his eyes to the hard nipples scraping against the chemise. I'm aching, desperate for more when he leans over me and drags down the silk covering my breast, exposing me to him. For a full minute, he just stares at me, his eyes moving over the sensitive, swollen flesh like he's memorizing the way I look in this moment. I can tell he's at war with himself in his mind, even as his finger moves inside of me. He wants more, but something is holding him back.

I look up at him pleadingly, arching my body in offer. His eyes lock with mine, and then flare as a flame stirs inside of him. Slowly, he surrenders, dipping his head toward my breast. The scruff on his jaw scrapes against the tender flesh as he rubs against me, bringing every nerve in my body to attention. But when his mouth latches onto my nipple, it feels like liquid heroin in my veins.

Oh, God. I did not expect it to be ... so intense.

I curl my hands into his hair, breathing him in as he rocks his pelvis against me. He stuffs another finger inside of me, fucking me while the length of his erection jars against my clit. I don't have to look down to know I'm soaking his pants, and I don't know why he's not taking them off, but I'm too dazed to give it much thought. His teeth graze my nipple, and I hiss as pleasure rolls through me, blindsiding me with its power.

I want to call out his name. I want to beg him for more, but it's all coming too fast. He's rocking against me, branding my flesh with his lips and his teeth. I'm greedy for every touch. Every kiss. Every shudder. The more I respond, the harder he thrusts. His neck muscles strain as he bites back the sounds of his rough approval and I just want to freeze this moment. I want to memorize that drunken bliss on his face as he abandons himself to me.

Inevitably, I'm lost to his control far too soon. Blinding light flashes behind my eyes as my body begins to convulse, the orgasm tearing through me violently. His grip on me tightens, his breath skittering across my nipple as my liberation tips him over the edge. He growls, a low painful sound as his body jerks against mine.

I'm breathless, shaking, and dumbfounded when I glance down and see he never even unbuckled his belt, and then it occurs to me. This was my opportunity. It was right there. All I had to do was reach beneath the pillow, take that knife, and plunge it into his neck.

One glance at his face when he drags himself up, hovering over me with as much uncertainty and torment as I feel, I know that I can't. I can't fucking do it because I don't want to.

"Knock, knock." The bedroom door swings open unexpectedly, startling both of us.

I swing my gaze past Alessio, who's still between my thighs, to see a woman I don't recognize standing there. She surveys us, her face souring as I yank at my nightgown, trying to cover myself up.

"Alessio." She narrows her gaze. "What the hell is going on?"

12

NATALIA

"Christ," Alessio mutters under his breath, dragging his gaze back to mine.

I can't discern the meaning behind the look on his face. He's on edge, like he was caught doing something wrong. A surge of irrational jealousy takes hold of me as I glance behind him at the woman who's currently staring daggers at me. I don't want to believe she could have any kind of intimate relationship with him, given that she's at least twenty years older, but nothing is out of the realm of possibility, is it? Why else would she come up here as if she has the right to do so?

"You should go get dressed," Alessio tells me in a low voice. "Wake Nino up and bring him downstairs."

I don't understand what's happening, but there isn't time to think about it. I lose the protective shield of his body as he pulls away from me and turns to face the woman. Something seems to pass between them, but I'm not a mind reader, so I don't have any idea what it is.

A sick, panicky feeling washes over me when I realize they're both waiting for me to leave, and my knife is still hidden beneath the middle pillow.

Oh, God. This is so bad.

I linger for another moment, trying to figure out what to do, but they're both staring at me, and there's no way I can grab it without being noticed. This plan of mine has turned out to be a colossal fuckup. I don't know when Angelina comes to make Alessio's bed, but I assume she does. Then, I have no doubt the truth will be discovered. I could be dead before lunchtime. To make matters worse, I think I'm way too reactive to the fact that Alessio is asking me to leave him here with this woman. I know it doesn't make sense. I'm not entitled to anything from him. But ten minutes ago, his fingers were inside me. His lips were on me. The sounds of pleasure that tore from his throat were mine, and now it's like none of it even mattered.

There is no graceful way to do the walk of shame past her. I'm in a skimpy nightgown that shows much more than I'd care to admit. She takes note of me as I pass by, her eyes moving over me in sharp disapproval. I maintain a neutral expression, but it isn't without difficulty.

She is, admittedly, a beautiful woman. She's tall, shapely, and well dressed. Her blonde hair is styled in a way that highlights her angular cheekbones. Even though I'm sure she's at least twenty years older than Alessio, I could see how she might appeal to him. In comparison, I feel plain, but I hold my head high as I pass her by because I'm good at faking it.

Once I'm in the hall, however, it's a different story. I take a deep breath and pause, glancing back over my shoulder. The door is still open, and I think a part of me is waiting to see if she shuts it. I'm desperate to hear what she has to say, but I'm still too close. Reluctantly, I inch toward the staircase as her voice rings out.

"Really, Alessio? Please don't tell me that's the nanny. Don't tell me you've fallen for that old cliché."

My throat squeezes as I wait for his response.

"It was a mistake," he answers callously.

Those words are like a hot knife to my chest, and I find myself shrinking back against the wall, humiliated. It's so stupid. I shouldn't be this sensitive. If anything, I should feel the same way about what just happened between us.

"You have to get rid of her," the woman says. "It's the only way. You can't let this go on while she's supposed to be looking after Nino."

There's another pause, and I'm still holding my breath, waiting for him to defend me, but he doesn't. This is the absolute worst-case scenario, and I'm not prepared with a backup plan if he wants to send me packing.

"I can have Marianna here this afternoon—"

"No," he grunts.

I perk up, but I'm not sure whether I'm hopeful or relieved.

"I'm in charge of Nino's care," Alessio replies. "I won't allow my poor decision to interfere with that. He cares for Natalia. It would only hurt him to remove her from his life abruptly."

"Hurt him?" the woman scoffs, her voice laced with resentment. "He barely knows her."

"He spends most of his time with her," Alessio admits regretfully. "He prefers her company, and they have already bonded. Making her leave would be equal to punishing him without merit."

"I'll never understand you men," she sighs. "You have your choice of the most beautiful women in the city at your disposal, women who would do anything you asked of them, yet you choose a shabby, disfigured simpleton out of convenience."

"Gwen." His tone is low and dark, a clear warning that softens the blow of her harsh words. "You will treat her with respect while you're in this house. You may not agree with all my decisions, but you need to trust that I know what's best for Nino."

I'm trying to figure out who she is in Nino's life when she sniffles. I don't have to see her to know she's putting on crocodile tears.

"Alessio, you know I only have the utmost respect for you. I'm just looking out for you, and I admit, sometimes I may come across as harsh, but you and I are the same. You are the only person in my life who knows what it's like to lose everyone they've ever loved. To me, you'll always be like a son."

"I know," he answers softly. "I'll never forget what you've done for me, Gwen. You are my family. Nothing will ever change that."

I can hear her moving, and I wonder if she's hugging him. But I'm still stuck on what she just said about him losing everyone he's ever loved.

"It's too late for me to find happiness," she says. "But you still can. I truly believe if you'd just give Marianna a chance—"

"I'll consider it."

His concession prickles me, and I can't help wondering who the hell Marianna is. Does he like her? Does he mean what he just said, or is he pacifying her?

"You will?" Her voice rises with excitement. "Oh, Alessio, you'll see. She's amazing. What about this weekend? I could arrange for you to take her out on the boat? Or dinner downtown? What do you think?"

He sighs. "I think I haven't slept all night, and I can't make any plans right now. I need to take a shower. Can you just wait for me downstairs? Angelina will make you a cup of coffee."

"Okay," she answers with a smile in her voice. "I'll wait for you in the dining room."

I fling myself around the corner as the sound of her footsteps approach the door. Taking the stairs as quickly and quietly as I can, I make good time. Her heels are so loud they seem to echo right behind me. This flight of stairs didn't seem quite so long last night. Now, it feels like an eternity until I get to the bottom. When I do, I glance over my shoulder long enough to see her rounding the landing. I dart back to my room, relieved I left the door cracked. I shut myself inside with a soft click, hoping she didn't notice, but by the pause of her heels on the second floor, I'm guessing she might have. Not that it matters. I already have a target on my back, apparently. My most important concern right now is finding that knife before Angelina does.

My eavesdropping didn't leave me much time to get ready. I don't want to miss a second of whatever's about to transpire downstairs, and I need to be on guard. There isn't time for a shower, so I wash my face and the mess between my thighs from Alessio's hands, trying not to think about it. I can unpack everything that happened later. Right now, I need to focus.

I dress and pull my hair into a bun in record time. My teeth are brushed hastily, and makeup applied as neatly as I can manage with my heart nearly beating out of my chest. I'm not sure what it is about that woman, apart from her obvious desire to see me gone, but something is prickling at my anxiety. People often talk about bad energy, and it comes to mind when I think of her. I didn't have to hear what she said about me to feel this pit in my gut. I've had it before, and it didn't lead me astray, but it didn't protect me either. I know Gwen is bad news. I just need time to figure out why.

I close my door behind me and walk quietly to Nino's room. When I open his door, I'm surprised to find him on the bed watching cartoons. It appears he woke early and took it upon himself to get ready. When he sees me, he smiles, and I return it eagerly. If there is one thing I know in all of this mess, it's that I will never tire of seeing that beautiful face.

I sign to tell him good morning, and he does the same in return.

Breakfast? I ask.

He nods, sliding across the large bed with the out-of-place alien comforter to jump onto the bench below. Admittedly, the room looks a little strange with the comforter and the painting Alessio chose as the only bright pieces amongst everything else. But Nino is happy, and that's all that matters.

He takes my hand in his without prompting, and together, we exit to the hall and walk downstairs. We only manage to make it to the foyer before Gwen comes out to greet us. Her eyes cut over me again and then move to Nino.

"Nino!" She shrieks. "Come here, my little lamb. Give your grandmother a hug."

Grandmother? I'm trying to digest that information when Nino's grip on me tightens. When I glance down at him, he's staring at her with obvious discomfort.

"Nino," she says, her voice a little firmer this time. "Don't be rude. You should be happy to see me. Now give me a smile and a hug before you upset me."

He looks up at me, his eyes betraying his reluctance. Nino isn't overly affectionate. He holds my hand, but he likes to keep to himself. He's quiet and introspective, and if Gwen is truly his grandmother, as she claims, she should know that about him.

You don't have to, I sign to him. *If you don't like it.*

His brows draw together as he replies. *I don't want to.*

Gwen watches the interaction between us with hawk-like attention. "What are you doing?"

I glance down at Nino reassuringly, then retrieve my phone to write out a message for her.

Nino doesn't feel like smiling right now, and he doesn't want to be hugged. I told him he doesn't have to.

Her eyes are practically spitting flames as she listens to the message. "Who the hell do you think you are?"

Nino. I glance down at him and sign. *Can you wait for me at the breakfast table?*

He nods, skirting around Gwen while she watches him go in disbelief. Then she turns her venomous gaze back to me.

"What do you think you're doing turning my grandson against me?"

I'm not turning anyone against you, I write. *He expressed his feelings about it quite clearly. He did not want to smile, and he did not want a hug. I will not force him to mask his emotions or show affection if he doesn't feel like it.*

"He will respect me," she shrieks. "You have no idea how our world works, and I'm telling you now, I am not a woman you want to cross. I won't stand for this."

Regardless of how your world may work, Nino is entitled to body autonomy. His emotions are valid, and when he's in my care, I won't force him to perform for the benefit of anyone. I am sorry if what happened hurt your feelings, but I stand by what I said. I'm here to look after Nino, and that includes his mental wellbeing. I do not subscribe to outdated philosophies that children should be raised to mask their emotions for the sake of an adult's ego.

She listens to my response and scoffs, clearly not getting it. "He is a Sovereign Son. He'll have to do plenty of things that make him uncomfortable. You can't even wrap your simple-minded head around that notion."

"Is there a problem here?" Alessio's voice alerts me to his presence behind me. I didn't even hear him coming. I turn to face him as Gwen answers for the both of us.

"Yes, there's a problem. This fucking nanny is trying to turn Nino against me!"

"Gwen." Alessio narrows his eyes at her before turning to me in question. "What is the issue?"

"The issue is she's a devious little snake, Alessio," Gwen barks. "Did someone cut out her tongue, because she couldn't learn to hold it? She needs to understand her place."

"Enough!" Alessio roars, shocking all of us into stillness. I've never heard him raise his voice, but right now, it's clear he's not mincing words. "If you have an issue, you can take it up with me in private."

Gwen considers it, her eyes drifting back to me. I think she knows there isn't anything else she can say in this situation that will make her sound rational at this point, but she's not ready to accept her defeat.

"Natalia, can you please assist Nino with his breakfast?" Alessio asks. "We'll be in shortly."

I nod and walk away, listening as I go, but they are both quiet until I'm out of earshot. There's no way I can hide here with Angelina in the kitchen. When she sees me, she snickers, and it's clear she heard the entire confrontation.

"That's what you get," she mutters under her breath.

Ignoring her, I head for the dining room to find Nino looking quite worried as he sits at the large table alone. His cheeks are stained with tears, and it breaks me to see them.

Hey. I kneel before him. *What's wrong, little prince?*

"Did I get you in trouble?" he sniffles.

No. I shake my head and write him a text note. *You don't ever have to worry about that, okay? I'm sorry you had to hear that yelling. It must have been scary.*

He winces. "She yells a lot. I don't like it."

It's okay to say you don't like it, I reassure him. *And it's okay to say no to a hug if you don't want one. If you would rather give a high five or handshake or even a wave, you can do that. But if you don't want to, you don't have to. If someone else gets upset about that, it's not your fault. It's your body, and you're the only one who can say what you do or don't want. You did nothing wrong. You can still tell friends or family you love them with words if you prefer.*

"But I don't love her," he whispers. "She always tells me I should come live with her when I don't want to. She drinks wine for breakfast, and smears lipstick on my face when she kisses me."

I offer him a sad smile, and there's only one thing I can think to say. *Have you talked to Alessio about this?*

He shakes his head. "I don't want to make him mad."

Does Alessio get mad at you often? I ask, knowing that he doesn't. I want to talk Nino through this to show him that his fears are bigger than reality. There's a major disconnect between them, and neither of them knows how to bridge that gap.

He casts his eyes to the table and shrugs. "I don't know. He doesn't yell, but I think he could get mad."

Why is that?

"He looks grumpy all the time."

Despite my efforts to remain serious, I laugh silently. There's no lie in what he's telling me. Nino peeks up at me, a tiny smile curling his lips when he sees me laughing.

You know, I think some people just look that way. Most of the time it isn't because of us. Sometimes, they might be busy or have a lot on their mind. They might even be sad, but they look angry to keep others away.

Why? Nino signs, his brows furrowed with concern.

Well, what do you do when you're sad?

He considers it for a moment. "I like to draw."

Do you ever tell anyone you're sad?

He shakes his head, and I wish I hadn't been right about that.

Why not?

"I don't know," he murmurs.

It can be scary to admit when you're feeling a big emotion. It's not always easy, and adults might hide it too. I think Alessio looks mad sometimes because he's really sad. He doesn't tell anyone either, but it's good to say how you feel. You just told me. Did it make things better or worse?

"Better," he says. "I like talking to you."

That's good. I want you to know you can talk to me any time about anything. I'll always listen, okay?

Okay. He signs and then surprises me when he leans down and hugs me. It's the first time he's ever done that, and knowing that he doesn't give hugs freely, it makes me feel ... too much.

I'm choking up when Alessio walks in and sees us that way, followed by a somber Gwen. I don't know what happened during their conversation, but she looks well and truly put in her place, and I can only hope that means I'm not fired.

Nino pulls away when he sees them, hops down from his chair as I rise, and walks over to Alessio. Then, he shocks all of us when he leans in and hugs him too, grasping at his waist, which is about as high as he can reach. Alessio looks visibly distraught and confused when his gaze collides with mine. I make a gesture with my hands as a signal to hug him back. It's such a simple thing, but Alessio has to be told how to do it, and that's how I know I'm right about him. We learn affection from our families, and whatever the case may be, it's quite obvious Alessio missed out on some or all of those lessons. I don't want to empathize with him after everything that's transpired today, but it's hard not to when I recall what Gwen said.

He's lost everyone he ever loved.

I still don't know what that means, but I want to. That is until I remember his words from earlier about me being a mistake. Those words seem to play in my head repeatedly as we all sit down for the most uncomfortable breakfast ever.

I help Nino make his selections from the food on the table while Gwen starts prattling on about some event at something called IVI. I'm not fully listening until it occurs to me that Nino mentioned IVI. He said that's where Alessio took him on the nights they have a meeting that's not on the schedule. I'm curious if that's some type of headquarters for their mafia organization or whatever Alessio would refer to it as. It's the same principle, right? They are powerful. Dangerous. Criminal behavior takes place. So, tomayto, tomahto.

"Marianna's going to look so gorgeous at the gala," Gwen says, interrupting my silent stream of thoughts. "Just wait until you see the dress she chose, Alessio. You're going to love it."

When I glance up, she's wearing a smirk, and Alessio is staring at me uncomfortably. I maintain that eye contact for a few seconds longer than I should, and I'm afraid my emotions are all over my face.

He doesn't belong to me, so I don't know why it matters. This morning, I was planning on killing him. If he thinks I'm a mistake and wants to go to a gala with another woman, it shouldn't make any difference to me. In fact, the busier he is, the better it will be for me. He did me a favor by telling the truth. We are from two different worlds. There is no reality where he's going to take me to his super-secret organization as a date. I'm the hired staff, and he is the enemy. He just hasn't realized it yet.

I focus on eating the small croissant I chose as quickly and politely as I can manage. I distract myself by trying to figure out how I'm going to make it up to the third level before Angelina does. Right now, I know she's still in the kitchen, where she remains during breakfast service. At least I can count on that, but I have no idea what Alessio's plans are for the day. For all I know, he might be staying home, in which case, I'm definitely screwed.

Alessio gives me a curious glance as I finish in record time and set a napkin on my plate. I know the polite thing to do is wait for everyone else, and that's the expectation, but I can't chance it. I retrieve my phone and start writing.

May I be excused briefly? I need to use the powder room.

He gives me a tight nod. "I'll look after Nino."

"Take your time," Gwen calls after me as I go.

I don't dignify her with a response, but I do glance over my shoulder to see Alessio's. I'm not even certain he heard her because his eyes are on me, brows pinched tightly, jaw set. I can't tell what he's thinking, but I don't stick around to find out.

There's a bathroom on the first floor, of course, but I head for the stairs. If anyone questions me later, I can say I needed to take my vitamin, which is in my room. If by chance I'm caught on the third level by Angelina or even Alessio, I'll just have to tell them I thought I left my second phone there. That won't go over well with Angelina, but there's a good chance Alessio wouldn't question it. Unless, of course, he does have cameras on that level, in which case, I'm dead no matter what.

My chest feels like it's being squeezed in a vise as I quietly make it up to the second landing, pausing for a moment to check my surroundings and then rushing up to the third. I'm as quick and quiet as I can be and oddly relieved when I find Alessio's blood-stained door is still cracked open. It hasn't been cleaned yet, so at least on that front, I'm good.

The covers on his bed are still in disarray from what happened between us this morning. I do my best to delay thinking about it while I head straight for the middle pillow and slip my hand beneath it. Only, when I do, I come up empty.

Shit. It's not there.

I remove the pillow completely, scrambling to feel around the bedding on the chance that it was jarred from its place while I was sleeping or when Alessio was grinding all over me. But I can't find it. At about this point, I realize there's a narrow gap between the bedframe and the wall. When I lean over to peek down inside, I'm horrified to see the blade of the knife wedged deep into that tight space.

I know it's useless, but I try squeezing my hand down into the gap, only to pull back in frustration a second later. It's way too narrow. I can't go in from underneath because there's not enough room. There's no way I could get the knife without completely pulling the massive bed frame away from the wall, and that's not going to happen without making a lot of noise on the marble floor.

There's a tightness in my throat I can't seem to shake as I search around for something, anything, that can help me in this situation. Right now, there's no possibility of me retrieving it, and I doubt Angelina will be moving the bed any time soon. On the off chance she glances down there when she's making it, she could see it. My only hope is to hide it.

I don't have time to come up with a better plan. I grab a pair of Alessio's socks from his dresser and dart back to the bed, leaning over and stuffing them down as far as I can get them. There's a very small likelihood Angelina will notice the dark socks against the dark panel without looking closely. I've bought myself some time, but I don't know how much. Regardless, it's going to have to do until I can figure something out.

13

ALESSIO

"Good morning, Nino."

"Good morning." He offers me a small smile, and I'm still not quite sure how to handle it. I make an attempt to smile back, but I know it's awkward and stiff. He doesn't hold it against me.

I don't know what Natalia said to him that day Gwen was here, but Nino has been much more receptive to conversation with me, and then there are the hugs. The first one I thought was a fluke, but by the fifth, I realized this was a new thing. One I don't mind, if I'm honest.

Natalia glances up from her plate to offer me a forced acknowledgment, and I nod at her. It's been like this for four days now. We haven't talked. We can barely look at each other. But it doesn't stop me from thinking about her every night when I fall into bed exhausted.

Logically, I know I need to have a conversation with her at some point, but my clients have kept me busy all week. After the shit show when I was ambushed during what was supposed to be a simple contract, I've been tracking down everyone who has even a chance of being involved and eliminating them. It isn't often that shit goes sideways with my clients, but every once in a blue moon, someone catches word somehow that I've been hired, and they prepare for it. The clients who end up getting a visit from me are either traitors to The Society or affiliated with some other criminal network. It's no surprise that they are paranoid as fuck already, but I can honestly say I wasn't expecting to walk into the target's house that night to be greeted by eight hired morons. In the end, I killed four of them and the target before the other four fled. Now, they've been dealt with too, but at the expense of my time and energy.

I have a suspicion none of it would have happened if I hadn't been distracted by the current situation at home. I'm accustomed to putting in long hours researching my targets. I always go in one hundred percent confident that I'm the one who will be walking out alive. In my line of work, carelessness isn't an option. But lately, I've been cutting corners. Becoming more complacent, I've been doing less recon while I try to juggle my responsibilities here, like watching Natalia and spending time with Nino.

When I glance at her now, I can't help feeling resentful for that. She can sense my weakness for her. That's the only logical explanation for her showing up in my room that night. A problem I have since resolved by keeping my door locked at all times.

I told Gwen it was a mistake, and at the time, I meant it. I was angry that she'd tempted me and even more irritable with myself for caving in, but distance has done nothing to dispel the increasingly alarming thoughts in my mind. My unreasonable conscience insists it wouldn't matter if it happens again. We've already crossed a line. What would one more time hurt? Maybe a few more times? I keep trying to convince myself I would still have control, but I know that's a lie.

When I look at her, I can still taste her skin. I can still smell the sweet scent of her arousal coating my fingers, and no matter how much I try, I can't purge the image of her tipping her head back and shuddering beneath me.

Fuck.

She glances up at me with a pinched expression. I've been staring at her for way too long. It's moments like this that remind me I can be so goddamned awkward sometimes. Natalia always handles it smoothly, just like she handles Nino. She knows what to do in every situation, and she stands her ground when she believes she's right. I can respect her for that, but there's a part of me that hates her, too. A part who wishes I'd never hired her, because right now, she's complicating the hell out of my life.

We eat our breakfast in silence, and Nino says goodbye before she starts to usher him out of the dining room to get ready for school. I stop her.

"I'm taking him today. When I get back, I'd like to meet with you in my office."

Her lips press together, but she dips her head and goes on her way.

I spend some time talking to Nino while Manuel drives us to school. Since I've been away most of the week, I wanted to make an effort like Natalia said I should, especially since he's been more receptive to it. He tells me about some of his classes and then asks if we can go out on the boat again soon. I consider it, aware that I have a contract this weekend, and Gwen has plans for some bullshit gala at IVI next Saturday that I'm supposed to attend. Marianna will be there, and she'll be expecting me even though I didn't agree to appear together. If I don't, Gwen will be breathing down my neck again, like she has been all week. I never should have told her I'd consider it in the first place. She caught me when I was tired and irritable, and she took advantage of that the way Gwen has the tendency to do.

I tell Nino we can go out on the boat next Sunday, and his excitement erases my frustrations over the gala. Once we've dropped him off, Manuel glances at me in the mirror.

"Just a heads up, sir. The security cameras have been acting up again. I had to reset them."

"Well, that's fucking annoying," I mutter.

He gives me an odd look. Manuel knows I take security at the house seriously, but he doesn't know I've been using the cameras to watch Natalia's movements like a goddamned fiend. This week, I've barely had time to breathe, let alone check up on her. I know from previous experience that we lose all the recently saved footage when Manuel resets the cameras. Typically, I would have already reviewed anything of importance before then, as it's Manuel's job to inform me, but there's been nothing of note. So, to him, my response is likely a little strange and more revealing than I care to admit.

He doesn't mention it again for the remainder of the drive, and neither do I. When we get back to the house, I find Natalia sitting outside, watching the lake ripple under the morning sky. For a second, I just stand there, observing her, hoping she won't notice me. She must feel my gaze on her because she turns, and if I didn't know any better, it looks like she's dreading this meeting.

I told her we'd talk in my office, but now that I'm here, I decide this might be a better setting. She sits up straighter as I approach her and take a seat in the Adirondack chair across from her.

"Is there an issue we need to discuss, Natalia?"

Her face pales, and her reaction catches me off guard. At first, I think maybe she's not feeling well, but when she wrings her hands together in her lap, I realize she's nervous. I often forget that people say I'm intimidating, so I suspect that might be the reason, but Natalia's never allowed that to bother her before.

"You've been avoiding me." I clarify. "I want to know what the issue is."

She dips her head, her shoulders relaxing slightly as she considers it for a moment. Then she reaches for her phone to write out a response.

I'm not avoiding you. And there is no issue.

She's lying, and she's not doing a very good job of hiding it. She can barely look at me. When I pass her in the house, she continues without so much as an acknowledgment. It's grating at me, and even more so, because I want to know why.

"I don't want to let what happened interfere with Nino's care," I tell her.

I would never. She shakes her head. *It's already forgotten.*

My jaw clenches, and I can't tell if she's intentionally goading me, but it feels like it. I should let it go, but I can't.

"You're angry with me."

No, I'm not, she insists.

I study her, searching for a deeper answer. "Is it because of Gwen?"

She shakes her head again, and it's infuriating. I want her to look at me. I want … something, but I don't even know what it is.

"She can come off harsh," I grit out. "She struggles with her emotions because she's been through a lot, but I've spoken to her, and there shouldn't be any more trouble."

Natalia nods, and that's all I get. Her response only serves to irritate me further.

"She has a point, though," I say. "It's not your place to tell Nino what he should and shouldn't do. She is his grandmother."

I know I'm goading her now, but I'm not expecting her eyes to alight with fire as she glares back at me. Suddenly, she has plenty to say.

No, it's not my place, Alessio. But someone had to do it. You aren't around, and when you are, you have no idea what's going on with him. He needs guidance. He needs reassurance. And I will die on this hill before I allow a grown woman to bully him into feeling responsible for her bruised ego. It's important for children to feel safe to set boundaries around their bodies. He did that, and she wanted to trample right over it. And when that didn't work, she used emotional manipulation. If she's been through hard times, that sucks, but we all have to accept responsibility for our own healing. Nino isn't comfortable doing what she asks of him, and it's your job to protect him and tell him that's okay, but clearly, you haven't.

My temples throb as I listen to her words and lift my gaze back to her. It isn't often I can't rein in my emotions, but right now there's no holding back from either of us.

"Everything I do is to protect him," I snarl, rising to my feet to glare down at her. "You know nothing about his life. You know nothing about Gwen or me, and if you ever talk about her that way again, you are fucking done here. Do you understand that?"

She flinches back as if she's preparing for a personal attack, and before I can make sense of it, her lip begins to tremble. She lowers her gaze to hide the hurt and fear in her eyes, but I can't unsee them. For a second, I'm questioning myself. I'm questioning everything. I'm starting to think Gwen was right all along. This was never going to work.

I stare at Natalia, wishing I could just say the goddamned words. To go get her shit and leave and never come back. That would be the best thing for both of us, but we both know we're in far too deep for that. She knows what I do. She's seen too much.

Despite her best efforts to hold them back, a tear splashes against her face, and I feel like a fucking asshole. My instinct is to fix this somehow, but I'm still too raw over what she said, and even if I wasn't, I don't know how. This is exactly what I don't want. These complications. The messiness that comes with human connections.

I need space. I need to go to the gym and punish my body, and then fist my dick until I purge every indecent thought I've ever had about her.

It's the only logical solution.

I SPEND the day trying to dispel the reminder of what happened this afternoon. I put my body through the paces of hell in the gym. I have a couple of stiff drinks for lunch. I consider going to the Cat House for a release, because I want to prove a point to Natalia, but the idea is driven by my anger and not desire. The truth is none of those women sound even remotely appealing right now.

I want her, and apparently, nothing can alter that.

I use Manuel as my carrier pigeon to deliver the news to Natalia that she has the rest of the day off. I don't ask him how she takes it, and I don't want to know. I give him the rest of the day off, too, opting to pick up Nino myself. He's supposed to have piano lessons and Italian studies this afternoon, but I think perhaps he could use a break.

"What do you want to do?" I ask him after we're secured in the car.

He studies me carefully, the way he always does when I ask him a direct question. I consider what Natalia said about giving him guidance and reassurance. I don't want to admit that the flaws she pointed out in me were accurate. Despite what appearances might suggest, I have tried.

"You can tell me." I soften my tone. "We can do anything you'd like."

"Anything?" he asks hesitantly.

I nod.

"Can we go to the Great Wheel?"

Well, shit. I wasn't expecting that. I know he's visited there before with his previous nanny, Rose. As for myself, I can say with certainty I've never been on a Ferris wheel, but I did say anything he wanted.

"Okay. The Great Wheel it is." I pull away from his school and head for Pier 57.

It's a cooler day, so luckily, there doesn't appear to be a horde of tourists when we arrive. I park the car, and Nino holds out his hand in offer. Another first. I take it, and something pinches in my chest when I feel how small his fingers are compared to mine. Logically, I'm always aware of how vulnerable he is. When I first took him in, I was admittedly petrified by the possibilities of something going wrong. I went overboard with Rose, directing her to babyproof the entire house and keep him safe at any cost. She was much older, and she told me not to worry so much. She had already raised many Society children by that time. But I never stopped worrying. I didn't have a fucking clue what to do with a toddler, and I think perhaps I let those fears get the best of me. Over time, I realized he was in safe hands with Rose, along with Manuel's observant eye, and I pulled back more and more, allowing them to actively partici-pate in his life while I remained a passive observer. I was so concerned about screwing up I didn't put myself in the game at all, and now I can see that was a grave mistake. I have missed out on so much.

Nino leads me toward the giant wheel, over the pavers, and through the small groups of people coming and going. He finds the ticket booth easily enough, and we wait our turn together before I pay. We enter the line for the Wheel, and Nino peers out over the water, eyeing the boats. It's one of the things we both enjoy, and I decide that there's no reason we can't take the boat out every week-end. It isn't out of the realm of possibility to charter a yacht in the summer and travel somewhere too. I think he would like that.

The attendant gestures us forward with a bored expression and helps us into the gondola. The seats are larger than I expected, but we get the cabin to ourselves because of the sparse crowd. Nino sits opposite me, close to the window, smiling as we slowly begin our ascent.

"This is my favorite," he whispers. "Rose used to bring me here all the time."

His confession dislodges something painful deep inside my gut, and I feel a need to address it. I'm not sure I know how.

"She was special to you," I say. "I'm sorry that she's no longer here. It must make you ... sad sometimes."

He looks over at me, and for the first time, I can see how much he truly does miss her. The woman was more of a grandmother to him, even more so than Gwen is, realistically.

"I do miss her," he says. "But she's in heaven now, and she told me someday we'll see each other again."

I nod, grateful that Rose found a way to comfort him even as she was slowly dying.

"You have Natalia now," I add, curious how he might respond.

"I love Natalia," he answers softly. "I want her to stay forever."

I swallow hard, hoping he doesn't see the tension on my face. He's never said that about me.

"If you like her, then I suppose we'll have to keep her."

This earns me a lopsided grin. He presses his fingers against the glass and looks out the window while I try to figure out how to address what Natalia said.

"Nino."

"Yeah?" He returns his attention to me.

"The other day, when Gwen was at the house, you didn't want to hug her. Can you tell me why?"

A frown pinches at his lips as he dips his gaze, and I notice this is something he does quite often, presumably because he thinks he's in trouble.

"It's okay that you didn't want to," I reassure him, taking a page from Natalia's book. "You did nothing wrong. I just want to know why you don't like to hug her."

"I don't know," he says. "I just don't like it. She gets lipstick all over me and smells like wine."

"Okay." I consider that for a moment. "But do you like spending time with her?"

He's quiet for a long beat, and I have a gut-wrenching feeling I already know what he's going to say before he finally answers.

"Not really," he admits. "She yells a lot, and it scares me."

I lean back, trying to digest those words. From a child's perspective, I can understand where he's coming from. Gwen was loud and blunt when I first met her too. She has the personality of a bull, and it's not for everyone. Over the years, with every devasting blow she's received, her grief has slowly whittled away at her sanity. Now she's on a heavy cocktail of psychiatric drugs for various maladies. Little things become big things to her, and I've witnessed her come unhinged often. She's under the close supervision of an entire medical team who continually assure me of her progress. If she weren't, I would never have left Nino with her for short periods of time. Now, I realize that too may have been a mistake. I don't know how to navigate the balance between protecting Nino and allowing Gwen to be a part of his life. She is the closest thing to a mother I've had since my own was murdered in front of me. She took me in and cared for me when I was at my lowest. I owe her everything, and sometimes that loyalty can be blinding. As much as I hate to admit it, Natalia had a point. Gwen is a grown woman, and Nino is still a child. If he isn't comfortable around her, I can't force him to spend time with her. It's something I'll have to deal with, and I only hope she won't have another breakdown when I do.

"It's okay if you don't want to spend time at Gwen's," I tell Nino. "I won't make you do that anymore. How do you feel about her coming to the house?"

He relaxes back against his seat, relieved. Guilt weighs heavy on my conscience that it took me so long to see something that was right in front of me.

"I don't care if she comes to the house," he says. "If you or Natalia are with me."

I rub the pressure from my neck, silently contemplating how the hell I'm going to bring this up with Enzo without him coming unhinged too. I'll have to be the one to address it first before Gwen goes to visit him in hysterics without giving him any context.

"Alessio." Nino's voice pulls me from my thoughts.

"Yes?"

He tangles his fingers together in his lap, tension returning to his face. "What if there's someone else I don't like?"

I lean forward, hoping to be as approachable as a man like me can be. "You can tell me, Nino. You can tell me anything. I'll never get angry at you for being honest."

He fidgets some more, eventually working up the courage to say what's on his mind.

"What if I don't want to visit Enzo anymore?"

His words blindside me.

"You don't want to visit your father?" I ask.

He shakes his head quickly, clearly ashamed of his admission.

Now, part of me feels like a liar because I told him he could trust me with his thoughts, but I also made a promise to Enzo that I would bring his son to visit as often as I could. Nino can't comprehend the gravity of what he's asking me. My loyalty to Enzo is the reason I took Nino into my care in the first place. To betray him would be unthinkable.

"Why don't you want to see him?" I adopt a neutral tone, despite the turmoil raging inside of me.

Nino stares down at his shoes, wiggling them back and forth to distract himself. "He's mean to me."

I let those words settle over us, but I need clarification. When I take Nino to visit Enzo in the Tribunal's prison, I'm only with them for the first ten minutes, and then his visits are supervised by the guards. Faithfully, I have brought Nino there to see his father from the beginning of his incarceration. I always assumed he was sad when he left because he was leaving, not because he had to visit in the first place.

"Can you explain how he's mean to you?" I ask.

Nino hesitates, and he still won't look at me. "He gets mad at me because he says I don't talk, but I always answer him. Sometimes he pinches my arm or squeezes my face. He says I'm weak, and I need to be strong like him, but I don't know how."

He's on the verge of tears by the time he gets the words out, and I'm in too much shock to comprehend it. I can't imagine Enzo doing any of those things. If I consider that Nino is a quiet, introverted child, much like I was, Enzo has always been the opposite. He is the charmer. He's loud and free with his thoughts, consequences be damned. It triggers a memory long forgotten when we were in school together, and he would get on my case about talking more. He told me it was the only way I'd get some action, and everyone would think I was weak if I didn't. I ignored him as I often did, letting Enzo get his say in because he'd usually forget about it five minutes later. But it bothered me then the way I can see it bothers Nino now.

"Thank you for being honest," I tell Nino. "Leave this with me for now. We can revisit it later."

"Does that mean I have to go this Sunday?" he asks.

"No. We will skip this weekend."

He sits back against the seat and peers over the water again. "Thank you, Alessio."

We are both quiet for the remainder of the ride. I'm lost in my thoughts, and Nino observes everything from a bird's eye view with keen interest. When we disembark, he asks if we can go to the carousel, and I cave to that request too. After several of the longest rides of my life, he decides he's hungry, so we stop for a frankfurter on the pier and find a bench to eat them on.

By the time we leave, the sun is starting to set. I'm considering what else we might do for the remainder of the evening when he informs me he has homework. I ask him if he wants my help, and he says he can do it by himself. Before we go our separate ways at the house, he gives me another hug.

"I hope we can go again," he says.

"We will," I answer gruffly.

He heads upstairs, and I take a sauna and a cold plunge in an attempt to clear my head. It usually helps, but in this case, my thoughts only seem more complicated. I realize it's almost Nino's bedtime when I check the clock, and I need to get him ready.

Upstairs, his door is cracked, and the sound of the TV floats out into the hall. When I ease it open, I'm surprised to see him and Natalia on the bed together, tears staining both their cheeks as they watch the screen credits roll.

"What's going on?" I demand.

They both look at me, and Nino sniffles at the same time Natalia does.

"ET had to go home," Nino says.

I stare at them in confusion. "The movie?"

Nino nods.

Natalia signs something to him, and he looks back at me. "But it's okay. Natalia says he's safe. It's just that goodbyes are hard."

I don't even know how to deal with that, so I jerk my chin in agreement. For a second, Natalia's eyes clash with mine, and I find myself wishing I could speak her language right now because there's so much I want to say.

"I did my homework," Nino informs me.

Natalia and I both glance at him.

"Okay, well, it's time for bed. Did you brush your teeth yet?"

"Already did," he says. "Natalia told me I should get ready after homework if I want to watch the movie."

"Alright, well ..." I linger awkwardly. "I came to say goodnight."

"Good night, Alessio." He climbs under the covers and flashes a dimple at me. "Don't let the bed bugs bite."

14

NATALIA

I say goodnight to Nino and follow Alessio into the hall, fully expecting more of his wrath. I was supposed to have the day off, but I wanted to spend time with Nino this evening. At this point, I have no idea what Alessio's mood will be like, and it's difficult to discern from his expression.

"I need to talk to you," he says.

I nod, and we both enter my room together. It feels natural to have conversations in here, even though it probably shouldn't. I wanted to put distance between us, but it only seems to irritate him more. By some small miracle, he still hasn't learned about the knife incident, and I can only imagine how he'll react when he does. Though I've made multiple attempts to retrieve it, I've been impeded by his locked bedroom door. That discovery was admittedly another blow to my fragile heart.

I know I need to leave this place. I need to do it soon. Every day I remain here, waiting for him to discover the truth, I'm playing with fire. There is no doubt in my mind he'll kill me without a second thought when he figures out my real motives, but there's a part of me that has been lulled into a false sense of security here. Some days, it feels as if there's no safer place for me than in the heart of my enemy's home. I can watch his every move. I can learn more about him. Those activities come with an unwelcomed side effect though. The more I learn, the more I warm to him.

I walk to the nightstand to grab my phone. Usually, I have it on me, but Nino and I have been working overtime on his ASL, and not having it gives us the chance to find creative ways to learn new words.

"I want to revisit our conversation from earlier," Alessio informs me.

His discomfort is obvious, and I know I need to fix this. I let my emotions overtake me before, and I can't do that again. I'm on the verge of issuing an apology when he continues.

"I think, perhaps, I was a bit harsh." He stuffs his hands into his pockets. "I will admit that you struck a nerve. I take Nino's care seriously, despite what it may look like. I have done the best I could with the skills I have, but I can see that I have failed him in some ways. Your blunt observations did not sit well with me, because they were so accurate."

The turmoil in his eyes triggers an overwhelming sense of guilt in me. I know he's being honest and sincere. He cares about Nino, and I think that somehow makes it both better and worse. It would be easier if he didn't, but it's better for Nino's sake that he does.

My delivery was not what it should have been, I write. *I'm sorry, Alessio. I know you have taken great measures to protect and care for Nino. I allowed my feelings to cloud my judgment, and I lashed out at you for it.*

"What do you mean your feelings?" His voice betrays his concern.

I stare at the keypad, wondering if this is a mistake. I shouldn't be so honest with him, but I think at this point, it can't hurt.

You said what happened with me was a mistake, and admittedly, it struck a nerve with me too. I should not have allowed my feelings about that to interfere with our professional relationship, but I did.

His eyes soften. "I didn't realize you'd heard that."

It was hard not to, I reply. It might be a little white lie, but the truth is, I probably would have heard it no matter what.

"Things with Gwen are complicated," he says. "Sometimes, it's easier to tell her what she wants to hear."

He's not denying that he meant it, and I can't tell if he did. More than anything, it feels like Gwen is an excuse not to divulge his feelings on the matter. The truth is, he's locking his door for a reason, and I know it's to keep me out.

We stand there, staring at each other, uncertainty lingering between us. I'm not going to make myself vulnerable again, but it's hard to deny that I can see he still wants me, no matter what he might say. Every time he's near me, I can feel it. This energy between us has a mind of its own.

"I suppose I should let you get some sleep," he tells me.

Goodnight, Alessio.

"Goodnight." He utters the word back to me but doesn't go. He's standing there like he can't move, like he doesn't want to.

I don't know what to say. Clearly, he doesn't either. When he struggles to pull himself away at times like this, it makes me feel like I'm not crazy for imagining there could be more. For a second, just a split second, I wonder if it would ever be safe to reveal my truth to him.

"Alright." He turns abruptly and leaves without another word.

I release a deep breath and wander into the bathroom to begin my evening ritual of brushing my teeth and washing my face. I strip out of my clothes and change into a tank and shorts, and then I find myself staring at my reflection in the mirror. The scars that litter my body have left me with a permanent reminder of the worst day of my life. For so long, I have cringed when I see them. I have avoided looking at myself out of disgust, and I can't help wondering if Alessio feels conflicted about them too.

I lift my shirt, fingers moving over the deep red mutilations scattered across my torso. When I touch them, I still feel the pain as if it were yesterday. I'm dead inside all over again. I close my eyes and my shoulders shake with emotion. I hate that it still has power over me. I have done so much work to overcome, rise above it, and still, it is not enough.

A warm hand settles over mine, and I blink in surprise, horrified to find Alessio standing behind me. Our gazes lock in the mirror, and my first instinct is to hide the evidence, wipe away the moisture at the edges of my eyes, but he's already seen it, and he stills my hand when I try.

"They are only scars," he murmurs against my hair as his fingers move over one of the raised red lines. "Wear them like a badge of honor. Show the world you are a survivor. There is nothing to be ashamed of."

I shiver beneath his touch, his body pressed so close to mine. I don't know why he came back, or how long he must have been standing there, observing my self-flagellation. Part of me thinks I should care, but the tenderness of his touch steals that rational thought. I feel safe in his arms right now, and it's unexpected. Terrifying even. Still, I take refuge against him, allowing him to shelter me from my storm.

He strokes every jagged line, closing his eyes as he leans into my hair and inhales me again. If there was ever a question in my mind about his attraction, the evidence is undeniable now. His hard cock is pressed against my back, and in response, my body begins to ache for more. More of everything. More of anything. I could stand here all night with him stroking my skin.

"I shouldn't have come back here." He circles his arm around my waist and pulls me closer. "You're making me break all my rules."

I lean my head back against his shoulder, closing my eyes as his palm slips up beneath my tank to grope my breast. His fingers send tiny shocks through my nerve endings, and I squirm against him, desperate for him to keep going. I know it has to be him this time. He has to take the lead. I couldn't handle his rejection now. Not tonight. Alessio seems to understand that, or maybe he's just done pretending.

He kisses his way over my jaw and then tilts my face up to his.

Our lips collide, and our tongues clash. The time for exploration is done. Alessio is unleashing himself, transforming from the silent, methodical killer to a man whose passion burns hotter than the sun.

I want him. Oh, God, do I want him. I'm done convincing myself otherwise, and when his other hand slips down into my shorts and between my thighs, he knows it too. He growls into my mouth as his fingers slide through my arousal, soaking him.

"This is for me." His voice is hoarse but possessive.

I nod against him, and he releases his grip on my breast to reach down and hoist me up against his body, never removing his other hand from between my legs. The fact that he can carry me so easily should probably terrify me, but it doesn't.

He hauls me into the bedroom, setting me down on the bed and tugging my shorts off. The loss of the warmth of his fingers leaves me achy and miserable, but those thoughts disappear as he drags my ass to the edge of the bed and lowers himself to his knees.

I watch him nervously as he splays my thighs apart, staring at the most vulnerable part of me with heated eyes. Nobody has ever been this intimate with me, and I can't tell what he's thinking. It's an unsettling feeling, but when he dips forward and kisses me over my center, I forget everything else.

He drags his nose against my skin, inhaling me deeply, and a flush spreads over my chest.

"You smell so fucking good," he growls. "I have to taste you."

I release a silent whimper as his tongue lashes against me. There's something so insanely hot about this powerful man on his knees before me, pleasuring me like I'm a goddess.

I want to say his name. It would be worth the pain to say it until my throat gives out, but I settle for curling my fingers into his dark hair and wringing out every last ounce of bliss as he learns my body. That's exactly what he's doing. He takes note of every muscle contraction, every silent shudder, and he catalogs them into one complete manual I want him to use again and again.

His fingers dig into my thighs, holding me wide open for him as he swirls his tongue over my clit. He tortures me as he hums his approval against me, alternating his soft strokes with his tongue thrusting inside of me. It feels so intense I can't hold back. The rapture builds. I'm at my breaking point. My release is violent and wet, and it still doesn't stop Alessio from dragging it out as long as he can. It's only when I become too sensitive that he pulls away, staring up at me with eyes so beautiful, I become overwhelmed by a sudden swell of emotion. I don't like this feeling. I don't know how to guard my heart with him, so I do the next best thing and reach for him, tugging him up against me.

He lets me unbutton his shirt, but before I can remove it completely, he's taking back control. Looming over me, large and indomitable, he eases me back onto the bed and settles his body between my thighs. Again, he makes no move to unzip his pants as he rocks his pelvis against me. I can't make sense of it. I don't know how he has so much self-control or why.

His hands are everywhere on me, touching, pawing, feeling. His lips are too. He kisses his way down my jaw, pausing at my neck scarf, and a moment of panic sinks in. I know he wants to remove it, but I can't let him. As he lingers there, I slip my hand down between us, stroking his cock through the material of his trousers. He sucks in a sharp breath, his eyes shuddering open and closed before he returns his focus to my face.

"Natalia," he chokes out.

I don't know how to tell him that I want to touch him. So, I reach for his zipper, searching his eyes. He looks at me uncertainly, torn between wanting this and holding on to something I don't yet understand. And then, finally, he decides for us.

"I have to feel you," he rumbles.

There seems to be some deeper meaning to those words, as if the decision has been agonizing for him. He reaches down and helps me unzip his trousers, revealing a bulging pair of black briefs. Before I even touch him, the heat radiating from him warms my skin. Our gazes lock, and he's so still, I'm not sure he's even breathing. I reach for him, slowly sliding my palm over his engorged cock. A visible tremor moves through his entire body as I do, and it stirs a deep want within me. I never knew my body could feel so empty, but right now, it does. It's screaming for him. Desperate for him. Willing to do anything to have him inside me. There's just one problem.

He's so ... *huge.*

I've only ever been with one man, and it was painful. I don't have any idea what Alessio will feel like stretching me apart. But I want to find out regardless.

I slip my fingers beneath the waistband of his briefs to touch him for real and he jerks at the contact, a muffled curse heaving from his lips. He's so hard for me, it produces a strange flutter in my belly. Maybe it's butterflies. Maybe it's hunger pangs. I don't know. I just know I like it.

He looks down at me, losing himself to the moment as I wrap my palm around his thick base and stroke him. His eyes take on a drunken intensity and then he tips his head back, rocking into my fist like he can't help himself. Every muscle in his body strains under the confines of his clothes, and I wish more than anything he'd let me peel them off. But I can sense there's something lingering just beneath the surface. He's surrendering to me inch by inch, but one wrong move might send him reeling in the other direction.

I memorize every detail of his face like this. Every agonized sound that erupts from his chest. Every muscle contraction. The way his lips fall apart before he forces them back together. He's trying not to reveal too much, but he's just as vulnerable as I am. I want more. I want everything. His skin against my skin. His breath on my neck when he slides deep inside me. I want him to change what I know about sex, but he's fucking my fisted palm, pressure coiling in his body with every thrust, and I don't know if he's going to take it any further. His dick is starting to pulse against me. It's just a matter of time. Then abruptly, right before the inevitable fall, he stops. He opens his eyes, looks down at me, and repeats the same thing he said before.

"I have to feel you."

Those words have significance, and I'm trying to figure out exactly how much, when he pulls back slightly and yanks his trousers down to his knees. It's the first glimpse I've had of his whole body since the sauna, and it's even better up close. His thighs are strong and muscular. Between them, his cock hangs heavy, bobbing as he lowers his body over mine. I splay my legs further apart to accommodate him.

Once he's close, he stops to search my eyes. I can't tell what he's trying to find there, but whatever it is seems to relax him.

"Just ... once," he grits out.

He fists his cock and slides it against my arousal, stifling a groan as I arch up into him. He tortures me that way, drawing it out, rocking his pelvis against me, using my come as his lubricant. It seems to go on forever, another orgasm building in me as his cock strains against the friction. I know he's on the verge too. He doesn't seem like he wants to stop, but eventually, he does, long enough to press the head against my opening.

Our eyes meet, and slowly, he starts to sink into me. I feel every penetrating inch. My fists tangle in the bedsheets, and even though there's a slight bite of pain from his girth, I'm trying to absorb every second of it. He clenches his jaw, his tension palpable as he goes deeper and deeper until finally, he's fully rooted inside me. For a minute, he closes his eyes, arms shaking, body tight, and I think he's trying to hold himself in check.

I reach up and touch his face, and he opens his eyes, staring down at me with an expression I've never seen. He looks totally and utterly owned by me right now. I recognize it because I know I feel the same about him. He's branded himself on me somehow, and I fear that I'll never be able to cut him out. Even worse, I don't think I want to.

"You feel so fucking good," he chokes out. "I've wanted to do this from the moment I saw you."

My heart bangs against my chest, and I nod to indicate I understand. He leans down and kisses me, and I wrap my legs around him, stroking my palms over the length of his back. Together, we start to move. Me arching, and him rocking. It's slow at first. He's still trying to make it last. I want to make it last too, but inevitably, as I get closer and closer to the edge and my body squeezes around him, his responds. He starts to roll his hips harder. Faster. My fingertips dig into his back as my head falls deeper into the pillow. His head tips back as he leans up, gritting his teeth.

I shatter around him first, and he rides it out long enough to let me have it before he jerks his cock out of me and pumps his fist over his length. He releases a tormented sound, and jets of his come spray across my stomach.

When he can't wring any more out of himself, he collapses beside me, chest heaving. I roll my head to the side and watch him as his pulse slows. I never knew a man could be beautiful, but that's exactly what he is. We're both hot and sticky, limp from the intensity of our connection. I don't know what happens next, but I know I don't want him to leave. Then he looks at me, and I can see the stress is already returning to his body. I'm not certain if he regrets what just happened, or he's worried this will complicate things.

"I'll get something to clean you up," he says.

He drags himself from the bed before pulling up his trousers and disappearing into the bathroom. The faucet runs for a few minutes, and when he comes back, he has a damp cloth he uses to wipe over my belly. It's an intimate act, but there's no intimacy in his touch right now. He's back to efficiency, barely looking at me, and I know I'm going to lose him. I don't want to, because I'm afraid of the feelings his absence will provoke, so in an act of desperation, I reach for my phone and type out a question to distract him.

What happened to Nino's birth parents?

He frowns when I show it to him. I'm not sure he'll even answer it, honestly. He sits down beside me and watches as I cover myself with part of the blanket. His pants are zipped back up, but he didn't adjust his shirt yet.

"Nino's mother was young," he says quietly. "She's a member of our Society, and with that comes expectations. She wasn't married to his father when she got pregnant, and it all became too much for her. She went into hiding until she had the baby, and then sent for the father to retrieve him. She didn't want to be involved in his life."

My jaw clenches in disbelief. There is so much I could say. I'm hurt on Nino's behalf. What must he feel like to be told that his mother didn't want him? It had to leave a wound, because I'm certain at some point, he must have asked.

And his father? I write.

Alessio is quiet, a dark expression on his face, and I can't quite tell what's behind it. Anger? Grief? I don't know, but when I reach up and stroke one of the scars on his chest, he freezes, his hand coming to mine.

"His father is gone too." He rises abruptly, my hand falling away from him as he glances down at me. "I have some work to do. Good-night, Natalia."

His formal goodbye leaves me cold and uncertain as he walks away without a glance back. He doesn't wait for a response. He doesn't even look at me again. In my heart, I knew I was right. This doesn't feel good. It feels pretty fucking terrible, actually.

My eyes sting, and I don't even know why I'm letting this get to me. I'm sad that he's gone and that eventually, I'll have to hurt him if he doesn't hurt me first. Most of all, I'm sad for Nino.

I don't know where his father is, but if I had to draw a conclusion from Alessio's statement, I could only guess that he must be dead.

15

NATALIA

WHEN I GO DOWN TO BREAKFAST, I'M HALF EXPECTING TO FIND Alessio gone. I've convinced myself avoidance will be how he deals with this situation, but it comes as a shock to find he's there as usual. We greet each other wordlessly, and there isn't much to talk about at the table today. Nino is tired, but he mentions his excitement about the boat outing planned for next weekend. I focus on him, but I can feel Alessio's gaze on me. I just can't return it, because I'm afraid of what I might find there.

Silently, I consider what his plans are today. If he'll be gone, then maybe I can check his room again. There must be a set of keys around here somewhere, but I have a feeling they're with Angelina or Manuel, and the likelihood of getting them is nonexistent.

Once Nino is finished with his meal, we retreat from the dining room. Manuel and I usher him to school uneventfully, and when I return, I find that Alessio is, in fact, gone. However, when I make my way up to the third level, his door is still locked. I stand there for several minutes, staring at it in frustration. That lock represents more than just the threat of discovery. It also represents Alessio's feelings. He has a lock around his heart too, and if I'm naïve enough to believe for a second that what happened between us might change anything, then I deserve to be caught.

With a sigh, I go back to my room and spend the afternoon considering my escape. It has to be done. I can't stay here in limbo forever, but my choices now are different. I'll either have to hurt the man I have obviously come to care about or leave loose ends that will probably tie a noose around my neck.

The rest of the day passes slowly. I help Nino with his homework and put him to bed early since he can barely keep his eyes open. Once I'm back in my room, going through my nightly ritual, part of me hopes I'll open my eyes again to find Alessio standing behind me, but it doesn't happen. So instead, I crawl into bed and touch myself while I think about him. I come, but it's not the same. The last thought I have before I drift off is if he'll be touching himself too.

Something stirs me from my sleep, and I don't know what it is. Only a feeling. Slowly, I sit upright, recognizing the silhouette of the man standing at the end of my bed. He's watching me, silent, like the predator he is. That's the dichotomy of Alessio Scarcello. As lethal as he can be, there's another side of him. One that seems less nurtured. More innocent, sometimes awkward, and endearing in his own way.

I know what he's doing here. Before, when I found him standing at the end of my bed, I knew he had probably come to kill me. Tonight, his intentions are of a different nature. I should send him away. After last night, it became clear to me what this is to him. The smartest thing to do would be to protect my heart before I entangle myself any deeper. Still, I can't. I don't want to.

Wordlessly, I pull back the covers to welcome him in. He stays there for a moment, lingering on the threshold of uncertainty himself. I slip my fingers beneath the waistband of my shorts and shimmy out of them, and I swear I can hear his heart beating from where I sit. In the end, it appears we are both afflicted by the same condition. He comes to me willingly, slowly unbuttoning his shirt and unzipping his trousers.

Tonight, he doesn't say a word. He lowers his body over mine, spreading my legs apart and rolling his hard cock against me. His fingers tangle in my hair. His lips meet mine, and we kiss. We kiss like it's the first time. I get lost in his scent, his warmth, his weight pressing down on me. I dig my fingers into his back, and he kisses his way from my lips down to my breast while his hand settles between us, teasing me with several long strokes before he nudges his cock inside of me. I arch up into him, sucking in a breath as he fills me. I'm still sensitive from the night before, and I can feel every agonizing inch of him.

He tilts my chin, and when I open my eyes to look up at him, I wonder what he sees. What's going through his mind when he looks at me? When he kisses me? His lips graze my jaw as his body stays completely still above me. He brushes my hair back with his fingers and rolls his hips slightly, a test. My body has relaxed around him, and now, where there was pressure, there is only pleasure.

I arch my hips up to greet him, and he groans as he thrusts deep. I drag his face back to mine and kiss my way over his jaw, down his neck to where his pulse beats. The very place I foolishly believed I could bleed him dry. Now, I'm worshipping that vitality.

For a moment, I fantasize about what it would be like to confess that sin to him. In my mind's scenario, he tells me he doesn't care. He tells me he'll protect me, and I'm safe with him. I wonder if he can feel it too, in this silent declaration he's making with every thrust. Every shuddered breath.

I come hard around him, and Alessio isn't far behind. I'm still convulsing around him when he pulls out, stroking his dick as his head falls back and he milks out his release. His warmth spills across my skin, soaking into me, and I reach down and smear it with my fingers. He watches, eyes flaring with heated possession. His dick is still hard. I think he might push back inside of me, and I want him to, but he doesn't.

The room goes cold as he drags himself from the bed, picking up his clothes on his way into the bathroom. This time, when he returns, his eyes move over my come-soaked skin. I think he likes what he sees. He likes it too much to clean it up himself. He hands me the cloth instead, fingers brushing against mine. And then, as quietly as he came, he disappears again.

THE NEXT WEEK passes in a consistent pattern. Every night, Alessio comes to my room, fucks me, and leaves. Oddly enough, this has become our only interaction. At breakfast, he avoids eye contact and focuses on Nino instead, asking him questions to break up the silence.

Every day, I find myself wondering if I imagined the night before. If I couldn't still smell him on my sheets, I would think I had. He's like a switch. Completely shut off during the day, and at night, he comes alive. The intensity between us only gets hotter, and I find that I can hardly lie in stillness waiting for the sound of him entering my bedroom. I'm desperate for more, but he only gives me enough to get my fix, and then he leaves me cold. I've turned into an anxious mess. My thoughts are constantly at war, and my heart is battered more than I'd care to admit.

These feelings in me are too big to be contained. Too big for words. I'm afraid at some point he's going to see it, and then he's going to remind me who he is. At times, I'm so certain he can't possibly feel anything when he refuses to even look at me. But at night, when he touches me, I can't deny the power of our connection. If he didn't feel anything, why does he kiss me like he can't live without it? Why does he worship my body, or linger for just a moment longer with every visit? I want to believe there's something real, something tangible, but at the same time, reality is knocking on the door.

Gwen has been by the house almost every day this week. I don't know why she feels the sudden need to lurk so often, but it's obvious her suspicion of me is growing. I've noticed the way she looks at me. The way she studies my features with a familiarity that produces a feeling of dread deep in my gut. Sometimes, I think I'm being para-noid, and then there are moments like today when I noticed her holding her phone as if she were taking a photo of Nino. Except, it looked like it was pointed straight at me. Panic ripples through me every time I think about it. I don't know who Gwen really is, but is it possible she could find out more about me?

As I'm considering it, my door creaks open and then shuts. Alessio finds his way to me in the dim light, already unbuttoning his shirt. He left me waiting for so long, I wasn't certain he would even come tonight.

I reach over and turn on the lamp, and he freezes, his eyes locking with mine. It surprises me to see vulnerability there, like the darkness was his shield, and I just stripped it away. I don't know what reason a man like him would have to be vulnerable, but I suspect it has everything to do with keeping his emotions at a baseline.

I reach for my phone and write a note for him. *I'm on my period.*

His brows furrow, and it seems like this is a complication he never even considered. How couldn't he have? He's never once used any kind of protection with me, and even though he hasn't come inside me, I have to admit I was slightly panicked over that small chance regardless. I assumed he would be too. The fact that he hasn't considered it leaves me even more confused. Now, he doesn't look like he knows what to do.

I set the phone back onto the nightstand and pull myself out of bed. When I walk toward him, he looks down at me hesitantly. I reach for his hand, and his arm is stiff, but he allows me to lead him to the chair next to the bed. Before he can sit, I stroke the bulge in his trousers, and his eyes fall shut. He relaxes beneath my touch, and I unzip his pants, tugging his briefs down to reveal his cock. When I slide my palm over his hot skin, his eyes open half-mast, staring into mine.

I point at the chair and then kneel before him, easing my body between his legs, my breath blowing across his cock. A shiver moves over him, and his hand comes to rest in my hair as I suck him into my mouth.

"Christ," he hisses under his breath.

I peer up at him, noting the way his muscles are already straining. He looks completely out of his mind, and it doesn't make much sense. I've never given a blow job before. I know I can't possibly be that good at it, but whatever I'm doing appears to be working.

"Natalia." His grip on my hair tightens. "Oh, fuck."

I suck him deeper, harder, watching him closely to see what it is that drives him over the edge, but there doesn't seem to be one particular thing. It's just ... all of it. The pieces are starting to fall together in my mind as I consider the progression of our interactions. At first, he wouldn't even unzip his pants. Then there was the way he said he wanted to feel me, just once. Those words have stayed with me, floating around my mind like a tumbleweed. Now, there's this. A man so hot I'm certain he's had many willing participants who've offered before me. The real question on my mind is, why does it seem like he's never felt this before? And why does it make me so happy to think I could be the first?

I throw myself into it, flicking my tongue against his head, swirling him around my mouth, and dragging my nails over his muscular thighs. He tastes like salt and man. As I bring him closer to the edge of no return, I decide I want to taste all of him. I want to feel his release spilling down my throat, marking me with a part of him. I want the intimacy I crave from him.

"Natalia," he chokes out again, his forearm straining as he grips the chair with one hand and holds my head with the other.

He's trying to warn me, but I keep going. I keep going until he releases so violently, he's shaking beneath me. His cock jerks into my mouth, and I swallow willingly. I swallow until there's nothing left but the sound of his ragged breaths.

When I finally free his cock from my mouth, I find him staring down at me like I'm the devil incarnate. He wishes he could just stay away. Instead of letting him put a wall between us, I slide up onto his lap, and force him to acknowledge me by grabbing his face. I want him to kiss me, but he doesn't, so I kiss him. He grunts on impact, his hand coming to rest on my ass in his lap. I can tell how much he doesn't want to like it, but already, he's hardening beneath me. I kiss along his jaw, all the way down his neck, sucking the skin between my teeth until it leaves a mark. I don't know why, only that I want to.

"Natalia," he murmurs.

I ignore him, desperate for him to stay. Just a little longer. It's pathetic. I'm pathetic. I don't care. I want this. Need this. I know he does, too. So why is he fighting it?

"Natalia." This time he grabs my hands to still them, trapping them between his. "I have to go."

I shake my head in protest. He stares back at me in frustration. I lean over and grab the phone, writing out the question that's been haunting me.

Have you ever been with another woman?

His eyes darken, and he picks me up without warning, setting me onto my feet. He won't look me in the eyes as he tucks himself back into his pants, zipping them up and fixing his shirt.

"I have to go," he says again.

And he does.

16

ALESSIO

"Alessio?"

"What?" I blink up at Gwen, and she's staring at me with a tight expression.

"Are you even listening to me?" she huffs.

I want to tell her that I am, but that would be a lie. My head is foggy. I'm tired and unfocused, and this is the last thing I want to be doing right now.

I start going through some of the footage on the computer to provide a distraction while Gwen glares at me. She's been popping up here incessantly. I don't know how she can sense something is off, but she always knows. She picks it up like a bloodhound, homing in on it until she's right on top of it.

"Can this wait for another time?" I ask. "I have work to do."

"Bullshit." She crosses her arms and holds her ground.

I toss her a sharp look. I have always regarded Gwen highly, but she forgets that it works both ways. If she ever spoke to me in front of another member of The Society this way, I would be considered weak if I didn't address it. The hierarchy of IVI dictates as much.

Perhaps, I should address it, but sending Gwen into a tailspin right now is the last thing I have the energy for.

"I want Nino to come stay with me for the weekend," she says.

My jaw sets as I shake my head. "That's not on the table for this weekend."

Or ever, I still have to tell her. At least until Nino comes around to her, if he ever comes around, that is. It's an issue that still needs to be addressed. Right now doesn't seem like the appropriate time to do it, but there's never going to be a time when she handles this news well.

"And why not?" she challenges. "You'll be at the gala. You won't even be here. I can take him Saturday and spend the day with him, and on Sunday, we will go see Enzo together."

"He won't be able to visit with Enzo this weekend either." I click through the series of footage from the week, deleting the unnecessary.

"What do you mean he won't be visiting Enzo?" Gwen's voice rises. "Does Enzo know that?"

"Not yet, no." I accidentally delete a subfolder in my haste, becoming irritated by this conversation.

"Enzo will not be happy about this," Gwen says. "Are you trying to keep him from us?"

"That is not my intention," I answer dryly, minimizing my folder to open the trash. I'm scrolling through it when I notice there are still folders in there from when the cameras were reset. The footage I thought was deleted. I move them back to the desktop, curious to see what I may have missed.

"It's because of that fucking nanny, isn't it? I know it is. She's getting in your head. Poisoning you against us. Can't you see—"

"Enough," I clip out. "I'm done having this argument with you. This has nothing to do with Natalia. It's Nino who doesn't want to see you."

Immediately, I regret the delivery of my message when her face falls in disbelief, but it had to be done. I clear my throat and try for a measured voice, though I can already see Gwen is starting to become hysterical.

"What I meant was Nino prefers it if you visit him here. He feels most comfortable at home."

"Because of her." She stabs a finger at the ceiling to indicate Natalia. "It's because she's fucking poisoning him against me!"

"This has nothing to do with her." I release a ragged breath as my blood pressure rises. "I don't know how many times I have to tell you."

"It does!" she screeches. "You are too blind. Led by your goddamned dick. A weak man just like your father—"

Heat flushes my skin as I rise abruptly, slicing my hand through the air as I gesture to the door.

"Get. Out!" I roar.

Her eyes widen at the vitriol I can no longer contain. It only gets worse the longer she stands there, staring at me innocently as if she doesn't know what she just said to provoke me.

"Get. The. Fuck. Out!" I repeat. "Get out of my house, or so help me, God, I will have Manuel drag you out on your ass."

"Alessio." Her lip trembles. "Please. I didn't mean it. You know I didn't mean it."

"But you did, Gwen. You always fucking mean what you say." I slam the computer shut and stalk around the desk. "I'm not your goddamned punching bag. I have always treated you with respect, but what you just said to me is unforgivable. I don't want to see you. I don't want to speak to you. I need you to go home and leave me the fuck alone until I decide otherwise. Is that clear enough for you?"

Tears stream down her face, but my sympathy has run dry. I leave her there to pick up the broken pieces by herself this time.

Her words play on repeat in my head as I punish myself in the gym to the point of exhaustion. I brutalize my body until my muscles give out, and I collapse onto the floor, head between my knees as I try to hold back the urge to retch.

I'm not like my fucking father, and I never will be. That's the mantra I've lived by. Over and over, I have tried to convince myself of that. But the truth is, I don't know. I have lived with this uncertainty inside of me. This pervasive fear that I will be weak like him. It's why I have avoided relationships. I decided long ago I would never marry. I would never have a family. The undiluted anguish and betrayal on my mother's face before she died was enough to cure me of those notions forever. If that was what a marriage became, I didn't want to be part of it. I wanted to believe I was better for those choices. I would never hurt anyone the way he had, and yet I am.

Every time I'm too weak to resist Natalia, I can see the hurt on her face when I leave. She wants more from me. She probably wants things I'll never be able to give her. She deserves someone who can, but I'm too selfish to let her have that either. I'd kill him. I'd fucking murder anyone who thought they could take her from me, but, inevitably, I know it can't last. She won't remain in this purgatory I've trapped her in. She will decide I'm not worth the pain, and she will leave, sentencing me to a life of emptiness. It's the only thing that was meant to be mine.

I drag myself up from the floor and head for the shower. It's late, and she's probably already asleep, but I want to go to her now. I want to tell her I'm done. For every truth in my mind, I will tell her a lie. Instead of confessing that she occupies my thoughts day and night, I will tell her I never think of her. I could tell her that she was a mistake. I could tell her the thing that I know would wound the deepest. She isn't what I want or need.

A sick feeling churns my gut as I consider that this is what I have to do. When it comes to her, I am too weak. The only solution is to make her hate me now before she allows me to destroy her life.

I focus on the mechanics of my actions as I wash, dry off, and dress in a fresh shirt and trousers. My mind is clear, determination heavy on my shoulders as I carry myself up the stairs to the second floor. Her door is cracked for my arrival, a welcome I don't deserve.

When I push it open, my chest tightens at the sight of her propped up against the headboard, staring at me. She's been waiting.

I swallow, prepared to make my speech without delay before I can regret it. Before I can reconsider it. But Natalia beats me to it, reaching for her phone, playing the message she's already written.

Don't come in if you aren't going to stay the night with me.

Those words rattle around inside my head. She wants me to stay the night with her. When my eyes move over her face, I can see she already knows I can't. She's shut down. Empty, just like me.

"Natalia," I choke out her name, trying to find the words I'd rehearsed so many times on the way up here. But they don't come. "Goodnight."

"YOU'RE NOT GOING to like this part much." I drag the sorry son of a bitch I've been torturing for the better part of the morning from the ice bath. He flops onto the floor like a fish, staring up at the ceiling, mouth gaping. His face is a bloody fucking mess, and he's managed to get it all over me. It makes me more irritable than I already am, though I have to give the asshole credit. He's held out longer than most, but he's about to break. I can sense it. I always do.

I grab him by the arms and drag him across the concrete floor to the large masonry oven I converted myself. As soon as he sees it, he starts kicking and clawing in resistance, but there's not much fight left in him.

"Don't make this more difficult than it has to be." I grab him by the jaw and stare into his beady eyes. "If you want to take it to your grave, what do I fucking care? Most men only last ten minutes at three hundred and fifty degrees. It will all be over soon enough."

"Fuck you, you goddamned psychopath," he wheezes. "There's something wrong with you. You're not right in the fucking head."

"You think I don't already know that?" Sarcasm tinges my voice as I roll him onto the platform that doubles as a door and shove him inside.

He clings to the frame, his bloody fingers slipping over the stone.

"Come on, man. We can work something out. You want money? Is that it?"

I stare at him with a bored expression. "Money? I've got more money than God, asshole. There's only one thing I want from you, which I made clear from the beginning. If I don't get it in the next ten minutes, you'll be dead, and I'll be on my way out to lunch for a burger."

I yank the door up, slamming it against his fingers, and he releases a violent yelp before removing the broken appendages. With his hands out of the way, I shut the door again, securing it with the external locking mechanism before turning the crank.

"Have fun." I lean down and tap on the glass.

He attempts to maneuver around and kick his way out of the box, but he's not going anywhere. With time to kill, I rejoin Angelo at the abandoned bar where he's been watching the show, grabbing a drink of water for myself.

"I can see you haven't lost your touch," he muses.

I shrug, suspecting he has more to say. Angelo is my cousin and another Sovereign Son within The Society. He's spent the last six years in the Tribunal prison for a crime he didn't commit. Now that he's free, he's on the warpath, and I have been busier than usual helping him extract information from anyone who participated in setting him up.

"Are you really going to roast him in there for ten minutes?" he asks.

"It's only one hundred and ninety in there," I tell him. "Basically, a very hot sauna. The point is, he thinks it's hotter than that. He'll cave. If he doesn't, I'll do this one for free."

Angelo snorts. "You do them for free regardless."

"It breaks up the monotony of my day."

"So you say." He studies me. "But it doesn't seem to hold the same shine as it once used to."

He's right, but I'm not about to admit that out loud. Something has been different. Off. When I started this work, it felt like a way to right some universal wrongs. The scales of justice aren't always favorable. Some people, such as myself, prefer more biblical measures. An eye for an eye. Every man I've tortured over the years has been different, but in the most important sense, they were all the same. They were all my father.

In my mind, I've killed him a thousand times over. It has been the only way I could avenge the deaths of my mother, sister, and brother. I was only a boy when the Tribunal sentenced him to death, and they looked upon me with pity as they denied my request to kill him myself. In the end, he and his mistress were hanged, as was the man who carried out her orders. There was nobody left for me to destroy, so I learned to channel my rage into something productive. For many years, I found satisfaction in that. Now, the dopamine rush is gone, and in its place is a stagnant feeling I can't quite identify. Like something needs to change, but I don't know what.

"You could do something else," Angelo says. "It's never too late. There are many respectable jobs within The Society."

"Yes, there are," I concede. I just don't know that I'm comfortable leaving the familiar behind.

The asshole in the oven starts slamming his body against the glass, interrupting us. "Okay, I'll talk. I'll fucking talk. Let me out. Let me the fuck out!"

Angelo glances at me and shakes his head in quiet amusement. "You win, Alessio."

This time, he accompanies me, helping me open the oven to retrieve the tomato-faced prick who thought he could withstand anything.

"Water?" he croaks. "Please—"

I dump the glass of water in my hand over his head. "Talk."

He glances at Angelo, then back to me. "I know who did it," he says. "I know who set it up, and I know why. I'll tell you everything if you give me your word he'll never find out who told you."

"You have it," Angelo snarls at him. "Now tell me."

17

ALESSIO

I'm a gruesome sight to behold when I get back to the house. I wasn't thinking clearly when I left today and forgot my bag with extra clothes, a side effect of the lack of sleep I've had.

I make it to the second level without encountering anyone, but my luck runs out there. Natalia is walking down the hallway when she seems to sense me. She turns around, freezing when she notices my shirt. In a normal world, I'd expect her to faint. Or scream. Perhaps even try to call the police, as I suspected she might've the first time she saw me bloodied. Her eyes are absent of the fear one would expect when she looks at me this way. There is only concern in her expression and perhaps curiosity. I want to know why she is the way she is. It's unsettling to encounter someone so calm in the face of something so out of the ordinary.

I'm not a fool. Whatever lies she tried to spoon-feed me were a feeble attempt to keep me from a deeper exploration of the real cause of her scars. Scars that were obviously inflicted by a knife. The defensive wounds over her hands and arms most likely saved her life, limiting the number of blows I found on her torso. It's what's under her neck scarf that has me most curious. I want to know who. I want to know why. Then I want to torture them until their blood runs dry.

She turns hesitantly, like she's trying to decide if I need her help, but I can't let her near me. If she gets close, I'm going to fuck her again. I'm going to fuck her until my body gives out. Already, I'm having withdrawals, and one second in her presence is too much.

It takes every ounce of willpower I possess to drag my gaze away from hers and walk up to my room without a glance back. I am equally relieved and annoyed that she doesn't follow.

I take a scalding hot shower, scrubbing my skin violently. I consider jacking myself off until my dick is raw, but it no longer appeals to me now that I know the warmth of a woman. I want her, and to my horror, I'm quite certain she's the only one who will do.

Twenty minutes later, I'm still feeling restless when I go downstairs to grab something for dinner. I don't even make it to the kitchen before Manuel approaches me wearing a strained expression.

"Sir, you should know that—"

"There you are, Alessio!" Gwen appears from the hallway, flitting into the room. She's dressed in an elaborate ballgown, and to my dismay, Marianna is right behind her, looking just the same. Apparently, I seem to have forgotten all about the fucking gala this evening.

"Why aren't you dressed?" Gwen looks me over with concern. She doesn't acknowledge the scowl on my face or the obvious anger radiating from me. She knows I meant what I told her before, but Gwen can never admit when she's wrong.

"Manuel, where is Nino?" I ask, forcing myself to remain calm.

"He's in the kitchen with Miss Cabrera."

"I think he could use some fresh air," I say. "Maybe some ice cream."

"No problem." He disappears into the kitchen.

I stare at Gwen in silence. She stares back at me. Marianna clears her throat. She's smiling at me like victory is in her grasp. I'm sure she's waiting for me to flatter her. To tell her how radiant she looks this evening. It's what she's used to hearing. She's a spoiled princess who's been so sheltered her whole life, she wouldn't have the first clue about the type of man I am. We don't have a single thing in common, and I can't comprehend why Gwen is so fucking insistent on shoving her down my throat at every opportunity. I've reached my goddamned limit, and I don't know that I've ever been as angry with her as I am right now.

Manuel returns with Nino, and Gwen doesn't say a word or even look in his direction as they walk out the door. Her attention is on Natalia, who has made an appearance in the doorway to the kitchen, concern etched onto her face.

"Oh, good. You're here." Gwen crooks a finger at her. "Nanny, come say hello to Marianna. She's Alessio's date for this evening, and who knows, perhaps even the lady of this household someday."

Natalia glances at me, and while she is usually composed, it's obvious Gwen's jab has wounded her as intended. I catch a glimpse of that hurt in her eyes before she dips her head at Marianna and retreats to the kitchen.

"Don't mind her," Gwen mutters to Marianna. "She doesn't know how to interact with people. I still haven't figured out if she's just mute or slow."

"Enough," I snarl. "I told you not to talk about her that way again. I told you not to fucking come here."

Marianna's eyes widen at my tone, and she shifts uncomfortably as Gwen gasps as if I've actually wounded her.

"Alessio, please. We had plans for this evening. Let's not allow anything to spoil our fun. We can discuss other matters later, but—"

"Marianna." I cut my gaze to her so there can be no mistaking my intentions. "You are a respectful Society daughter, and it's clear to me you are looking for a husband. So, allow me to be clear to you. I apologize for Gwen wasting your time this evening, but I won't be attending the gala. I am not in the market for a girlfriend or even a wife. Especially not a wife. It's time for you to set your sights upon someone else. With that said, I hope you have a pleasant evening."

"Alessio!" Gwen screeches.

"If you'll excuse me, I'm going to get a drink." I nod to Marianna and narrow my gaze at Gwen. "I want you gone when I return."

Gwen immediately starts to wail, and I can hear Marianna trying to console her as I enter the kitchen, but I don't stop to listen. I glance around the space, searching for Natalia, but I don't see her. Upon checking the adjoining dining room, I realize that's empty too. Curious, I head for the pantry, and when I open it, I'm surprised to find her hiding in there. She's standing in the corner, her eyes red with emotion she tries to conceal as she dips her head.

"Natalia, look at me."

She doesn't. I hover in the doorway, torn between maintaining the promise I made to myself and the desire I feel to shatter it right now.

She gestures at me to go and then turns away, staring at the wall. Her obstinance makes my dick swell, but it's the overwhelming realization I have that urges me toward her. I approach her slowly, quietly, lingering behind her. Close enough to touch. Close enough to smell. She shivers as I lean into her, my breath whispering over her ear.

"Are you jealous, Natalia?"

She glares up at me. My lips curve into a smile that feels foreign as I wrap my arm around her waist and pull her back against me, so she can feel my cock pressing into her spine.

"Do you think this is yours?"

Another glare. She shakes her head, clearly at a loss for how to speak to me without her phone.

I told myself I wasn't going to do this, but when she's in my arms, I seem to forget why I ever decided so in the first place.

My lips graze her neck, and I kiss a path down to her collar bone, worshipping the sweetness of her skin. "If you want it, take it."

A warm flush spreads over her skin, and her head falls back against me as I slip my palm into her blouse, grazing her nipple beneath her soft silk bra. She melts into me, and I quickly find myself losing control as I yank up her skirt and tug down her tights and panties. When I slide my fingers between her thighs, she's so fucking soaked for me I can't help but rumble in satisfaction.

"This belongs to me." I palm her pussy. "Only me. Same with your mouth. Your tits. Your whole fucking body. If you ever get the notion that anyone else can touch you like I do, I will slaughter him, Natalia. Do you understand?"

She hisses out a breath between her teeth, nodding frantically as she starts to rock her pelvis against me in need. I think the little fiend actually likes the idea of me bloody and violent. I suspect in her mind, she'd like to do the same to Marianna, and perhaps Angelina too. The thought of her possessive nature gets me so fucking hard, I can barely refrain from shoving my cock inside her before she comes.

I thrust my fingers into her over and over, fucking her wet cunt so hard I could swear I heard her whine. I'm trying to decide if I imagined it as she arches her back and comes so violently, she squirts all over my hand.

"Fucking Christ," I choke on the words as she nearly collapses in my arms.

She's still breathless and weak as she reaches back and strokes my dick through the material of my trousers, grinding her ass against me. If I was clinging to the idea that I could stop this insanity, it's drowned out by the overwhelming need I have to lay claim to her. I unzip my pants, yanking my cock out and spinning her around in my arms. I hoist her up against me, and she wraps her legs around my waist, using her free hand to nudge me inside of her. Her pussy slides over me, taking me straight to paradise as she squeezes my cock.

"Now tell me." I bite her lip and tease it between my teeth. "Do you think this belongs to you?"

She stares up at me, fire blazing in her eyes as she cups my face between her palms and nods. I groan in response, fucking her like a madman as she starts to kiss and bite my neck. I want to come in her. I want to empty my seed into her over and over until I own her.

The thought terrifies me, and I try to push it away. Watching her like this, wild as she rocks down against me, claiming me like she's never going to let me go, it does something to me. She's tormenting me. Forcing me to break every rule I've ever made for myself. At times, I hate her for it. Right now, I never want it to end.

She drags her fingers over my chest and down to my waist, sliding them beneath my shirt. When they find my back, her nails rake over my spine, making me grunt. She's leaving marks any way she can. Biting at my skin, sucking me sweetly and then rough. Her pussy soaks my trousers, and I know she's going to come again. The pressure is torturing her. The anticipation has me on edge, and I need it to happen now before I blow my load inside her. I dig my fingers into her ass cheeks, slamming my hips against her as she rides out every deep thrust.

"Come on, Natalia," I growl. "Show me it's yours. Show me you'll never let anyone else take it from you."

My words tip her over the edge, and her entire body vibrates in my arms as her pussy convulses around me.

"Fuck." I yank my cock from her warmth as it starts to pulse, and she reaches down to milk it until my come sprays across her pussy.

In the back of my mind, there's a realization of how close that was. How I almost didn't make it, yet there's another part of me that likes seeing her pussy soaked with my come. I adjust my grip on her, holding her up with one arm as I reach down with the other and rub it into her clit. She pants against me, still sensitive from her orgasm, yet she rides my fingers like she'd gladly take another.

When she opens her eyes again, she glances over my shoulder, her lips curving into a smirk. I'm still fingering her when I look back to find Gwen and Marianna standing behind us, slack mouthed.

"What the fuck is wrong with you?" I bark. "I told you to get out."

Gwen shoots Natalia a scathing look, and then they turn to go. I don't see the rest, because Natalia grabs my face and kisses me. She kisses me until we're both breathless and our lips are raw, and still, it isn't enough.

I don't know what the fuck she's doing to me, but I know it's going to be a problem.

18

ALESSIO

I COLLAPSE NEXT TO NATALIA, EVERY MUSCLE IN MY BODY straining as I try to catch my breath. We've been going at it for hours. I've lost count of how many times I've made her come, and I think it's safe to say that she's officially fucked me dry.

After Gwen and Marianna left, Manuel returned with Nino and put him to bed at my request. I carried Natalia up to her room, getting her naked as soon as we crossed the threshold. I've spent more time between her legs today than I've ever spent with anyone in my life.

I lift my gaze to hers, and I just can't stop fucking staring at her. Her cheeks are flushed, and her hair's a mess from my fingers. The evidence of my possession is all over her body, and I like it too much.

She reaches down, stroking my hair back with a gentleness I've never known. Her eyes seem to reflect the war waging in my head. I'm sure she's wondering if I'm going to leave now. It's what I always do. When I rest my head against her chest and massage her breast with my palm, I'm wondering that myself. She continues to stroke my hair, and it feels ... nice. My eyes are so heavy I just want to rest them for a second. I just want to lay right here and feel her for a little longer.

The sound of a creaking door jolts me awake, and Natalia's panicked gaze meets mine as she looks down at me, trying to convey her silent thoughts.

"What is it?" I ask, voice rough from sleep.

The morning sunlight pouring through the window is a good indication I've been here all night. As is the comforter currently covering my body. I sit up, following Natalia's gaze to Nino, who's currently standing at the end of her bed with a curious expression on his face.

"Alessio, why are you in Natalia's bed?" he asks.

I look at her for an answer, and she tries to hide her nerves as she leans up, signing something with her hands.

Nino nods as if to say he understands and then looks at me. "It's okay. I have nightmares sometimes too."

Natalia stifles a laugh when she sees the confusion on my face.

"When are we going on the boat?" Nino looks toward the window, the water beckoning him.

"Right, the boat." I glance at my watch, surprised to see we've all slept in. "Today's Sunday."

Natalia takes over the conversation, signing to him again. Nino signs back and hurries off, shutting the door behind him as he goes.

"What did you tell him?" I ask.

She grabs her phone from the nightstand and uses it to respond.

I told him to get ready and said he could watch cartoons until I get him for breakfast.

"And the part about me having nightmares?"

She flashes me a smile, and it catches me completely off guard. I've seen her smile at Nino, but I've never seen her smile at me. Not like this. It's unguarded and beautiful.

Without overthinking it, I lean in and kiss her, rolling her onto her back as I rock my painfully hard cock against her pelvis. Before I can get back inside of her, she makes a gesture to the bathroom, which I take to mean as the shower.

Showering together seems ... intimate. I can tell she's worried Nino could come back, and we do need to be careful, so I take her to the shower. Then I fuck her up against the wall, making her come twice before I blow my load over her back. When I'm finished, she washes me, and I close my eyes, trying not to overthink this. It feels good. It feels like something I could do every day, until that voice in my head reminds me I can't have her. Not really. Having her means I would inevitably fuck it up somehow. I would destroy her. It's in my DNA.

When I open my eyes again, she's watching me with a guarded expression. She can sense the change in me. She always does. She reaches up, smoothing the concern from my face. Somehow, I earn another smile from her, and she shakes her head when she sees my cock getting hard again. She taps my wrist to indicate the time, and I grunt.

I ask her if she wants me to help her wash, and she shakes her head, making a gesture to Nino's room. I tell her I'll get him downstairs for breakfast, and she nods.

Leaving her behind feels different this time, and I don't know why. I just know every step I take away from her, something is trying to drag me back. However, it isn't possible to spend the day buried inside of her, and I made a promise to Nino.

We're downstairs at the breakfast table when she joins us thirty minutes later. Her typical uniform is gone, and in its place is the pair of jeans that have made more than a few appearances in my thoughts when I'm jacking off. They emphasize the curve of her hips, reminding me of the softness I know is just beneath the surface. I can still feel her skin against me when I close my eyes, and I think I've got a goddamned problem because I'm getting hard again just looking at her.

She takes the empty seat between us, her long hair cascading down her back the way I like it. I'm wondering if she did that for me when her hand finds my thigh beneath the table. She gives it a little squeeze, and when I meet her gaze, she looks amused.

You're staring, she writes.

"Yes, well," I mutter into a bite of toast, leaving the rest unsaid.

We eat our breakfast, and Nino's excitement grows as we venture out onto the water again. It's a nice day to be out on the lake, and we make the most of it, cruising around for hours before stopping to eat lunch in a cove. This time, Natalia and Nino help with preparations, and I watch him with interest as I notice how relaxed he's become just over the last several weeks.

Guilt settles over me as I consider the burden of the thoughts he must have been carrying before. There is no denying that Natalia has helped him, or that she has helped me too. Every day, Nino seems to enjoy my company a little more. He has started to tell me little things throughout the day, completely unprovoked. He will ask me questions or tell me about something that happened at school. Today, he seems more at ease than he's ever been with me, but it's the question he asks me when Natalia sets the table that truly catches me off guard.

"Alessio, are you going to be my dad now?"

I blink at him and then notice that Natalia's frozen, her expression strained as she waits for my response. I don't know how to answer that question, and I think it's evident to all of us. Nino is aware that he already has a father, but Enzo isn't coming home, and he gave the responsibility to me. Biologically, Nino will always be Enzo's son, but I'm the one who will raise him. It's something we discussed long ago when I took over his care. Enzo told me he knew that one day Nino would come to see me as his dad, and he trusted me to take on that role. It was never something I wanted to force, and I honestly didn't expect it to happen naturally. Now that it is, I'm rather unprepared for it.

I kneel so I'm at his level, hoping I don't royally fuck this up. "You and I will always be family, Nino," I tell him in a rough voice. "I'm here to protect you and take care of you, and whatever you want that to mean, I'm okay with it. You can call me Alessio, or you can call me ... something else if you prefer."

"I want you to be my dad," he says quietly. "If that's okay."

Emotion steals my voice as he hugs me. I hug him back, squeezing my eyes shut, so they stop burning. Quietly, from a distance, I have always loved Nino, but I never thought that he could love me too.

When I open my eyes again, I catch Natalia swiping away tears as she watches us. She looks distraught, but I don't know why. Before I can ask, she scurries over to the door and disappears below deck.

Nino looks up at me. "Is Natalia okay?"

"She's okay." I ruffle his hair, but honestly, I'm not so sure.

"DOMINUS ET DEUS, MR. SCARCELLO." The guard behind the gate greets me. "You're here for Enzo Marcone?"

"Yes." I nod. "But I'd like to have a word with you first."

His expression pinches as he opens the gate, gesturing for me to come in. "What can I do for you, sir?"

I consider my words carefully. This is a Tribunal prison, so the guards are expected to have unwavering loyalty to The Society. Even though Enzo is a prisoner, he is still a Sovereign Son. I don't know what the guards' relationships with him are really like, other than the little I've seen during my visits. They always seem to treat him with respect, and Enzo would tell me if they weren't. Now I need them to do the same with me by answering my questions honestly.

After he lets me through, I follow the guard to the holding area for visitors. It's currently empty, as it always is at this hour. This time block is reserved specifically for me to bring Nino here. It's an arrangement I made with the Tribunal after many debates.

"Would you care for a drink, sir?" The guard asks.

"No, thank you." I glance at his uniform, but unlike civilian prisons, he doesn't have any identification. "What is your name?"

"It's Thomas," he answers. "Thomas Thorne."

"Thomas," I repeat. "I've seen you here often. Is it safe to assume you interact with Enzo regularly?"

He swallows, glancing over my shoulder at the door. His nerves are unsettling, and I'm curious about the cause of them.

"Yes. I interact with him frequently, sir. Mostly on weekends, as you know."

"Can you tell me how he's doing here?" I ask. "What sort of prisoner is he, compared to the rest?"

He frowns, shifting his weight from one foot to the other. "I don't want any trouble, Mr. Scarcello."

I can see the open door is a problem for him, so I walk over and shut it. "What do you mean you don't want any trouble?"

"If I did something to upset him..." He trails off, and I'm surprised by the terror in his eyes. "I didn't mean to."

"Why would you think that you had?"

"I don't know." He stuffs his hands into his pockets. "Can you tell me what this is about?"

I had only intended to ask him about Nino, but now I'm interested in what else might be taking place.

"You aren't in trouble," I assure him. "I didn't come here to harass you about Enzo's care. I suspect there's more going on that I'm not aware of, and I'd like to be informed on the matter. If he's causing trouble here, you have a duty to The Society to report that behavior."

"I've tried." He lowers his voice, even though nobody can hear him in here. "It's not me. It's the other guards."

I stare at him, annoyed. "Don't be vague. Tell me what the problem is, Thomas."

"He's your friend," he says. "You two are practically brothers."

"We are," I concede. "But my loyalty is to IVI, first and always. As yours should be too."

My warning doesn't sway his uncertainty, so I suppose I'll have to throw him a breadcrumb.

"Look, Thomas. Nino has given me a rather disturbing account of his visits with Enzo, and I'm concerned. I want to know what's really happening."

He grimaces, lowering his gaze to the floor. "He's a cute kid."

"He is, and as his guardian, it's my job to protect him. I need to know if this place is safe."

He collapses into a chair and sighs, dragging a hand through his hair like he's still expecting this to be a trap.

"I know it's his kid," Thomas says. "And I'm not the sort of man to tell someone how they should raise a kid, especially a Sovereign Son, but Nino always cries during their visits. I don't like watching it. I'll tell you that much."

"Why does he cry?" I demand.

"Because Enzo criticizes him the whole time. He talks down to him. Treats him like he treats everybody else, I guess . . . sometimes, he gets a little rough with the kid too."

My jaw clenches as I try to maintain my composure. "Rough how?"

"He pinches him. Socks him in the arm. Makes him do pushups. I've seen him smack the kid in the face a few times."

"And you let this happen?" I bark. "Why hasn't anyone informed me?"

"I tried to put a stop to it, but it's the other guards. As long as he's paying them extra, he gets whatever he wants. I reported him to the Tribunal once, and do you know what happened?" He glances up at me, eyes gleaming. "The other guards brought my wife in here when I was gone and made her fuck him. They told her she had to do it, or they were going to make me disappear. Enzo never lets me forget it. He asks about her every time I see him."

I turn away from him and stare at the window to the hall. I don't want to believe that any of this is true. I know Enzo. He can be a prick, but not like this. This is not the way I know him to be.

"He fucks women from the Cat House every week," Thomas goes on. "The guards sneak them in here every Wednesday. He didn't have to have my wife. He did it because he could."

I want to tell him to stop, but it seems he's come uncorked.

"They bring him fucking steak dinners. Lobster. Coke. You name it. Anything he wants, they'll get it for him. He has a phone, a laptop, internet. An actual bed in his cell—"

"How?" I turn back to him.

"His mother," Thomas answers. "She pays the guards every week, and I'm not talking about just money. She fucks them too."

I cringe at the image, and again, my instinct is to deny it, but his story aligns with what Nino told me. And I know Gwen would do anything for her son. What he's saying isn't that farfetched, all things considered. She has always proclaimed Enzo's innocence, as have I, but now I'm realizing I don't know him as well as I thought.

"Where is he now?" I ask.

"He's in the visitor's room waiting for you and Nino. Gwen has already been by today."

Of course, she has.

"Can you show me his cell without the other guards seeing us?"

"Not physically," he says. "But I can show you."

He stands up and heads for the door. I follow him out and into the control room. He enters his login details and pulls up the monitors, clicking on the thumbnail of a cell. Sure enough, when he enlarges it, I can see it's not like the others. There's a bed, a TV, and a refrigerator. He has all the amenities a prisoner could hope for in here.

"The guards like to watch him fuck the women," he says quietly. "That's part of their arrangement."

My head is a throbbing fucking mess as I attempt to process all this information. Enzo has always made it seem like he was so hard off in here. For years, he has begged me to do everything in my power to appeal to the Tribunal on his behalf, and I have done it. Again and again, I have gone back there and pleaded with them for a case review. I have sunk hundreds of thousands of dollars into my own investigation, trying desperately to prove his innocence. For years, I have stared at the ceiling at night, too frustrated to sleep, thinking that he was in here suffering immensely. Now, I can see he has made a fool of me.

"I need their names," I tell Thomas. "I want the identity of every guard who has betrayed The Society."

His eyes widen in terror. "What are you going to do?"

"Leave it with me."

THE MOMENT I walk into the visitor's room, Enzo greets me with a withering glare.

"Where is my son, Alessio?"

"Nino won't be visiting today," I inform him.

"And why is that?"

There's something in his expression I don't think I've ever seen before. Perhaps he's toying with me, but it seems deeper than that. Something is off, and I can't quite figure out what it is. He's too calm. I know Gwen has been here already, and I don't doubt she got him as worked up as much as she is. Enzo has never had great impulse control. He flies off the handle easily, and I expect that from him. The fact that he isn't right now is somewhat disturbing.

"Nino expressed that he is no longer comfortable visiting you," I answer bluntly. "He told me you hurt him."

"Oh, for fucks sake, Alessio. You coddle him too much. He needs to learn to be a man."

"He's a child." I scowl at him.

"Yes, he's a giant fucking baby. You've made him soft, and I don't like it. If he were with me, he would know how a Sovereign Son should act."

I take a breath to temper my rage. I knew this discussion wasn't going to go over well, but with every word he utters, I'm tempted to lean over and smash his goddamned face in the table. This is the same man I've stood by for years. The man I gave my unwavering loyalty and support to when he needed it most, but right now, he feels like a fucking stranger.

"He won't be coming back." I stare at him, waiting for the inevitable blowout that will surely come.

"Is that what you think?" he laughs caustically. "He's my son, Alessio. If I want him to visit me, he will."

"Biologically, he may be yours," I clip out. "But I am the only father he's really known, and in case you've forgotten, you granted me the customary rite when you were sentenced. I'm sure I don't need to remind you that means I have full discretion to decide who he sees and when."

"Is that a threat?" Enzo narrows his eyes. "Are you actually fucking threatening me, Scarcello? After everything my family has done for you?"

"Take it as you will. I'm not bringing Nino here so you can torment him. I thought you were better than that, Enzo. I expected more from you."

"My mother was right about you." He leans across the table, snarling his words in a low voice. "That fucking nanny is wrapped around your dick so hard, it seems to have cut off the blood supply to your brain. If you think for one goddamned second I will stand for this, you will come to regret it. Do. Not. Fuck. With. Me."

I rise from my seat and turn to go. I want to believe there will be a better time to discuss this after he's cooled down. There are things to consider. He needs some intervention, obviously, but I don't know that it will make a difference. He's not getting out of here, and he'll never truly be a part of Nino's life. As things stand, I'm not sure we'll ever get to a point where we can agree. I know Enzo well enough to know he's not backing down from this. I don't want to believe the worst in him, but I don't know who he is right now.

"I mean it, Alessio," he calls after me. "He better be here next Sunday. I'm not going to ask twice."

19

NATALIA

NINO AND I ARE CUDDLED UP ON HIS BED, WATCHING A MOVIE together when the house loses power. He clings to me nervously as we wait for it to come back on, but it doesn't. A weird feeling lodges in my chest as I remember Manuel told me he had the night off. I don't actually know what he does on his time off or if he's even still in the house. Sometimes he sticks around, but there are other times when I don't see him. Alessio is gone too, which means there's a chance Nino and I are here alone.

"Natalia?" Nino whispers into the darkness. "I'm scared."

I hug him close to me as I pull my phone out and turn on the flashlight. He seems to relax when he sees my face, but a noise from downstairs makes us both jump.

"What was that?" he asks.

I hold a finger up to my lips and listen. There's a long pause before we hear it again. Something crashes, and it's loud. Chillingly loud. My heart races as I try to reassure Nino. If Manuel were here, I'm certain he would have called out by now. Unless that's him downstairs, or maybe Alessio is back. But it sounds like someone is breaking something, and I have a gut feeling it's not either of them.

My fingers tremble as I type out a text to Alessio and try to send it, but it doesn't go through. That's when I notice my phone has no service or WIFI. I try again a few more times, but it's not working, and my immediate thought is that someone is blocking the signal.

I lift Nino off the bed as I consider my options. The first thing I have to do is get him somewhere safe. There's no way for us to get to the ground level besides the stairs, and I don't know who's down there. Going up to the third level is an option, but if someone has broken in, they could probably break through Alessio's door too. I'm terrified, but I can't let Nino see that. I have to figure out what's going on. I have to protect him.

I take him with me into the hall, using my phone light to check the path to the third floor. There's nobody up here yet, but I suspect it's only a matter of time. I take the stairs quietly, hoping Alessio left his door unlocked. If he didn't, I'll have to hide Nino in one of the guest suites.

I turn the handle on his door and say a silent prayer of relief when it opens. His room is empty and quiet, and for now, it's the safest place I can think to keep Nino. I shuttle him into the closet, and then I write out a message for him and lower the volume before I play it.

Nino, I need you to be brave for me, okay? I'm going to check downstairs for Manuel. While I do that, I need you to stay in here and be very quiet until I come back for you.

His lip trembles, and his eyes shine with tears. "Do you promise you'll come back?"

I promise. I take him into my arms and hug him. *Just don't come out no matter what you hear. I want you to lock the door behind me and don't open it until I tap four times.*

"Okay," he says.

Can you do me a favor and keep trying to send this text to Alessio?

He nods.

I give him one last glance, smoothing his hair over with my fingers. The phone is clutched in his hand as I quietly shut the closet door behind me, waiting for the lock to engage. My other phone is in my room, and I need to grab it so I have a source of light. As I creep down the stairs, I'm trying to remember if I've ever seen a landline in the house, but I don't think I have.

I make it to the second landing without hearing anything. Whatever that sound was downstairs, it seems to have stopped now. It's eerily quiet as I turn the corner and then freeze. Standing in the doorway to my room is a figure I know immediately isn't Manuel or Alessio.

"There you are, you little bitch." She starts to move as soon as she sees me, and my instincts tell me I need to lead her away, so I run down the stairs and out the front door. I don't know what her intent is, but my gut is telling me I need to put as much distance as I can between her and Nino.

She gains on me as I tumble out onto the lawn, slipping on the wet grass. I don't have any way to communicate with her to ask what she wants, but I don't think it matters. She didn't come here to talk. That much is clear.

I dart into the garden, seeking out cover from anything I can while I try to think. I don't have a weapon, but I don't know if Gwen has one either.

"I know who you are," she calls into the darkness as I lower myself to the ground and crawl behind the barrier of some rose bushes.

Her accusation sends a chill down my spine, but I don't believe her. She's toying with me. She has to be. She's been suspicious of me from day one. I want to assume that's all this is. Alessio mentioned she has issues. I think maybe she's having an episode now.

"You were right there under our noses the entire time," she says. "You thought you were so clever. That nobody would notice. But I did. I recognized something in you the first time I saw you."

My blood runs cold as I move faster, trying to be quiet as she tromps around the garden, seeking me out.

"It was your face," she muses. "Your features are so much like his.

You thought it would be easy to fool a man, but you underestimated me. I know who you are and why you're here. You don't belong in our world. You were nothing more than a mistake."

A sour taste bubbles up my throat and I realize it's all over. She really does know. The worst-case scenario is happening, and I'm not prepared. I don't know how to get out of this trap, and when Alessio gets here, I fear that he will have no choice but to end my life when he discovers the truth.

A thorn splinters my palm, tearing the flesh open, and I hiss through my teeth. Blood drips from the wound, but I keep crawling through the thorns. I have no choice. I didn't come this far to give up now. I swore to myself I'd do whatever it takes, regardless of who stood in my way. I need to find something to defend myself. Anything.

"It's over now," Gwen yells. "You might as well come out. There's only one way this can end, Natalia. We both know that."

I swallow the painful reality that she's planning to kill me. I reach the edge of the garden, and the rustling of her clothing alerts me to her presence. She's right behind me.

"Come here, you little bitch!" she snarls as her claws narrowly miss my arm.

Somehow, I manage to stagger to my feet, and I launch myself into a run. I head toward the dock, stopping once I reach the shoreline to scoop up a large rock. Gwen approaches me from the shadows. She is relentless as she follows me with one intention.

I step onto the dock, walking backward as she comes toward me. In the moonlight, I can see there's a syringe in her hand. I have a feeling if she stabs me with it, I won't last more than a few minutes.

I can't negotiate with her. My breathing is too tense, my heart too fast. My throat is spasming, squeezing as I try to force air in and out of my lungs. Somehow, I know it wouldn't matter. She's as much of a monster as he is.

"Accept your fate," she snaps. "I can promise you this is me being merciful. If Alessio were to find out, you couldn't even begin to imagine how painful he would make your death. With me, it will be quick. You won't feel anything."

I shake my head, my hands trembling around the rock in my grasp. She offers me a pathetic laugh.

"Did you think he actually cared about you?" She snorts. "Alessio isn't capable. He sees you as something to use. Something to entertain him until he's bored of you. He's just like his father in that way, but I suppose you wouldn't know that, would you?"

My silence is answer enough, and I think Gwen enjoys the fact that he hasn't opened up to me. She wants to be the one to drive the stake through my heart.

"His father was weak when it came to women too," she says. "But what man isn't? It's a curse, I think. They can't control it. Their minds are designed that way. They will always be led by their dicks, but eventually, logic wins. Alessio's father destroyed his entire family for an affair with a nobody. She was as deluded as you are, believing she could have him for herself. She decided the only way was to slaughter the competition."

My gut wrenches as I remember those scars on his chest. I had assumed they were collateral damage from his work, but this is much darker than anything I could have imagined. Then there are those portraits on the wall along the third level. I thought they might be his family, but it must be a shrine to what he lost.

"His mistress hired someone to come to the house in the middle of the night while she was fucking him." Gwen waves the needle in her hand theatrically. "While Alessio's father was balls deep in that woman, a stranger was busy shooting his wife right in front of their children. When he finished with her, he moved onto the kids, but Alessio's a survivor. He always has been. He took three bullets to the chest at ten years old. I'm sure I don't have to tell you that going through something like that changes a person. He stopped feeling. He stopped being human, I think. If it wasn't for me taking him in, I don't know what would have become of him. He's like a son to me. Whether he understands it or not, I will always do what's necessary to protect him."

I want her to stop talking. I don't want to hear anymore. As I walk backward, I realize I'm slowly running out of dock. I'll have to do something soon.

"Don't you want to know what happened to the poor delusional woman who thought she could have the man she loved to herself?" Gwen asks.

I shake my head slowly, trying to formulate a plan. I've had years of training. I've kept in shape, and I've prepared for every scenario I could imagine. Gwen doesn't know that. I want to believe it gives me an edge, but the truth is, I know nothing about her skills either.

"Alessio's father sold her out in the end," she says wistfully. "They hanged her in a courtyard full of spectators. Her love for him didn't save her, and your obsession with Alessio won't save you."

Without warning, she lunges at me, and I topple backward, dropping the rock as I fall. She follows, launching herself on top of me as she tries to plunge the needle into my neck. I grab her wrist with both hands, holding her off, but she's stronger than I assumed.

"Give it up," she snarls. "You can't have this life."

The image of Nino locked in the closet upstairs compels me to fight harder than I've ever fought in my life. Gwen underestimates that I'm a survivor too. I grapple with her, kneeing her in the gut and punching her in the side of the head with one of my fists. Instead of weakening her defenses, it only seems to drive her harder. She grabs my hair with one hand, entangling it in her claws before she slams my head down against the wood planks. Darkness flashes in my vision, disorienting me. I need to get a grip. I need to get control before she punctures my skin with the tip of that needle.

I reach up and sink my teeth into her forearm, biting down as hard as I can until I taste blood. She screams in agony, releasing her grip on my hair, and it gives me the moment of distraction I need to reach for the rock. It's slippery in my grasp, but I hold on for dear life, heaving it up with all the strength I can muster until it collides with her skull. The first blow stuns her, and the second disarms her. The needle falls from her fingers, and she tries to fight me off with her hands. The rage inside of me has returned with a vengeance, and I can't hold back anymore.

It isn't Gwen I see as I roll on top of her and smash her face in with the rock. For all intents and purposes, she may as well be him. She knew about me. All this time, she knew, and instead of feeling a shred of humanity for what he did, she came here to destroy me.

I beat her face bloody, and at some point, her hands grow weaker. She's still trying to fight, but she can't even see me. There isn't even a second that I consider letting her go. When the rock becomes too slick with her blood, I toss it aside and grab her by the hair, dragging her to the edge of the dock, I heave her shoulders over the edge. She lets out one last gurgle before I plunge her head under water and hold her there. I don't know how long it goes on, but I keep her there until her body goes limp and everything falls silent. I'm more animal than human as I pull myself away, retrieving the needle she brought for me. It isn't necessary at this point, but I'm not taking any chances. I stab it into the back of her neck, staring down at what I've done with an emptiness I haven't felt in years. It isn't him lying there, but I wish it were.

I can't find it in me to feel shame. She deserved what she got, but in my gut, I know Alessio won't feel that way.

Alessio loves her. He thinks of her as a mother. As family.

I told Nino to keep trying to send that text to come home. A chill moves over me as I consider that he could be here at any moment. I can't face him. Not after this. I can't let him see what I've done, because I know I won't survive his grief over this betrayal.

My thoughts move toward survival as I search Gwen's clothes. When I find her keys, I remove them and stuff them into my pocket. There won't be time to search the office for the boathouse keys. This is the only option that makes sense.

Robotically, I wash the blood from my hands before I run back to the house. I stop on the second level for my bag and then head straight for the closet in Alessio's room. I tap on the door four times, and Nino opens it. He can see something isn't right, and guilt washes over me when he shines the phone light at my shirt. There's still blood there, but there isn't time to think about it. I grab one of Alessio's coats from the closet and take Nino's hand.

"Is everything okay?" he asks. "Did you find Manuel?"

I force a nod and sign that it's okay.

Downstairs, I secure him into the backseat of Gwen's car. The entire time, my heart is beating out of my chest, and I'm paranoid Alessio will show up any second, but I have to manage one problem at a time.

I smooth my hands over Nino's arms in reassurance before I take the phone from him and toss it onto the lawn.

We're going on a car ride. Don't worry, okay. You're safe now.

He nods, and I climb into the driver's seat. My fingers fumble with the keys before I realize there's not a place for them. It's a start button ignition. It takes me three attempts to figure out I have to apply the brake to get it to work. I'm on the verge of a panic attack when the engine finally fires up. When it does, a silent sob of relief bursts from my lips.

We make it to the gate, and I'm paranoid it won't open. As if somehow, in the span of what has probably only been fifteen minutes, Manuel has disabled my access. But it does open, and I drive right out. I drive down the street, and then another and another until I finally hit the freeway. Then I keep driving. I drive for hours until there's no choice but to stop.

NINO IS asleep in the backseat when I pull into the gas station. I glance back at him nervously, considering how to handle this situation. There's no way I can use the debit card tied to my account, because Alessio has that information. I don't doubt he's probably already accessed it by now, searching for clues. I'll have to pay cash inside, and I can't leave Nino out here, even with the doors locked.

I feel horrible for waking him up, but I have to do it. He stirs slowly, looking around in confusion when he notices where we are.

Are you thirsty? I ask.

He shakes his head, and I comb his hair away from his face with my fingers.

I have to go inside. Do you need to use the bathroom?

This time, he nods. I'm relieved when he starts to move on his own, unbuckling and climbing out of the car. He takes my hand, and I walk him inside where he uses the bathroom, and then we grab a bottle of water just in case. I don't know where I'll stop again. We need to find somewhere to stay for the night. I have some cash on me, but at some point, I'll have to access more. That's a problem for another time. Right now, I just need to get back on the road.

We pay the cashier and walk back to the car. I help Nino inside and buckle him in, giving him the water. I'm a nervous wreck as I try to figure out how to open the gas tank, which turns out to be another button inside. The car smells like Gwen's perfume, and it makes me nauseous as images of her dead body flicker in and out of my mind.

I wasn't sorry when I killed her, but the numbness I enveloped myself in is beginning to dissipate. All I've been able to think about for the last hour is Alessio's reaction when he realizes what I've done. I know they had their problems, but he thought of Gwen as his family. I can't regret killing her when she would have done the same to me, but it sickens me that I have inevitably hurt Alessio by doing so.

He'll never forgive me for this. I know it in my heart. It takes everything I have to hold it together as I fill the gas tank, fingers trembling, stomach churning. I close my eyes for a second. A mere second. In that second, everything changes.

The sound of brakes engaging next to the car makes my spine rigid. A car door shuts. There's movement as I'm turning just in time to see Manuel slipping into the driver's seat. My heart jumps into my throat as the locks engage, and Alessio gets out of his car, fury in his gaze as he stalks toward me.

My eyes move to Nino in the backseat. He's fallen asleep again. All I can think is I'm not going to get to say goodbye. This is it. This is the last image I'll have of him.

Alessio corners me, returning the fuel nozzle and shutting the gas cap. His voice is low and terrifying as he pries the keys from my fingers.

"Get in the car."

He doesn't mean Gwen's car. I can't make myself move. I can't stop staring at Nino, thinking of all the ways I've failed him. What will become of him when I'm not here? Alessio grabs me by the arm and drags me away forcefully. Fighting back is useless. I know that now.

He hands the keys off to Manuel through the window and leads me to the passenger seat of his car, slamming the door once I'm inside. When Manuel drives away, it feels like a part of me has died already. I press my fingers to the glass, sobbing silently as I mourn a loss so deep it cuts me to the bone.

Alessio takes his place in the driver's seat, staring at me with a hatred so pure, it only makes it that much more painful. He doesn't speak as he pulls away. There isn't a word uttered from his lips for the entirety of the long drive back to Seattle. I don't even know where we were. I wasn't following a map. I was just trying to get as much distance as I could. In hindsight of my failure, I realize my fatal mistake. Gwen's car likely had some sort of GPS tracker on it. Of course, Alessio would know that. The question is, why didn't I think of it before?

Anger, frustration, and sadness mix into a toxic cocktail inside of me. Briefly, I consider throwing myself out of the car and onto the freeway. Surely, it would be less painful to die that way, because I can't even bear the thought of the alternative. I can't look into his eyes as he kills me.

I cry some more, grieving for the life I never got to have. The one

I swore I would claw back if it was the last thing I did. Now, I realize how foolish it was. Death was inevitable, and all I did was delay it.

I'm numb by the time we reach the house. Reluctantly, my eyes move to the dock as the car comes to a stop, but Gwen's body is no longer there. I don't know if that's better or worse.

Alessio turns off the ignition and steps out, coming around to drag me out too. He doesn't speak as he hauls me toward the boat house. Agony makes me weak as he opens the door and forces me onto the deck, guiding me to a passenger seat in the cockpit. He shoves me onto the cushion and retrieves a tie-down rope. There's no resistance on my part as he secures my wrists painfully, looping the restraint through the metal bar beneath the seat cushion.

This is how he's going to kill me. I understand that as he moves away and begins his preparations. The external door to the boathouse slides open, and he takes his seat without a word, guiding us out onto the lake. He drives for what feels like hours, but everything is warped right now, including my sense of time. I'm still wondering how he's going to do it as I watch the side of his face, studying the man I've come to know during my time with him.

Even now, my pitiful heart skips a beat when I look at him. There's still a sense of hope that reality hasn't diminished, as if there could be another alternative to what I know to be true. Gwen told me he was only using me. She told me it would have always come to this. I don't want to believe it, but the longer I watch him, the more I wonder.

Did he ever feel anything at all?

More tears stream down my face, and I'm still crying when he adjusts the speed and starts to slow. When he stops the boat completely, I try to shut down too. Locking my emotions away, putting on a brave face, I remember who I am. I remember why I'm here. I'm a survivor. I came here to fight, and I'm not giving up. Not until there's no hope left.

Alessio stares out over the water, unmoving, and I think he's trying to remember who he is too. When he finally turns, approaching me with empty eyes, terror chokes the air from my lungs. He's reverting to what he knows, his ability to dissociate more powerful than my own. I can see it in the mechanical way he unties my wrists and tosses me a notepad and pen from his bag, staring down at me with disgust.

"Why?" he demands.

My throat burns with emotion, but I know it doesn't matter what I tell him. He's not here to listen or accept my explanation. He thinks he wants it, but there's nothing I can say to make him feel better about what happened.

She tried to kill me.

"Bullshit," he snarls. "You destroyed my security system. You cut the power to the house and used a signal jammer. There was something you didn't want me to see. Tell me what it was."

I shake my head in denial, but he's already made up his mind.

"Where did you get the poison, Natalia?" He leans down into my face, his biceps rippling with rage. "Who the fuck are you working for?"

I release a stuttered breath. There's no deceiving him now. He accepted my half-truths before, but he's done playing this game, and I'm tired of lying too.

I'm not working for anyone, and the poison wasn't mine. If it were, I'd have nothing to lose by admitting it now. I'm not a spy, Alessio. I have no idea how your security system works, but Gwen did.

"Lie to me one more time." He stares at me with hollow eyes, slowly removing a pistol from the holster at his side.

I'm not proclaiming my innocence. I'll admit freely that I came here to destroy you and your kingdom. I intended to take back my life and I didn't care who I had to kill to do it. That included you. Especially you. Because you were always my biggest threat. Except, when it came down to it, I couldn't do it. I didn't know who you were when I made those plans, but I know now. Having feelings for you wasn't in the cards, but it happened regardless. So many times, I thought about telling you the truth, but Gwen figured out who I was. And then, I had no choice.

"Who, Natalia?" he demands. "Tell me who the fuck you're supposed to be."

I dip my head, choking on my thoughts as I try to avoid his gaze. But he grabs me by the throat, wrenching my head back as he shoves the pistol into my mouth, gnashing it against my teeth.

"I can't believe a goddamned word you say." His fingers dig into my flesh. "You don't talk to me about your fucking feelings because it's all bullshit. There is one thing I'd like to know, though. Do you like sucking on this as much as you liked my cock in your mouth? You filthy fucking liar."

I sob silently, torn apart by the grief radiating from him. He isn't just angry. His hand is shaking as he tries to hold onto me, and his voice is raw. I thought he was empty, but I was wrong. I was so wrong. Alessio is full of emotions, and they are spilling all over me.

"Give me one reason why I shouldn't." He cocks the pistol and stares deep into my eyes. "One fucking reason, Natalia."

I swallow, carefully moving my hand up to his. He allows me to retreat slightly, and I push past the pain in my broken vocal cords as I force them to cooperate.

"Because I'm Nino's mother."

20

ALESSIO

HER CHOKED VOICE STARTLES ME, AND IT'S SO FAINT, I THOUGHT I misheard her. But after several moments of replaying it in my mind, I realize I couldn't have.

I'm Nino's mother.

I dissect her words, staring deep into the eyes that have betrayed me for months. I think she could have told me anything else, but the conviction in her gaze is more painful than I thought it could be. I realize now she's not just a liar, she's insane. She's literally fucking insane.

"You aren't Nino's mother." My fingers fall away from her as I remove the pistol from between her lips.

I feel like I've been shot in the chest all over again. Everything aches. It aches so much, the only logical thing to do is put her down like a rabid animal. Insane or not, I can't forgive her for what she's done, but I can see that she believes it. She believes in her twisted mind that this is her reality.

I try to make sense of it, but I can't. I can't accept this as the reason. I need more from her. I need to understand the path she took to arrive at this conclusion. I need to know what drove her to destroy me this way.

I retreat to my bag, disarming the pistol and replacing it with the vial I carry with me to all my jobs. This is always a last resort. It's effective, but it takes patience and time I don't like to waste. I don't usually know a subject well enough to wade through all the deepest caverns of their consciousness, trying to discern truth from fear, but I need to know Natalia's every truth. I need to mindfuck her until every lie she's ever spun unravels.

I remove the dropper and grab her by the face. She squirms in my grasp, fear swallowing the light from her eyes as I force her mouth open.

"It's a psychedelic," I tell her as the tincture splashes against her tongue. "You should know this about me, Natalia. I always get the answers I want, even if I have to cut them out."

Her eyes well with tears as I force her lips closed and make her swallow. Inevitably, she does. I'm impatient, strung too tight to sit here and wait, but I have no choice. It takes time.

I take the seat opposite of her, watching her as she watches me. Minutes pass. It's dark and silent in this part of the water. At the bottom of the lake, nobody would ever know she was here. My mind is a warzone of those images. I'm torn between killing her and kissing her one last time.

It goes on forever, an endless sea of stillness. I need a reaction from her. She's resistant, fighting it off as she tries to hold it together. Slowly, it starts to happen. She's sweating. Her leg starts to bounce up and down. She moves her hand in front of her face, sucking in a sharp breath.

I rise from my seat and lean over her, doing what I've wanted to do since she arrived. I reach for her neck scarf, and she stares up at my face as I release the knot. As the silk unravels, falling into her lap, I'm not surprised to see the scar I always suspected was there. I am surprised, however, by the anguish I feel when my fingers move over the jagged flesh.

Somebody cut her throat.

Her hands come up to mine, and when my eyes meet hers, there is a wall of raw grief behind them.

"I'm scared," she croaks.

The tincture is bringing her fears to life, and she's seeking reassurance from me. I swallow the discomfort in my own throat as I pull away, tapping the notepad in her lap.

"Tell me who you are."

She takes the pen in hand, writing in jerky letters.

Natalia Cabrera is my real name. I didn't have the resources to change it credibly. I had to bank on the fact that you wouldn't know who I was. My son's name was Camilo, before he changed it. I am Nino's mother.

"No." I glare at her. "You aren't."

She taps the pen against the paper in frustration, and I don't know how this is going to work. It will take forever to get the answers I need. I'm starting to doubt this plan, wondering if I can force her to talk, even though it's obviously painful for her. As I'm considering it, she starts to write again. I wait for her to stop, but she doesn't. She keeps going as if she's in a trance. Filling up pages in big block letters as she gazes into the paper like she's reliving a memory. I don't speak. I don't even want to breathe. I think this could be important, but when she finally shows it to me, I don't know if I can even stomach reading it.

I stare at her for a long moment, and she shoves the notepad at me, forcing me to acknowledge it. Slowly, my gaze dips to the words, and I find myself entrapped.

I went to college in New York City, taking classes during the day, cleaning office buildings at night. One of my regular clients was on Pearl Street. I didn't know what kind of business it was. It was just an old building with a bunch of empty offices and only one that ever got used. The guy's name was Nathaniel. I always suspected something wasn't entirely right about his operation, but he paid me cash and never bothered me, even though he stayed in the office when I cleaned.

Occasionally, Nathaniel would have visitors come through, and one of them was always watching me when he stopped by. He creeped me out, but I didn't see him often enough to think it was a real concern. Then one night, Nathaniel stepped out, and the guy showed up when I was there alone. He cornered me in one of the empty offices and asked me if I was afraid of him. I told him no, but I knew he could sense I was lying. I think he enjoyed it.

He told me I was pretty. I thanked him and tried to finish my work. I was young, and I didn't know how to handle the situation. I'd never even had a boyfriend before. I thought if I told him no, he would respect that. He said he wanted to take me out that night. I declined, and he got angry. He asked me if I thought I was too good for him. I tried to leave the office, but he grabbed me by the arm. It happened so fast I didn't have time to think about it. One minute, I was trying to escape, and the next, he had me pinned against the desk. I think I screamed. He punched me in the face. After that, it was a blur. Mostly, I remember the senses around me. The sound of his zipper coming undone. Nausea as he pulled down my pants. His fingertips digging into my skin. He smelled like strong laundry soap. There was pain between my legs. It hurt because I wasn't prepared for it. It was my first time. And I kept thinking I should have been fighting back, but I was paralyzed. I couldn't move. All I could do was cling to the desk as he took what he wanted. I don't know how long it lasted. It felt like hours, but I think it was only minutes. When he was done, he tucked himself away and said he thought I'd have more fight in me. He said I was disappointing. Before he left, he paused and then turned and asked me if I knew who he was. I shook my head, and he said you don't want to find out. Keep your fucking mouth shut, and you get to live. I knew he meant it, so I didn't say anything. Not right away. But after that, nothing was the same. I couldn't sleep. I couldn't eat. I lived in constant fear, looking over my shoulder.

I went to the police station a couple of weeks after it happened. There was an officer who interviewed me. He seemed nice at first. I thought he was going to help me. I left feeling like everything might be *okay, but it wasn't. The cop started showing up at my apartment. My work. My school. He had been watching me, and he knew my entire schedule. He told me some things were better left unsaid, and if I were smart, I'd forget that I had a one night stand I regretted. It was the first time I realized the guy had connections. I moved. I changed jobs. And I kept quiet, but I never stopped being afraid. There were times I thought about leaving the city altogether, but I was only a year away from finishing school. I didn't want to give that up.*

Time passed. I was trying to move on with my life. And then, one day, he saw me on the street. He wasn't following me. It just happened. Millions of people in New York and I ran into him on the street. I could see it on his face. He'd forgotten about me. I was just a number to him. But when he saw the baby in my arms and the fear on my face, he remembered. Something changed then. I didn't know it at the time, but it was there in his expression. I wasn't just a nobody to him anymore. I had something he wanted.

I ran from him. I went back to my apartment, packed a bag, and set out to leave. But he was already there. When I went downstairs, he was waiting outside with more men I didn't recognize. It was too late, but I still tried to escape. They caught me in seconds, prying my son from my arms while he screamed in terror. I didn't know what was going to happen to him. I fought harder than I ever thought I could, but it didn't matter. Two of the men took him away, and the rest shoved me into a van, locking me in the back with the devil. I begged him. Over and over, I begged him for mercy, but he had none. He tortured me for hours. Burning me. Stabbing me. Strangling me. It wasn't going to end, but I couldn't tell him what he wanted to know.

Was it his son? That's all he kept asking. Was it his? Like my baby was a possession. Something that could be taken from me. I told him no. Again and again, I told him no. And then he got the text. Someone had sent him the birth record, and when he saw the date, I knew it was over. I fought him. I fought for my life. But I was too weak. He slashed my throat and directed his men to toss me into the river while I choked on my blood. I floated away, thinking I'd never see my baby again. I'd never get to hold him, or kiss him, or protect him from the evil in this world. I didn't know what would become of him, but I was certain I was already dead.

When I woke up in the hospital, they told me some tourists in the park had seen me and pulled me out of the water. At the time, I couldn't remember what had happened, so they had to tell me. They said I'd been attacked, and I had only survived because the knife missed my artery. It took months for me to recover. They sent me to a facility. I did the treatments, and slowly the pieces came back to me. At first, I was too terrified to tell them. But there was one doctor I trusted. She was kind to me. She knew I wasn't imagining things. I needed her to help me, so I told her the truth. I begged her to help me get my son back, and she promised she would. She tried talking to the police simply to see if they had ever heard of this man. She didn't mention me, but her asking was enough. The next week, she was murdered in her bed.

I released myself from the treatment center and went to stay with a friend and her husband. He worked in tech, and he was able to dig up some information for me. That's when I found out the man who took my baby was involved in some type of criminal network. His reach was far more powerful than mine. It seemed hopeless, and I was scared, but I couldn't give up. My friends kept telling me it would be okay. They were trying to dig up anything they could, and then one day, they just didn't come home. They'd been tortured and mutilated because they were trying to investigate him. He didn't even know what they were looking for. I guess it didn't matter to him. All I can think is they must not have told him about me. Even as he brutalized them. They died to protect me.

You wanted to know why I came here. This is why. I didn't have any other choice. He took everything from me. He stole my innocence, took my son, and killed people I cared about. I had to do it on my own. I had to come back for him, Alessio. I just didn't expect you to change everything. I didn't want to care about you, but I do. I'm not telling you this because I think it will save my life because I know it won't.

I'm telling you this because if you're going to kill me tonight, I want you to know that it was real. It was all real for me. And all I can ask is that you continue to love Nino the way I know you do. Because as crazy as it sounds, I am so grateful that it was you he ended up with. You saved him, and I know you always will. I can be at peace now, as long as he's with you. As long as you have each other.

The story ends there, and I stare at the paper for a long time, pain radiating through my chest. The imagery of her words is scarred in my mind, and I can't unsee it, no matter how much I want to. I can't deny that Natalia was tortured. I knew it the moment I saw her scars. She carries the burden of that pain with her, and it enrages me that anyone could do that to her. So much of what she says makes sense. The details wouldn't be out of the realm of possibility if she were dealing with some type of underworld network. Corruption is rife, and in The Society, our reach is all-powerful. Judges, police, NSA, CIA, FBI. We have a foothold in every sector, and not just nationally. All of that isn't difficult to believe. But there's one glaring problem with her story. Nino is not her son. He never was, and he never could be. I know his mother. I grew up with her. The only logical conclusion I can draw is that she is mistaken. Either the trauma altered her memory of what happened to her, or her story is real, but she has the wrong child.

When I look at her, I don't know. I don't know anything anymore, except the one thing I can't forget. She murdered Gwen. She beat her, drowned her, and poisoned her. The agony of that reality settles over me like a dark cloud, and I can't pardon her from the consequences of her actions. I can't allow myself to sympathize with her when she set out to destroy me. The last words I spoke to Gwen were in anger. I had dismissed her so I could fuck Natalia. It was all I cared about at the moment, and I realize now that Gwen was right. I am just like my father.

I turn away, stomach churning. I need to fucking kill her. It's the only way to right this wrong. She's obviously sick in the head. There's something wrong with her. She's living in a false reality, and even if she weren't, it wouldn't matter. This is the last thing I can do for Gwen. This is the only way to honor who she was. She took me in and cared for me. She was my family, and Natalia destroyed that without a second thought. She betrayed me, and there is no coming back from that.

I turn back to her, my fury driving me to wrap my hands around her neck and squeeze. She doesn't fight me. She just looks up at me with devastated eyes, accepting that I'm a fucking monster too. As I try to separate my guilt from my actions, I can see myself as the man from her story. Torturing her. Making her cry and beg for mercy, only for her to realize there is none. Are we any different? Am I any different from the man who killed my mother without a second thought?

My hands fall away from her, and I stumble back as she gasps for air, clawing at her throat. *What the fuck am I doing? What the fuck have I done to her?* She just told me every gut-wrenching detail of the worst moments of her life, and my response was to repeat it. I shake my head, tempted to rip my fucking hair out. I'm sick. I'm so goddamned sick.

I turn away, heading for the door to the cabin entry. I need space. I need to think. I know it's a stupid fucking move, considering I've just left her up there with all my weapons. Maybe it would be better if she tried to kill me. Maybe it would make it easier to do what I came here to do. There's a part of me that wishes she would come down here with my pistol. I have a feeling Natalia would aim straight for my heart.

I collapse onto the lounger, scrubbing my hands over my face. My grief is still too raw to comprehend, but I'm only beginning to realize it's not just Gwen that I'm grieving for. It's the loss of Natalia too. The trust I had in her is shattered. Without her to soften the jagged edges of myself, I don't know who I'll become. Who will Nino have to keep him from becoming just like me?

Moisture soaks the edges of my eyes, and I squeeze them shut, trying to turn off these fucking feelings I never wanted. I don't know how I got here. I don't know when I changed, but I blame her for it. I blame her for every goddamned thing.

Soft fingertips touch my face, and when I open my eyes, Natalia is kneeling in front of me, as gentle as I've ever known her to be when she wipes the evidence of my emotion away. I don't need her gentility. I need her fucking violence. I need her to brutalize me like she brutalized Gwen.

"I fucking hate you," I snarl.

She flinches but doesn't retreat. Instead, she shakes her head as if to say I'm a liar. I watch her with bleary eyes as she rises slowly, her warmth pressing against me as she closes the distance between us. When she tries to kiss me, I grab her face, squeezing her hard as I hold her there in front of me, a mere inch away from my lips. I want to destroy her, but I can't deny that I want to fuck her too.

She senses that weakness in me, and she grabs onto it with both hands, prying my fingers from her face. This time, I'm ashamed to admit there's no resistance on my part when her lips collide with mine. I let her kiss me, convincing myself it will be the last time. When she crawls up into my lap, I let that happen too.

Her fingers cup the base of my skull as she delves deeper into my mouth with her tongue, grinding down against my cock. I release myself from the grip of rational thought as I start to rip at her clothes, forcing them out of the way to access the thing I can't admit I need.

She unbuckles my belt, unzips my trousers, and takes my cock into her palm. I bite back a resentful groan, jerking my hips up into her fist. I'm so fucking hard it's painful, and I hate myself for it. I hate that I could still want her after everything she's done, but she tries to make me forget. She kisses me all over, working her way over my jaw and down my neck as she lifts her hips and rubs the head of my dick against her wet cunt. I close my eyes and let it happen. She sinks down on me, and my fingers dig into her waist, holding onto her as she rolls her hips against me. It feels so fucking good it makes me sick. It makes me sick that I could do this with her when Gwen's body is barely cold.

I stop abruptly and pick her up, carrying her to the bed and tossing her onto it. She looks up at me uncertainly as I lower myself over her and spread her thighs apart. I don't want to look into her lying eyes, but I have to, because this will be the last time I ever do. I shove my dick back inside of her, and she arches up into me, her fingers clawing the bedding as I thrust deep and hard. I fuck her into oblivion. I fuck her until all the stress from the day accumulates in the base of my spine and explodes out of my balls inside of her. My cock jerks, spewing come into her womb without a second thought about the consequences. It's what I've wanted to do from the first moment I saw her. There's a twisted sense of satisfaction in me when I pull away and watch the evidence of my possession leak from her pussy. It lasts for a matter of seconds before I'm questioning what I've done. She follows my gaze, glancing between her thighs, and her face begins to shift. I don't think I've ever seen such an empty expression on her, and instinctively, I know she's no longer here. She's somewhere else. Without warning, she starts hyperventilating, bolting upright as she shakes her head violently.

"No. No. No. No. No. No." Her voice cracks. "You aren't taking my baby."

Her chest heaves as she crawls around me, flinging herself from the bed. Her bare feet slap against the floor as she starts to run, and I watch in disbelief as she heads for the stairs. I yank up my pants, following after her, cursing myself for letting this happen. She's on fucking psychedelics, deep in the grasp of an obvious hallucination, and right now, I'm her goddamned tormentor.

"Natalia," I call after her as I climb the stairs, giving chase.

I'm expecting her to grab a weapon. I'm expecting her to try to end me. But when I reach the top deck, I find her at the edge of the bow, stepping over the railing as if she's going to jump. One of the dock lines is tangled around her foot, but she doesn't seem to notice.

My heart hammers against my chest as I call out to her, but she doesn't hear me. She's too far gone, captive to her mind.

She's got one foot over the railing, her hair blowing in the breeze as she stares over the water. She's never looked so fucking tragic, and it destroys me.

"Natalia." I soften my voice, approaching her carefully. "It's okay. You're safe."

She doesn't respond. I'm still two feet away when she starts to lift the foot that's tangled in the dock line. She's walked right into it, too dazed to understand the magnitude of this situation. If I don't reach her first, she's going to trip. I rush forward at the same time she lifts her arms and leans toward the edge.

"I'll float away again," she croaks. "I'm taking my baby away."

I catch her by the shirt, barely grasping onto her as we both topple forward. Gravity works against us, my shins smacking against the railing as I try to stop the inevitable. Her weight yanks me forward, and the rope catches my trousers before we both tumble overboard, crashing into the water and bouncing off each other. The cold water stabs my skin like a thousand tiny needles as I rise to the surface, gasping for air.

I wipe my eyes, seeking her out, but I can't find her. One second passes and then two. I call out for her, my chest squeezing in pain as I move around. There's no response. She couldn't respond if she wanted to because someone tried to silence her forever. Now, she's reliving that history as she drowns in the ice-cold fucking lake I was determined to bury her in.

I dive back under, slicing my arms around me as I try to see through the darkness. But I can't. I can't see shit, and every second that passes torments me. I'm not ready yet. Not this way. I can't let her go like this.

Something brushes against my fingertips, and I swim closer, grabbing onto what I realize is the rope. I burst up to the surface again, pulling it through my hands as the weight at the other end resists. She's still tangled in its grasp. I can feel it as I pull harder, my breath heaving as I work faster and faster. And then, instead of rope, I finally touch her foot. I dive under again and pull her against my chest, exhaustion weighing me down as I swim toward the stern. She's limp in my arms, and in the back of my mind, there's a voice telling me I'm already too late, but I can't accept that. I won't.

When I reach the swim platform, I heave her body up first, my muscles straining from the exertion. I'm out of breath, shaking as I climb up after her. There isn't time for weakness. I reposition her onto her back and tilt her head before I start compressions. She looks so fucking fragile beneath my palms, and I'm afraid I'm going to break her, but the alternative is much worse. I keep going, counting down the compressions before I pause to breathe air into her lungs. I repeat the process continually, long past the moment the darkest thoughts start to creep into my mind.

"You're not fucking leaving me," I grunt. "Come on, Natalia. Wake up. Show me those pretty eyes."

She's so still beneath me it terrifies me. Death has her in its ugly grip, but I'm not willing to relinquish her.

"Come on. You're stronger than this." Thrust. "You can do this." Thrust. "I know you're in there." Thrust. "I'm not letting you go."

Agony makes me desperate. I push harder. Faster. Pleading with God and the Devil alike, I beg for one more chance. In exchange, I offer them my soul. I make promises I know I can't keep, but I don't care. I'm willing to do anything, whatever it takes to bring her back.

"Come on, baby," I cry out. "Don't fucking do this to me."

Her chest heaves, and I freeze when she starts to vomit. It takes a second for me to realize what I need to do, and I turn her onto her side, rubbing her back with one hand while I make sure her mouth is clear with the other.

"That's it." My voice fractures. "Good girl, Natalia. You did it."

Her eyes flutter open and shut several times, and I know she's not out of danger yet. I need to warm her up.

"I've got you." I scoop her up into my arms and force my legs to cooperate as I carry her downstairs to the shower.

I hold her against me while the water warms up, and her teeth begin to chatter as she starts to come back to her senses. Her head lolls against my chest as I step beneath the spray, allowing it to warm her body. I keep her there until the color comes back to her skin and then I carry her to the bed, wrapping her up in the blankets. Once she's secure, I brush her wet hair away from her forehead and she looks up at me, disoriented and uncertain.

"You fell off the boat," I tell her. "I think you hit your head. Just stay here and keep warm. I'll be right back."

She blinks at me, and it's the only response I get. I ascend the stairs and go to the cockpit, checking my location before I call Manuel.

"Yes, sir?" He answers on the first ring.

"I just sent you my location. I need a Society doctor out here now."

"I'm on it," he assures me.

"Thank you." I disconnect the line and stare out into the distance, gulping in air as I come to grips with everything that just happened.

I came out here to kill her, but now I know with horrific certainty it's not an option. I don't think it ever was.

21

ALESSIO

I HOLD NATALIA IN MY ARMS UNTIL THE DOCTOR ARRIVES WITH several other men in tow. He doesn't even blink as I confess to drugging her and explain the events that followed. He tells me she'll need to go to The Society hospital, which I already knew was a given. IVI maintains its own network of healthcare where discretion is a priority. The doctors won't ask unnecessary questions, and they respect the hierarchy, which means they'll abide by my orders. Right now, I need further assurances about her condition, and I'm not getting them.

The doctor directs me to pilot the boat while his guard leaves on the one he arrived on. He remains below deck with Natalia while I guide the boat to the port nearest the hospital. When we arrive, there's another crew waiting for us. Within minutes, they've got her transferred to an ambulance.

The doctor and I both climb aboard, and I watch silently as he checks her vitals repeatedly for the duration of the journey. It doesn't take long to arrive at this time of night, but there's still a part of me that's wondering if I was too late. Natalia's awake but unresponsive to questions, and I don't know what that means. She's too weak to try to communicate. I have to assume that's the reason. There's nothing I can do but sit there helplessly as we pull to a stop, and they wheel her inside to undergo tests and an evaluation.

"I should stay with her," I tell the doctor.

"You can join her after she has imaging done," he says. "But I think it would be wise if you had an evaluation too."

"I'm fine." My eyes move to Natalia as they wheel her down the hall. She doesn't look back at me. "Where should I wait?"

"It may be a while. I can call you once I know—"

"Where can I wait?" My tone dissuades him from any further argument.

He sighs and points to a room down the corridor. "In there, if you'd like."

I go to the room and collapse into one of the chairs, leaning my head back against the wall as I stare up at the ceiling. For the next three hours, I dissect every second of our interaction this evening. I think of everything I should have done differently, and in every scenario, I'm questioning how I could have saved her. That's not right, not when I took her out there to end her life. My nerves are shot, and I'm fucking exhausted, and her confession is stuck on replay in my head. I'm trying to be rational as I consider every valid explanation for her thought process. If she's confused, I will have to find a way to give her clarity. But what if she's not? What if she's just insane?

I realize I don't care. If she is, it doesn't change the glaring truth I can no longer deny. Killing her isn't an option. Neither is letting her go. Right now, looking at her really isn't an option either, because every time I do, I feel these fucking feelings I don't want. I'm still not any closer to a solution when the doctor finally makes an appearance in the early morning hours. He gives me a rundown of the tests and the results of her evaluation, informing me Natalia has a concussion, but otherwise, she appears to be doing well. They want to keep her for observation to be safe, and I decide that's for the best. Then he asks me if I want to see her.

I hesitate, trying to consider what would be smartest for both of us. They can keep her safe here under lock and key until she's released. That will buy me some time to figure shit out, but I also know I can't go without seeing that she's alright for myself. Tonight, I was so certain that she was gone forever. I don't want to admit how much that terrified me.

I nod to the doctor, and he leads the way to the elevator bank and then up to the third floor. Her room isn't far from the hall, and the door is cracked open, so I catch a glimpse of her before I even enter. She's lying there, asleep, monitors beeping quietly in the darkness around her.

"Did she communicate with you?" I ask.

"Yes," the doctor replies. "She was able to communicate via ASL with one of our interpreters."

Some of the tension in my body ebbs away. "And you're sure she's okay?"

"She's okay," he repeats. "She was responsive, alert, and cooperative during the evaluation. What she needs most right now is rest, and I suggest you get some too."

"What if she wakes up?" I look around the sterile room. "Will she know where she is?"

"She is already aware."

Part of me is held hostage by my desire to stay, but my self-preservation shuts it down, reminding me why I have to go. I can't think straight when I'm around her. The only logical solution is to send Manuel to keep an eye on her. He's a familiar face, and I know he won't let her out of his sight.

"I'd like two guards at her door," I say. "I'll send my own as well. She's not to leave unless she's discharged under my approval."

"Understood," he agrees.

I linger uncertainly before I make one last request. It's a matter of formality at this point. Something concrete I can give Natalia when we inevitably revisit the conversation about Nino.

"I need you to run a maternity test too. How long will that take?"

He stares at me in question. "I'll need the child's DNA as well. But once I have both, I should have results in three to five days, give or take."

"When can you come to collect it?" I ask.

He checks his watch, noting the time. "Will ten o'clock work?"

I meet his gaze, lowering my voice. "Nobody else is to know this is happening."

His brows draw together. "Of course, Mr. Scarcello."

"Ten o'clock," I repeat. "We'll see you then."

BACK AT HOME, I give Manuel my instructions and send him to the hospital. I still need to handle Gwen's remains, but I can't do that with Nino alone here.

I climb the stairs, pausing on the second landing. I'm fucking spent, but the sanctuary of my room doesn't beckon to me as it typically would. Instead, I find myself moving down the corridor, opening the door to Nino's room. He's asleep, huddled beneath the alien comforter Natalia insisted he should have. The recollection makes my throat tight, and I try not to dwell on it as I approach him. For a long moment, I stand beside the bed, studying his features. He looks like Enzo in some ways. He has his eyes, his hair, and his skin tone, but some attributes don't match. His nose, jawline, and cheeks are different. Softer. I always credited that to his still being a child, but now I'm trying to recall his mother's characteristics in more detail.

He opens his eyes unexpectedly, blinking away sleep when he sees me standing there.

"Daddy?"

That word hits me straight in the heart.

"Hi," I choke out.

"Is everything okay?" he asks.

I attempt a smile. "Yes, it's okay. You should go back to sleep."

He peeks around the room nervously. "Can you stay with me?"

I'm stunned into silence. He's never asked that before. I can only assume he's still scared from whatever took place here last night. I don't know how much he heard or even what he witnessed. It's something we'll need to discuss, but not right now.

"I'll stay." I pull back the covers, and he moves over for me.

It feels strange settling into this bed with the alien comforter. But it also feels like it's exactly what I need right now. Nino covers us both up and then lays his head on the pillow next to mine. We're shoulder to shoulder, both of us staring up at the ceiling when I glance over at him.

"Comfortable?"

He hesitates and then slowly rolls onto his side, wiggling his way into the crook of my arm so he can rest his head on my chest. Once he does, he yawns.

"Comfortable," he whispers.

Sleep takes us both quickly and doesn't let us go until Angelina wakes me by clearing her throat hours later.

"What is it?" I grumble.

"There's a doctor here for you."

Shit. I sit up, rubbing the sleep from my eyes before I glance at Nino, wondering how I'm going to explain this to him. He'll have questions, and I didn't even think about how I would deal with this part yet.

"Nino." I settle my hand on his back and stir him from sleep. "It's time to wake up. There's something I need you to do."

22

ALESSIO

"WILL THAT TEST REALLY TELL ME IF I HAVE ALIEN DNA?" Nino scoops a raspberry up with his spoon and shovels it into his mouth.

He's eyeing me skeptically, and I feel like an asshole for lying to him, but there's no rational way to spare his feelings if he knew the reality. He would hope for something that could never be.

"There's only one way to find out, I suppose," I murmur into my coffee cup.

He's quiet for a moment, and his lip starts to tremble. "If I am, does that mean I have to leave earth like ET?"

Christ, I am not good at this. "No, Nino. It doesn't mean you have to leave earth. It was a bad joke. I'm sorry. The test wasn't really for alien DNA."

"Then what was it for?" he asks.

I consider his question for way longer than I should. "It is a DNA test, but it's for humans. There's nothing wrong with you, okay? I promise."

He nods.

I check my watch. There's not much time before Angelo is due to arrive, but I know we need to have another conversation I've been putting off.

"Nino, I want to talk to you about what happened last night."

He rips a piece of toast off and chomps on it. "Okay."

"Were you afraid by anything you saw or heard?"

He swallows his food and stares at his plate. "Yes."

"Can you tell me what happened?"

"We were watching Toy Story, and the lights went out. It was scary when they didn't come back on, and then there were loud noises downstairs."

The hair on the back of my neck prickles as I study him. "The lights went out while you and Natalia were together?"

"Yes. I didn't like it, but she gave me her phone so I could see."

"You're sure you were together when they went out?"

He gives me an annoyed look. "Yes, dad."

I try to soften my tone. "Okay, Nino. This is very important. I just need you to tell me everything you can remember about what happened after that."

He wipes his mouth with his napkin and turns to look at me, his expression serious. "Natalia took me up to your room and left me in the closet. She told me to keep trying to text you, and to lock the door behind her. We had a secret code for when she came back so I would know it was her. She told me she would knock four times. I hid in the back of the closet and texted you like she said. She went downstairs to see what was making the noise, but it stopped. I don't know what happened after that, because it was quiet for a long time. Then she finally came back and tapped on the door like she promised. There was red on her shirt, and she looked scared. We got into Grandma Gwen's car and drove away."

I sit in silence with my thoughts for a few moments, trying to make sense of it. His account leaves me with more questions than answers. Natalia said Gwen knew how to disarm the security system, and I didn't believe it was her, but Nino's story aligns with hers, and now I don't know what to think.

"Thank you, Nino," I tell him softly. "You were very brave last night."

"When is Natalia coming back?" he asks.

This is the question I've been dreading, and I don't have a response for him. To my relief, I'm saved from answering when Angelo makes an appearance, interrupting us. He jerks his chin in greeting and then looks at Nino uncertainly. They've spent some time around each other, but Angelo doesn't have any clue how to interact with a child. Today he's going to have a crash course.

"Hello, Nino." He pulls out a chair and sits down. "Looks like you're stuck with me for the day."

Nino arches a brow at him. "Why?"

"Because I have some things to take care of," I tell him. "And Manuel is busy at the moment."

Nino shrugs and goes back to eating his toast.

"If you have any trouble, let me know." I rise from my seat, and Angelo looks concerned.

"You're going now?"

"Yes." I grab my suit jacket from the chair, slipping it over my shoulders. "Why?"

"I don't know." He glances at Nino. "I thought you'd finish breakfast first."

"It will be alright," I assure him. "Just watch a few movies with him. I'll be back as soon as I can."

He nods unenthusiastically, and I ruffle Nino's hair as he glances up at me.

"Have fun with Angelo. If you need anything, you can text me from his phone."

"Okay," he says quietly.

I hate to leave him right now, but I have no choice.

Outside, I glance at the shed where I have Gwen's body stored in the freezer. Tonight, I'll have to deal with that. She deserves more than what I can give her. She deserves a headstone, a Society funeral, and closure for everyone who knew her, but the only way to give her those things is by turning Natalia over to the Tribunal. In doing so, the consequences would certainly mean her death. I can't accept that option until I understand what happened.

My first order of business takes me to the same house Nino visits every week for his piano lessons. The Hudsons live in an estate in a gated community with a large IVI presence. Their family is well established and widely respected. At least, they were until their daughter's absence and abandonment of her child cast a shadow over their name.

Mrs. Hudson greets me at the door when the guard calls out for her. She's a reserved woman with dark hair and brown eyes that seem to look through me. I've always known she wasn't fond of me, judging by the way her shoulders tense in my presence. I couldn't blame her for the reaction. I've never been the type of man who makes people feel particularly at ease.

Our relationship consisted of a simple agreement. They wanted time with Nino because he's their grandson, and Mrs. Hudson was able to provide that in the form of piano lessons. They never speak of his mother Elizabeth in his presence, and he only knows Mrs. Hudson as a teacher. Their family typically only ever sees Manuel when he drops Nino off for lessons, and I can tell she's not sure what to make of my appearance on her doorstep today.

"Mr. Hudson isn't here," she informs me carefully.

"I know." I try for a smile, but I think it only scares her more. "I came to see you."

Her brows knit together, and I question if I've made the right decision. Out of respect, she will communicate with me, but it doesn't mean she will answer my questions honestly. I've always dealt with her husband. He's a hardened man, one who takes the expectations of IVI seriously. Reputation is everything to him, and when his daughter left, he was humiliated and angry. Mrs. Hudson is different. There has never been shame in her eyes when she spoke of Elizabeth. There was only ever pain.

"Please, come in." She steps back reluctantly, allowing me to enter. "Would you care for any refreshments?"

"I'm okay. Thank you."

She offers me a tight smile and leads me to the same sitting room where she gives Nino his lessons. It's a large space, well furnished, but absent of any family photos, as was necessary for our arrangement. We both take a seat, a small table separating us.

"What can I do for you, Mr. Scarcello?" she asks.

"Please, call me Alessio."

She bows her head. "Very well. What can I do for you, Alessio?"

"I want to talk about Elizabeth."

The color drains from her face, and she shakes her head immediately, moving to rise from her chair. "Then you should wait for Mr. Hudson."

I reach over and settle my hand on her arm, gesturing for her to stay. "I don't wish to speak to Mr. Hudson. As I told you before, I came to see you."

She hesitates, torn by her desire to flee and the expectations of The Society. Normally, I would be the last man to leverage my rank against her family, but right now, I don't care why she stays so long as she does.

"What do you want to know?" she asks in a hushed voice.

"My knowledge of the situation is second-hand," I confess. "I've never felt the need to delve into it further, and I'm not here to seek her out. I just have some questions. I'd like to hear your thoughts on why she left."

She's quiet for a very long time. So long, I don't know that she'll even answer me. Her fingers have a death grip on the edge of the chair. She's not comfortable with me, and I don't know if I'll ever disarm her.

"You don't know me very well, Mrs. Hudson." I lean back against the chair, considering my words carefully. "But I can assure you I'm a man of my word. Something I should hope I've proven by now, given that you've had regular visits with Nino. Whatever you tell me today will stay between us. I'm not here to tarnish your reputation further. I'm not here to track your daughter down. I simply want to know the truth."

She considers me for a moment, then gestures to the piano. "May I?"

I nod, and she rises from her seat, moving to the bench. She sits down and starts to play, humming along as she does. It's an odd thing to do, but I suspect the music calms her nerves.

"She didn't leave me," she says after a few minutes, the words hanging between us. "And she never would have left her son."

I stare at her back, confused by her statement. "What are you implying?"

She turns to look at me, her eyes brimming with tears. "I'm implying that your friend is a liar. I don't know where Elizabeth is, but I know she didn't abandon her baby. She didn't run away. Wherever she is, she's dead. I accepted that a long time ago."

Her candor leaves me speechless. I expected her to express her dislike of Enzo, but I never expected her to accuse him of lying. It troubles me, adding to a long list of growing uncertainties about the man I thought I knew. I also have to consider that Mrs. Hudson is a grieving mother who doesn't want to believe that her daughter could abandon her. Enzo courted Elizabeth for a year. If there was any indication of a problem, I have to wonder why she never thought to address it during that time. The Society abides by ancient philosophies when it comes to dating and marriage. Women are expected to remain pure for their husbands. Agreements are often made, and arranged marriages aren't uncommon, but the family always has a right to refuse the match.

"Is it out of the realm of possibility that she simply wasn't ready to be a mother?" I ask. "That she was ashamed of what the other members might think once they realized the child was had out of wedlock?"

"No." Mrs. Hudson looks me dead in the eye, her expression leaving little doubt to her uncertainty on the matter. "Elizabeth wanted to be a mother more than anything else in this world, just not by him. She was getting ready to break it off, but she was scared."

"Why? She had the right to do so if that was her wish."

"Because she was in love with someone else, and that man turned up dead a week before she disappeared."

"PEACE BE WITH YOU, GWEN." I make the sign of the cross over her remains one last time before sealing up the cremation chamber.

I'm not a particularly religious man. Catholicism heavily influences The Society, and I was raised in that environment, but I always found it a little hypocritical. We were expected to attend Catholic schools, go to mass, and extol the virtues of the church in our daily lives. Essentially, what those virtues boiled down to were wealth, power, and influence. As long as we showed up, donated our money, and asked for forgiveness, it didn't matter what we did in our free time. That became evident to me over the years as I watched my brethren lie, steal, and cheat everyone but themselves.

Men could be forgiven for being weak. Their extramarital dalliances were to be expected, and wives were taught to turn a blind eye. As long as their households were abundant and they had their reputation, they were deemed righteous.

Gwen was a devoted wife and mother who followed the rules for decades. She kept her mouth shut until that silence began to choke her to death. While her husband partook in sins of the flesh with every other woman he could manage, she stayed home and raised the children, drowning herself in pills and booze.

I was fifteen years old when she came to my room in the middle of the night and asked me to kill him. I suppose she saw something in me that others didn't. She recognized the darkness, and she knew I could do it because when I looked at him, all I saw was a coward like my father.

Gwen was torn between her desire for revenge and her love for him, and she hated herself for it. She wanted it to be violent, but she also just wanted it to be over. It happened to be a Thursday that I found myself at his mistress's house. She was passed out on the sofa, too intoxicated to notice my presence. It made it easier for when he arrived. I waited by the door and hit him in the back of the head first, rendering him unconscious before I dragged him to her bedroom.

I gagged him and performed the task Gwen asked of me with efficiency and a numbness that surprised me. Mr. Marcone cried as I sawed off his cock and shoved it down his throat until he choked on it. I never felt any remorse for what I did, even as I left there with the knowledge that his mistress would probably be hanged for the crime. Gwen praised me when I returned. She told me I'd saved her, and I had done a good thing, but her sadness never truly left her. Over the years, she withered into a shell of her former self. She never tried to love again. She never wanted to. When her other son Ricardo was murdered, I think she stopped living altogether.

Enzo and I were all she had left. She relied on me, and I failed her. Again and again, I failed her. If I had truly been there for her, I wouldn't be burning her body right now. I wouldn't have ever let it come to this. It only further proves the one unyielding truth I've lived with all these years. I am my father's son. This is why I can't allow anyone to get close to me. I can't trust myself to take care of them.

My phone chimes and I'm reluctant to look at it, but I know it's Manuel. He's sending me updates as he promised he would after I gave the hospital permission to discharge Natalia this afternoon. She's at home now, locked in one of the guest suites. Nino doesn't know she's there, and I've given Manuel strict instructions to call for the doctor if she becomes too overwhelmed, but so far, his texts indicate it won't come to that.

I retrieve my phone from my pocket and read his message.

Just checking in, boss. She's still despondent. Refusing to eat. Won't communicate with me. But she is safe. No signs of harming herself.

His report is bothersome, but I can't do anything about it right now. I suspect it's only going to get worse once I receive the maternity report and relay it to her. She'll realize everything she believed was a lie. Mrs. Hudson made a convincing argument for Elizabeth, however, it doesn't negate the fact that she was deemed the mother by the Tribunal.

"All good, Mr. Scarcello?"

John's voice startles me, and I turn to face him. He's the owner of the crematorium, another member of IVI, and I have an ongoing arrangement with him. I bring the bodies, and he allows me to use his facilities with no questions asked.

"Everything is fine, John. Thank you."

"You want me to call you when it's done?" he asks.

"No." I return my phone to my pocket. "I'm going to stay for this one."

23

ALESSIO

Over the next three days, I spend my time cleaning up Gwen's house. During the process, I discover that her security system has also been disabled, and the footage of her last day is frustratingly absent. I leave everything from that week as is for when IVI will inevitably come to do their own investigation. I've already scoured every second of the footage myself, and there's nothing of note. There are other things I don't have time to comb over just yet, so I take them as a precaution. I find a stash of old hard drives in her private office, documents belonging to Mr. Marcone, and a copy of the case files for Ricardo's death. There's a lot to go through, but I could use the distraction.

Enzo has already left me multiple messages asking if I've seen or heard from his mother. This evening, I'll have to report her missing, and the Tribunal will break the news to him. I'll have to talk to him at some point, but not until I've figured out this situation with Natalia.

She's still locked in the guest suite at home. Manuel has been checking her hourly, delivering meals, and ensuring her safety. With every report he gives me, my discomfort only grows. She's eaten very little, and he tells me she's still despondent. Once, she asked to see me, and I couldn't bring myself to inquire how she responded when he told her no.

I'm anxious for the results from the doctor and even more so for the conversation that will follow. But right now, I can only focus on putting out one fire at a time.

At four o'clock, I make a formal appearance before the Tribunal. IVI is a self-governed organization, which means we don't file grievances through civilian channels. Everything is dealt with at a court specific to each city, fates determined by three Councilors appointed by The Society. In Seattle, this process takes place within the IVI headquarters downtown.

I lodge my missing person report for Gwen, laying out the details of her absence for Councilor Guillory, the head judge. I'm not expecting it to take long, as I've provided a rather detailed account of her schedule and anything else they may need, but I'm caught off guard when Councilor Guillory peers down at me from the dais, studying me with interest.

"Might this be related to the emergency review of your guardianship over Nino Marcone?" he asks.

"Pardon me?" I blink at him, clearly unaware of such a request.

He shuffles through some papers before him, gathering details. "Enzo Marcone and Gwen Marcone requested an emergency review of your guardianship just last week. It is rather strange that she should go missing shortly after that, is it not?"

The news is sobering but not entirely unexpected. Enzo is angry with me, and he's flexing whatever muscle he has available to prove it, but it feels like a betrayal to hear that Gwen participated in the scheme too. This is a problem I didn't foresee. Not only will they be digging into Gwen's life, now they'll be digging into mine too.

"I have nothing to hide," I answer somberly. "You are welcome to interview me with any questions you might have. As you know, Gwen is like a mother to me, but she is not without her problems. She has been in and out of rehab for alcohol abuse and has required the care of a psychiatric team for years. She hasn't been quite herself since the loss of her husband and son. The reason Enzo granted the rite of Nino's care to me was because she was no longer capable of raising a child. I will concede that recently, there have been some issues. It was brought to my attention that Nino was uncomfortable visiting her due to her drinking and yelling. Also, as you are aware, the guards in the Tribunal prison have been turning a blind eye to Enzo's mistreatment of Nino during his visits. That's something I brought forward weeks ago."

"Yes, we are aware of those issues," Councilor Guillory responds. "The guards in question were replaced, and Enzo is under constant supervision. This is how we know that Gwen came to visit him on Monday."

Pressure creeps up my spine, and I can already tell I'm not going to like whatever it is they have to say. They've blindsided me with this information, and they know it.

"We would have warned you earlier," Councilor Guillory says. "But the footage was only reviewed last night, and it landed on my desk this morning."

"Forgive me," I grit out. "I'm not aware of any recent conversation between them."

He pushes up his glasses, leaning forward to review what I'm assuming is a transcript. "It appears that Gwen came to him with a photo on her cell phone. She showed him the image and asked if the woman was familiar. Mr. Marcone became visibly upset and told her it was impossible. She responded by informing him it wasn't, since she was alive and breathing and living in your house with his son. There was a brief acknowledgment from Mr. Marcone followed by an assurance from Gwendolyn Marcone that she would handle it. This was the last time she was seen alive if what you tell us is correct." He pauses to hold up a photo of Natalia. "Does this woman look familiar, Mr. Scarcello?"

I swallow, at a complete loss for words. My mind is reeling, and I'm desperate to see those transcripts for myself. If what Guillory says is true, then everything I thought I knew is a lie. Enzo really does know Natalia, and Gwen came to the house that night to kill her just as she said. If that's the case, then how does Elizabeth Hudson fit into this scenario? How is it possible that IVI declared her to be Nino's mother?

"Mr. Scarcello?" Councilor Guillory snaps his fingers. "We are waiting for your response."

"My apologies." I choke on the words. "Yes, I do recognize her. She is my ... nanny."

"I'm sure you won't insult our intelligence by denying that you know how she is connected to Enzo as well."

My blood runs cold as I realize they have me cornered. Lying to them now would be a grave mistake. There is only one way out of this situation. It isn't ideal but telling them the truth may draw on their sense of morality. It's the only hope I have.

"I believe I do know how they are connected," I answer cautiously. "But I am waiting for confirmation from a DNA test."

All three men stare at me, waiting for me to go on.

"At first, I was not certain. Elizabeth Hudson was deemed to be his birth mother. That was the declaration made by IVI, which you can confirm through the Tribunal's records."

"Yes, we are aware," Guillory replies. "But there was never a DNA test. We took Enzo's word as a Sovereign Son. Of course, that was before his incarceration for the murder of his brother. Are you telling us you believe this nanny of yours to be his rightful mother?"

"Yes." It physically hurts to admit after my assumption that Natalia was deranged for believing so. "She only recently informed me that she is. She told me that Enzo had attacked her. He forced himself on her, and Nino was the result of that encounter. When Enzo found out, he tortured her and left her for dead so he could take the baby."

The room falls silent for a long moment while they consider my words. It's a serious accusation against Enzo, but that isn't my concern. I am concerned that Natalia has no ties to IVI, and they won't want this to get out.

"Do you believe that he is capable of the things she accused him of?" Guillory asks.

I lower my gaze to the floor, ashamed that it took me so long to see who he really is. "The truth is undeniably slashed into her skin."

"And yet..." He taps his pen against the wooden desk before him. "You came to this Tribunal many times over the years, declaring that we'd gotten the details wrong in his case. You told us it was implausible, unthinkable, that he could commit such a heinous crime. You denied that he would ever assault his brother's wife. You laid blame on his brother for starting the altercation that led to his death. You denied that you'd ever known Enzo to be violent in general."

"I am aware." I cringe at the reminder. "I will admit I was blinded by my loyalty to him. He was a lifelong friend, and I had never witnessed any indication of his disposition for violence. Those blinders have been removed now, and I can see things for what they are. All I can do is apologize for wasting your time and ask for your forgiveness on that matter."

There's another long pause, and the three Councilors speak quietly amongst themselves before returning their attention to me.

"It is an unfortunate circumstance if Gwendolyn perished during her attempt to veil the truth of her son's nature. However, this court believes our time is better served pursuing other matters. Despite your dark family history and the stain on your father's name, you are a well-respected member of this community, Scarcello. On the matter of Nino Marcone, we find that you are fully capable of providing for him and ensuring his safety, as you have done for the last four years. We will not be reviewing the case Enzo has brought forth, and from this day forward, we will grant you full legal custody of the child if that is your wish."

"It is my wish," I reply gruffly. "Thank you, Councilors."

"However." Guillory holds up a finger. "There is a problem we must discuss, and that is the matter of the nanny."

"I understand," I grit out.

"It is this court's understanding that by your own admission, she infiltrated your household under the guise of being a nanny when in truth, she is the child's mother. She has no ties to IVI, no loyalty to prevent this from becoming an outside problem, and while we are sympathetic to her plight, this is a glaring issue."

"I take full responsibility for her," I tell them. "She doesn't mean to cause harm to The Society. She simply wants to be close to her son."

"That's admirable of you," Guillory replies coldly. "But we need more."

"Such as?"

"Pending the results of the DNA test, we have prepared three viable options." He glances between his fellow Councilors. "The first is that she will enter The Society and marry an eligible member from the lower echelon."

"No." My nostrils flare. "Absolutely not."

"The second," Guillory goes on as if I didn't speak. "Is that she will marry you if you are partial to her."

Heat crawls up the base of my neck as I shake my head. "I have already made it known I have no intentions to marry."

"Then you have one other option," Guillory says.

"Which is?"

His face is stoic as he delivers the blow. "You can kill her."

24

ALESSIO

I'm pulling into the driveway when the email I've been waiting for finally comes through. There's a note from the doctor telling me to let him know if I need anything else. Attached is a PDF of the results.

I turn off the ignition and stare at it for a moment. Selfishly, there's still a part of me that wishes it weren't true. It would be so much easier if it weren't, but when I open it, the confirmation is undeniable. Natalia is Nino's mother. Everything she told me on the boat was true, and I'm a goddamned asshole.

I don't bother delaying the inevitable. I forward the email to the Tribunal immediately, with my assurances that I'll follow up with them tomorrow.

Inside, I find Manuel in the office. He managed to restore the previously saved security footage from the hard drive, and he's been combing over it for days while Nino is occupied with school or his other activities. We won't be able to see what happened the day Gwen was here, but I'd like to know for certain if there's anything else I need to be aware of.

"How is she?" I ask him as I take off my suit jacket and discard it on the chair.

He glances up at me with a grim expression. "Still the same, sir."

I loosen my tie and then yank it off. "I'll be moving her back to her room today."

He stares at me curiously. "Okay. Would you still like me to check on her?"

"No. I will take care of it."

He grunts and goes back to his work.

I venture to the kitchen, grab a pre-made lunch from the fridge, and head upstairs. Outside the door, I listen for Natalia, but it's silent. I've avoided her since the boat incident, and I'm not certain how she'll react when she does see me, but the clock is ticking, and I need to deal with this now.

I draw in a staggered breath and open the door. She's sitting in a chair, staring out the window. Her hair is a tangled mess, a far cry from her usual styled bun, and she's still wearing the sweats the hospital sent her home in. She doesn't seem to hear me enter. She doesn't acknowledge me at all, even as I walk around and stand directly in front of her.

"Natalia?"

Nothing. She gives me nothing. She stares through me, completely cut off from her surroundings.

"Natalia," I say her name louder this time, but it still doesn't elicit a response.

There's a long, tense moment of silence as I consider how to handle this situation. I understand dissociation. I recognize the mechanism I've used myself many times throughout my life. If I had to guess, I suspect I probably looked just as she does now while I was recovering in the hospital, the sole survivor of my massacred family. The problem is, I don't know how to pull her from it delicately.

I'm accountable for her current state. I accept full responsibility for it, and I have no desire to traumatize her further, but time isn't favorable toward a gentle recovery. I need her alert and involved in the decision before I deliver it tomorrow.

Setting the sandwich aside, I see no other alternative. I bend down and scoop her into my arms. Her head lolls against my chest, and she does not make a sound as I carry her from the room and down the stairs. She feels too light, and it bothers me. I should have come to see her sooner. I should have forced her to eat if that's what it took, but I can't go back and change it now.

I open the door to the pool room and carry her over to the cold plunge. She still won't look at me. Her eyes are unfocused, staring off into the distance as I walk down the stairs into the ice-cold water. When I lower myself and cover her body, it has the intended effect of shocking her back to life, but not in the way that I had hoped.

Her eyes are empty when they move to mine, and her voice is barely a whisper when she forces herself to speak.

"Kill me fast."

She closes her eyes, and I adjust my grip on her, freeing one hand to stroke her face.

"Natalia."

She shakes her head, refusing to look at me.

"I'm not going to kill you."

Her teeth begin to chatter, but she opens her eyes, staring up at me with a fragility that makes my chest ache. I need to explain further, but first, I need to get her warm. I lift her into my arms again, cradling her against me as I exit the cold plunge and head for the shower. It takes me a minute to get it warm, and then I set her on her feet, leaving her in her soaked clothes as we stand beneath the spray together.

"You're not giving up now." I let the words settle between us as she hugs her arms to her chest.

She gives me a gentle nod.

"I was wrong." My voice betrays the depth of my regret. "I know it now, and I'm sorry. I'm sorry for everything that happened to you. I'm sorry for what Enzo did, and I'm sorry that I made it worse."

I'm not good at apologies, but Natalia surprises me when she reaches out and takes my hand in hers. When I look at her, her eyes are soft, and I wish they weren't. I wish she could hate me like she should.

"You're Nino's mother," I tell her. "And he needs you in his life."

She trembles with relief, and I can see the burden she's carried for so long dissolving. If only she knew what it was about to cost her.

"It isn't as simple as letting you go, Natalia. I can't allow you to leave with him. If you try again, I won't be able to protect you from the consequences. As far as The Society is concerned, I'm his father, and he is a Sovereign Son."

Her fingers tighten around mine, and I force the rest of the words out as quickly as I can.

"There's another option. It's not ideal, but it's the only way to keep you alive."

She stares at me intently, holding her breath, and I suspect she already knows. Perhaps she can feel the terror radiating from me.

"You can marry me," I say somberly.

I don't know what sort of response I'm expecting from her exactly, but she gives me none. Before she can get any ideas about what it will be like, I decide it's best to lay it out for her, so there are no questions.

"It will be a marriage in name only. We will live together and raise Nino. You'll have my protection and your freedom, within reason."

She exhales a shaky breath, and I release her hand before she can express her thoughts.

"You have twenty hours to decide. For now, I'd like you to eat something and visit your son. He's missed you."

AS THE DEADLINE LOOMS, I leave Natalia to spend time with Nino, periodically checking in on them through the surveillance system. He doesn't know that she's his mother yet, but someday he will. I think that's more than enough to entice her into the shitty proposition of marriage I made, but I can't help feeling sorry for it, and I also can't help resenting her for it either.

I didn't want this. I never wanted to marry. Now, my hand is being forced. Giving her the option to marry someone else in The Society wasn't going to happen, not even over my dead body.

There's a part of me that suspects she still might turn me down, even at the risk of death. If I were her, I probably would. I have little to offer her in the way of marital bliss. I can provide for her, I can protect her, but I can never give her the things she'll probably want.

Love. Loyalty. Trust.

Those things are off the table. They have to be. It's the only way to make this work. If she has no expectations of me, then she can never be disappointed.

When the hour finally approaches, I don't have to seek her out. She comes to me in my office, phone in hand, and plays the message she's already written.

I've been thinking about what you said, and there's something I'd like to address first. I know Nino is a part of your world, and the connection to The Society is nonnegotiable, but I need your assurances that he won't be a prisoner to it. I need to know that he will be free to make his own choices about his career path when the time comes. Who he marries. How many children he wants. I want him to make these decisions on his own even if they do not align with their standards. His happiness is the most important thing to me. I need your word he'll have it.

I consider my answer carefully. Natalia doesn't understand how The Society works. From her perspective, I can see how it might seem like a prison. Some of the practices are archaic, I can admit, but as a Sovereign Son, Nino will have more opportunities than most could ever dream of. In time, I believe she will come to see those advantages.

"He will always be free to make his own decisions," I promise her. "As long as I have breath in my lungs, I will ensure that. The Society has expectations for members, but there are always choices. I want the same things for him that you do. I want him to be happy."

Her posture relaxes, and she takes a seat across from me, writing a new note.

There's one other thing I need to know.

"Okay." I shift uncomfortably, wondering if she's going to mention feelings.

I need to know if Enzo is dead.

"Yes." My response is immediate.

It isn't something I even have to think about, because I already knew she would ask. She won't feel safe with me, or in The Society, if she knows he's still alive. The lie is for her sake, but soon enough, it will be the truth. I had decided upon it before I even left the Tribunal. Enzo will pay for the crimes he's committed, and it will be by my hand. First, I need to build my case against him, so they will grant my request.

In the meantime, I'm relying on Nino not to mention him, which shouldn't be a problem since he never does. I've already begun to gather evidence against Enzo. The stronger my argument is, the quicker I can end him.

Natalia seems to be lost in her own thoughts for a moment. I can't tell if she's disappointed or relieved by my answer. But eventually, she moves on with the conversation.

The name I gave my son was Camilo, but he doesn't know that. It wouldn't be fair to ask him to change it now. He is Nino to me and everyone else that matters, but I can't live with him carrying the name of that monster. I want his last name changed to Scarcello.

Her request relieves me more than she could ever imagine. I had already planned on it, but it gives me a strange sense of pride to know that she wants her son to have my last name too.

"It will be done," I tell her.

Thank you, she writes. *Can I ask you something else?*

"I'm listening."

Why did you save me? From the lake?

Her question catches me off guard and makes me uncomfortable. I'm not certain how much of it she remembers, or even how much of it she may have heard. My pleading. My bargaining. My desperation. I don't have an answer for her that won't betray me.

I drag my fingertip along the edge of my desk, using that as a distraction. "You're Nino's mother. It was the right thing to do."

She offers me a sad smile and doesn't call me on the lie.

Okay, Alessio. In answer to your proposition, I will marry you.

25

NATALIA

"Hello there. You must be Natalia?"

I offer a nervous smile to the beautiful raven-haired woman as she strides toward me. She's elegant in a red dress and heels, and I'm relieved to see she looks to be around my age. Her stunning green eyes move over me with a warmth I wasn't expecting, and her smile disarms me almost immediately.

"I'm Abella Moretti," she introduces herself. "It's so lovely to meet you."

I'm already reaching for my phone when she surprises me by signing with a fluidity that only comes to someone well versed in ASL.

No need for that. Alessio informed me that you speak ASL, and so do I. My mother was deaf, so our family is fluent.

I relax as I communicate a response to her.

Thank you. I had no idea. It's lovely to meet you as well.

She glances at Manuel. "I take it you'll be joining us today?"

"Yes," he grunts. "Mr. Scarcello's orders."

Abella looks at me, her eyes twinkling with amusement. *Don't worry. You get used to it.*

I notice she has a tag along too, her own version of a Manuel. He's big, bulky, and stone-faced as he scans the shopping center, seeking out potential threats.

Shall we get started then? Abella asks. *We have a busy day ahead of us.*

Yes, I think we should. Thank you for taking time out of your schedule to meet with me.

It's not a problem. She walks, and I fall into step beside her. *Shopping is one of my favorite sports.*

I'm glad for it, because it's been years since I've been shopping for myself. When Alessio informed me I'd need a new wardrobe for Society functions, as well as a wedding dress, I seriously thought I might throw up. I didn't even know where to begin. He arranged this meeting with Abella, explaining that she'd be like a mentor for me. She's been raised in IVI, and it's obvious she knows how everything works. I already love her sense of style, and I just hope she can give me the sort of help I desperately need.

Abella leads the way through the shopping center while Manuel and her guard follow behind. It does feel strange having them with us while I'm shopping for clothes, and I'm not sure I'll ever be able to relax. Abella gives me a sideways glance.

Don't worry. They'll be busy watching everyone else around us. Just pretend they aren't even here.

I nod, though I think it will take a while for that to happen.

She leads me to the door of an upscale Boutique, pausing to knock on the glass. At first glance, it appears to be closed, but a moment later, a woman appears, greeting us with a respectful nod.

"Miss Moretti, always a pleasure to see you, and it's lovely to meet you, Miss Cabrera."

I smile politely, and Abella gestures me in with her.

"Thank you, Katherine."

"Can I get you a glass of champagne before we begin?" Katherine asks.

I fold my hands together in front of me as I consider it. Since the boat incident, I've had my period, so I know I'm not pregnant, but I'm not sure if alcohol is the best thing to settle my nerves. Although I figure it couldn't really hurt either. I sign my answer to Abella and then distract myself by taking in the space, decorated in clean shades of black and white and a touch of mood lighting. It looks expensive, and I'm tempted to check one of the labels before we even get started.

Abella chats with Katherine for a moment before she disappears into the back to retrieve our champagne.

I wander over to one of the displays, noting the price on the first dress I examine is four thousand dollars. It makes me dizzy and nauseous, but Abella is quick to shut it down.

Don't think about the prices. I've ordered a special selection of clothes for you to try on and they all come from Society owned boutiques, which means we get a discount. Regardless, the price doesn't matter. Alessio gave me explicit instructions not to include tags, so there won't be any on your items. I want you to choose what you feel comfortable in.

But he'll still be paying for them, I protest. *I'm not sure I'll be able to pick anything if I don't know the prices.*

She smiles at me. *Please don't feel guilty. You may not realize this yet, but you could buy every item in this store ten times over, and it wouldn't even begin to put a dent in Alessio's bank account. He wants you to have nice things. This is one of the perks of being a Society woman, so you may as well enjoy it.*

Katherine arrives with our champagne before I can respond, and I drink mine quickly, wondering how much exactly Alessio earns when he's torturing or killing someone for The Society.

Good girl, Abella praises me when I finish my glass. "Katherine, I think we'll need another."

Katherine brings us the entire bottle on ice, and we begin. Abella and I take a seat on the lush velvet loungers and watch as Katherine and her assistant wheel out rack after rack of clothing. There seems to be one for every occasion. I'm overwhelmed and already slightly tipsy when Abella rises and starts pulling items off the first one.

They are conservative outfits, much like what I'm wearing now, only more expensive and a lot nicer. I'm not entirely sure if it's the champagne, but all I can do is stare at them with a blank expression.

Are you okay? Abella looks me over with concern. *Do you not like the selection? We have a lot more options to choose from.*

The selection is beautiful. I grimace at my rudeness. *I'm sorry. I don't want to seem ungrateful. I know you must have spent hours putting this together. It's just that...* I smooth my hands over the shapeless skirt I've worn like a shield, trying to find the right words. I don't know Abella all that well, but I do feel at ease with her.

What is it? She sits down beside me, her eyes kind as she encourages me. *I promise you won't hurt my feelings.*

I don't wear these clothes because I'm comfortable in them, I confess. *I wear them because I've spent years hiding who I am. Trying to go unnoticed. And now, I'm not sure I want to do that anymore. I want to feel pretty. Like you.*

Abella's lips curve into a dazzling smile. *Darling, you aren't just pretty. You're fucking gorgeous. And can I just say thank God you told me.* She laughs, her eyes twinkling. *I'll admit I thought it was a crime to cover you in these fabrics. But if you are ready to let the world see you, I will light the path for you.*

My chest squeezes, my emotions overwhelming me. It's been so long since I let myself have a friend. I'd forgotten what it was like, but I think Abella and I could be good friends. I think I kind of love her already.

"Katherine," she calls out. "Could you please do us a favor and take these away? We're going to consider some other options. We'd like a selection fit for a Society wife. All your best fabrics. And red. Lots of red. A few little black dresses, some jeans, we need the whole works."

"Of course." Katherine steps into action, removing the racks and returning minutes later with new ones. Abella and I have already had another glass of champagne in that time, and I think my nerves are finally settling.

"Come on." She ushers me from my seat. "You're going to love this. I promise."

Two hours later, I think I've officially tried on more clothes than I have in my entire life. After the first piece took fifteen minutes to coax me out of the dressing room, Abella came and sat with me once she realized what the problem was.

Hold your head high, she told me. *You can't hide your scars forever, nor should you want to. If you hide them, it means he wins.*

I don't even know how she knew it was a him that caused them, but I suspect it's intuition. Abella is probably one of the most perceptive souls I've ever met. She gets me, and I don't know how. But every time I was uncertain about something, she would talk it through with me. She discovered pieces that I would never have looked twice at, and now I think they might be my favorites. We've acquired an entirely new wardrobe, including casual wear, evening gowns, winter apparel, heels, sandals, and everything in between. When they brought out the lingerie selection, I studied the beautiful silk and lace with a sadness I couldn't shake. I told Abella I wasn't sure I'd even need them, and her eyes crinkled as she told me I definitely would.

I want to agree, but Alessio has made it known that this marriage won't be one of love. Regardless of what I see in his eyes when he looks at me, he can't bring himself to admit that he has real feelings. Something is holding him back, and I suspect it's partially due to the fact he's still grieving the loss of Gwen. But I think a larger part of it has to do with what happened to his own family. He hasn't dealt with his pain. He just created protective mechanisms to keep it from happening again. The walls he's built are so thick, nobody can ever hurt him, but it means he won't let anyone love him either.

He hasn't returned to my room in the two weeks since we agreed to marry, and we've barely spoken other than to discuss Nino and the upcoming wedding preparations. It's not really a wedding, but more of an elopement. We leave tomorrow, and I'm not entirely certain what I'm getting into, but he's given me a cliff notes version. Abella has been filling me in on the rest of the details throughout our morning, explaining how The Society works, the type of functions we'll probably attend, and what my life will be like as Alessio's wife.

It still seems surreal to think about it. *I'm going to be his wife.*

Maybe it's foolish and naïve, but the thought warms me. It makes me feel safe and slightly drunk. It also makes me feel slightly stupid, because I'm marrying a man who might never be able to admit he cares about me. I'm becoming a part of his world, a world I had only ever dreamed about destroying. Now, I'll be one of them, following their rules, and rubbing elbows with the dangerous elite. There's still a part of me that thinks I shouldn't be okay with it. This isn't a fairy tale. It's a hostage situation. I'll be negotiating with them for the rest of my life.

"Alright then." Abella hiccups, discarding her champagne glass. "We better pick out your dress before Manuel has to carry you home."

We both laugh, and Katherine discreetly removes the champagne bottle before snapping her fingers at her assistant. "We're ready for the dresses."

They wheel out five more racks full of wedding dresses, and I'm glad we saved this part for last. I probably would have had a panic attack if I had to choose it first, but now I'm boozy and my cheeks are warm, and my inhibitions are just low enough that I think I can try one on without hyperventilating.

Abella goes through the first rack, holding up each dress, swishing it in front of her as she models them on the hanger. We both laugh at some of the faces I make, and the elimination process goes rather quickly. We have a decent selection pile for me to try on when she holds up a simple, white silk trumpet dress with off-the-shoulder straps and an open back. I pause, staring at it with a sudden overwhelming sense of emotion.

That one, I sign. *That's the one I want to try.*

Abella offers me a curious glance. *Right now?*

I nod. Her eyes light up, and she gestures for me to join her in the dressing room.

I don't know how I know. It just feels like the one. I wasn't expecting to get attached to any of these dresses, honestly. I kept telling myself it just had to fit the role as if I were an actress in a play, but as Abella helps me into it, it doesn't feel like a role. I feel like a woman preparing to marry the man she loves. It doesn't fully hit me until I look at my reflection in the mirror and break down in full-on sobs.

"Hey." Abella rubs my back, trying to comfort me. "It's okay. It's going to be okay. Take some deep breaths."

I nod at her, calming my breathing and forcing myself to relax.

"We can take it off," she says. "If you hate it."

I don't. I shake my head. *It's the opposite. I just wasn't expecting to love it so much.*

"Oh, thank God," she whispers. "Because you look fucking amazing right now. I think this is the one."

Me too.

We both glance at my reflection in the mirror, and after a long moment, she lets out a little shriek. *Did we seriously just pick out your dress in one try?*

My heart flutters as I smooth my fingers over the beautiful fabric. *I think we did.*

I COULD GET USED to this, I tell Abella.

She smiles over at me, bobbing her head in agreement. "You should. You're about to be Mrs. Scarcello. You could come here every week if you wanted to."

The therapist adjusts her pressure on my foot, kneading into a spot that's still sore from our full morning of shopping. After buying what feels like entirely too many clothes, Abella brought me to a spa for an afternoon of pampering. I've been massaged, waxed, scrubbed, and turned over with a fresh haircut and a full face of makeup. My fingers and toes are a glossy shade of red to match my new lipstick, and I feel like an entirely new woman. It's been an amazing experience but getting used to it seems a bit too self-indulgent.

I don't know that I'll be spending much time at the spa, I sign. *I want to do something productive with my time when Nino's at school. Maybe I could get a part-time job. I have an education. I'd like to put it to use.*

Abella studies me, and I catch a glimpse of sadness in her features for the first time since I've met her.

"I get it," she says. "You can do something else. The sky's the limit, right? And when you're not working, I will keep you busy. We can do lunch dates, afternoon movies, you name it. I'm there."

I'd like that.

There is work you can do for The Society as well. She signs back. *Just about every industry you could probably imagine. You'd have your choice being the wife of a Sovereign Son.*

What does that even mean?

Just think of this as a kingdom. She laughs. *In this kingdom, Sovereign Sons are nobility, and everyone else is just noise. Your husband will always be your king, and you are his queen. If you're one of the lucky few, you may even learn to love each other.*

I glance at the engagement ring on her finger. I've wanted to ask about it all day, but it never seemed like the right time until now.

Are you one of the lucky ones?

She follows my gaze, and her eyes shine with emotion. *I thought I was, but we have to make the most of the cards we're dealt, right?*

I'm so sorry. I didn't mean to upset you.

No. It's okay. She forces a smile. *It's life, right? Nothing ever works out the way we plan.*

Are you okay? I ask. *You're not being forced into anything, are you?*

I'm okay, she answers, sitting up straighter. *My situation is complicated. A conversation better saved for another time.*

I nod, not wanting to press her.

"I suppose I should let you get home." She glances down at the therapists. "Thank you so much for your assistance today."

"It was our pleasure." They rise from their stools and leave us.

I follow Abella to the changing rooms, and I can't help feeling guilty for upsetting her. The mood is noticeably different as we dress and prepare to say our goodbyes. She seems lost in her thoughts, and I hope it won't prevent us from meeting again.

I finger comb my hair back while she reapplies her lipstick. The silence is unsettling, but Abella bounces back a moment later as if nothing ever happened.

"Before you go, I have one more thing for you." She retrieves a box from one of the shopping bags she brought in with her.

You've already done so much. I glance at the box reluctantly. *I feel like I owe you.*

"You do." She teases. "And you can repay me by keeping me busy with frequent get-togethers. Promise me you will."

Of course, I sign. *You're the only friend I have here.*

"You'll have plenty more soon," she informs me. "But be warned that many of them will just be curious about Alessio. So many have tried and failed to snatch him up for themselves. You've caused quite the stir by doing what they couldn't."

An uncomfortable heat crawls over my skin. *Really?*

"Don't sweat it," she says. "He chose you. Nobody else matters now."

I can't bring myself to tell her that he only chose me so I could live, not because he wants to marry me. It casts a shadow over the entire day, and now I can't help feeling ridiculous for picking out a wedding dress as if it means something. This is all an act, and at the end of the day, Alessio made it clear it's not going to be a traditional marriage. We won't sleep in the same bed. We won't have conversations as we lie together, naked and satisfied. There's a very strong possibility that if he's not doing those things with me, he will find someone else to provide it. Someone from the large pool of opportunities he apparently has.

My heart hurts as Abella gestures to my scarf, distracting me. "May I?"

I release a shaky breath, my eyes drifting to the box in her hands. I don't know what's in it, but I know I trust her. She hasn't stared at my scars. In fact, she hasn't shown any discomfort around them at all, and she's already seen me at my most vulnerable today. I reach up and untie the neck scarf for her, unwrapping it with care.

She watches curiously, and her only reaction is to swallow when she sees the disfigurement left on my neck.

"Whoever he is." She opens the box and pulls out a beautiful black lace choker. "I hope he's rotting in hell."

She helps me secure the choker, and I turn to look at myself in the mirror, my fingers moving over the lace in appreciation. It's strange and surreal how much a simple piece can change the way I look and make me more comfortable in my skin.

Thank you. I glance at her in the reflection. *I hope he is too.*

26

ALESSIO

"Anything?" I ask Angelo.

He glances up from the computer screen with bleary eyes. We've been taking shifts going through the hard drives from Gwen's house, working long hours as I try to build my case against Enzo for the Tribunal. I have a pre-arranged court date set in one month. I'm not married to the idea of letting things sit that long, but I'm also not ready to go in unprepared.

Regardless of their approval, I am determined to end Enzo's life. There is no future where he'll get to live, as far as I'm concerned, but it would be wiser to go through the proper channels first rather than risking the Tribunal's wrath.

"Nothing much on these folders," Angelo says. "Just a lot of shit if you ask me."

I scrub my hand over my face and sigh. It's been the same for me. I have no earthly idea why Gwen kept so much useless information stored on these hard drives. I'm beginning to think it might be a lost cause, but the fact that she did keep everything also tells me there might be something of note in the void.

"Did you know Enzo dated Ricardo's wife in high school?" he asks.

"What?" I stretch the muscles in my neck, trying to recall that time in our lives.

"Right here." Angelo turns the screen and shows me a photo of the two of them, and it jogs my memory.

"That was the annual Society gala," I say. "I wouldn't call it dating. Ricardo and Enzo had an intense rivalry. They were always trying to outdo each other, making outlandish bets. That year Enzo had challenged Ricardo to give up his girlfriend for a night at the gala if Enzo got better marks at school. Ricardo thought he could never do it, and he was stupid enough to agree to the bet. Of course, Enzo cheated, but it didn't come out until after the fact. He took Nicolette to the gala, and it burned Ricardo up. I had forgotten all about that."

Angelo seems to sense what I'm thinking as I explain the story to him. At the time, I never thought of it as anything more than harmless fun. Looking back now, it's obvious that Enzo always had a thing for Nicolette. Her rejection irked him, and he could never understand why she thought Ricardo was a better match. As we grew older and Enzo dated his way through half the eligible Society daughters, I assumed he had forgotten all about it. When he told the Tribunal it was Nicolette who had come onto him that fateful night of the murders, I had attributed it to a marriage gone sour between her and Ricardo. She and Enzo had known each other for so long, it wasn't a stretch of the imagination to think she would seek comfort from him. At the time, I believed his version of events. Now looking at it through a new lens, with all the information, the truth is obvious. She had rejected Enzo for years, and he felt entitled to her. Just as he felt entitled to brutalize Natalia on a whim and dispose of her like she was nothing.

"He never showed any signs." I shake my head in disbelief. "It's strange to think you know someone, and then you're completely blindsided like this."

"Don't blame yourself," Angelo says. "I never saw it either. Not with him, and not with my own flesh and blood."

A dark look comes over his face, and I know he's thinking about his revenge. He'll have it soon now, but probably not soon enough to satisfy him.

"You should get some sleep," I suggest. "No need to keep at this all night. We can resume when I return from New York."

"With your bride in tow." His lip twitches as if the thought amuses him. "Never thought I'd utter those words."

"Yes, well, I should probably go make sure she's ready. She had a busy day with Abella Moretti."

His nostrils flare at the mention of her name, as I knew they would. We can't help goading each other. I have a feeling he's dying to ask more about it, but his pride won't let him.

"You should tell her to watch the company she keeps," he grunts. "Wouldn't want her falling in with a bad crowd."

"No, I wouldn't," I agree. "Which is exactly why I chose Abella to help her, but I suppose you wouldn't know her character, given that it's been years since you've spoken to her."

"I know everything I need to." He closes the computer and reaches for his jacket. "I won't keep you, Alessio. Please give your bride my regards. Enjoy the festivities in New York. I will see you when you return."

"Likewise." I walk him out into the hall. "Thanks for your help."

He nods and takes his leave, and I trudge up to the second floor, heading for Natalia's door. I haven't had a chance to speak with her since Manuel returned her home this evening. After I picked up Nino from school, I was busy taking him to his regular activities, and then I handed him over to Manuel so I could do some work. I'll need to hire another guard for Natalia, but it will take time and caution to vet them. For now, we will have to juggle Nino's care and Manuel's time between the two of them.

I hesitate outside her door, trying to determine the standard I want to set from here on out. I've been maintaining my distance, though she never leaves my mind. If we are to survive this life together, I need to set aside any conflicting feelings.

My hand settles on the knob, and then I take it back, opting to knock instead. There's a long moment of nothingness before Natalia opens the door, and I'm shocked into silence.

Her skirt suit is gone, and in its place is a simple black dress that displays the soft swells of her breasts and the curve of her hips much more than I'd care for. There's nothing particularly wrong with it, but the discomfort in my cock is growing by the second, and I'm having difficulty looking away. The situation doesn't improve as my eyes roam over her face. She's wearing some sort of makeup that seems to intensify the color of her eyes and red lipstick that draws me in like a goddamned magnet.

I don't even realize I'm taking a step closer until my chest brushes against hers. She has to strain her neck to look up at me, and when she does, I notice the simple lace choker around her neck.

"I like this," I murmur, my fingers moving to touch it against my will.

She offers me a nervous smile and then gestures into her room, silently asking me if I want to come in.

"I can't," I reply gruffly. I don't tell her it's because I know if I step inside, I won't have the self-control I need to resist touching her. "I just came to see if you were ready for tomorrow morning."

She nods, giving me her assurances. Then it gets awkward again, because I'm standing so close to her, and now I've stuffed my hands in my pockets to keep control of them.

"We'll leave at ten."

She doesn't say anything because she can't without her phone or a great deal of pain from using her own voice. For a moment, I consider how ridiculous it is that I haven't even attempted to learn the basics of how to communicate with her in the language she can use.

I linger for far too long trying to think of something else to say, but I have nothing really. I just don't want to leave. Instead, I pull my hand from my pocket and do the one fucking thing I shouldn't.

"It's going to be okay." I reach out and allow my fingers to stroke her cheek.

She shivers beneath my touch, and I'm not sure who moves first, but inevitably the gap narrows until our lips are a breath away. This time it's undeniable that I'm the instigator as my lips brush against hers. I lose all my senses, grabbing her by the waist and pinning her against the door frame as I smear her lipstick with the intensity of my kiss. She melts against me, body soft and pliable against mine. I inhale her, I grope her, and I'm not proud of the fact that I'm practically dry fucking her in the hall. This is what she does to me, and I can't stand it.

I yank away from her, breathless. She's gone from elegant and beautiful to looking thoroughly fucked in a matter of seconds, and I didn't even manage to get my dick inside of her. I want to. I really fucking want to, but I can't. I keep telling myself I can't, because it's a recipe for disaster.

"Alright." I drag my fingers through my hair, returning some of the strands that fell loose. "Well, goodnight then."

I leave her standing there, wide-eyed and confused as I stalk down the hall and up the stairs. It looks like I'll be spending my night in the shower with my worthless fucking palm.

I THROW open the door to my bedroom, already unbuttoning my shirt with a determination to get to the bathroom as quickly as I can, but as soon as I lift my gaze, I freeze at the sight of Angelina.

"What are you doing?"

She's sitting in the chair next to my bed, obviously waiting for me. Immediately, her eyes drift to my tented trousers, where my goddamned erection is throbbing so painfully, I couldn't hide it if I wanted to. Fucking Christ.

"Mr. Scarcello." She rises slowly, offering me a coy smile. "I'm so sorry for the intrusion. I was waiting to speak with you, but you look distressed. Is there anything I can help you with?"

I don't have to ask what she means. Her attention on my groin makes it quite obvious. Angelina has always dropped subtle hints about her interest, but I suspect this is her last-ditch effort now that she knows I'm eloping with Natalia tomorrow.

"Did you need something?" I grit out, walking to the dresser where my decanter rests, using the distraction to calm myself.

She's quiet for a long moment, and I'm not sure what she's going to say or do next. "Are you sure there's nothing I can assist you with, Mr. Scarcello?"

"You can assist me by telling me what you're doing here." I pour myself a drink. "I've had a long day and an even longer one planned for tomorrow, as you're aware."

She straightens her spine in the face of my rejection, her lips pursing. "You're really going to marry her?"

"Yes. Is that a problem for you, Angelina?"

Her eyes flare in indignation. "Yes, it's a problem. I won't take orders from her. If that's what you expect, then I think it's best I give you my notice."

She's watching me like she thinks I will protest. This was never just a job to her. She could have done plenty of other things with her time within IVI, but she volunteered her services here. I paid her well, and I never indicated that this was anything other than a professional relationship, and yet it's clear she never gave up on the idea. She's still not ready to give up, judging by the challenge in her eyes.

"Angelina, I've appreciated your time here," I reply with a guarded tone. "But if you can't respect my wife, then I agree it's best you leave. I'll issue a severance payment to your account by the end of the week."

She shakes her head in disbelief, her vitriol spilling freely as she heads for the door. "Very well. I wish you the best of luck in your marriage, Alessio. But I suggest you watch your back. That knife on the nightstand was hidden under your bed beneath a pair of socks. I'm sure I don't have to tell you how it probably got there."

I turn to look at the nightstand, and something twists in my gut. Angelina doesn't linger waiting for a response. She leaves me standing there, staring at the proof of betrayal. I walk over to examine it, but there's no need. I know exactly who's knife that is. The only question I have is how the fuck did it get here.

I toss back my drink, leaving the damning evidence sitting there while I head back downstairs. I had planned to get some sleep tonight. Now, I won't rest until I see the fucking truth for myself.

27

ALESSIO

It's well past five in the morning when I drag my bloodshot eyes away from the screen in frustration. I've been searching the restored footage for hours, but I haven't seen a goddamned thing so far. My gaze drifts to the wall, and I sit there, silently contemplating when this must have happened.

At first, I wanted to believe it was tied to the incident with Gwen. It would make sense if Natalia grabbed her knife before she took Nino upstairs to my room, but it still doesn't explain how the knife ended up behind the bed. The explanation for that is far more disturbing, though I've already begun to piece it together. Natalia didn't mince words when she told me she came here to destroy me and my kingdom. She was willing to do whatever it took to get her son back.

Then it hits me. The night she was in my bedroom when I came home, bloodied and wounded. At the time, it had seemed to come out of left field. There had been an attraction between us, I thought, but I never expected to find her waiting in my room. I never expected her to offer herself to me after so little provocation on my part. A sickening feeling washes over me as I realize why.

She didn't want me. She came to my room that night to kill me.

I'm numb, too dazed by the clarity of my thoughts to move. I count back the dates, recalling the contract I made for that night. It's not difficult to remember since it turned out to be such a clusterfuck. Then, I recall the folder I had restored. Neither Manuel nor I had a chance to search the footage. I had intended to but never got around to it.

Mechanically, I turn my focus back to the screen and click through the folders until I find what I'm looking for. I check the time-stamps of each thumbnail, and when I find the image of me returning to the house that night, I go back a little further. I pull up her bedroom, and I watch with growing resentment and hostility as she selects the black silk nightgown to distract me. She packs her bags and creeps down the corridor, out of sight once she hits the third landing. There is no surveillance on that level, so I can't see what she did next. I can, however, see how many hours she waited for me. I can see that the next morning, during breakfast, she tried to go back. Over the next week, she repeated the process, meeting what could have only been my locked door.

She tried to retrieve the knife before she was discovered. I don't know why this lie feels like the worst, but I want to know what her plans were. Had she decided to stab me while I was inside of her? Had she only failed because it fell beneath the bed?

My eyes burn as I watch the clip on repeat, studying the method-ical way she moves. The absence of emotion on her face. In many ways, it feels like I'm looking at myself, and I don't like what I see. Pain radiates down the center of my chest, and I curse at the image on the screen. I curse at her for making me a goddamned fool.

I slam the computer shut and throw my glass at the wall, shat-tering it to pieces. As I rise from the chair, I consider what I've sacri-ficed for her. I consider what she's cost me, and then I consider changing my mind. It's not too late to tell the Tribunal to find her another husband. She could be someone else's problem.

Only, the thought of it boils my fucking blood. Fucking witch of a woman. She has her talons in me, and I can't let her go. I can't give her to someone else. I'll never let anyone else touch her, but there's one thing I know for certain after tonight.

I'll never make the mistake of trusting her again.

THE PILOT'S voice comes over the speakers, welcoming us to New York. I unbuckle my belt and rise from my seat while Natalia does the same beside me. I can feel her gaze on me, but I refuse to look at her. Not right now.

We've spoken no more than three words this morning. I asked her if she was ready, and she replied with a nod. She could tell that I had shut down, and she didn't try to make conversation during the flight. I kept to my papers, and she stared out the window, silent.

Now, Luca is here to deliver us to the Catholic church where the ceremonies in New York are performed for IVI. That ride is also silent. Natalia seems to be growing more concerned by the second, and I can't even bring myself to look her in the eyes. I don't know what I'll find there, but I know I'm tired of the lies.

Logically, I'm aware that her circumstances made her desperate. I've asked myself again and again what I would have done had I been in her position. She doesn't have the same options as me. She doesn't have an army of guards at her disposal or a powerful network behind her, but that doesn't change the fact that she didn't trust me enough to talk to me about it. Instead, she would have rather bled me dry while I was inside of her.

The wound that reality leaves behind is still too fresh, and I'm too raw to be kind to her right now, even if that's what she needs. She's terrified, I'm sure, but so am I. Last night I gave her my assurances, and now I'm wondering how this sham of a marriage will ever fucking work. What's going to become of us? Will she spend her days outside of the house, distracting herself from the realities of our life like my mother did while I drink myself into oblivion? When the temptations of a warm body become too much, but we can no longer stand to look at each other, then what? If she ever seeks comfort from another man, I'll give him a bloody and violent end. She has to know that this is her life now. She can't have me, but I won't let her have anyone else either.

When Luca delivers us to the church, my tie feels like it's choking me, and I exit the car without preamble.

"Take her to get ready," I tell him.

I don't look back at her. I can't. I head inside to the space reserved for the groom, grabbing the first bottle of whiskey they stocked for me. There isn't a need to bother with a glass. I bring it straight to my lips and chug, savoring the burn in my throat and the warmth in my stomach.

I collapse onto a chair, staring at nothing as I wait for the alcohol to numb me. It takes a few minutes before I feel anything, and it's still not enough. She's twisting me inside out, wreaking havoc on my nerves. I'm tempted to obliterate myself completely, but even after everything, I can't do that to her.

"Sir?" Luca pokes his head through the door, his eyes drifting to the bottle of whiskey in my hands. "We'll begin in thirty minutes. Would you like me to wait here with you?"

"That's fine," I tell him.

He enters, hands me a note from his pocket, and takes a seat in the chair opposite me. "Miss Cabrera asked me to give that to you."

I swallow, wondering if she's changed her mind. Perhaps she's decided death is a better alternative than marrying me after all. I unfold it reluctantly, reading the words written in the handwriting I've come to know well.

Alessio,

I've been waiting to tell you this, but it never felt like the right time. It's important that you know before we marry that I am truly sorry for any pain I have caused you. I'm sorry about the lies I told you, and most of all, I'm sorry about what happened with Gwen. I can't go back and change it, and I can't take away your grief. But I hope that one day, we can move on from it together.

When you made your proposal, you told me that this situation wasn't ideal. But that wasn't true. I didn't say yes to save myself. I said yes because this is what I want. And I hope someday you will feel the same way too.

Thank you for being the man who saves me, even at my worst.

Natalia

I RELAX BACK into the seat, staring at the letter. Quietly, I try to pick apart every nuance of the words. The silence is overbearing, and I don't know why I even fucking ask, but I do.

"How is she?"

"She's nervous," Luca says reluctantly. "But she seems to be doing okay."

I nod. His response does nothing to settle me, but time passes regardless. And then, inevitably, it's up.

"Shall we?" Luca stands, gesturing for me.

I swallow, rise, and take one last look at myself in the mirror. My eyes are hollow from a lack of sleep, and I'm not acting like myself, but there's a strange new feeling settling over me as I prepare to meet my bride at the altar. I don't recognize this feeling. It's warm, soft, and all-consuming. There's a name for it, I think, but it can't be that.

It certainly can't be that.

28

NATALIA

Between Alessio and Abella, I've been given enough information to have a pretty solid understanding of how today is supposed to go. I've been told Society weddings are often elaborate affairs, but that won't be the case for ours. Alessio didn't want to have the wedding in Seattle because that would require him to invite all his associates and their wives. Here, in New York, it will just be the witnesses and us.

I'm okay with that because my nerves are already shot. Alessio's coldness toward me today isn't making this any easier. He's barely looked at me, and it's unsettling. I can't help feeling like I've trapped him into this situation, and I hate it. But most of all, I hate that he doesn't want it the way I do.

It's hard to breathe when a guard I don't recognize comes to retrieve me. He tells me it's time and escorts me out into the main church. When the doors open, the men in masks and cloaks turn to regard me. They are the witnesses from IVI. Alessio told me they'd be here as a requirement, and I wouldn't know who they are. It all feels a bit strange, but this is part of their marriage ritual, and I know it will only get more intense as the day goes on.

My eyes drift to the front, where Alessio is waiting for me. He towers over the priest in an all-black suit, overshadowing everyone else in the room. He's the perfect mixture of dark looks and handsome features. A villain and a reluctant hero. When his gaze settles on me, it pulls me forward like a magnet.

Music plays as I walk down the aisle, but I'm not sure I hear any of it. My head feels like it's underwater. I'm dizzy and nervous over the doubt I might find in Alessio's eyes when I reach him.

It seems to take forever. My body feels like it's weighted down with bricks, and it's hard to move. When I first put on the dress, it felt beautiful, but it's claustrophobic right now. Somehow, by some miracle, I make it to the man I'm going to marry. His eyes heat and then flare as they move over me with a slow-burning appreciation, and I feel like I can finally breathe again. This is the reaction I needed from him. I don't think I could have gone through with this if he wasn't as vulnerable as I am now.

He releases a breath too, and his shoulders relax as I offer him a small, nervous smile. The warmth has returned to his eyes, and it might be as temporary as the sun peeking through the storm clouds, but for now, I will take it.

The music draws to an end, and the priest welcomes us, beginning the ceremony with scripture. I catch only a few words because I can't seem to tear my gaze from Alessio. He doesn't look away either. It might be the longest we've ever gazed into each other's eyes, and it feels intimate. It feels ... sweet.

When the priest asks us to join hands, we do so willingly. His are warm and strong and firm around mine, and I take shelter in his touch. Even in the face of uncertainty over our future and what it may hold, I am comforted by the love I have for this man. It burns so deeply, I want to blurt the words out this very second, but there isn't time.

The priest begins the vow ceremony, and we are asked to declare our intent. Alessio recites his vows first. His gaze intensifies as he declares to forsake all others, remain faithful in good times and bad, in sickness and health, until death do us part. It feels so real. It feels like at this moment he means every word. I know I mean them when I sign and mouth the words back to him.

Luca delivers the rings, and the priest proceeds with the ceremony, blessing us before he asks us to exchange bands. Alessio's ring is a simple titanium band, and mine is a white gold halo diamond I chose from the selection his jeweler showed me. A surge of possession takes over me as I slip his onto his finger, and I am proud to wear the ring he carefully secures on mine. He holds my hand in his for a moment longer than necessary, his thumb brushing over the band. This moment is significant and not just for me. I can see it in his eyes. He's equally tormented and terrified by the impact of the journey we're embarking on together.

The priest directs us to kiss, and we both lean in, our lips soft against each other. It's not like the kisses he steals in the night. It's gentle yet possessive. He doesn't pull away, and neither do I. We seem to have forgotten that we have an audience, and I think he'd be content to stand here all afternoon, drinking me in like he owns me. I'd be content with it too, but the priest clears his throat before declaring that it's time to greet the witnesses.

I'm breathless when Alessio breaks away, staring at me like I've cursed him. I've seen that look before, and I know it usually precedes him pulling away. He's afraid of whatever he's feeling, and his reaction is to shut down. It's what he always does, but right now, I need him to be present.

I squeeze his hand in mine, silently pleading with him before the men in cloaks come to greet us. To my relief, he doesn't release me from his grip. The process is formal and efficient, each of them coming to offer their well wishes before stepping aside. I offer them a nervous acknowledgment and nothing else, aware that these same men will be there to witness what comes next. The one ritual Alessio was hesitant to inform me of.

After our last nuptial blessing from the priest, we are dismissed, and Luca whisks us away in the car to a high-rise building in Manhattan. There is no signage on the doors, and just inside, there are enough guards to take down a small army should the need arise. When they see Alessio, they bow their heads respectfully.

"Dominus et Deus, Mr. Scarcello."

I glance at him, but he doesn't say anything as he leads me to the elevator. Inside, we are both quiet, our hands still clutched as the carriage takes us to the top of the building. Alessio guides me out into the hall and then up a staircase that opens onto the rooftop.

The space looks like something out of a fairytale. There are cobblestone pavers weaving through lush foliage and ornate bubbling fountains. Gas lamps cast a soft glow over the pathways that open up to private seating areas. At the center of it all is a marble pavilion with a stone fire pit burning inside. That's where most of the cloaked men are gathered, waiting for us.

My eyes move to the solitary chair and table in front of the pavilion. Everything has already been set up for the ritual. Not only does every Society member have an inked inscription of IVI on their skin, but the wives are marked in an additional way. It's designed to be a testament of loyalty to your husband. And tonight, I will have my choice of a brand or a tattoo of Alessio's family crest on the nape of my neck just below the IVI lettering.

At first, I will admit I was reluctant to agree to such a ceremony. For years, I've bore the permanent marks of another man's hate. I've despised them. Revolted at them when I looked in the mirror. But when I talked it over with Abella, she helped me see the ritual from a different perspective. It's not just a brand. It's a permanent mark of our love. The more I considered the idea, the more I liked it. Alessio's mark on me won't be the same as the man who tried to kill me. His will be designed to show the world I belong to him and him alone. It's possessive, hot, and maybe a little demented, but I've decided I'm okay with that. I delivered my decision to him freely, without pressure or coercion.

Looking up at him now, I can tell this means something to him too. Before, his explanation of the process seemed like a formality, but as he helps me to kneel on the pavers in front of the chair, it's impossible to miss the fire in his eyes. He likes the thought of his ownership printed on my skin.

He moves around me, kicking away the chains attached to the anchors on the pavers. There are restraints at the end of those chains, and I know they are meant for show. It's a disappointment to the crowd he's chosen not to use them, and they make it known.

"Come on, Scarcello. Cuff her up. Show her how it's done."

There are cheers from the back, but Alessio freezes, his eyes darker than I've ever seen them as he stares back at the men.

"I invite whoever felt the need to speak so freely to come forward and say it to my face. Nothing would please me more than to remind you I am a Sovereign Son, and you are woefully out of turn."

Stillness meets his request, and the men all seem to regard him with lowered heads. I can't make out their eyes beneath the masks, but I suspect they have been effectively put into their places.

"Very well." Alessio comes around me, his fingers settling on my neck possessively. "Let the coward stay silent and leave me to handle my wife how I see fit."

His wife.

I should be bothered by what's happening between them, but right now, those words are the only thing I can seem to focus on. I really am his wife, and he's mine. Mine. I like the word way too much. That word comes with baggage, so many possibilities for heartache, but it also comes with hope. A hope that he will always protect me the way he's protecting me now.

He draws the chair closer behind me, taking his seat. His legs offer me shelter, and I focus on his warmth pressing against my sides as he starts to sanitize my skin. I'm wearing the choker Abella gifted me, and Alessio is careful to select the area beneath it, so he doesn't have to remove it.

"Relax." He leans forward, his lips brushing against my ear. "I'll be gentle."

I nod and dip my head forward, giving him adequate room to

work. He presses the template against my skin, carefully peeling away the film before he turns on the gun. I've already seen the design, so I know his family crest is a shield bearing the Scarcello name. Behind the shield, dueling swords are exposed, while Laurel branches along the sides complete the finer details. It's beautiful and simple.

The vibrations of the gun seem to echo around me as he draws closer, and the needle contacts my skin. It stings, as I expected, but not unbearably so. I've been through worse, and I realize at this moment that I trust Alessio. His hand is steady and efficient, and I don't think the entire process takes more than fifteen minutes. It's over before I expect it to be, and then his voice reverberates through the crowd.

"It is done."

Some men come to look at his work, but the rest remain at a distance, much to my relief. He doesn't let them get too close, and I suspect he's glaring at the ones who try, judging by the way they move back.

He applies the salve and then bandages it before helping me up. I'm lightheaded from the process, swaying slightly as I rise to my feet. Alessio stabilizes me with his palm on the bare skin of my back.

"Alright?" he asks.

I nod, leaning into the support he offers. He stares out into the crowd, his face devoid of any emotion.

"Let's go."

LUCA DELIVERS us to Alessio's apartment in Tribeca. I've only ever seen it from the outside, something I've yet to tell Alessio, so I'm not sure what to expect within. It's a high-rise, with more guards from IVI waiting just inside. They greet Alessio with bowed heads, and I can see Abella wasn't exaggerating when she said Sovereign Sons are like royalty.

Alessio seems slightly uncomfortable with the formality of it all, and now I understand his amusement whenever I held my ground with him. He's used to being treated this way. Most women probably wouldn't dare speak out of turn in his presence. If there is one thing I've learned during my time with him, it's that Alessio is not a man who wants a woman that doesn't speak her mind. In fact, I think when I don't, it drives him nuts.

The private elevator delivers us directly to his apartment, and I follow him inside, watching as he removes his jacket and loosens his tie. This is the version of him I like best. The man the world doesn't get to see.

My eyes drift over the space, taking in the floor-to-ceiling windows and the beautiful view of the skyline. It's bright, airy, and comfortable. I'm already tempted to sink into the soft gray sofa, but more importantly, what I really want to do is help Alessio out of his clothes. I've missed his touch desperately, but I haven't tried to push him for more. Even though he's married me, I'm aware he's been grieving the loss of Gwen. I wanted to respect that by giving him time and space, but I'd be lying if I said I didn't have hopes we could lose ourselves in each other tonight.

"There are two rooms down the left of the hall." He doesn't look at me when he speaks, but his voice is notably distant again. "Take your pick. Make yourself comfortable."

With that, he leaves, disappearing into the hall and turning to the right. He doesn't hesitate or glance back. The lines have been drawn, and he has retreated into his armor again.

I clutch at my dress, tempted to rip it off as I stagger over to the sofa, trying to hold back my emotions. It hurts to breathe when I sit down, and yet I can't help feeling stupid for it. What did I expect, really? That we'd come here, and he would forget all the walls he's built around himself? But how could I have known? Alessio runs hot and cold at every turn. There is no consistency. Last night, he kissed me like he could drown in me, and today, he couldn't hide his feelings when we said our vows. Now, he's returned to the familiarity of his routine, determined to shut me out.

I stand up and stare out at the skyline, reaching around to unzip my dress. For a second, I feel foolish for agonizing over the lingerie I'm wearing beneath it. I thought he would see it, and it would make him want me.

I remove the straps from my shoulders and shimmy out of the fabric, letting it pool on the floor beneath me. The woman in the reflection of the glass is wearing a white bustier, a matching garter, and thigh-high stockings. I barely recognize her, and I know it's because I'm not ashamed of my skin for the first time in as long as I can remember. We won't get this day back, and I'm not willing to let it slip away because we're both too scared to admit the truth. If Alessio wants to push me away, he needs to look me in the eye when he does it. He needs to tell me how he really feels.

I move toward the hall, heading in the direction he went. It isn't difficult to find his suite. The bedroom door is cracked, and when I peer through it, I'm surprised to see him sitting on the bed. His elbows are on his knees, head bowed as he turns over a velvet box in his fingers. He looks tormented by his thoughts, and I hate it. I hate that he can't let me in.

I press my fingers to the door, opening it softly. He looks up, his nostrils flaring as he burns a path over my body. I approach him the way one might approach a wounded animal. I don't want to scare him away, and I know it doesn't matter how much he wants me. I understand that now. It's not a matter of want. It's a matter of what he'll allow himself to have.

I stop in front of him, slowly reaching out to stroke his face. He closes his eyes, falling into stillness as I remove the box from his hands and set it aside. I climb onto his lap, settling against him as my lips hover over his.

"It's our wedding day." I force the words out. "We only get one."

His jaw clenches, and he shakes his head. "You don't have to pretend anymore. We're married. It's done."

I grab his face with both my palms, forcing him to look at me. "I'm not pretending."

My lips fall into his, and he digs his fingers into the flesh of my hips. There's a long moment of uncertainty as I kiss him, and he doesn't return it. He's so rigid I have no idea if he's going to take me or toss me away. Inevitably, he loses himself to the moment, coming unraveled little by little. His tongue sweeps across the seam of my lips, and then he invades my mouth. Our teeth gnash against each other, and he yanks me down over his erection, grinding my body into his. We tear at each other's clothes, and I manage to get his shirt unbuttoned and his trousers unzipped, but he's still struggling with the clasps on my bustier.

"How do you get this fucking thing off?" he grunts in frustration.

I pause to reach back and undo it, and when it falls loose, he tosses it aside and kneads my aching breasts in his palms. I reach down between us to stroke his cock, but he stops, lifts me, and splays me out on the bed. He yanks down his trousers and then moves his attention to the triangle of white lace between my thighs, glaring at the obstacle between us. He slides his fingers beneath the strings, dragging my panties down over the garter. My stockings and heels are all that's left, but he doesn't bother with those when he lowers his body over mine.

Foreplay isn't on the table. I'm already soaked for him, and he's desperately hard for me. We've gone without for far too long, and it's painfully obvious when he nudges his cock against me and sinks inside with little resistance.

I arch into him, already on the knife's edge of losing it. The tension from the day dissolves as he dips his mouth to my nipple, teasing me with his tongue before he sucks me in completely. He rolls his hips and thrusts as I cling to him, fingers dragging over his muscular ass, silently pleading for more.

I ache with every touch, every lick, every deep thrust. I'm in awe of the way his muscles strain. The vein in his neck throbs in time with my heart hammering against my chest. His fingers tangle in my hair, and we're both lingering on the precipice when he growls into my skin.

"Fucking show me, Natalia. Come if you want it."

I don't know what he means by that, and I can't make sense of it right now. I'm already there. My breath hisses between my teeth as my head falls back, and my body starts to spasm as wave after wave of pleasure rolls over me. It feels so good I'm milking out every last second, and then Alessio tips his head back, growling as his cock begins to pulse.

He doesn't pull out. He doesn't even try. He comes hard, emptying his seed inside of me. Instinctively, my fingers dig into his back, terrified that he'll think it was a mistake. I'm convinced of it, but it doesn't happen the way I think.

When he opens his eyes, they are still dark and hungry. He's not even remotely close to satiated, and neither am I. I want it to go on forever, and I'm relieved when he returns his lips to mine and settles his body against me. He's still inside of me, and he's still hard. Within seconds, we're pawing at each other, and then he's thrusting into me all over again. His fingers move between us, teasing my clit, and pressure builds in me as I squeeze around him. He fucks me for what feels like hours, drawing out every second. We taste each other. We touch each other. I stare into his eyes, and he stares back into mine. It's intimate. It's powerful. It's fucking terrifying.

We both come a second time, and again, he doesn't pull out. I'm overwhelmed by my emotions, desperate to let them spill from my lips when he rolls beside me, and we gaze at each other. I take his hand in mine, reverently touching the band on his finger. He watches me, his eyes guarded but warm. I don't think there will ever be a better time, so bravely, I use my hands to sign to him.

"What does that mean?" he asks.

I reach up and touch my neck as I speak, pushing past the pain. "It means I love you."

He goes rigid beside me, and I become aware that I've made a grave mistake. It seems to happen in slow motion as he sits up, turns away, and shuts down completely. He's silent, his muscles tensing more with every passing second, and all I can do is watch.

"Don't," he says finally. "Save yourself the heartache, Natalia. It's a mistake to think this means anything more than what it is."

"You're my husband," I whisper. "I saw it in your eyes when you said your vows. Why can't you admit it?"

"You saw what you wanted to see." He stands up and gathers his pants. "All I saw was a noose around my neck. I never fucking wanted any of this."

His words cut me to the bone. I'm shaking, barely holding it together, when he reaches down and grabs the velvet box he had in his hands earlier. He opens it, revealing the knife I brought to his bedroom to kill him. He tosses it onto the bed, and his eyes cut over me with a coldness so stark it physically hurts.

"What just happened between us? That was the last time. You may be my wife, but I don't want you in my fucking bed. So, the next time you think about coming to me, don't."

29

NATALIA

HELLO, DARLING. I KNEEL IN FRONT OF NINO TO UNZIP HIS COAT. *Did you have fun?*

"Yes." He bobs his head, his cheeks red from the cold outside. "Daddy let me get a hot chocolate after dinner."

My eyes crinkle at the chocolate evidence left behind on his face. *I can see that.*

I dare a glance up at Alessio. He's stiff, waiting for me to finish with Nino so they can get on with their night. Every other day we take turns spending time with Nino, shuttling him to activities, eating dinner together, and putting him to bed. We have a schedule that works to Alessio's benefit because it means we rarely see each other, except for the breakfast table, where we no longer talk. So far, Nino hasn't seemed to be affected by the tension between us, but I suspect it's only a matter of time.

My heart thumps pathetically as I wait for Alessio to return my gaze, but he doesn't. He checks his watch and then retrieves his phone from his pocket, using it as a distraction.

I return my attention to Nino, giving him a watery smile. *It's time to let you get back to your night with daddy.*

He presses his cold fingers to my face like he's trying to comfort me. "You can come too, Mommy."

I nearly cry every time he calls me that. It's a recent development, one that evolved naturally. Shortly after our return from New York, Alessio left the results of the DNA test in my room along with a handwritten note to tell Nino whenever I thought it was best. I didn't wait long to have the conversation with him, but I made a point to say that I didn't want him to feel pressured to call me anything he wasn't comfortable with. At first, I think there was some confusion on his part, and there are still some details we'll have to discuss when he's older. But eventually, he accepted the concept on his own and shyly began to call me Mommy instead of Natalia. Even though the rest of my life was in chaos, it meant everything to hear those words from him.

I wish I could stay with you. I sign to him. *But tonight is daddy's night, and I have to go Christmas shopping.*

His eyes move between us, and he seems to be considering something for a moment. I'm sure he knows something isn't right. He's already asked me why Mommy and Daddy don't sleep in the same room like the parents on TV do. He's made some other innocent observations too, and quite frankly, I'm tired of giving him excuses. He deserves more than that. I don't know how to be a good example to him when Alessio and I are both miserable. This isn't the life I wanted. My husband is so cold, I get a chill every time he walks into the room. Every day, my heart breaks a little more. It's too painful to keep up this charade.

Nino tugs on my sleeve and then signs to me. *Can you buy daddy the present I told you about? The alien socks.*

Of course, my love. I nod. *I will take care of it.*

"Okay." He flashes a dimple. "Then I'll see you later."

In the morning, I tell him. *I won't be back before you're in bed. So, sleep well.*

"I will," he says.

I ruffle his hair and pull him in for a hug before releasing him. *I love you so, so much. You know that, right?*

I love you too, Mommy.

We say goodbye, and I don't bother to glance at Alessio again, but I can feel his gaze on me as I walk out the door. Manuel is already waiting outside with the car, ready to deliver me to the shopping center.

The drive is quiet, and I use the time to check my emails. A few weeks after Alessio and I returned from New York, I managed to land a part-time job working as a coordinator for some of the children's services within IVI. I've spent my first three weeks in the new position getting my bearings, but so far, I love it. I have to admit I'm impressed by the range of mental health, education, and after-school programs on offer. The Society is ahead of the curve from what I can tell, but I already have some ideas I'm hoping to implement in the future. I'm working on more interactive programs for children like mindfulness and yoga. It keeps me busy when I'm not with Nino, and occupying my mind is the only thing saving me right now.

We arrive at the shopping center, and Manuel escorts me inside to meet Abella. She greets me with a hug and a kiss on each cheek and then steps back to look at me.

You look like you could use a drink, she signs.

I laugh silently, shaking my head. I actually could use a drink, but I haven't told her yet that I won't be having one anytime soon. I haven't even told Alessio about the pregnancy test I took two weeks ago, but eventually, I'll have to. Right now, I just can't think about that conversation.

I could use a meal. I reply. *I'm starving.*

"Me too." She reaches for my arm, looping it through hers. "Come on, then. Let's get you fed."

We end up at the martini bar and cafe that's become one of our regular haunts. Abella and I get our own table while Manuel and her guard watch from a few tables back. It's still awkward, but she was right that I'd get used to it. Manuel has always been professional, and I feel safe in his presence, but he informed me that I'd have a new guard starting this weekend. Apparently, it's customary for every member to have their own guard in families of Sovereign Sons. When I asked if it was because they were a target, Manuel skirted around the subject, but it was obvious that was the reason. It makes me nervous, but I'm grateful that Manuel looks out for Nino, and I'll have someone to look out for me too. I know Alessio can take care of himself, and that brings me some relief.

The waitress comes to take our drink order, and Abella orders herself a martini and a burger. I order a Sprite and fries with cheese dip.

"That's an interesting combination." She wrinkles her nose. "Why aren't you having a—"

She stops midsentence as something seems to occur to her. Before I can say anything, her eyes drift to my stomach, widening, and she switches to ASL.

No way. Are you pregnant already?

I bite my lip, holding back tears as I nod. There's no point trying to hide it from her. She'll know anyway, and I trust that she won't let my secret slip. If anything, her excitement is a welcome reprieve from the turmoil in my mind. I'm happy about this baby, but I don't know if Alessio will be.

How long? She asks.

It has to be from the wedding night. That's the only time it could have happened.

Her face falls, and she reaches her hand across the table briefly to squeeze mine. *Things are still not good?*

No. I reach for my napkin, folding over the edges to give my fingers something to do. *I don't know how much longer I can take it. He's miserable. I'm miserable. But mostly, I'm just heartbroken. I don't even know why he married me. Who wants to live this way?*

Abella considers the question for a few moments. *Do you think it has something to do with his family?*

Yes, I admit. *But I don't know for sure because he doesn't talk to me about it. He's never said anything.*

I don't know him that well, Abella says. *But we grew up in the same circles. I know he's never had a girlfriend before you. It seems like he was avoiding any kind of intimate relationship.*

I stare at her in confusion. *He's never had a girlfriend before me? I thought you said there were a bunch of women trying to land him.*

Yes, trying. She emphasizes the word with her hands. *But he never dated any of them. Even in high school, as far as I'm aware. It's weird. I think what his father did to his mother really screwed with his head.*

I lean back against my seat, grateful for the interruption when the waitress delivers our drinks. It gives me a moment to contemplate what Abella just said. It makes sense that Alessio is having difficulty navigating his emotions with me if I'm the first woman in his life. The first real relationship he's had. He's my first intimate relationship, too, other than a few innocent dates I had in college before Enzo happened. It doesn't change anything though, does it? At the end of the day, I'm the one willing to make an effort, and he isn't. We can't work through his issues if he's not willing to let me in.

Look, I'm no expert. Abella leans forward as the waitress leaves. *But I think you should try again. I know he's been a total dick, but men have the emotional maturity of children sometimes. Maybe he just doesn't know how to fix things.*

I shake my head, my temples throbbing at the idea of putting myself out there again. He hurt me, and I know I hurt him, but he hasn't forgiven me, and I don't think I can stand one more of his rejections.

If he wants to fix it, then he needs to say so. If he doesn't, then I guess we'll both need to figure out a way to move on.

I get it, Abella says. *But if you love him, and you want to make this work, what do you have to lose at this point? If he hurts you again, then wash your hands of it. But I think you two could have something special, and real love is rare. So, if that's what you think this is, grab onto it with both hands and don't let go.*

I offer her a sad smile, agreeing that she has a point. I need time and space to think about it, and one thing I've noticed about Abella is that she's good at talking about everyone else's problems except for her own.

You never told me when you're getting married, I say.

She downs the rest of her martini in one long gulp and sets the glass onto the table, her eyes taking on a cloudy hue. "As long as I can avoid it."

I want to ask her more, but our dinner arrives, and she changes the subject. We eat and laugh and talk for an hour before we finally get around to our Christmas shopping. If there's one thing I can be grateful for in all of this, it's that Alessio has given me a true friend in her.

30

ALESSIO

"Mr. Scarcello, you wanted me to check in when I arrived?"

I glance up from my computer to the man standing in my office doorway. "Yes. Have a seat, Damien."

He does as I request, and I size him up for what feels like the hundredth time. I've spent the last six weeks interviewing guards and trying to find a solid match for my requirements. Not only do I need a candidate who speaks fluent ASL, but I need them to be someone I trust wholeheartedly with Natalia's safety. It's important they understand I will fucking slaughter them if they even look at her wrong. As it turns out, it's a tall order. I managed to find a guard from Germany who's willing to relocate, but he can't be here for another month. However, between Natalia and Nino's schedules, Manuel isn't able to be with them both at all times, and I need a temporary solution, which is where Damien comes in. IVI sent him over as a courtesy until the new guard arrives, and I've spent the last week giving him the rundown repeatedly. He needs to know this job comes with a zero fuck-up policy.

"My wife's safety is a priority," I tell him. "I'll need bi-hourly updates."

"Yes, sir." He smirks. "You've told me. Several times."

"I'm aware." I narrow my eyes at him. "But I'll reiterate as many times as I deem necessary."

"Of course, Mr. Scarcello. I understand."

"Today will be busy." I check my watch. It's the day before Christmas Eve, and I'm waiting on word from Angelo regarding the emergency court hearing I requested. "I'll need you to remain with Natalia at work this morning and then keep watch over the house this afternoon. Manuel needs to leave by noon today to catch his flight back home. He'll return on Tuesday, after the holiday, and we'll resume our normal schedule."

"It won't be a problem," Damien assures me.

He looks far too self-assured for my liking. I suspect he thinks his skills are superior to the demands of this position. It rubs me the wrong way, but right now, short of duplicating myself, there aren't many options at my disposal. With the upcoming holiday, I have to use the resources I have. I may not like this asshole, but he's vetted by IVI and has references from two other families. I'm also aware that I'll never be completely comfortable hiring anyone with male anatomy to watch over her, but the IVI security team is a male-domi-nated industry. I'll have to get used to the idea eventually, and I only need him around for a month until her other guard arrives.

There isn't time to consider it further because a moment later, Angelo appears in the doorway. I'm eager to hear what he has to say. Since the discovery of Angelo's false conviction, he's been working closely with the Tribunal to ensure the responsible party will pay. He knows the Councilors better than I do on a personal level, and he requested an emergency hearing for today on my behalf. When he nods at me, it's a quiet indication that he was able to sway them. It's a welcome reprieve after the hell of the last few weeks.

I slam the computer shut and rise from my chair, my eyes cutting to Natalia's new guard. "You can wait for my wife in the parlor room, Damien. She'll be downstairs soon."

"No problem."

He leaves quietly, and Angelo arches a brow at me.

"When?" I ask.

"Now."

"Fucking finally," I mutter, grabbing my suit jacket from the back of the chair.

"You're welcome," Angelo grouses.

"Thank you." I walk around the desk to join him. "Now, let's go get this over with."

He follows me into the hall, and I feel like a thousand-pound weight has been lifted off my shoulders. I've been in negotiations with the Tribunal for weeks after they rejected my first proposal. They said I didn't have sufficient evidence against Enzo to warrant his death. It was bullshit. If he were a lower echelon member, he'd already be dead. Because he's a Sovereign Son, they want undisputable proof about the new accusations I've made against him.

I've spent weeks digging and following up on leads. Part of that meant excavating Natalia's background and linking Enzo to the murders of the people who tried to help her. I created timelines of his visits to New York and the subsequent wire transfers made to the cop who helped him. A cop that later died under mysterious circumstances.

Then there was the issue of Elizabeth, the woman he claimed was Nino's mother. I've been working with Mrs. Hudson, and she turned over Elizabeth's journals which detailed Enzo's threats and abuse. Her last entry was an admission that she believed he would kill her, and the next day, she was gone. Enzo covered his tracks well, which is why he managed to fool so many of us for so long, but I knew his defense wasn't bulletproof. He slipped up in his brother's murder by leaving his own blood at the scene. His actions have proven that he acts on impulse, and he's not a criminal mastermind. I was counting on that weakness to reveal a fatal flaw in at least one of his covers, but as it turned out, it wasn't Enzo who fucked up and left something behind. It was Gwen.

On her hard drives, she had saved years' worth of security footage from her house, including the day that Enzo assaulted Ricardo's wife. Manuel discovered it late one night while he was helping in the search. He handed it over to me and told me to watch it before excusing himself from the room. He couldn't stomach seeing it a second time, so I was prepared for the worst. I only managed to watch the footage exactly once, vomiting after I witnessed the things Enzo did to Ricardo's wife. The situation took a violent turn when Ricardo showed up in the middle of it and tried to stop Enzo. Ricardo managed to pull him off her briefly but was subsequently stabbed to death with the knife Enzo carried. With his brother's blood on his hands, he forced himself on Nicolette a second time before he killed her too.

The images have haunted me every night since. The thought I keep coming back to is that Gwen knew. She had to have known, because IVI searched for the footage but turned up nothing. She had hidden it, only returning it when Enzo was convicted, and there was no hope left. Why she would keep the video is beyond my comprehension, but I'm beginning to understand that Gwen was possibly just as sick in the head as Enzo is. She had always laid the blame for Ricardo's death with Nicolette, condemning her for seducing Enzo. She had spent her life protecting Enzo and cleaning up his mistakes at the expense of everyone else. When she tried to kill Natalia, I was so blinded by my loyalty to the Marcone family I couldn't see how deranged they were, but I see it now.

Enzo tried to portray himself as the victim in this situation. He reasoned away the DNA evidence left behind with the fact that Nicolette had come onto him, and he had a moment of weakness. He maintained that Ricardo killed her in a fit of rage and that Enzo had tried to stop him, but Ricardo had then turned on him. He said he had no choice but to kill his brother to save himself. The Tribunal never fully believed his version of events, and the evidence was contradictory. Without witnesses or footage, they could not determine that what had occurred warranted death. They'd sentenced him to life in prison instead. Now that they've received the actual footage, they can have no doubt to Enzo's brutality. If all goes as planned at this hearing, it means Enzo could be dead by this evening. Natalia can rest peacefully, and I can be content that I've made him pay for the crimes he committed against her and the others.

"Traffic's going to be a bitch right now," I tell Angelo as I check my watch again. "Perhaps you should let them know we could be delayed."

"Don't worry, they'll wait," he assures me.

We reach the front door, and the sound of heels approaching makes me pause. Angelo taps me on the shoulder to get my attention, and when I turn, Natalia is lingering at the bottom of the staircase.

She looks beautiful today, but then she looks beautiful every day. Her long, dark hair is loose and free, the way I like it best. Her lipstick is red, and her dress is too. It kills me every time I see her in that color. Or any other color, really. It doesn't matter what she wears. This hunger never goes away. The constant ache in my chest doesn't either. She's more than I deserve. More than anyone deserves.

Her eyes are soft as she looks up at me hesitantly. I think it's the first time I've even made direct eye contact with her since the night in New York. I've done my best to avoid her, but right now, my thoughts are all over the place, and I wasn't prepared for this. She holds out the phone in her hand, indicating that she has something to say.

I step away from Angelo and meet her in the middle of the foyer. From this close, I can smell her new perfume. It's something soft and sweet she picked up on a shopping trip with Abella. That scent has been haunting the halls of this house ever since, and it's driving me crazy.

I'm already on edge, and I try to justify that as the reason I feel so disconcerted in her presence. Truthfully, I'm half expecting this to be a goodbye note, even though I'm certain she knows she can't leave.

Instead, I'm greeted with something even more unnerving when she hits play.

Can I talk to you? It's important.

"I.." My voice fractures and I shake my head. "I can't right now."

She reaches out and touches my arm, her throat working as she forces herself to speak. "I'm your wife, Alessio."

"I know." I swallow painfully, repressing the truth I've wanted to tell her for far too long. "I just... I have to be somewhere."

She lowers her lashes, nodding without further protest. Why would she? I've done everything in my power to fuck this up for us. If she doesn't hate me yet, it's only a matter of time.

She turns to go, and I watch her walk away. It's the only time I can watch her. What I really want to do is drag her back and kiss her. I want to tell her I never meant to hurt her, but it would be a lie. I had to hurt her so I couldn't destroy her later. It was always inevitable that I would.

Angelo clears his throat, and I drag my gaze away, forcing myself out the door. Later. Everything else will have to wait until Enzo is dead. Until then, there can be no peace.

Outside, we get into his car, and he drives because I'm too amped up to focus. I need to prepare my thoughts for the Tribunal. It's been consuming my mind for so long I haven't been able to see anything else. Angelo has other plans, apparently.

"Why didn't you hear what she had to say?" he asks.

I glance over at him. "We had to leave."

"When you have a beautiful wife at home who wants to talk to you, who gives a fuck what's waiting for you. You should listen to what she has to say."

I laugh at the absurdity of his statement. "Ironic, coming from you. Would you listen to Abella if she asked you to talk?"

His grip on the wheel tightens, and so does his jaw. "It's not the same."

"No?"

"No." He glares at me. "What Abella did was unforgivable. In your case, I think it's safe to say it's the other way around. Natalia's loyalty to you is unwavering. All you have to do is look at her to see that."

"You don't know anything." I stare out the window.

"I know you've been moping around for weeks, acting like a fucking lunatic. You've convinced yourself you can't rest until you deal with Enzo, but it's just an excuse to avoid your real problem."

"And what problem would that be?" I grit out.

"I've known you forever, Alessio." He guides the car onto the interstate, checking the mirror as he accelerates. "This is what you always do. You push the people who care about you away. That's the real reason you went to live with the Marcone's instead of us when you lost your family. With them, you had nothing to lose. It's a pattern. A survival instinct. You think it will hurt less if you fail everyone from the beginning than if you fail them in the end, so you don't even try. You did it with Nino, and now you're doing it with her. It's not going to save you or anyone else. All you're doing is making everyone miserable, including yourself."

His words hit me like a goddamned bullet I didn't see coming. I can't deny their accuracy. It's exactly what I do, what I've always done, because deep down, I'm fucking terrified I'm going to hurt someone the way my father hurt me. It's crippled me in more ways than I can count, but Angelo is wrong about one thing. It's protected the people in my life too.

"I couldn't live with myself if I caused them that type of pain," I answer quietly. "You can't understand."

"It's because you've been through that type of pain that I know you'll never hurt them that way." Angelo dodges in and out of the morning traffic, his eyes focused on the road ahead. "What are you even afraid of? I know you'd never be unfaithful to her, so it isn't that."

"It's not about being unfaithful." I glance out at the passing scenery. "It's about making one wrong choice, one move that has the potential to be devastating. Do you think my father had any idea that night when he walked out of our house that his decision would cost him so much? He made a careless choice in a moment of weakness, and it changed everything. It fucking paralyzes me every time I think about it. I question everything I do, wondering if it's right. Just because it hasn't happened yet, doesn't mean it won't. There will come a day that I fuck it up. It's inevitable."

I can feel Angelo's gaze on my face as he quietly acknowledges that I just told him more than I've probably ever told anyone.

"It is inevitable," he agrees. "You will fuck it up."

I turn to him, meeting his gaze.

"Because you're human, Alessio. That's what we do. We fuck up. We hurt each other. I can guarantee you it's a species-wide problem. You've condemned yourself to a life of isolation, and for what? Your fears won't protect your family and distancing yourself won't protect you. There are no guarantees in life. You can't stop the clock or change their fate. But you can pull your head out of your ass and make the most of the time you've been given. You have a wife and son who care about you, and if you don't stop shutting them out, there will come a day when it will be too late. They won't forgive you for the time you've lost. When it's all said and done, you'll be remembered as the man who couldn't love them."

I close my eyes and lean my head against the seat. My chest hurts, and it feels like I'm fucking dying.

"You aren't dying," Angelo mutters. "That's what us other humans call an emotion. Get used to it."

"Did I say that out loud?" I groan.

"Yes, you did. Now do me a favor. Do us both a favor. Fix this shit."

"The Tribunal?"

"No." He snorts. "Your marriage."

"THANK you for taking the time to meet with me today." I stand before the Councilors, waiting for any indication that they will reconsider their position. This is the last attempt I will make to go through the proper channels. If they deny my request again, I will walk into the prison and kill Enzo there, consequences be damned.

"We've watched the footage you sent over," Guillory responds. "But I must say this is quite unfortunate timing. Why the urgency, Scarcello? Enzo is already locked up. Couldn't this wait until after the holiday?"

I hand the guard the transcripts of Enzo's voicemails. "This is why."

The guard delivers them to the dais, and the room falls into silence as the Councilors read through them.

"He's threatening your family." Guillory peers at me over the rim of his glasses. "The man is clearly unhinged, but what can he do locked away in prison?"

My jaw works as I force myself to keep a level head. "Does it matter if he's locked away? His access to the outside might be limited, but he has proven himself resourceful in the past. I'm imploring you to consider your response if it was your own family. Would you determine his threats to be harmless then?"

Guillory narrows his gaze at me. "Leave my family out of this. Your point has been made."

I cut my gaze to Angelo briefly, recalling the rest of our conversation in the car. He encourages me with a nod, and I continue, choosing the words from my heart rather than my head.

"I stand before you today as a Sovereign Son who wishes to avenge the deaths of Ricardo, Nicolette, Elizabeth, and anyone else's life Enzo's time on this earth has cut short. But I'm also standing before you as a man who..." My throat works as I stumble over the words. "A man who watched that footage with the knowledge that Enzo perpetrated those same acts against my wife. Not only did he violate her body, but he ripped an innocent child from her arms, depriving him of a mother for years. Enzo tortured my wife, slashed her throat, and tossed her into a river like garbage. I have no choice but to ask when will enough be enough? At what point will this Tribunal deem him unfit to live? Once his body count reaches double digits? The crimes he has committed are heinous, and he is undeserving of another second of your leniency. The only equitable punishment is a slaughter as vicious as he has doled out himself."

The three Councilors stare down at me, stone-faced, and I'm not certain whether I've managed to sway them. They turn to each other, speaking quietly amongst themselves before returning their focus to me.

"Merry Christmas, Scarcello. You've got your wish. At this time, the court finds the evidence you've brought forth sufficient to move forward with a penalty of death. Now, end him and be done with it."

31

NATALIA

AFTER AN EXTENDED MEETING, MY HALF-DAY AT WORK RAN later than I had anticipated. When I say goodbye to the group of Society women who have been assisting with my class development, I realize Nino needs to be picked up from school.

Damien, we have to go. I play him a message as I rush around the desk.

"Of course, Mrs. Scarcello." He opens the door for me and leads me out of the building, scanning the street as we walk to the car.

He's been with me all day, and I don't know if it's just that I need to get used to him, but it's strange having his eyes on me so frequently. Manuel has a way of watching you without making you overly aware you're being watched, and Damien definitely does not. If I'm completely honest, I feel a little uneasy when he looks at me. It's a problem I'll have to address with Alessio, but I can't imagine he'll be responsive to hearing it.

We'll need to go straight to Nino's school. I type out another note as Damien opens the back door for me.

"No problem."

He settles into the driver's seat and pulls out into the afternoon traffic. I check a few emails along the way and then notice I have a missed text.

Abella: *Sooooo?*

Me: *He wouldn't talk to me.*

The three dots appear immediately, and she sends me a string of crying emojis followed by another text.

Abella: *Give it time.*

I send her a hug emoji and rest the phone in my lap, rubbing my aching temples. I don't want to cry again. I'm not going to cry again. I've already had three spontaneous outbursts of emotion throughout the day. I want to blame it on the pregnancy hormones, but I know it isn't just that.

When I glance up, I catch Damien staring at me in the rearview mirror. It irritates me, and I'm tempted to tell him so. In the office, I could understand his attention, but this is beyond excessive.

I'm grateful when we pull up to the school so I can get out of the car, even if it's just for a few minutes. Damien seems to know how this situation works already as he follows me inside to retrieve Nino. He told me this morning that both Manuel and Alessio gave him detailed instructions. I can't imagine Alessio telling him anything other than grunting not to let me out of his sight, but those are thoughts better saved for another time.

Nino beams at me as soon as he sees me, and I greet him with a hug and a kiss on the cheek.

How was school, darling?

"It was okay," he says. "But I'm ready to go."

Me too, I laugh.

We walk out to the car, and Damien drives us to Nino's piano lessons as planned. He eats his afternoon snack along the way and then asks me what we're doing on Christmas day.

I smile at him, brushing his hair aside. *I don't know yet, but let me talk to dad about it, okay?*

He nods, and we arrive too quickly. It's tempting to skip today altogether, but Nino enjoys visiting with Mrs. Hudson. Abella was the one to inform me that their daughter was who everyone thought was Nino's mother. She disappeared, and then months later, Enzo came back with Nino. He told the other Society members she didn't want the baby, and she was too ashamed to return. I have a sick feeling Elizabeth met a terrible fate with Enzo before he ever realized I'd had a baby.

I took it upon myself to have a heart-to-heart with Mrs. Hudson after I wed Alessio, and she told me she always knew Nino wasn't really her grandson. She wanted to continue their visits regardless, and I saw no reason to deprive her of that request when it's something Nino enjoys too.

When we arrive, I walk him to the door with Damien, and Nino glances up at me.

"See you after?" he asks.

I nod, ruffling his hair. I tried to go in with him a few times, but he was too nervous to play with me watching him, and he promised he would tell me when he was ready. We made a deal that it would be on his terms, so for now, I use the time to catch up on emails or read in the car.

Damien opens the door for me when I return, and I remove my phone from my pocket as I sit down. I'm reaching for my seatbelt when I catch a movement from my periphery. It's too late for me to react when Damien punches me in the side of the head, blindsiding me. My body slumps against the seat, and I'm barely clinging to consciousness as he grabs my phone and pockets it.

"You and I are going to have a little fun, Mrs. Scarcello."

His words are garbled like I'm underwater, and my head throbs furiously as he shuts me inside and starts the engine. It takes me a few minutes to come back to my senses, fighting off the subsequent nausea as the adrenaline response takes over me. I flutter my eyes open, and the afternoon light makes them water. It burns, but I fight off the instinct to close them as I peek up at the back of his head. Damien doesn't think I'm a threat right now, and I have to use this time to think. But my thoughts are distorted, and everything is blurry. It feels like a dream because none of it makes sense.

Why would he do this?

Then it hits me. It's a dark thought, but one I have to acknowledge. Alessio hired him to watch me, and this is only his first day. Is this why? Did he ask him to do this to me? Did he hire him to do the thing he couldn't?

Ice numbs my heart, and I swallow the pain that feels unbearable, forcing it down. There isn't time to focus on that now. I have to think about survival. I have to find a way to get back to Nino like I promised.

I turn my gaze toward the window, studying the familiar foliage of the Hudson's long driveway before Damien merges onto the street. He starts to turn in his seat, and I close my eyes, hoping he can't tell that I'm awake. I remain in the same position for a good three minutes as he drives, and then slowly, as quietly as I can, I use my hand to search for my bag. When I find it, I dip into the largest pocket where I've kept my butterfly knife since Alessio returned it to me.

For years, I've carried this knife as protection. I familiarized myself with it. I practiced with it. I trained in self-defense, maintaining a physical routine that made every strategic move feel like second nature. I've never actually used it on anyone before today, but there isn't a doubt in my mind that I will. Damien doesn't know me. If he did, he would have never left me unsecured in the back the way that he has. He underestimated me, and that mistake will cost him his life, so help me, God.

From my position on the seat, I watch the passing scenery through the top of the window, but I can't see anything more than clouds now. I relax my breathing, trying to think this through rationally. Attacking him in the car would be easier, but we're going too fast, and I'm not wearing a seatbelt. Killing myself isn't part of the plan, so I sit tight, cataloging my advantages. He thinks I'm unconscious, and he doesn't know I have a weapon. I don't want to wait because I don't know where he's driving me but catching him off guard is the best chance of my survival.

The car slows and turns once and then a second time before Damien lowers his window, and I recognize the familiar sound of the security gate unlocking. He's taking me back home.

The first thought in my mind is that Manuel is gone, and I know Alessio is too. He won't be here to watch it. He just wants to know it's done.

My eyes blur with tears, and I blink them away rapidly, pulling myself together. I can't fucking do this right now. I have to win this fight for Nino. That's it. There is no other choice.

The car comes to a stop, and I lie as still as I can, opening the blade when he gets out. I hide it beneath my palm and wait. I'm not sure which door he'll open first, but I'm prepared with my heels at one end and my blade at the other. I count the seconds, forcing myself not to look, and then I hear the handle above my head. The door opens, cool air rushes in, and he grabs me by the hair. He yanks on my head to drag me back, and the pain is excruciating, but I don't make a sound. I don't give him any indication that I'm conscious.

"Wake up, bitch." He slaps my face when my dead weight flops against the seat cushion, and again, I don't move.

"And here I thought you were a fighter," he grumbles, leaning down to lift my shoulders with his hands.

The moment I feel his breath on my face, I open my eyes and lock my gaze on the target of his artery. I swing my arm, and he mutters a stunned curse right before the knife plunges into his neck. He drops me immediately, staggering back as he grabs at the blade, yanking it free. It's only once he does that, he realizes his mistake. Blood spurts from the wound rapidly, and he slaps his palm over it in a desperate attempt to stop it.

"You fucking bitch," he gurgles the words as he drops to his knees.

He collapses onto the ground, his body twitching as he continues to bleed out. He's dying quickly, but I can't let him go until I have the answer I need.

"Who asked you to do this?" I force the words from deep within as I stare down at the face I'll never forget.

He digs his fingers into his flesh, his last words so faint, they barely register. "You know who."

"NATALIA, ARE YOU OKAY?" Mrs. Hudson stares at me, wide-eyed with concern as she examines the wound on the side of my face. It's swollen and bruised, so there's no hiding it, but I can't think about that right now.

I play the message from my phone, hoping she can't see the tremor in my arm.

Everything is okay. I just fell, and Damien had an emergency arise, so I need to take Nino now.

She seems uncertain, glancing over my shoulder. When she notices Alessio's car in the driveway and not the Rolls Royce, she looks even more doubtful. But I don't have time to waste convincing her. I move around her just as Nino comes into the entryway.

"Mom?"

We have to go. I sign to him. *Come here, darling. Quick, quick.*

He doesn't hesitate, scurrying over to join me. Mrs. Hudson eyes my Burberry coat curiously. It wasn't what I was wearing when I dropped him off, and she knows it. But I don't have time to care. I just need to go.

"Are you sure you're okay?" She calls after us as I take Nino to the car. "I could have the Society doctor come here. It's no trouble."

I wave at her and shake my head, helping Nino into the backseat. Once he's secured, he starts asking questions the minute I've got the car started. I turn back to him long enough to tell him that I'll explain everything as soon as I can, but right now, I have to drive.

It would be tempting to tell him that everything will be okay, but

I don't know that. What I do know is I'm more prepared this time. When I turn onto the main road, I only drive a few blocks before I stop to park Alessio's car on the street. I help Nino out, and we walk two blocks to the grocery store where the taxi I ordered is waiting. We get inside, and the driver gives me a bored expression, asking where I want to go. I check my phone to make sure the GPS is disabled and it's in airplane mode and then write out a message for him.

The ferry terminal.

He nods and pulls out into traffic, leaving me to check on Nino. He seems to understand that something's not right, and he looks scared, and I wish more than anything I could give him my assurances.

Guess what? I sign to him.

What? he asks.

We're going on a really big boat.

He leans up, peering out the window as if we might be there already. "Where to?"

You'll see, I tell him. *It's a surprise.*

It will be a surprise for both of us.

I have more than enough cash on me to hold us over for a while. I've been pulling it out of my account every week when I meet Abella, just in case. I have no idea how long it will take Alessio to track his car to where I left it, but I'm hoping it will take him longer to track down the taxi.

The ride to the ferry terminal seems to go on forever, and I find myself glancing over my shoulder every few minutes, expecting Alessio to appear behind us, but he hasn't yet. I won't be relieved until we're on the ferry, and even then, I have to consider that he might figure out what I'm doing. In the meantime, I plan my next steps, writing two notes in advance.

The taxi driver drops us off, and I pay him in cash, scrambling out onto the pavement with Nino in tow. We head for the terminal and go straight to the passenger-only line, purchasing two tickets for Bainbridge Island. Then, we head for the bathroom, and I pull out a different set of clothes and tell Nino he needs to change before we get on the ferry. An older woman comes out of the stall, offering me a sympathetic glance before she heads to the sink. Once Nino is in the stall, I approach her apologetically and use my app to ask her for a favor.

I'm so sorry to bother you, but my son is feeling unwell, and we really need to catch the ferry to Bremerton. I'm worried we won't make it in time to purchase the tickets, and I can't leave him in here alone. Would it be a huge imposition to ask if you could buy us two tickets if I give you the cash?

She reads the note, and her eyes move to the bruise on the side of my face. Obviously, she thinks there's more to the story, but she takes pity on me and accepts the cash from my hand.

"Of course, dear. Don't you worry. I'll get the tickets and bring them right back here."

Thank you so much, I write. *You don't know how much this means.*

She nods and disappears, and I tap on the stall Nino's in. He opens the door for me, and I make quick work of slipping on a pair of jeans, some sneakers, and a different coat. When we exit together, I direct him to wash his hands and wait for her to return. To my relief, she does, handing over the two tickets with a gracious smile.

"I hope you feel better, young man."

Nino gives her a confused glance, and I smile at her, typing out one last message. *Thank you again. You're a lifesaver.*

She checks her watch and sighs. "I have to be going myself. Safe travels, you two."

She leaves, and I hand Nino a winter hat and secure my hair in my coat before putting mine on as well.

Okay, ready? I ask.

He nods.

Let's play a game, I sign. *I want you to look for any cracks on the floor. Whoever spots the most wins.*

"Cool," he says.

I take his hand, guilt eating at me as we step out of the bathrooms, both of our gazes on the floor. I don't know how many cameras are around here, and I don't think I'll be able to fool Alessio completely, but right now, I just need to buy time.

We board the Bremerton ferry with only a few minutes to spare, and Nino proudly declares that he won the game before his excitement turns to the ferry.

"Can we go look around?" he asks.

Yes.

He leads the way, weaving through people as the ferry glides out into the water. The journey is only a little over thirty minutes, but it feels much longer. I find myself scanning the passengers for anyone who looks like they might be associated with IVI, but realistically, I don't know.

When we arrive, Nino and I exit with the first wave of passengers, blending into the crowd before it disperses. We walk down the street, and I flag a taxi before they pull away from the curb. The driver, a woman with pink hair, gives me a curious glance as I approach her window.

I write out a quick note, playing it out for her.

Could you drive us to Port Angeles?

"Do you have any idea how much that's gonna cost?" She snaps the gum in her mouth. "That's an hour and a half each way."

I pull out a thousand dollars and show it to her.

She whistles and gestures for us to get in. I help Nino into the back, buckling him first.

"Cash first." The driver holds her palm up through the divider.

I hand it to her through the slot, and she counts it before she takes off. Once we're on the interstate, I take a deep breath and try to relax.

"I'm hungry," Nino says. "When are we going to eat dinner?"

I reach into my bag and grab two granola bars, handing them both to him. *Eat those for now, and when we stop again, I'll buy you dinner, okay?*

He nods and chomps through his granola bars, then promptly falls asleep. The ride is long, and I can't use my phone to distract myself or figure out the next steps. I know there's a bus station in Port Angeles because I checked when I was planning my escape route before. It will take time for Alessio to track me at each location, and the safest thing I can do is change routes and transportation methods often.

We arrive just before seven, and the driver drops us off. The first bus scheduled to leave is going to Moses Lake, so those are the tickets I buy. I grab Nino a burger and a few snacks for the road, and we board the bus. The journey is long, and I don't get much sleep, but Nino does.

From Moses Lake, we take a taxi into Spokane and then board an Amtrak to Portland. In Portland, I pay a woman five thousand dollars for a van that's probably only worth about five hundred, and we drive. We keep driving until I'm so lost myself that I'm certain Alessio won't find us.

32

ALESSIO

"Remove the hood." I nod to Thomas.

He does as I ask, skirting around the chair he used to secure Enzo. When Thomas unveils his bloodied face, I can see that he didn't go gently.

His eyes find mine, and there's a split second when his reality sinks in. It's only a moment, but at that moment, I see him for the coward he is.

"I take it you have been getting my messages then," he spits. "Fucking traitor. After everything I've done for you, this is how you thank me."

"I know who you are now," I answer without emotion. "The only traitor I see is you."

"I hear congratulations are in order." He yanks against the restraints, shaking the chains. "You finally got a taste of pussy. How does it feel to know I had it first?"

"You never had her." I stare down at him in disgust. "You took what she wouldn't give you freely. That's what you still don't understand, Enzo. It doesn't make you a man. It makes you fucking pathetic."

"Pathetic," he sneers. "Coming from the man who has me tied up like a dog. Give me a fair fight. If you want to end me, let's do this man to man."

"You want to take a shot?" I shrug and gesture for Thomas. "Fine. Give me a hand with these."

"Are you sure, Mr. Scarcello?"

Enzo snorts at Thomas's remark, and I nod.

We release him from his restraints, and Enzo sits up, cracking his neck from side to side. In his mind, this is a foregone conclusion, but Enzo has always underestimated me. He's known me for many years, but he's never seen me work. He's never even seen me angry. He doesn't have any idea about the quiet rage that lives in me, but he's about to learn.

"I'll tell you what." Enzo rises to his feet and shakes out his arms. "I'll even give you the first one for free, so you can feel like you accomplished something."

"I'm not looking for favors. You said you wanted a fair fight, so take your shot, Marcone."

He chuckles to himself and then throws out a left hook that collides with my jaw. The impact reverberates through my skull, but it doesn't drop me like he was expecting. I let him have that one, because he's foolish enough to think it will happen twice. When he throws a second one at me in quick succession, I dodge it and smash my fist straight into his nose.

He howls out in pain as blood spews from his nostrils, but it teaches him nothing. He tries to come at me again, and this time, I break teeth with a fist to his mouth.

"You motherfucker." He spits the fragments onto the floor.

When he charges at me again, I swerve, grabbing his arm as I swing around behind him and yank back. At the same time, I thrust my palm into the base of his skull, sending him face down into the floor. He grunts when his shoulder dislocates, rendering that arm useless. I use my weight to kneel into his back and smash his face into the cement with a satisfying crunch.

"Have anything to say now?" I snarl.

"Fuck you." He gurgles on his blood.

I leave him lying there in a heap as I rise to my feet and gesture for Thomas. "Give me a hand, will you?"

He walks around and grabs Enzo's good arm while I drag him by his injured one. He snarls and grunts like a pig from the pain before he vomits all over himself when we throw him back into the chair.

"Fucking disgusting," I spit at him.

Luckily for me, there's a hose attachment in the prison basement, so I set that up at the sink while Thomas works on securing Enzo's restraints.

"His legs need to be wider," I inform him. "Drag him to the edge of the chair. He shouldn't be able to move at all."

"Okay." Thomas yanks him forward, widening Enzo's legs.

Once he's secure, Thomas steps away. I blast Enzo with the hose, cleaning the blood and vomit away. Enzo chokes on the water, coughing and sputtering when it hits his face, and I do it again just because I fucking feel like it.

"Do me a favor." I toss the hose aside and point to my bag. "Grab the scissors out of there and cut off his pants and underwear."

"You've got to be fucking kidding me," Enzo groans. "Just kill me, Scarcello. Get it the fuck over with."

I pause to look at him. "Did you get it over with when you were torturing my wife?"

His eyes flare, and he doesn't answer.

"Or how about his wife, for that matter?" I gesture to Thomas, and he freezes, turning to see the vacant expression on Enzo's face. "What about Nicolette? Or Elizabeth? How about your own fucking brother?"

His silence is deafening, and it fucking enrages me.

"How many were there, Enzo? How many times did you have to throw your limp dick around to feel like a man?"

"You don't know anything," he roars. "They all fucking loved it.

Every one of them. Especially his wife." He looks at Thomas, taunting him. "She begged me for more. Over and over and—"

Thomas slams his fist into Enzo's face, and his head jerks back as another bloody tooth flies onto the cement. It renders Enzo unconscious for a few seconds, and Thomas offers me an apologetic shrug.

"I had to."

"Just work on that." I point to Enzo's pants. "Will you?"

Thomas nods and grabs the scissors, getting to work. He rips through the material efficiently, and when he's finished, there are nothing but scraps on the floor. Enzo's flaccid dick is on full display, and it's not something I particularly care to see, but I've given this day a lot of thought. I've had nothing but time to plan how I would do this. The only suitable punishment in my mind was an eye for an eye. So, for everything he did to Natalia, I'm going to give it back, ten times worse.

I drag over the mechanical sex machine I borrowed from the Cat House and adjust the height until it looks right. Thomas watches me curiously as I grab my bag and pull out three huge dildo attachments.

"Oh, for fucks sake," Enzo wheezes as he stirs and looks down. "Come on, man. Are you kidding me?"

"Which one do you think?" I ask Thomas.

A dark sense of satisfaction flashes in his eyes as he points at the largest model.

"I thought so too." I toss the others aside and screw it onto the machine.

"How's that work exactly?" Thomas asks. "Does it just go right in?"

"I don't know," I admit. "I guess we're going to find out."

Enzo starts to freak the fuck out, thrashing against the chair, but it does him no good. The legs are bolted to the floor, and Thomas bound him so tight there's no chance of him moving.

With the dildo attached, I turn on the machine, and it thrusts forward, pounding against Enzo's puckered flesh. He squeals.

Thomas and I cringe. The dildo rams but doesn't make entry because it's on the lowest setting. I solve that problem by cranking it up to the max, and on the next rotation, it splits his skin wide open. Enzo lets out a blood-curdling wail, and Thomas gags, but neither of us can look away from the horror show.

"How does it feel?" I ask Enzo. "What's it like being on the other end of it?"

His eyes water, the moisture dripping down his cheeks, and for the first time in his life, he has nothing to say. He's still squirming, trying to test the limits of his restraints. His attempts get him nowhere, and eventually, he starts to beg like I suspected he would.

"Okay, okay, I'm fucking sorry, alright. Is that what you want to hear? I'm sorry. Just quit already."

I cock my head to the side curiously. "Did you quit when they asked you to?"

He retches again, but this time nothing comes up. "Just kill me. Just fucking kill me."

I lean down to look him in the eyes. "We haven't even begun yet."

He turns away, his knuckles white as he grips the arms of the chair. For the next fifteen minutes, we let him suffer before I decide he's become too accustomed to the pain to reap anything more from it. Then I turn off the machine and grab my knife, offering it to Thomas first.

"You take a couple," I tell him. "For your wife."

He glances at the knife, and for a second, I'm not sure he's going to do it. Then he looks at Enzo, and the rage he's repressed comes back all over again. He stabs him in the gut twice, twisting the blade to inflict as much damage as possible before he hands it back to me. I wasn't expecting him to go that deep, but it's too late to turn back now. Enzo's already delirious, and I don't want him to die on me before I finish the plan I started.

I stab him once in the gut myself, and he grunts, his chin tipping forward as he starts to murmur something I can't quite understand.

"What?" I squeeze his face in my palm.

"Where's my mother?" he whispers. "Just tell me. Did you kill her after everything she did for you?"

I wipe the blade on his shirt to clean off the blood. "Tell me where Elizabeth is, and I'll tell you what happened to Gwen."

"She's fucking dead," he chokes out. "Buried in the yard beneath the rose bushes."

I don't have to ask him if Gwen knew about that too. At this point, I wouldn't doubt if she helped him dig the grave.

"Where is my mother?" Blood coats his lips, and I know I'm losing time.

"Natalia killed her," I answer coldly. "She's fish bait now."

He wails at the lie like I knew he would, renewing his fight against the restraints. "You motherfucker."

I hand the knife to Thomas and gesture at Enzo's cock. "We're running out of time. Cut it off."

He blinks at me, and I arch a brow at him, waiting. His fingers curl around the handle, and he lowers himself on one knee, reaching out to grab the useless tube of flesh.

"For my wife," Thomas murmurs as he begins to slice.

Enzo releases a silent scream, his lips opening and closing as he tries to suck in air. He's dying. It's a matter of a few minutes now. I can't draw it out any longer, as much as I'd like to.

"Before you leave this earth, I think it might interest you to know this is the same way I killed your father."

He looks up at me, gurgles, and shakes his head.

"Gwen asked that of me. She said it was the only suitable punishment for a man with no integrity left. It's only fitting that you'll die choking down the bitter memory of your crimes too."

He tries to speak, his neck muscles working, but nothing comes out. I don't care what he has to say anymore. Thomas has finished sawing off his favorite appendage, and the time for talking is over.

"May I?" he gestures to Enzo's mouth.

"Be my guest."

"Wait," Enzo chokes, using the last of his strength to smile through his bloody teeth. He's staring at me, and there's something unsettling about his expression. I don't understand what it is until he gets the last word.

"I've already ruined your life. You just don't know it yet."

33

ALESSIO

"WHAT THE FUCK IS GOING ON?" I STAB MY FINGER AGAINST THE phone, disconnecting my tenth unanswered call to Damien.

"I'm sure there's an explanation," Angelo tries to reassure me, but even as he says it, I can hear the uncertainty in his voice.

"No." I try Natalia's phone again, but there's no response. "This isn't right."

I don't want to admit that Enzo's last words are ringing in my ears. When he said them, I tried to discredit them, but I've known him too long to doubt his certainty. It was written in his eyes. He didn't care that he was dying because he thought he'd won.

It's not a coincidence that I can't get a response from Damien or Natalia. There's a sickness in my gut I want to ignore, but I can't. It only gets stronger as Angelo finally pulls up to the gate at the house.

My phone rings as we drive through, and my pulse pounds in my ears as I rush to check it, only to see that it's Mrs. Hudson. For a second, I consider rejecting it, but then I wonder if Nino ever made it to her house today.

"Mrs. Hudson," I answer briskly. "Is Nino there?"

"What? No, he's not here."

There's a pause, and I'm trying to formulate the necessary words to respond when she fills the silence.

"Mrs. Scarcello picked him up two hours ago. That's why I was calling. I wanted to make sure she was alright."

"What do you mean was she alright?" I demand.

Mrs. Hudson clears her throat. "She had an awful bruise on her face. When I asked her about it, she said she fell, but something didn't feel right. Her guard wasn't with her, and I didn't think she should be driving, but I couldn't get her to listen. She was so jumpy."

"Did she say where she was going?" I croak.

"No. I assumed home," Mrs. Hudson answers just as Angelo stops the car abruptly.

When I glance over at him, he looks rattled, and it isn't until I follow his gaze that I realize why.

"Mrs. Hudson, I have to go."

I don't know if she says goodbye before I disconnect the call, but I'm already scrambling out the door. Angelo calls after me as I move past Damien's dead body in a daze, heading straight for the house.

"Alessio." He calls again, but I can't respond.

I gain entry through the security system, and the house is eerily quiet. So much so that the sound of my footsteps seem to ricochet off the walls until I come to a stop in the middle of the foyer.

"Natalia," I call out for her as my chest caves inward. "Natalia!"

Angelo puts a hand on my shoulder, startling me, and when I turn, he seems haunted by whatever it is he sees in my eyes.

"Natalia!" I bellow.

"Alessio." Angelo tries to halt me, but I can't stop.

"Natalia!" I scream her name until my lungs burn, moving through the house like a phantom.

When I reach her room and find it empty, I tear through her closet. Her clothes are here. Her suitcases are too. In the bathroom, her toiletries are still sitting on the counter. But it doesn't bring me relief. I know. She left everything behind. *She left me behind.*

"Nino." My voice is hoarse by the time I make it to his room, but it's as vacant as my heart.

I stand there like a fool, staring at that goddamned alien comforter, and my eyes burn. They're gone. My whole fucking life is gone.

"Alessio." Angelo calls out from the doorway, and when I turn to face him, he jerks his chin in a gesture for me to follow him. "I think you're going to want to see this."

Ten minutes later, I'm staring at the computer screen, dead silent. Angelo is beside me, waiting for a reaction. Some kind of response to let him know I'm still fucking alive after watching that footage.

"Damien," I snarl his name as I rise from my chair.

"Alessio, we need to—"

Angelo's voice fades as I walk out the door and into the kitchen, grabbing the first knife I see from the butcher block.

He joins me again as I stalk toward the front door and out onto the lawn. When I come to a stop over Damien's corpse, a rage unlike any I've ever felt washes over me. I kneel onto his chest and stab him in the eye, and it feels fucking good. So good, I do it again and again, slashing at him as I scream out my agony. I mutilate him beyond recognition, nearly severing his head from his body before Angelo finally grabs me and drags me up.

"Enough." He grabs my face and stares into my eyes. "Alessio, we have to find them."

34

ALESSIO

I walk down the hall in a daze, the sound of my footsteps echoing off the marble. It's the only thing I've found to break the mind-numbing silence. The quiet was what I used to value more than anything, but now it feels like a prison.

It's Christmas Day, and the house has fallen into stillness. Everything is closed, and the city is stagnant. I haven't slept in two days, and my leads have run dry after we tracked Natalia and Nino to Portland. She bought a vehicle, and the last known sighting I have is from a gas station off the interstate. From there, they could have gone anywhere. The maps in my office have provided possibilities but no solution. Her room has turned up nothing. The witnesses have been less than helpful, all of them reiterating the same story. They didn't have any sort of conversation with her. They delivered her to her destination, and that was it.

I've watched the footage so many times it feels like my eyes are bleeding. Everything hurts. She was so meticulous in her plans it leaves little doubt that she's been thinking of this for some time. Was it before we married or after? Regardless, it makes little difference.

What it boils down to is that I lied to her about Enzo, and now the worst has happened as a result.

I don't know where they are. I don't know if they're safe, or warm, or scared. It's a hopeless feeling, one I'm not accustomed to. There's an army of guards searching for them, but every minute that passes feels like this is the beginning of a lifelong sentence. I can't say I don't deserve it, but I'm not willing to let them go.

I find myself standing in the middle of the parlor room, staring at the Christmas tree that looks like it's been frosted with snow. Natalia ordered it, and she and Nino decorated it together. It's the first time I've ever had one in the house. I barely gave it a passing glance before, but now all I can see are missed opportunities. While I was busy dividing the household, they were living. They were living without me.

I stagger forward, collapsing onto the floor. I can't fucking breathe. I never wanted to feel this way again. I did everything in my power to prevent it, and yet here I am. I stare at the presents beneath the tree, blinking away my endless existence. Natalia took so much care to wrap Nino's gifts. She left me lists of the things she was buying him, so there wouldn't be duplicates.

I was too caught up in the war in my head to see what was right in front of me, but I can see it now. There's a gift with my name on it. A small square box wrapped in red paper with Natalia's handwriting. Unlike the other gifts that Nino addressed to me, this one is just from her.

Curiosity has me dragging it into my lap. I can't remember the last time I opened a gift from someone. When I was a boy, my mother would give us thoughtful gifts every year. Then I moved in with Gwen and her family, and her version of Christmas gifts was stacks of cash in each of our stockings. I didn't need the money. I had more than I could ever want after I inherited my family's estate, but Gwen told us we should just buy ourselves whatever we wanted. Over time, I came to see Christmas as a commercial holiday, forgetting the sentiment involved.

Somehow, I know Natalia's gift won't be something random she grabbed from a shelf at the department store, and selfishly, I want to know what it is.

I rip off the paper, tossing it aside to find a box of white gauze bandages with a small envelope taped to the side. When I open the envelope, there's a stack of paper in Natalia's handwriting. I glance at the first sheet, reading the words she left me.

Because I'd rather be a source of comfort than pain. Keep these for a time when you need them, and I'll be there to bandage your wounds.

I didn't fail to execute my plan in your bedroom that night. My plan failed me. We can't destroy what we love without killing ourselves in the process. I wasn't pretending then, and I'm not pretending now.

I love you still.

Natalia

PAIN RADIATES THROUGH ME, and my eyes blur as I flip the page. It takes me a minute to realize what I'm seeing. They are her notes from her search for Nino.

-FIRST SIGHTING of Enzo in over a year and a half. He returned to the building on Pearl Street to meet with Nathaniel. Consider the risk of approaching Nathaniel? Need confirmation of Camilo's location first. Will continue to track Enzo's movements.

-Followed Enzo to a building in Tribeca today. He met with another associate, unknown name. Tall, well presented in a suit and tie. Handsome man, but terrifying. His eyes are so stark. Is he mafia too?

-Lost Enzo in traffic. Haven't seen him in three days. Followed his associate to a dinner meeting with another unknown. The next day, the associate left and didn't return.

-Nathaniel is dead. They removed his body from the Pearl Street building this afternoon. Was it related to Enzo?

-Three months since I've seen Enzo. No good leads. Starting to lose hope. No sign of associate either.

-Six months with no updates.

-Another year gone. No sign of Enzo. Where is Camilo?

-Three years in. Losing hope. No Enzo. No associate. Check the building periodically, but nothing new.

-Lead on Enzo's New York address. PI managed to dig up his last name. It's Marcone. But nothing comes up for him other than this rental he never uses. No other ties to this city, job or otherwise. Will keep searching.

-Enzo's associate has returned. Followed him upstate in the middle of the night. The taxi driver got spooked, and the associate lost us.

-Associate still in New York. Followed him to a coffee shop this morning, meeting with another unknown. Have a name from the conversation. Alessio Scarcello. Will continue to track.

-Alessio Scarcello lives in the building in Tribeca. The building has guards and no access to outsiders. He has a driver. Searches for him turn up nothing. Who is this man?

-Followed Alessio to the coffee shop this morning. He had a phone conversation and said he's leaving soon. Must act now. Paid a guy from the subway a hundred bucks to bump into Alessio's table and spill his drink. Please don't let this guy die because of me.

-Plan executed. Alessio didn't kill subway guy, and I made the swap when he went to the bathroom. He has my pen now, and I have his.

-Spent the rest of the night listening to audio from pen. One phone call from Alessio to unknown. Asked about someone named Nino. Says he's flying back home to Seattle tomorrow morning at ten a.m. Will follow.

-In Seattle. Landed early, waiting for his arrival. No signs yet.

-He arrived on a private jet. Did not see him but was able to verify his location through GPS. Outside his home. Locked gate.

-*He has a little boy he calls Nino. Have yet to see him but heard him speak. Nino does not refer to him as his father. Could it be Camilo?*

-*Alessio rarely leaves his house, except for at night or at random times during the day. There does not appear to be any set schedule for him. The guard drives the boy to school. Hoping to get a better look tomorrow.*

-*Neighbor caught me lurking on the street. Asked me what I was doing. Need to lay low for a few days. Hired PI.*

-*PI couldn't find any birth record with Alessio listed as the father. Feel like I'm getting closer.*

-*Alessio mentioned Enzo to Nino today. He referred to him as his father in a past context. I've finally found him.*

-*Saw Nino for the first time outside his school. He's so beautiful, I cried. When can I hold him again? I have to get him back.*

-*Alessio seems kind to Nino, although distant. He's not as intimidating when he speaks to Nino. Does Nino love him?*

-*No information on Enzo. Alessio has Nino full time. Is Enzo dead?*

-*Pen battery is running low. Need to make a plan. Taking him from school isn't an option. I won't get past the security and definitely won't make it out of there with the guard watching. How will I ever get Nino to trust me when he doesn't know who I am?*

-*Overheard Alessio speaking of interviews for a nanny position. This is my chance. Must find ad.*

-*Found ad, applied, and got interview!*

-*Alessio Scarcello is more terrifying in person. But he's different. He doesn't give me that sick feeling Enzo did. In fact, I'm not really sure what I feel about him. It's strange and new. I want to believe he's a good man. Does he love Nino?*

-*I'm here. I'm actually in Seattle, at Alessio's house. I spoke to my son for the first time since Enzo took him from me. He's such a sweet, quiet boy. My heart isn't broken anymore. Alessio has taken good care of him, though emotionally, he seems absent.*

-*This might be harder than I thought.*

-*Alessio is watching me. It should scare me, but it doesn't. Why?*

-*Nino is getting more comfortable around me every day. He's flourishing here. Part of me feels guilty. He does care about Alessio. What will happen when I take him away?*

-*We need to leave soon. Things are getting too confusing. Alessio is confusing me.*

-*I went to Alessio's room to kill him. I couldn't go through with it. I don't want to hurt him. That's a problem.*

-*Alessio comes to me at night. We have sex, and I like it. I like it way too much. But then he leaves me, and I feel ... empty. I'm scared of these feelings. I'm scared because sometimes I think I wish I could stay. I wish he could want me the way that I want him.*

-*So much to update, but I think this will be my last. I don't even know why I'm writing these anymore. Alessio married me, but not for love. I love him, though. I got my son back, and I love him with my whole heart too. I just don't know if I can survive here without Alessio's warmth. Will he ever give me a chance?*

IT'S the last entry on the page, and I can't take my eyes off of it as the weight of her words settles over me. This woman ... this fucking witch of a woman stalked me, researched me, and created an elaborate plan to inject herself into my life without me even realizing it. I don't know whether I'm more impressed or terrified by her, but there's one glaring certainty. She is my equal in every way, and after all of that, she thinks she can just leave me?

"Alessio?" Angelo's voice startles me, and when I look up, he's watching me with concern. "Damien's been disposed of. I went through his apartment, and it looks like he and Enzo had been exchanging letters. Apparently, they knew each other from the Cat House. Damien had roughed up one of the women, and Enzo helped him clean it up without anyone finding out. They've been writing to each other for years, and Enzo called on him to repay the favor now.

He gave Damien instructions to access the safe at Gwen's house. I found a large amount of cash hidden in his closet and a plane ticket to Mexico. It looks like he was going to kill Natalia and bail the country."

I absorb that information, and my pulse slows, my voice barely audible as I speak.

"Natalia thinks I did this. She thinks it was me."

35

NATALIA

"Nino." I try to call out his name, but my voice is too weak.

I open the door to the hall closet, checking in there, but it's empty too. I'm trying not to panic, but the longer I walk around the house in my robe, the harder it's becoming to reel in my emotions. I was only in the shower for fifteen minutes. I didn't hear anything, but I can't find him. The house is small, only a one-bedroom on a half-acre of property in a rural area. There aren't many places for him to go.

Sweat trickles down my neck as I glance out the windows into the yard. There's no sign of him there either. I stuff my feet into a pair of boots near the door and trudge outside.

"Nino," I try again, but the cold air makes it even harder to speak.

Immediately, the worst thoughts enter my mind. It's the same scenario that plays through my head every time I lose sight of him, or I hear a noise at night, or a strange car drives by. If someone looks at me funny in the grocery store, or a neighbor stops by to be friendly, that thought is always there. I'm constantly looking over my shoulder and wondering if today is going to be the day.

After three months of this, my nerves are shot, and it isn't getting better with time. It's only getting worse. I'm pregnant, hormonal, and I feel like I'm losing my mind every second of every day. At times, it's unbearable, and I find myself questioning everything. This was always the end goal before Alessio came into the picture. I was supposed to run off into the sunset with Nino and make a life for us, but this isn't a life. It's a prison.

I'm terrified to let him out of my sight. I live in fear that at any moment, someone else will show up at my door, and this time, I won't survive. It feels like I've only bought myself time, but time will eventually run out. For so long, I had thought about what it would be like to get my life back. In theory, I knew that I'd never really be free. We'd have to be careful. That was a given, but imagining it and living it are two different things. I don't know how to make this work. The Society's reach is too powerful, and realistically, there isn't anywhere on this planet that we could ever really be safe. Alessio told me that if I ran again, he wouldn't be able to protect me, but he left me no choice, and now here I am.

I'm ashamed to admit that I miss him. I miss his scent, his warmth, his presence. I miss the way he felt against my body and the safety I thought I had with him. I had convinced myself that he just needed to learn to trust his feelings for me. Foolishly, I thought that in time, he would come back to me, and we'd be okay. We'd make it through. I felt that in my heart. Maybe it was an illusion, but I don't want to believe it was. Even now, I question it. Did I make a mistake? What if he wasn't the one who sent Damien?

Then reality kicks in, and I feel stupid all over again. I can't keep doing this. I can't keep making excuses when the explanation is right in front of me. It was there all along, and I just didn't want to see it.

I slog through the mud, rounding the side of the house, and my heart jumps when I find Nino sitting on a log staring up at the birds in the sky. A silent sob bursts from my chest, and I stagger forward, nearly tripping in the mud as I reach for him.

"Mom?" He turns to look at me with scrunched brows.

What are you doing? My hands move quickly as I sign the words, frustration getting the best of me. *I told you not to come out here unless you're with me.*

"I'm sorry." He lowers his gaze and comes to join me. "I was bored."

Come on. Let's go inside. I reach for his hand, and he gives it to me.

By the time we get back in, both our shoes are coated in mud, and I'm too exhausted to care. We kick them off by the door, leaving them as they are.

I'm going to get dressed. I tell Nino. *Then we'll talk.*

He nods, settling onto the couch and grabbing the throw blanket to warm himself.

In my room, I change into some leggings and a sweatshirt. We don't have a lot of clothes between us, apart from the basics I picked up at a cheap store along the way. In my hurry to leave Seattle, I didn't grab much. I have money to survive on, but I don't know how long. Eventually, I'll need to get another job, and I can't imagine how I'll do that without Alessio finding out. It would have to be something under the table, and then there's the question of what I'll do with Nino during that time. Who will watch him and the baby? I can't trust anyone, and just the idea of it nearly sends me into a panic attack.

Those thoughts are overwhelming, and I don't have any answers. I've considered leaving the country, but that isn't even a real possibility. I can't get us new passports, and the moment our names are registered on any travel document, I'm certain Alessio would know. I don't know what would happen then. Would he come to deal with me himself, or would he let someone from The Society do it? I've become so used to the idea my concern isn't even dying anymore. It's the trauma it would leave behind if Nino saw or heard it. I know Alessio would never allow him to witness something like that, but I can't say the same for anyone else who might come. Every time I consider it, it feels like there's a vise around my neck. I don't know how to fix any of this.

I walk back down the hall and find Nino scribbling in his art book. He's not drawing anything, just scribbling lines. He's been doing that a lot lately. This conversation we're about to have is long overdue. I've been putting it off, because I don't have a solution that's fair to him.

I sit down beside him, touching his arm to get his attention. When he looks up at me, his eyes are still glassy.

I'm sorry I got upset, I tell him. *I was worried about you. Can you tell me why you went outside without me when you know you shouldn't?*

"Because I don't understand why I can't," he says. "We used to go outside all the time at home, and now you hardly ever want to. It's boring in Montana, and I hate it here."

I'm reluctant to ask because I already know the answer, but we have to figure out how to work through this. *Why do you hate it here?*

"Because I have no friends." He wipes the moisture that starts to leak from his eyes. "I have to do homeschool, and I can't play the piano or go swimming, and there are no boats. I miss the lake. I miss daddy, and I want to see him. I don't understand why we had to go away."

His words gut me, and before I can help it, I'm crying too. Nino, being the sweet boy he is, forgets all about his own discomfort and crawls over to hug me.

"I'm sorry, mom. I didn't mean to upset you."

No, I'm sorry, I sign to him. *I know this isn't fair to you. I miss all those things too.*

"Then why can't we go back?" he asks.

I don't have an answer for him. I don't know how to explain that we can't go back because, if we do, it means I might die. It feels selfish to hold him hostage in a life of misery, because of the target on my back. He deserves more than this, and I can't help thinking I've made a huge mistake. I came back into his life when he already had a life of his own, and I think maybe I was too late. Maybe he was better off with Alessio, where he was happy and safe.

Nothing makes sense, and everything's a mess. So, I do the only thing I can. I hold him, and we cry together.

36

NATALIA

Something stirs me from my sleep, and at first, I think it's Nino. Our bedroom has twin beds, which were free with the house when I rented it. I sleep in one, and he sleeps in the other, but he often gets up once in the middle of the night to use the bathroom, which always wakes me. When I glance over at his bed, it's empty, and it takes me a second to realize the bathroom light isn't on either.

I sit up, and my heart jumps into my throat when I notice the dark silhouette standing at the end of the bed, watching me. Fear wraps its ugly claws around me as I toss the blankets aside and stand up. I didn't get to say goodbye. That's the only thing I can think about as I dart around the shadow and out into the living room.

"He's already gone," Alessio's voice follows me as I run toward the window. "Manuel is taking him home."

I press my fingers against the glass, a muted sob falling from my lips as I scan the driveway. There's a dark car out there, but nobody's in it. He's not lying. Nino is already gone. They swept in and took him quietly in the middle of the night. They didn't even give me a chance to hug him one last time.

"It doesn't feel very good, does it?" Alessio's voice draws nearer.

I'm afraid to look at him. I'm terrified of what I might find when I do. I can't forget what he did, and I'm still hurting because of it. I'm angry at him for destroying what we could have been. I'm devastated that he could be so merciless to take Nino away without a goodbye, but love is the most complicated human emotion. It doesn't go away just because someone gravely wounds us. We have to be willing to let it go, and I never was.

The warmth of his body presses against mine, and I shiver, blinking away the tears that begin to fall. He pulls me closer, his fingertips sweeping over my jaw as he turns my head toward him. Moonlight pours in through the window, highlighting the features I've come to know so well. He's still Alessio. The same man who can manage to intimidate you one second and soften you the next. His eyes are just as piercing as they ever were. His jaw is just as strong, and I suspect his hair is still as soft as it was when I dragged my fingers through it more times than I can count. There is something different about him though. He looks thinner, the hollows of his eyes darker. I want to believe it's because he's been as tormented as I have, but it feels foolish even to consider it.

"You smell the same." He drags his nose through my hair, inhaling me, and my knees nearly buckle. It shouldn't feel so good. I shouldn't be so relaxed in the arms of the man who's most certainly come to kill me.

His grip on my face tightens, and he pulls me closer, his lips hovering a breath away from mine. When he kisses me, it feels like it might be the last time. Maybe it's the first. I can't tell anymore. It starts soft, and then my lips give way to him. His tongue enters my mouth, and he tastes me with a growl, the sound reverberating down my throat. We fall back into the same old pattern, and I melt against his body despite the adrenaline coursing through my veins. Maybe it's sick to want this one last time, but I do. If he's going to destroy me, the least he can do is satisfy me first.

His free hand slides over the curve of my hip, and he yanks my ass back against his erection, grinding it into me. My staggered breaths fall between his lips, and he drinks them, swallowing the taste of me like it gives him life. He releases my jaw, his fingers drifting down the sensitive skin on my neck. I wonder if this is it, but then his palm is sliding beneath my nightgown, groping my breast. He bunches up the hem of the silky fabric around my hip with his other fist, exposing me to the cool air. His teeth scrape against my lip, penetrating the flesh, and he releases it with a hum of approval when he tastes the metallic tang of my blood. I sway in his arms, lightheaded from the adrenaline crash and that kiss. He tightens his grip on me, holding me upright as his fingers glide through the slickness between my thighs.

"Still wet for me?" The guttural sound of his voice vibrates against my ear, making my entire body ache for him.

I nod against his chest, and he teases me with his fingers, dipping two of them inside of me. I'm swollen with need, and I can't bite back the sigh of pleasure that rolls over me as I arch my pelvis up to meet him. He fingers me, sliding in and out with a torturously slow rhythm as he sweeps my hair back over my shoulder. His lips come to rest on the tattoo he inked into my skin, and he kisses it reverently. It confuses me. It torments me. I can't think straight right now, because I'm on the verge of coming undone. My muscles clench around him, and I squeeze my eyes shut, trying to make it last. Then it happens. He tips me over the edge by dragging his teeth over my neck, sending sparks all the way down my spine.

Spasms rock through me, and I collapse into the strength of his body, allowing him to hold me upright while I succumb to the pleasure. When it finally ends, Alessio takes my hands in his and tips me forward, bracing me against the window before he releases me. He unzips his trousers, and I turn to watch him as he drags out his cock and slides it between my thighs, soaking himself in my arousal. He groans at the contact and air hisses through my teeth as I roll my hips against him, a silent plea.

Our eyes collide, and even with all the unknowns, I can't stop myself from wanting him. He's beautiful and terrifying and still perfect somehow. I can't decide if this is the best way to die or the worst. All I know is I need him, and at this moment, he needs me too.

His palm comes to rest on my back, and he shudders as he pushes the head of his cock against me. I'm so wet, there's little resistance, but he takes his time, entering me slowly. I watch his face, memorizing the way his lips part and his eyes fall shut. He finds stillness once he's fully inside of me, and he seems to be drawing it out, imprinting this feeling in his mind the way he's imprinted himself on my soul. Then his hands come to rest on my hips, and he starts to move, dragging his cock in and out. It's a slow, torturous rhythm that builds until his primal urges take over, and he fucks me like he'll die without it. I'm lost to the moment, completely consumed by him, and then he wraps an arm around my waist, pulling me upright. As he does, he feels the soft curve of my belly, and everything stops.

I freeze, and he does too. I can't bring myself to look at him, because I don't know what I'll see. I don't know when or if this will change the inevitable, but I couldn't bear it if I saw him making that decision. I wait for him to say something, but he doesn't. His arm goes lax on me, and his palm slides down over the small bump, as if he's checking to make sure he's not imagining it. There's a minute where everything is so quiet, I'm not even sure he's breathing. Then his lips find my neck, and he kisses me right where my pulse is beating a wild tempo. He rolls his hips, his cock throbbing inside of me, and a sound of pleasure gets caught in his throat.

He doesn't take his hand from my belly, branding it there while he starts to fuck me again. It feels bittersweet and slightly alarming because I don't know what he's thinking. Maybe I'm just delusional, but it feels like he wants this. Logically, I'm aware I can't trust this feeling, but I want it to be real. More than anything, I want it to be real.

I lose myself in him, soaking up this connection while it lasts. His thrusts become more desperate, and a tremor moves down his arm as he tries to bite back the sounds of his pleasure. The tension in his body builds, and I can feel it in his grip on me. He tries to resist it. He tries to make it last, but inevitably, he surrenders with an agonized groan. His cock pulses inside of me, and he doesn't bother to pull out. Warmth fills me, and he milks out his release, his hips rolling against me until it becomes too much. When he stills, he doesn't let go of me. He holds me against him for so long I don't know what to think.

"That was a careless mistake you made." His gravelly voice penetrates the silence. "Logging into your email on your new phone. You're too clever for that, Natalia. It leaves me to wonder if it was intentional."

My response isn't necessary. We both know it was. I did it for Nino. I did it because as much as it kills me, I can't give him the life he deserves. All I ever wanted was to have my son back, but I didn't realize what it would cost him. Imprisoning him with me isn't the life I envisioned. I can't outrun The Society forever, and I can't force him to live his life in fear to protect me. He was never a threat to IVI. He has a home there. He has a father who loves him, a man who will protect him and provide for him, and even if that man can't love me, I have to be okay with this decision. It's the only thing that makes sense.

Alessio pulls himself out of me, and his come drips down my thighs. He turns me in his arms, and I swallow as I look up at this brutal man. He is brutal, but he can be soft too. That's what confuses me so much. I don't ever know if he wants to kiss me or kill me.

I point to the envelope taped to the mail holder by the door, making three failed attempts before I get my vocal cords to function.

"For Nino."

He glances briefly at the letter I wrote for my son, but he doesn't move to retrieve it.

"That's it?" His thumb skims over my cheek. "I thought you came to destroy me. Now you're ready to give up?"

My eyes sting as I choke back the heartache I wish I could just stop feeling. "I can't..." I take a deep breath, struggling past the pain in my throat. "I can't kill you and live with myself."

His eyes soften, and he drags his thumb between my lips, parting them before he leans in to kiss me one last time. I close my eyes, and then I'm left cold when he moves away. I don't know what to expect, so I try not to expect anything at all.

I can hear him moving around the kitchen, turning on the faucet, and then tossing something into the bin before he zips his pants up. When he returns, he grabs my face, and I think this is it. I guess it doesn't matter that I have our baby inside of me.

I'm trying not to cry. My throat is already raw from using my voice, but it's the last thing I'll ever say, and I have to say it. I force the words from my gritted teeth, pleading with him for this one thing I know he can't deny me.

"You're his father. You're all he knows. Please take care of him."

"Natalia." His breath fans across my lips as he leans in. "Go pack your things."

ALESSIO CARRIES me onto the jet, my bare feet dangling over his arm as he lowers me into the seat. He didn't bother to grab my muddy shoes before we left the house, but he did wrap my long coat around me.

He hasn't said a word since we left, and he doesn't say anything now as he takes a seat beside me. My mind is reeling, and I think the baby must have changed his mind. He's going to wait, and then he'll do it. My palm comes to rest on my belly, and I want to be relieved, but it doesn't make it any better. I can't imagine going through this entire pregnancy, seeing our baby, and then dying at the end of it.

I'm struggling to breathe when he rests his hand on my knee and leaves it there. His wedding band gleams beneath the cabin lights, and it only confuses me more. Why is he still wearing it? Why does this simple touch, his skin on my skin, feel so possessive?

He stares out the window, seemingly lost in his thoughts as we take off. I don't have it in me to use my voice again, and I don't have my phone on me, so asking questions isn't on the table. All I can do is sit back and stew in the malignancy of my mind. Once we're up in the air, Alessio unbuckles both of us and helps me up from my seat. He leads me into the rear cabin, ushering me into the bedroom.

For a second, I'm wondering if this will be where it happens. He didn't want to leave any evidence behind at the house. That's why he had me take all our stuff. The Society wouldn't want my death linked back to them. Alessio is meticulous. He's probably done this a thousand times. He told me once that he'd never killed a woman. I'm staring at him, wondering if I'll be the first when he removes my coat and tells me to lay down.

I don't have anything left to lose, so I do. Alessio kicks off his shoes and walks around the other side, climbing in beside me. I'm lying on my back, but he rolls me onto my side, draping a throw blanket over us before he pulls me against him. His arm wraps around my waist, and he tucks his chin against the top of my head before his palm settles on my baby bump. Warmth moves over my body, and again, I can sense the possession in his touch, but I don't know what it means.

We don't talk. He just holds me there, safe in the cocoon of his body, until the pilot tells us it's time to prepare for landing. Then we get up, and he repeats the process in reverse, securing me in my coat, leading me back to my seat, and settling his palm on my knee.

Things only get stranger when we land, and he carries me to his car, securing me inside without another word. I don't know what he's thinking, but tension has crept into his features, and I'm a nervous wreck by the time we finally get back to the house. It's a welcome sight, but a bittersweet one too. This place feels like home. Nino was right about that. I miss him so much already, but I can only hope that he will be happy when Manuel returns him safely to these familiar surroundings.

I don't know if I'll see him again. I'm trying to imagine how this might work. Will Alessio keep me locked in a room until I give birth? When I look at him, I feel crazy for even thinking it. But how can I not?

He drives through the gate, parks the car, and lifts me out again. I try to gesture to let him know I can walk, but he ignores it, carrying me inside the house and up all three levels to his bedroom. When he finally sets me down onto his bed, his lips part as if he's about to say something, and then he looks away.

The numbness that's kept me alive in his absence begins to thaw when I realize he's being awkward again. He wants to tell me something, but he's nervous. These are the rare moments of uncertainty Alessio doesn't often show, but when he does, they tend to be with me.

He drags a hand through his hair, paces a little, and then stops, turning to look at me. "I lied to you."

If I wasn't worried already, it only gets worse when he grabs the tufted chair from near the window and drags it over in front of me. He sits down, and we're face to face. I can see all of him, and he can see all of me, and it feels intimate. Alessio has always avoided direct conversation, and I don't know how to prepare for whatever he might tell me.

"I've been lying to you," he says again.

I hug myself, waiting for an explanation. I have no idea what he's talking about, but I'm not going to interrupt him, not when he's finally talking to me.

"When I told you Enzo was dead, it wasn't true."

My blood runs cold, and I glance at the door, terror streaking through my veins like he might appear at any moment. Before I can take that thought and run with it, Alessio reaches for my hands, taking them in his.

"He was in the Tribunal prison for murdering his brother and sister-in-law. That's why I had Nino."

Those words settle over me like a dark cloud. I'm still shaken, trying to process the multitude of my emotions when Alessio goes on.

"He's dead now." His thumbs rub circles over my hands, and I realize he's trying to comfort me. "I swear it on my life. There's a video if you want to see it for yourself. I'd understand if that's what you need."

I pull my hands free, my mind too foggy to comprehend I'm trying to sign a response to him. Alessio leans over and grabs the notepad from the nightstand. When he hands it over, it still has my writing on it from the night I came to tend to his wounds. I stare at the ink for a second, recalling that memory, wondering why he kept it. I flip to a new page and begin to write.

Why did you lie?

His tormented eyes move over my face. "Once I knew the truth about you, there was never a question that I would kill him. I wanted to be the one. Maybe that was selfish, but I needed him to suffer. I thought I was protecting you by keeping his existence a secret. I didn't want his memory to haunt you. I didn't want you to feel unsafe here. Before I could kill him, I needed approval from The Tribunal, and it took longer than I had anticipated. When I finally got it, I realized it was too late. Enzo knew my schedule well from years of consistency. He was aware that Manuel takes time off at Christmas, and I'd need a guard for my new wife. That was the opportunity Enzo saw when Gwen's plan failed. He paid Damien to kill you, Natalia."

He pauses, bowing his head as he draws in a staggered breath. Alessio has always been in careful control of his emotions, but when he looks up at me again, there is so much pain behind his eyes he can't hide it.

"I had no idea," he chokes out. "I was so focused on ruining him I didn't see what was right in front of me. You needed me, and I wasn't there. I left you alone and vulnerable, and the worst part is you thought it was my doing. I had destroyed your trust in me so completely that you actually believed I hired that piece of shit to hurt you."

His admission stuns me. All this time, I had questioned the truth I thought I knew. Deep inside, it felt wrong, and now I know why. The weight of that realization relieves me, but it doesn't take away the hurt. For months, I've felt like I was dying inside, and it was all for nothing.

You did destroy me, I write. *I never needed you to protect me from the truth, Alessio. Your lies cost me my sanity and months of our lives. The pain of that betrayal was unbearable. What was it all for? What did it accomplish other than driving me away?*

"I know you don't need me to protect you." His voice is rough when he replies. "I don't doubt your capabilities, but I will always want to protect you because I'm your husband, and that's my job. It was the one thing I thought I could do for you. Perhaps it was misguided, but I didn't want to burden you with additional pain. I had already caused you enough by pushing you away. I can't change what happened, but I can promise you on my life I will never lie to you again."

His words soften me, and some of the pain I've carried for so long ebbs away, but I can't forgive him that easily. There is still so much I need to know.

Why didn't you tell me this as soon as you saw me today? Why bring me all the way back here, letting me think I was going to die?

"That wasn't my intention." He reaches out to touch my face, his fingers soft against my skin. "I knew you wouldn't want to come back here, but I couldn't take no for an answer. I had to bring you home so we could argue, and then you would see. I would make you see."

Make me see what?

He reaches over and grabs me, dragging me onto his lap, notebook, and all. His eyes are as vulnerable as I've ever seen them, and his voice is uncharacteristically gravelly when he speaks.

"I'm sorry, baby." He squeezes me so tight I can hardly breathe, his body shaking against mine. "I know I failed you. When I said I didn't want this, it wasn't true. I was a coward. I wanted it more than anything, but I didn't trust myself not to let you down."

Do you mean the way your father let you down? I ask.

Alessio looks at me with hollow eyes. "How did you know?"

Gwen, I admit. *She told me about your family. I wanted to bring it up before, but I didn't think you'd be receptive to it.*

He sits quietly with his thoughts as he strokes my arm. I'm not sure if he'll respond. Opening up is difficult for him, and I want him to, but I know I can't force it either.

"I never wanted a relationship," he confesses. "Experience taught me that happiness was an illusion. Then you came along, making me feel things I didn't want to feel. I resented you for it, and I pushed you away because you fucking terrified me. I thought it was the right thing to do until you left, and I had a glimpse of what life would be like without you and Nino. That's not a life I want, so even if I only get to keep you for a year, ten years, or however long fate decides, I want that. I'll do what's necessary to make it happen. You can be angry with me for as long as you feel like it, and I'll take it. I deserve that, but I'm not letting you go."

I stare at him, unmoving. I can't seem to find the words I need to respond. Two hours ago, I thought he was going to kill me. Now he's holding me like I'm the most precious thing in the world, and it's like something has switched on inside of him for the first time. It's everything I wanted, but it's happening so fast it still doesn't feel real. I don't know how to trust that he won't turn cold on me again.

"Natalia?" Concern creeps into his voice, and his grip on me tightens as if I might try to flee.

My vision blurs with tears, and I'm so sick of crying, but this time they are happy tears. Tears of relief.

Are we going to do this for real this time? I ask. *No more bullshit?*

"No more bullshit." His lip twitches and then curves into a smile.

You can't shut me out again, Alessio. I mean it. I won't accept that anymore.

"I know," he says. "It's going to take time, but I'll prove it to you. I swear it."

I reach up to touch his face, but he intercepts my hand and brings it to his lips, kissing my ring.

"You're still wearing it."

I smile, even as I'm quietly crying in his lap. My eyes move to his ring, and I nod, a silent acknowledgment that he is too.

He leans closer, his lips brushing against mine. "Marry me."

I thread our fingers together to show him that we're still married. That hasn't changed.

"Marry me again," he says. "Because you want to."

He pulls his hand free of mine, his brows pinching together in concentration. I'm not sure what he's doing until he touches his forehead and then starts to sign, slowly and awkwardly.

Because I love you.

I laugh and cry at the same time, nodding as he offers me a boyish grin.

"I've been learning, but I'm still slow. I think I'll need your help."

I tell him that he definitely does, and then I reach for his face, pulling him toward me. Our lips collide, and everything else melts away. We kiss ourselves into a frenzy, and it's only a matter of seconds before we're tearing at each other's clothes. He relocates us to the bed and gets me naked in record time, but I only manage to get his shirt off and his pants unzipped before he's in me. I suspect it's going to be a repeat of our earlier session, where we both come hard and fast, but Alessio sets a different pace this time. Now that he's inside of me, he doesn't seem to be in any hurry. He thrusts in and out of me leisurely while his hands roam over my body. It's unexpected, and I realize that he's not fucking me. He's making love to me.

"My beautiful wife," he whispers against my lips. "I'll never get tired of this. You're the only one, Natalia. My first and my last. I want you in my bed every night from now on."

His admission stirs something feral and possessive in me. I suspected it, but his confirmation makes me feel drunk with happiness. I love that he's only mine. I want him to only ever be mine, and I sign the words to him, which he repeats back to me. I know he means them. There's no doubt in my mind when I look into his eyes. Loyalty is everything to him.

I squeeze my body around him, and we kiss until our lips are swollen and we come together. When he collapses beside me, he takes my hand in his, our gazes still connected.

"We're having a baby."

I nod, warmed by the expression on his face. I can tell he's a little nervous but proud.

"I like this." His palm cradles the bump with reverence. "I'm going to put a lot of babies in you."

I laugh silently, and his lips tilt up in amusement.

He leans in and kisses my neck. "We're a family. You're my wife and the mother of my children, and nothing else will ever come before that. I promise you."

I edge myself closer, and he rolls onto his back, giving me the crook of his arm. My head finds sanctuary against his chest, his heartbeat lulling me into a comfortable, happy place. I could fall asleep right here, but there's something I need to do first.

I spell out Nino's name with my hands, and Alessio knows exactly what I'm asking. He really has been learning.

"He'll be here this afternoon." His voice vibrates against my cheek when he answers. "Manuel is driving him so we could have this time to talk. He's sending me hourly updates."

I nod, grateful that we have some time. I know Nino is safe with Manuel, and there's one thing I have to ask before I can move forward. For me.

I'd like to see the video of Enzo's death.

37

NATALIA

I'm nestled between Alessio's legs, the warmth of his body pressing against my back. His arms are wrapped around my waist, and his tension is palpable as I set the phone aside. The video has ended, but I think I'll be processing what I just saw for months to come.

"Are you okay?" He brushes the hair away from my face, studying me.

I turn to look at him, and I don't hesitate to nod. I love him. I love him so much, not only for who he is but for what he did. Maybe it's sick. Some might say it's unhealthy to be satisfied by such a grisly revenge, but I have no sympathy for Enzo, and I think what Alessio gave me is priceless. I know now, with certainty, that Enzo will never hurt me or anyone else again. He paid for his crimes, and he did so gruesomely. He got what he deserved.

I reach for the notepad, but Alessio hands me his phone and opens the notes app instead. I relax my body into his and write a note.

Thank you. I'm sure it must have been difficult to lose a friend, but you did the right thing.

"It wasn't difficult to lose someone I never really knew," he answers. "I'll do the same thing to anyone who hurts you."

I understand, I write. *I would do the same for you.*

His lips curve into a smile that I will never tire of seeing. "I don't know whether to be terrified or flattered now that I've seen what you are capable of."

I made a promise to myself after Enzo that nobody would ever do that to me again, I explain. *I'm okay with having blood on my hands if it means protecting my family and myself.*

He considers it for a long, quiet moment.

"I thought it might bother you to see me that way," he admits. "I didn't know how you would feel about it."

I shake my head, typing adamantly. *I know what you do, but I didn't come into this relationship with blinders on. I accept you for who you are. I just don't want that darkness spilling over into our lives. I need to know you're safe, that our children are safe.*

"Well, you shouldn't worry," he assures me. "I've decided to reserve those skills for as-needed cases only from here on out."

So that means you're retiring?

"Not retiring, exactly. I will be changing careers. I'm tired of the gore. I think I've had enough for one lifetime."

This news relieves me more than he could ever know. I will love Alessio no matter what, but that isn't the life I want for him. I want him to do whatever makes him happy, and I tell him so.

"I've been giving it some thought," he says. "Angelo and I have been talking it over, and we are going into business together."

What kind of business?

He gets that boyish look on his face again, and it makes my heart beat a little faster.

"I wanted to build something we can pass down to Nino if he wants it, something we both love."

Boats? I ask.

He nods. "The business will be charter brokerage exclusively for

IVI. Yachts, catamarans, sailboats. High-end luxury for our members all over the world."

There's a peacefulness in his eyes when he talks about his plans, and it brings me comfort to know that he'll be doing something he enjoys.

Nino is going to love it. You both get the same look on your face when you're on the water. He must come by it naturally.

Alessio chuckles, and it's such a beautiful sound, I could play it on repeat. He's so relaxed right now I don't ever want this day to end.

"It will give us an excuse to spend more time on the water, too," he says. "We can do some research as we expand locations."

Really? I turn into him.

"Yes, really." He kisses me, and then his phone rings.

It's Manuel, so I hand it to him anxiously. He answers, thanks him, and disconnects.

"They're here."

Neither of us wastes any time getting up. It hasn't even been a full day since I've seen Nino, but after this morning, I've missed him already. Alessio seems nervous as he waits for me to slip on the robe from his bathroom. It smells like him, and it's warm, and it will do until I get the energy to shower and change.

"Your clothes are in there." He nods to the closet. "Whenever you need them."

I peek over at the door, and it warms me to know he moved my things in here. No more division. No more separate rooms. We're really going to do this marriage thing. When I look back at him, I know we're not going to fuck it up this time.

I join him at the door, and he settles his hand on my lower back as we walk downstairs together.

"Should we move Nino up to the third level?" he asks.

Yes, I sign.

"I think I'd feel more comfortable having him close too," he says.

We reach his door, and Nino is inside, still in his pajamas from this morning. He's at the window, looking out over the lake. His home. There's a softness to his face that lets me know he's at peace again. It means everything to me.

"Nino," Alessio's voice cracks as he calls out to him, and it splinters my heart.

"Daddy!" Nino turns and barrels toward him, tears streaking down his cheeks before he even reaches him.

Alessio lowers himself on one knee, catching Nino in his arms as he collides with him. They hug, and Alessio visibly trembles as Nino squeezes him in his arms. Their reunion is far more emotional than I ever could have prepared for, and I start bawling too.

We're all crying when Nino starts to sniffle and looks up at Alessio. "When can we go on the boat?"

He laughs, and so do I. Nino glances between us innocently. "What?"

"I love you." Alessio ruffles his hair. "I've missed you."

"I love you too, daddy. I missed you so much."

They hug for another long minute, and then Alessio releases him. "Don't forget to say hello to your mother. She's missed you too."

Nino comes to me, and I squeeze him in my arms until he protests. "I just saw you before bed, Mommy."

I know. I let him go and sign to him. *But I missed you.*

"I missed you too."

He says it as he wanders back to Alessio, clinging to his arm. Alessio gazes down at him with so much warmth in his eyes, it devastates me that they were apart for so long, but I can't let it darken this day.

"Will you both come downstairs?" Alessio asks. "There's something I'd like to show you."

I DIDN'T KNOW what to expect when we came down here, but it certainly wasn't this. Nino lets out a squeal of excitement when we walk into the parlor and see that it's still decorated for Christmas, exactly the way we left it.

Alessio wraps his arms around me from behind, murmuring into my ear. "The first of many Christmases together."

I relax into him with a sigh, smiling when Nino darts toward the tree and starts checking the labels on the gifts.

"Can I open them?" He turns back, waiting for us to answer.

We both nod, watching as he sits on the floor and tears them open one by one. He thanks us for all of them, but I can see that Alessio has won the best gift award when Nino unwraps the remote-control boat.

"So cool!" He skims it over the tree skirt, making boat noises with his mouth while we laugh.

"There's one for you too," Alessio whispers in my ear. "I already opened yours."

I look up at him in question, and he growls against me. "There's nobody else I'd rather have tend to me, my creepy little stalker."

My chest shakes with laughter, and I shrug. It's true, and I can't deny it.

He releases me and walks over to the tree, retrieving a small box from beneath it before he gestures me over to the couch. I sit down with him, and he hands it over. I'm not sure what it could be, but when I open it, there's a note with words I recognize. They're the same words I wrote on his gift, except with a different ending.

Because I'd rather be a source of comfort than pain. Keep this for the times you need tending, and I'll be there to care for you. No matter the hour. No matter how large or small. This is my promise to you.

I open up the box beneath it, revealing a pavé diamond bracelet. It's stunning, and I'm certain it probably cost a fortune, because I've never seen anything like it. On the side, in place of one of the settings, there's a tiny button. I press it out of curiosity, and Alessio's phone rings from his pocket. He pulls it out to show me there's an alert on his screen that I've signaled for him. It shows my location and the time, and it keeps buzzing and ringing until he dismisses it.

I understand immediately this is for him just as much as it's for me. He wants to keep me safe, and I don't think I've ever had a more thoughtful gift. I hand it to him and then hold out my arm so he can secure it for me.

"Do you like it?" His fingers skim over the sensitive skin on my wrist.

I gesture for his phone and pull up the notes app.

I love it. I'll feel better knowing you're just a button push away.

"I wasn't there before when you needed me," he says. "But I will be now. I want you to use it. I don't care what it is. If you're sad, or you want to talk, or if you need me to hold you. Whatever it is, Natalia. I mean that."

Even if I just want your dick? I smile, amusing myself as I show him the question.

His eyes flare at the idea. "Especially when you want that. You already told me once it belongs to you."

EPILOGUE

Natalia

"You called for me?" Alessio's voice echoes through the chapel as the heavy wooden door shuts behind him.

I turn away from the altar, curving my lips as I sign to him.

I have a need.

His eyes heat as he watches me drag the hem of my dress up my thigh.

"In a church, Natalia?" He scolds me, signing the words as he speaks them. "Have you no shame?"

I shrug one shoulder, blinking at him innocently. *Is it a sin for a married woman to want her husband?*

"If it is, then let us be sinners." He teases the words against my lips when he reaches me, dragging his hands up over my hips, bunching the fabric of my dress. "Tell me about this need you have."

I reach down and stroke his cock through his trousers and then slowly unzip them before I respond.

Is that clear enough?

"This bracelet has turned into a full-time job." His voice is tinged with amusement as he turns me in his arms.

I smirk as he unbuckles his belt with one hand while palming my bare ass with the other. It's become an ongoing joke between us that I use the bracelet primarily for what he refers to as dick-on-demand. It was put to good use halfway into my pregnancy when my hormones were going completely nuts. I couldn't get enough of him, night or day. It didn't matter the hour. Regardless of where he was or what he was doing, he kept his word and came to please me. It's undeniably hot knowing I have that power any time I want it. I use and abuse it proudly, but Alessio doesn't mind.

"We only have ten minutes." He breathes into my neck as his fingers move between my thighs. "But I'm not stopping until you come for me."

I hum my quiet approval as I arch back into him, grinding my ass against his cock as he slides his fingers through my arousal.

"Always so wet for me," he rumbles. "My little deviant."

A protest of air puffs from my lips when he pauses to move some of the candles over on the altar, clearing a space. Then he grabs my hips, tilting me forward until I'm fully exposed to him. I don't try to hide myself. Alessio has witnessed it all, including during childbirth, and it never changed the way he sees me. He takes me as I am, scars and all, and I bare my body without shame. I'm a mother, and a wife, and a woman with imperfections. None of that matters because I'm his.

He kneads the flesh of my ass cheek while he starts to finger me. It feels so fucking good, I'm rocking back against him, begging him for more. Alessio knows how to push all my buttons now. He's made it his goal to study them, memorize them, and become a master of his craft. Mission accomplished.

He told me I had ten minutes, but I come for him in two. I'm clinging to the altar, silently pleading with him as I look over my shoulder.

"So greedy." He slides his cock against the mess he left between my thighs, sinking inside of me way too slowly.

His fingers dig into my hips, and he growls as he bottoms out. I'll never get tired of watching the way his head tips back and his mouth parts like he's just entered heaven. It's so hot I can't stop staring. He knows it too. When he opens his eyes, he's already starting to smirk at me.

"Creepy little stalker."

I roll my ass against him, and that effectively puts an end to the conversation and resets the clock. He pulls back and thrusts into me, his pelvis slapping against my ass exactly how I like it. Sometimes, it's a slow, torturous kind of love. Today, it's hard and fast and intense.

My nails scrape against the altar as another orgasm rips through me, stealing my senses for a full minute. Alessio responds to my body as he always does, his cock jerking and spasming inside me as he releases himself. He falls forward, stroking my back as he kisses my neck.

"Have I satisfied your needs, dear wife?"

I roll my hips against him, nodding.

"Very well." He pulls us both upright and then scoops me up into his arms, his cock swaying between his legs as he carries me to the bathroom. "I better wash this sin off you then. The ceremony's about to start."

THANKS FOR LOOKING AFTER HER. I smooth my hair back over my shoulders and glance down at our sleeping angel in her stroller.

"It's no problem." Abella gives us a sly smile as her eyes bounce between us. "What are godmothers for?"

I peek up at Alessio and roll my eyes. He always gets us caught. He looks far too content, and it's a dead giveaway every time.

Could you be any more obvious? I ask.

He shrugs and signs back. *You're the one that sent for me. I was just doing what was asked.*

"You do know I can understand everything you're saying, right?" Abella blushes.

I would never have known it until she admitted it, but she confessed to me one day after a few martinis that she's still a virgin. It literally stunned me. She's so confident and beautiful I can't imagine there hasn't been a man who's tried, but she explained to me that the expectations are different when you're from an upper-echelon family. She's basically the definition of a Society princess, and therefore she's supposed to save herself for her husband. Two years ago, I would have thought it sounded archaic, but admittedly, now I think it's sort of sweet. I'm grateful that Alessio and I share so many firsts. He may not be my first experience, but he's the first man I gave myself to freely, and I have no doubt in my mind he'll be the last too.

Abella doesn't talk much about her engagement, but I know she's marrying a Sovereign Son too. I can only hope that he'll make her as happy as I am.

A soft sound drifts up from the stroller, and Alessio edges closer, unable to resist himself. We both stare at our sleeping daughter in awe. Madalena Emilia Scarcello was born on a Tuesday, just after midnight. We named her after Alessio's mother and sister. Even though she's been here for six months, he still tells me often how much it means to him.

I never had any doubts that he'd be an amazing father because he already was, but Madalena has brought out a different side to him. He's so gentle and attentive to her. Sometimes I want to cry just watching them together. Publicly, he's still the same awkward, grouchy man that scares the shit out of everyone. At home, with our children, he's a marshmallow on the inside. He takes care of us. He never lets any of us feel second-rate.

I couldn't have asked for a better husband and friend. We juggle work and kids and Society things, and it keeps us busy, but at the end of the day, we always come back to each other. On the days when things aren't always smooth sailing, we argue, and then we get over it and move on. It's taken us both some time to trust that we can express our frustrations with each other, but we've learned to lean into the process. We hear each other out, and we deal with it together.

Next month, we'll be renewing our vows in Greece. Alessio chartered a yacht for the occasion, and Nino can't stop talking about it. It won't be anything over the top. It will just be our little family in a beautiful place where Alessio and I will recite the promises we've made with new meaning. It's important to him that he gets to do this over again. He still carries the guilt over his distance after our wedding, and this is his way of trying to make it right. It isn't necessary because I've already forgiven him, and I tell him so often, but I know he needs this, so I'm happy to oblige.

He seems to be aware that I'm thinking about him as he wraps his arm around my back, settling his palm on my hip. He kisses my temple, lowering his voice so only I can hear.

"Thank you."

I look up at him in question, and he regards me warmly.

"For being my wife."

I kiss him back, and someone clears their throat. When we look up, the representative from IVI is arching a brow at us. He's here as a witness for the ceremony of Madalena's baptism. It's something we were supposed to do after she was born, but we're just now getting around to it. Alessio was raised in the Catholic church, but neither one of us are devoted members. He tells me it's more about the ritual than anything. I could have said no, but I like the idea of our daughter being baptized. I wasn't here for Nino's, and that's what today is really about. *Family.*

"We'll be starting soon," the representative tells us. "Where's the godfather?"

Alessio checks his phone, but it's not necessary. On cue, Angelo walks in the door with Nino at his side. They're both dressed in suits, and Nino looks like a mini Alessio. I'm already plotting how many photos I'm going to sneak of them when Alessio speaks.

"There he is. It's about time."

Everyone turns to look at Angelo, including Abella. I anticipate that she probably knows him from The Society, but I'm not prepared when her mouth drops open, and she gasps. She brings a trembling hand to her face, rising from her seat as if she's seen a ghost.

"Angelo?"

His eyes cut over her, colder than I've ever seen them. "Hello, Abella. Nice to see you too."

THE END.

BOOKS BY A. ZAVARELLI

Boston Underworld Series

CROW

REAPER

GHOST

SAINT

THIEF

CONOR

Sin City Series

CONFESS

CONVICT

The Society Trilogy

REQUIEM OF THE SOUL

REPARATION OF SIN

RESURRECTION OF THE HEART

Ties that Bind Duet

MINE

HIS

Bleeding Hearts Series

ECHO

STUTTER

Standalones

BEAST

STEALING CINDERELLA

PRETTY WHEN SHE CRIES

HATE CRUSH

TAP LEFT

For a complete list of books and audios, visit http://www.
azavarelli.com/books

ABOUT THE AUTHOR

A. Zavarelli is a USA Today and Amazon bestselling author of dark and contemporary romance.

When she's not putting her characters through hell, she can usually be found watching bizarre and twisted documentaries in the name of research.

She currently lives in the Northwest with her lumberjack and an entire brood of fur babies.

Sign Up for A. Zavarelli's Newsletter:
www.subscribepage.com/AZavarelli

Like A. Zavarelli on Facebook:
www.facebook.com/azavarelliauthor

Join A. Zavarelli's Reader Group:
www.facebook.com/femmefatales

Follow A. Zavarelli on Instagram:
www.instagram.com/azavarelli

Printed in Great Britain
by Amazon